A stalke ... **life. And Lara hadn't even known.**

Her father's voice broke into her thoughts. "I need you to work this case, Lara, and so does Conley."

Lara swung her head around, her hands clenched at her sides. "You can fire me if you like, but I'm not taking this on. Conley doesn't need a bodyguard so much as he needs a baby-sitter. When he goes out, when he's in the office...someone has to be with him 24/7. And whoever it is has to be good. Someone no one will notice."

"That's right."

"You're going to have to find the perfect person."

"That's right."

His repetition registered, and Lara finally understood. She held up her hands as if she could ward off his suggestion. "No way. I am not—"

"You have to. You're the only one who can be around him that much and not raise any suspicions. No one will give your presence any thought. The setup's too great to ignore." Her father stared at her, his fingers tapping the steering wheel. "You're his wife," he said quietly. "And you're going to have to act like it whether you want to or not."

Dear Reader,

I married my husband when I was nineteen years old. He was five years older than I. He came from a small town in West Texas, and I grew up in a large metropolitan area. He was an engineer, and I wrote. He was intense, I wasn't. My parents were married, his were divorced. I'm Anglo, he's not.

When we walked down the aisle, money had to be changing hands. The odds were probably a thousand to one on the marriage lasting. We were too young and too different. But very much in love.

Twenty-seven years later, we're still together—and still much in love. We've moved fourteen times, from one end of the world to the other (literally). We've lost dreams and replaced them with new ones. We've lost hope and found it again. Like everyone else's, our marriage has had good times and bad.

And that's why I wanted to write *Marriage to a Stranger*. Sometimes, no matter how long you've been together, you wake up one morning and realize you don't really know the person next to you. Your partner's changed. Or most likely, you both have.

In this book, Conley Harrison knows he doesn't want a divorce. He hasn't been the best mate in the world, but he has his reasons and believes they're good ones. He decides he's not going to let Lara go, at least not before he tries to make things right one last time.

His success—or failure—depends not only on himself but on Lara, as well. Is their love strong enough to survive?

Sincerely,

Kay David

P.S. Visit my Web site at www.kaydavid.com.

Marriage to a Stranger
Kay David

HARLEQUIN®

TORONTO • NEW YORK • LONDON
AMSTERDAM • PARIS • SYDNEY • HAMBURG
STOCKHOLM • ATHENS • TOKYO • MILAN • MADRID
PRAGUE • WARSAW • BUDAPEST • AUCKLAND

ISBN 0-373-71045-3

MARRIAGE TO A STRANGER

Visit us at www.eHarlequin.com

Printed in U.S.A.

Marriage is one of the trickiest relationships. You have to be lucky to have a good one, but you have to be smart to make it last. This book is dedicated to everyone who has been brave enough to walk down the aisle and also to those who are contemplating taking the plunge. How do you know you're doing the right thing? You don't. You only know you can't do anything else!

CHAPTER ONE

"I WANT A DIVORCE."

Standing in the doorway of her kitchen, Lara Harrison spoke in a calm and deliberate manner. Last night, she had practiced saying the words over and over. Looking into her bathroom mirror, her face straight and her voice quiet, she had repeated herself until the fateful sentence had come out sounding both dignified and determined. At least until she'd started to cry.

By dawn, she'd run out of tears. Now, in the painful morning light, all she had left was the awful realization that her marriage was over.

From across the room where he sat at the breakfast table, Conley Harrison, her husband of seven years, put down his coffee mug and looked at Lara. Conley was always collected and composed, and her pronouncement did nothing to change this.

His reaction—or lack thereof—was exactly what she'd expected.

Conley's taciturn manner—the complete opposite of her father's nonstop agitation—had thrilled Lara when they'd first married. Quiet and mysterious, her husband had been everything she'd wanted in a man. Things had changed, though, and his attitude had begun to drive her insane. He didn't share his feelings or let her know what he thought about anything. If she wanted his opinion, she had to drag it out of him. Lately, as impossible as it seemed, he'd become even more reticent. He answered her questions with curt replies and appeared totally preoccupied. To make matters worse, all he did was work. On the rare occasions when he did have a free hour, he acted as if he had better things to do than be with her.

Which, she suspected, he did...and had for some time. She quickly shut her mind to that painful reality. It wasn't the primary motivation for her decision and there was nothing she could do about it one way or the other.

His jaw twitched, a reaction he couldn't control, and he repeated her words. "You want a divorce."

She looked at him steadily. "It's time to call this one over, Conley. Past time."

"I don't believe I understand."

Lara shrugged as if she didn't care, but deep inside she struggled to contain her churning emotions. They'd fallen in love so deeply it had almost hurt. She had meant it when she'd promised to love him "forever and ever." But now forever was over.

"There's nothing complicated about it," she replied. "I'm simply tired of living this way." She crossed her arms. "You do nothing but work. You're never at home. We aren't a married couple and we haven't been for quite a while. I think it'd be best—for both of us—to go our separate ways."

"And when did you come to this conclusion?"

"I've been thinking about it a long time."

The cold silence built, a reflection of the day outside. The snow had started last night after Lara had finally fallen into an exhausted sleep; she'd woken and heard the quiet in the middle of the night, had sensed the heavy blanket of white. Years ago, she'd loved the wild Colorado winters. They'd meant she and Conley had an excuse to stay at home in bed.

She couldn't even remember the last time that had happened, though. She'd moved out of their bedroom several months ago. Sleeping by herself in the room they'd once shared, night after night when Conley didn't come home, had become a special torture all its own.

The last time they had made love had been more than ten months ago. They'd been in the Turks and Caicos, a small group of islands in the Caribbean. The whole trip had been a foolish idea; Lara wasn't even sure why she'd agreed to go but she'd been so surprised when Conley had suggested a holiday, she'd said yes without thinking. Once there, they'd passed by the docks one evening on their way to dinner, and she'd caught an aching glimpse of the sailboats in the harbor. A long time ago, they'd promised each other they'd buy a boat and live on it someday. She'd even given Conley a compass when they'd barely had money enough for food.

The failed vacation had been awkward and uncomfortable; a heavy weight neither could carry by themselves.

She looked at Conley again. "You know how I've felt. Don't tell me you're surprised."

"I'm not surprised," he said stiffly, "but I would have thought there might be some discussion about it before...this."

She felt a surge of disbelief. "When would that have happened, Conley?" She lifted her hands helplessly. "You're never here. Would I have called you in Hong Kong and left a message? E-mailed you in Moscow? Paged you in Rio?" She paused, the awful quiet around them suffocating in its intensity. "It wouldn't have mattered," she finally said. "Even when you are here...you aren't. You wouldn't have heard me if I'd tried."

Their gazes met. The connection was painful and sharp, a bitter moment of truth for which Lara wasn't prepared. Regret immediately stabbed her. She didn't love Conley anymore, but this look hurt more than she could have expected.

With his eyes still holding hers, Conley stood up unexpectedly. For a moment, it seemed as if he were going to come toward her, but all at once, coffee mug in hand, he turned abruptly. Too abruptly. He bumped the edge of the carved oak table with his thigh. Hot coffee splashed over the edge of the mug and down his tan wool slacks, staining the expensive fabric and obviously burning his leg.

He looked at the splotch then froze, his mouth an angry slash. Lara thought he would say something then, scream at her, yell maybe, react somehow. With her breath caught in her throat, she wished for once that he'd just let go.

A moment later, he did.

But it wasn't what she expected.

Without a word of warning, he raised his arm and hurled his coffee mug into the sink. He'd been a pitcher in college. The mug landed in the drain with a crash, shattering into a thousand pieces.

His reaction was so out of character, so totally unexpected that Lara couldn't help herself. She gasped and stumbled backward, but Conley didn't appear to even notice. He tore out the back door and into the snowy morning. A few seconds later, the engine of his Suburban roared to life and a heartbeat after that he shot out the drive, the tires crunching, the big green vehicle a blur of movement as it passed the kitchen window.

Lara stared at the door, still vibrating from Conley's departure. With everything she knew, she'd assumed he'd be relieved. Bewildered and confused, she lurched toward the threshold. She was halfway across the room when a shard sliced into her heel.

Pain raced up her leg and she cried out. Bending over, she reached down and pulled out the shard, a red stain spreading across the bottom of her sock as dark as the one on Conley's slacks. She stared at the blood then blinked as the image began to waver. Covering her face with her sticky fingers, Lara moaned into her palms, the heartfelt sound of her sorrow filling the cold empty kitchen.

God, what had she done?

Even though she'd known she had to do it—to say the words that had been unspoken until now, to make the choice that Conley couldn't—she'd taken an irreversible step. With the utterance of one little word—*divorce*—she'd put into motion wheels no one could stop. A knot of sick grief lodged deep in her throat. Her foot throbbed hotly, but the pain was nothing compared to the ache in her heart.

CONLEY MANEUVERED the green Suburban down the side street with reckless speed. His mind wasn't on his driving; it was back in the kitchen with Lara. All he could see were her beautiful hazel eyes, filled with agony and anguish. He'd been prepared for her words, but not for the level of pain they'd caused him.

The SUV slid slightly to the right, and Conley cursed, his hands tightening on the steering wheel. The snow was thick, clouds of the white stuff shooting out from his tires to add to the drifts already in place. Driving in Red Feather could be difficult, but no one really minded. Snow made the place what it was—a wonderful ski resort that swelled with tourists in the winter season. The little town clung to the edge of the Rocky Mountains an hour north of Boulder and when the weather turned bitter, everyone who could came here, their skis strapped to their roofs, their minds on having fun.

Conley and Lara had met on the slopes but they had settled here for a much different reason than skiing. They'd needed their own space, away from Boulder, where Lara worked at Mesa Protection and Security, her father's firm. She hadn't wanted to be any closer to the office—or Ed—than was necessary during their time off, and Red Feather had offered the perfect getaway.

Or so they'd thought.

Cutting around another snow-covered corner, Conley reached the small lot outside his own office and parked, throwing the SUV out of gear with a jerky motion then killing the engine. For a few seconds, the sound of the huge motor echoed in the sudden silence, then the noise died out, leaving behind an emptiness that matched the one in Conley's heart. He stared down the street at the sign in front of his office.

Harrison's was all the sign said, but that was all that was necessary. Conley had started the firm after finishing college and now he had more than seventy-five employees. The company had grossed almost fifty million last year, the world-renowned computer chips they designed highly specialized and incredibly expensive. They helped run everything from the space station to mechanical hearts. But their very uniqueness was also their downfall. When someone had a question about a Harrison chip, Conley Harrison was the only person they could ask.

Big deal. Who in the hell cared? None of it really mattered to him anymore and it hadn't for quite some time. His throat closed tightly as Conley thought about the effort and hard work he'd put into his business over the years. His only goal had been to make a good life for Lara.

And for himself, as well, he confessed silently. The faces of his always weary parents came to mind. They'd been sharecroppers in Kentucky, hardworking, plainspoken people who'd managed to raise five children in the midst of a poverty that belonged to another country, in another time. Despite their problems, they'd taught Conley and his four siblings a lesson Conley had learned well—providing for your family meant everything. You took care of them first and the rest followed.

He tried to live his life that way, but things hadn't worked out like they should. He'd given Lara everything…but it hadn't been enough.

A blowing gust of wind caught his attention, snow scratching over his windshield. If he didn't leave the damn truck soon he might be stuck in it for good. He jumped out with his hand on his cell phone and hurried down the street, the wind cutting through his sweater as if it didn't exist. He'd been stupid to leave the house without a coat, but staying warm hadn't seemed important at the time. He'd only wanted to get away from Lara's accusing stare and hurtful words.

He'd been waiting, holding his breath for months, it seemed, but when she'd finally said what he'd been expecting, the reality had shocked him. He'd wanted to grab her and force her to take back the request, shake her until the words no longer existed. But he couldn't. She had every right to ask for a divorce and even though it felt as if she'd yanked his heart straight from his chest, he had to acknowledge her prerogative to do just that.

He hurried to the corner, then ducked his head and started across the street. The last few years had been tough ones, he'd be the first to admit, but the most recent couple of months had been even worse. Keeping her unaware of what was going on had been damn near impossible. It sounded crazy, even to him, but Conley *could not* let Lara find out about his problem. She handled situations similar to this all the time and for that very reason—as illogical as it sounded—he didn't want her involved. He didn't want to be just another case for her.

Without any warning, a stunningly cold sweep of

wind hit him from the side, searing his face and stripping away his breath. His excuses went with it, planting a blow he couldn't dodge. Who in the hell was he trying to kid? He didn't want Lara involved with this mess, yeah, but the truth was, he didn't think she'd even *want* to be involved.

Their marriage had been on the skids for a very long time. At some indeterminable point, they'd started drifting apart and neither of them had had the energy or time to do anything about it. Like so many couples everyone knew, they'd stopped listening to each other, stopped giving each other the time that every marriage needed.

They were both guilty, but he was the primary offender; he put everything before their marriage. His work. His company. His self. The painful realization stung, but he had to admit it.

He was almost on the other side of the street, and another burning gust of wind brought his head up— or maybe it was something else, he thought later— some kind of sixth sense, a warning he didn't consciously consider. Whatever it was that made him look, it didn't really matter.

The car was coming too fast.

Before he could react, Conley realized he didn't have a chance. The front bumper of the speeding coupe caught him at the knee and pitched him sideways, into the air. It took forever for him to come down and hit the drift of snow.

He thought of Lara as the whole world went quiet.

CHAPTER TWO

DESPITE HER throbbing foot, Lara was on the StairMaster when the doorbell rang. She'd halfheartedly swept the kitchen then jumped on the machine to try to clear her mind with some hard physical activity. The plan had been a good one, but it wasn't working.

The bell sounded again, and she ignored it again. By the time she got downstairs, whoever was waiting would be gone. She didn't even care anyway. She didn't want to see anyone right now. She was too upset.

Lifting a hand to wipe her forehead, she closed her eyes and tried to block out the chimes, but the noise persisted. With a curse, she finally gave up and made her way to the front door. When she reached the entry, Lara could see her neighbor and friend, Sandy Oakley staring inside, her hands cupped around her eyes to peer through one of the sidelights.

Lara moaned out loud. How could she have forgotten? She and Sandy had made a date last week to have breakfast this morning. She'd promised to pick Sandy up more than an hour ago! She hurried to the front door and threw it open, apologizing before Sandy could even get inside and shake off the snow.

"God, Sandy! I'm sorry! I completely forgot about our breakfast—"

"No problem, it's okay. Really. My car's in the shop again so I just trudged up the sidewalk in a snowstorm, that's all. I'm up to it."

She waved toward the street, and Lara followed her movement. Footsteps proved Sandy's point. She looked back at her friend. "Why did you walk, for heaven's sake? Couldn't Matthew have given you a ride?"

Sandy's husband, Matthew Oakley, was Conley's right-hand man and former college roommate. Conley depended a lot on the brilliant hardware designer.

"He had to go in early. Something about some chip or something..." Sandy patted her bulging stomach. "The baby didn't mind. He likes cold weather. Really..."

Lara rolled her eyes at Sandy's elaborate exaggeration. Friendly and outgoing, Sandy was the exact opposite of her quiet and intense husband, although just as smart. She and Lara had developed a close friendship over the years, mainly because Sandy was one of those people who never missed an opportunity to announce how she felt about anything. She kept Lara honest.

Shaking out of her coat, Sandy turned around to add to her litany of woes, then she saw Lara's face. "Oh, my God. You told him, didn't you?"

Lara nodded, her eyes filling. Sandy enveloped her in a hug; then, with her arm around Lara's shoulder, she guided them both back to Lara's kitchen. "Sit down," she said. "I'll fix us some tea." Sandy got out the mugs and tea bags, and within seconds, the smell of lemon and honey filled the kitchen.

"Tell me." She placed the steaming cups on the kitchen table and sat down in the chair Conley had vacated a scarce half hour before. "What'd he say?"

Lara shook her head. "It didn't go well. He...he wasn't thrilled."

"Did you expect him to be?"

"I thought he was ready."

"But he's not."

Lara sipped her tea and grimaced. Sandy always made it too sweet. "He threw a mug into the sink, then stormed out. It wasn't like him at all." She looked up. "You know how he is. Mr. Strong and Silent."

Sandy waited a heartbeat, then she said just what Lara expected, her reaction sharp and to the point. "You're an idiot, Lara. A total, complete idiot."

Outside the back door, the wind suddenly picked up. Snow swirled and the fir tree beside the window tapped a staccato beat against the glass as if it agreed with Sandy's pronouncement.

"I had to do it," Lara said stubbornly, not meeting her friend's eyes. "And you know why."

"I know why you *think* you had to do it, but I refuse to believe your suspicions. Conley isn't that kind of man. You don't really think that anyway. It's an excuse, that's all."

"It doesn't matter anymore." Lara spoke quietly, sadness coloring her words. "There's an emptiness between us that I can't fill by myself. We aren't the couple we used to be. We aren't close. We aren't a family. We don't even seem to care. And it hurts too much to keep trying." Her eyes went to her friend's swelling stomach. "Maybe if we'd had children…"

"Having a baby doesn't make you a family. Love makes you a family. You could get it back if you tried."

"I did try, Sandy. But it takes two."

"You and Conley just got on the wrong track, that's all. If you'd both—"

"There's nothing either of us can do now." Lara interrupted her friend. "It's over. Believe me, it's over."

The wind continued to howl, the gusts growing stronger. Sandy waited a beat. "I'm well aware that's what you think. But what if it isn't what Conley believes?"

Looking up at her friend, Lara gripped her tea mug a little too tightly. "I don't see—"

"Throwing dishes isn't a typical sign of consensus, is it? Did he say straight out that he'd agree to a divorce?"

"He stormed out the door, Sandy. It was obvious—"

Sandy cocked her head to one side and raised her right eyebrow. It was a familiar move; Lara had seen her do it a thousand times…usually right before she made some horrendous point Lara hadn't considered. "Did he or did he not actually say to you that he would give you a divorce?"

Lara felt her heart thump. "He—he didn't *actually* say the words but…"

"Lara, Lara, Lara…" Sandy shook her head slowly. "Colorado's a no-fault state and Conley's got plenty of money. You and I both know money makes the impossible…possible. And vice versa. If he doesn't *want* a divorce, it could get nasty." She put her teacup down carefully. The deliberate movement reminded Lara of Conley. Instead of mere hours, she felt as if a lifetime had passed since they'd talked.

"If he wants to fight you, he can." Sandy raised both eyebrows this time. "If I were you, I'd be worried about *that* possibility."

SANDY STAYED a little while longer, then Lara took her home. The streets were completely empty, the snow coming down in sheets of solid white. When they pulled into Sandy's driveway, she turned to Lara and paused, her fingers on the door handle.

One last question, Lara thought with dread. God, hadn't she said enough already?

"Have you told Ed?"

Lara grimaced. Her father would go ballistic when he heard her news, and then there'd be hell to pay. When Ed was unhappy, everyone was unhappy. He made sure of it.

"Not yet. I'm dreading it, though."

Sandy's expression turned sympathetic. "He's not an easy man to break bad news to, that's for certain."

Lara tucked her hair behind one ear and smiled grimly. "He's not an easy man, period." For just a second she was six years old again and in the first grade. That's when she'd learned other kids called their fathers "Dad" or "Pop" or even "Father." Anything but their first name. The argument had been short, and Lara had learned quickly how much her opinion—or anyone else's for that matter—meant to Ed.

"He won't like it," Sandy said.

"Yep. He told me when I got married to make it last. I guess I haven't followed his advice."

Sandy snorted. "He's a big one to be giving advice about marriage."

Ed had been to the altar four times. Lara's mother, his first wife, had deserted him when Lara was five. Unable to stand his overbearing ways and need to control, Alicia Bentley had fled, leaving her baby daughter behind. She'd died shortly after that in a skiing accident. And Ed had been with a number of women since.

"You're right," Lara conceded. "But I'm sure Ed would tell you he loved every one of them."

"Well, he can be charming." Sandy grinned. "But there's that other side of him…"

"You mean the side I'll see when I tell him about the divorce?" Lara gripped the steering wheel. "He likes Conley. He'll believe this is all my fault."

The silence stretched out, then Sandy reached across the seat and put her hand on Lara's right arm. Her expression held a wistful note. Married longer than Lara and Conley, Sandy and Matthew had never had a perfect relationship but since the pregnancy, things had gotten more tense. Sandy had always idealized Lara's marriage, mainly because she idealized Conley.

"Are you sure about this, Lara? I mean, really, really sure? Conley's the kind of man every woman dreams about…."

Lara stared through the windshield. She'd asked herself that very same question a thousand times the past few weeks, and each time, her answer had been the same. Yes. Absolutely. Positively. Without a doubt. She wanted a divorce.

She wanted it because things weren't working out, but for other reasons as well. Lara had vowed a long time ago that she would never be like the women her father had always married. Except for one—Bess MacDougal—they had been helpless and insecure, women who didn't know who they were without a man. When Ed's interest flagged, Lara had read the desperation in their eyes; she'd be damned before she'd see it in hers.

A few years ago, she and Conley had reached this same point and had almost separated. They'd decided to give the marriage another try, but after a while, a very painful while, it was clear to Lara nothing had really changed. The agony of that realization was something she never intended to experience again.

To top it all off, there was the *Other Problem*. She couldn't bring herself to use the actual term because then the situation would become too real for her so she always thought of it as the *Other Problem*.

She turned to her friend and spoke. "Yes," she said. "I'm absolutely sure. I don't love Conley anymore. It's time to move on."

WHEN SHE CAME BACK through the kitchen door, Lara's phone was ringing. It was probably Ed, she decided, wondering why she wasn't yet in the office. She loved her job, but sometimes she found herself wishing someone other than her father owned the company. He was a hard boss and it was a hard job. Bodyguards to night patrols, employee checkouts to prenuptial investigations, Mesa Security offered very discreet services to very wealthy clients. The firm kept a low profile—so much so it was known only in certain circles. But it was the best, and when someone needed help with a delicate situation, they called Mesa. Mainly responsible for the day-to-day operations, Lara left the heavy-duty bodyguard service to the fleet of freelancers Ed managed. A few years back, personal security was all she'd done, but she'd put that part of the business behind her.

She'd had to.

The phone rang again and with a moan, she shrugged out of her coat and grabbed the receiver off the wall. But the person at the other end wasn't Ed.

"Lara? This is Theresa. Did I...catch you at a bad time? You sound out of breath."

"I just came in the door. I had to run Sandy home. She'd stopped by."

Catching her reflection in the window over the sink, Lara pushed her hair out of her face and tried to imagine Theresa Marchante, Conley's attorney, appearing as Lara did right now. Sweats, no makeup, in need of a shower. The woman had to

exercise—she was too svelte and attractive not to—
but somehow Lara couldn't picture the lawyer be-
draggled and mussed. Theresa always looked wonderful, her suits tailored and in flawless taste, her
red hair shining and pulled back. Normally such perfection would have made Lara dislike Theresa immediately, but because of the attorney's attitude that
was impossible. Conley valued her opinion in all his
legal matters. Theresa was a hard worker and loyal
to her clients—she'd been Conley's counsel for several years now.

"I'm sorry to have to bother you, but..." She
paused and seemed to hesitate.

A rush of coldness swept over Lara, shaking her
to her toes. Theresa Marchante didn't flounder over
anything. God, had Conley already contacted her?
Had he already told her to start the paperwork for
the divorce?

Lara dropped her coat on a nearby kitchen chair
then gripped the phone with both hands. "It's okay,
Theresa. What can I do for you?"

"I...I have some bad news, Lara."

Lara's chest went tight. He *had* told her! Conley
had gone directly to his office and called his attorney!
Damn, he might have even called her from the Suburban. Lara's initial feeling of dismay, even though
she'd been the one to bring it all up, morphed illog-
ically into anger. His little act of rage this morning

had been just that—an act. He couldn't wait to be free of her, could he?

"I know what you're going to say, Theresa." She forced herself to speak. "I'm just surprised he told you this fast. Did he...ask you to start the paperwork already?"

"I don't think we're talking about the same thing, Lara. In fact, I know we aren't. I'm calling about Conley—"

"I don't know what he told you this morning, but the divorce is my idea, okay? I was the one who brought it up and I'm the one who—"

"Lara, look, I don't know anything about a divorce." In a voice uncharacteristically shaky, Theresa broke in, halting Lara's explanation. "I'm calling because Conley's been in an accident. I'm at the hospital right now. He asked me to phone and let you know."

"Wh-what? An accident?" She fumbled for the chair behind her and sat down, her coat falling to the floor. "What happened?"

"I'm not sure at this point. We were supposed to have a meeting early this morning. I was running late and when I got here, I found him in the street, right outside the building. He was shivering and banged up pretty good. He said something about a car hitting him, but I didn't get all the details. I took him straight to the hospital. The doctor's in with him right now."

"Oh, my God...is he okay?"

"He doesn't seem to be hurt too seriously, but he wanted you to know what was going on."

Lara jumped up from the chair. "I'll be right there, Theresa. I have to get dressed but it'll only take a minute then I'll—"

"Lara, don't! The weather's horrible and it's getting worse. You'll just cause another accident rushing over here." Theresa's voice returned to its usual firm and sensible tone. "It's not necessary. I can bring him home when they finish. If they keep him longer, then you can come after lunch. It's supposed to be better later this afternoon."

Lara jogged down the hall toward her bedroom. "No," she said firmly. "I want to see him. I *have* to see him. I'll throw on something and be there in twenty minutes."

Theresa was still talking as Lara clicked off the phone and tossed the cordless unit to her bed. The attorney meant well, but she didn't understand. When Conley got upset or worried, his mind was like a train on a single track. Lara yanked off her sweatshirt and Lycra pants. He'd been concentrating on their angry words; he'd never seen the car or whatever had hit him and she was to blame.

Pulling a pair of gray slacks from the closet and a black turtleneck, she dressed in record time, guilt fueling her every step. Five seconds later she had her hair slicked back and lipstick slapped on. Running through the kitchen, she grabbed her purse and cell phone and headed out the door, a missed shard crunching beneath her right boot.

She didn't stop to wonder why her heart was lodged in her throat.

"I DON'T KNOW the details. That's all I can tell you right now." Lara gripped the steering wheel of her truck and maneuvered out the driveway. The overhead speaker of her cell phone crackled in response.

"I don't care if he just has a hangnail, he's better off in Denver." Her father's gravelly voice boomed across the line. "That Podunk hospital in Red Feather is a disaster waiting to happen. He should be down here in Boulder, at the very least."

Before Lara could answer, she heard her father bark instructions to someone in his office, probably Larry, her stepbrother. "Get me International Helo Service outta Denver! Earl Stanley runs 'em and I want him on the phone—"

"Ed, Ed! Hold off." Lara spoke loudly, trying to get his attention back. "I want to check things out at the hospital before you start taking over the situation. I'll call you from there."

"But I can have a chopper at Red Feather in no time! We'll airlift him to Denver then Houston if we need to—"

"Let me see him first, okay? I promise I'll call

you after I get a handle on things, then we can decide what to do.''

Something in her voice must have registered. He spoke again, this time slower. "Are you sure, sweetheart? I can—"

"I know you 'can' anything, okay?" Lara reached the corner, the snowbound street before her virtually deserted, a blanket of white swirling down over the trees and parked cars. Another six inches of snow had fallen since she'd taken Sandy home. "But let me see what's going on before you go into action. The way Theresa talked, I don't think he's hurt that badly."

Silence was her only answer and Lara cursed to herself. He had his faults, but the old coot could read her like a well-worn book.

"If that's what you think, how come you're so upset?"

Lara tightened her hands, her leather gloves squeaking inside the still freezing cabin of the truck. "What makes you think I'm upset?"

"I can hear it in your voice, dammit. What kinda imbecile do you think I am? I've been your father for thirty-three years! You don't think—"

"Okay, okay…enough already!" She gunned the engine and turned the corner, fighting the skidding tires. She didn't want to explain but telling him this way did have its advantages; she could confess what was going on, then hang up on him. He could rant and rave to Larry and his wife, Stephanie. Stephanie was the sweetest person Lara knew—she could actually calm Ed down sometimes.

"So what it is?" he demanded. "If you think Con's okay what's wrong?"

"We had a fight this morning."

"Everyone fights. That's what marriage is about."

"Not us," she answered grimly. "Conley doesn't argue, you know that."

He grunted his agreement and waited for her to continue.

"We fought because…because I told him I want a divorce."

"A divorce! Are you nuts?" Her father's wrathful voice filled the interior of the truck. "Have you lost your mind?"

"You don't understand—"

"You're damn right I don't understand! Conley Harrison is the best thing in your life. The man's a brick! He makes more money than you can ever spend, he obviously loves you—"

"You don't know what you're talking about." Ed must have heard the pain and weariness in her voice because he instantly fell silent, an unusual state for her father. "I don't want to go into it right now, but you're going to have to trust me on this one. Things have gotten pretty bad around here."

When he remained silent, Lara knew exactly what

he was thinking. He'd told her more than once it'd almost killed him when her mother had left him. She'd been the only woman he'd truly loved, and it was Lara's theory he'd been searching ever since for the same feeling.

After a moment, he asked quietly, "Is it another man, baby? Are you in love with someone—"

"No," she interrupted. "I'm not in love with anyone else. It...it just isn't working, Ed, and hasn't been for years. That's all I can say for now." The vehicle's heater suddenly kicked in and sent a blast of feverish warmth toward her face. "I'll call you from the hospital as soon as I know something." She reached over and switched off the phone, then did the same with the heater.

After fifteen more minutes of fighting the snow and wind, she pulled under the overhang at the Red Feather hospital.

THE HOSPITAL WAS like hospitals everywhere. Cold, stark and sterile. Lara shivered as she raced down the corridor toward the emergency room. He had to be okay, she told herself. Theresa hadn't seemed too upset and God knew how competent she was. On the other hand, that was part of the problem. The world could be exploding and Theresa Marchante probably wouldn't react.

A flashing red light above one of the doors caught Lara's eye and she hurried toward its blinking beacon, the crimson letters ER standing out against the white of everything else. Her throat was tight and clogged as she pushed open the door and rushed inside.

In contrast to her own turmoil, the room inside was peaceful and quiet. It was too early for the skiers who'd be brought in later, and the drunk drivers from the night before were all long gone. The only people in the waiting area were a mother and father, a small child cradled between them who looked lethargic and stuffy.

Lara quickly crossed to the desk that lined one wall. ''I'm Lara Harrison,'' she said, leaning over a high Formica barrier. ''My husband, Conley was brought in a little while ago. I think it was a car accident—''

The woman behind the counter wore a brightly colored nurse's smock, her hair tied back in a no-nonsense fashion. She tilted her head in a puzzled way. ''You're Mrs. Harrison? I thought...'' She shook her head then finished her sentence. ''There's a woman with him. I got the impression *she* was Mrs. Harrison.''

A cold chill rippled over Lara before she understood, relief hitting her hard when she did. ''You must be thinking of Theresa. She's his attorney. She found him.''

A chagrined expression crossed the nurse's features. ''I'm so sorry...I just thought...'' She broke off her words. "Please go on back. He's in cubicle number one. I believe the doctor's with him right now."

Lara followed the woman's wave toward a door on one side. Stepping into a long corridor sectioned off by curtains, she quickly located the first one. She pushed aside the dark-blue fabric and her heart stuttered to a stop.

Conley sat on a metal examining table. Theresa Marchante stood close beside him, patting his bare shoulder in a comforting way. She nodded at Lara, touched Conley one more time, then dropped her hand as Lara stared at Conley in distress. It was obvious someone had cleaned him up, but just as obvious he was hurting. A huge bruise on his temple was already turning black, the edges of it ragged and painful looking. His right pant leg had been sliced from his hip to his ankle, an angry swelling distorting the calf, a long, nasty cut on the side. His eyes were what stopped her, though. They were full of something Lara had never seen before. She ran to his side, Theresa stepping away slowly.

"My God...Conley...are you...are you all right?" Lara touched his jaw and then his arm, her horrified eyes taking in a litany of minor wounds she hadn't seen from the doorway.

"It's not as bad as it looks."

From across the cubicle, an older man with his back to her spoke before Conley could, his voice deep and reassuring. He turned, a syringe in hand, a stethoscope around his neck. A name tag on his smock identified him as Dr. Sorelli.

"His injuries appear severe, but they're mostly insignificant. Landing in the snowdrift saved his bacon, big time. You're Mrs. Harrison, I presume?" The man's manner was forthright, almost crusty and Lara suddenly realized why his name sounded familiar. He was well-known in town, having been in the emergency room for almost two decades.

Lara nodded, but her eyes stayed on her husband's face. "Conley, I can't believe this happened. Good grief—"

"I'm fine, Lara." His words were brusque and curt, and somehow that made her feel better. He didn't *look* like himself, but he *sounded* like himself. "It was a stupid accident, that's all. I wasn't paying attention when I crossed the street in front of the office. A car came out of nowhere and clipped me as I stepped up on the curb."

Lara's knees went weak. She gripped the edge of the bed and held on, fighting nausea as well. "A car hit *you?*" She turned to Theresa then sent her horrified gaze back to Conley's face. "I thought you were in the Suburban...I thought there'd been a wreck, not this!"

The doctor came to where she stood. "If you're going to faint, do it outside. I need to give him this shot and we can't handle you, too."

Pulling herself together, Lara nodded numbly then watched Conley wince as the needle went in. The doctor stepped back to the counter, dropped the syringe into a red jug then he started to wash his hands.

Lara had more questions, but Sorelli grabbed a towel and turned around, speaking before she could. "I want to keep you for a couple of hours, Mr. Harrison. For observation. Sometimes nasty things develop that we can't see at first. After that you'll need to take it easy for a day or two—"

"I can't do that." Conley shook his head then grimaced. "I don't have time to be here as it is. I've got a flight to Baku tomorrow and work to do before I leave."

The doctor crossed his arms. "You're not going anywhere tomorrow. You'll be lucky if you can make it from the bed to the bathroom without these little white pills I'm going to give you."

"But I feel fine—"

"No, you don't," the doctor said, "and you definitely won't tomorrow. Especially after I sew up that leg. It's going to be stiff for at least a week."

Conley's mouth went into a familiar line of stubbornness and Lara stepped closer to the table. "You need to listen to him, Con."

"She's right." Theresa spoke up from the side of the room. "You were lucky out there, Conley. Don't be a fool. Stay home and take care of yourself."

"And Baku?" he asked.

"Matthew could go," Lara suggested.

Conley answered her, impatience heating his voice. "No, he can't. Matthew designs the damn chips but I can't let him near the clients, you know that. His people skills are nonexistent. We'd lose the account and then—"

"I can handle Baku." Lara and Conley both turned to Theresa when she spoke.

"You don't know the first thing about that account, Theresa."

"You're absolutely right," she agreed, "but I can *handle* it. I'll pick up the phone and tell them you've been delayed. If they don't like it, that's too bad."

He seemed to hesitate for just a second, and Lara held her breath. She felt a tug of anger that he'd consider Theresa's suggestion and not her own, but on the other hand, whatever worked, worked.

Reaching for the suture equipment he'd laid out on the counter, the doctor spoke again. "You'll have to talk to the police, too, you know. We've already called them."

Conley shot Lara a look, his gaze skimming hers in an unfamiliar way, something quick and fathomless shimmering there then swimming away before she could catch it. He turned to the doctor who was threading the needle. "That wasn't necessary," he protested. "It was a simple accident. All my fault, really. The car couldn't have avoided me—"

"It was a hit and run, Mr. Harrison. The police have been called." The doctor's words were blunt but his touch was swift and professional. Within seconds, he had Conley's wound closed with almost invisible stitches. He stepped back and appraised his work, then nodded, clearly pleased.

Snapping off his gloves he washed his hands once more and looked at his patient. "We'll find you a bed and let you settle in. If you're okay after a while, you can go home." Smiling at Lara, he spoke a final time. "Good luck keeping him quiet, Mrs. Harrison. Something tells me you're going to need it."

CHAPTER THREE

CONLEY HAD NO intention of sleeping, but as soon as his head hit the starched white pillowcase, he found he didn't have a choice. When he woke hours later, it was early evening. He was stiff and sore and felt as if...he'd been run over in the middle of the street.

Without moving, he opened his eyes. Lara sat in a padded chair on the other side of the bed, holding a magazine. She wasn't reading it, just holding it. The look on her face broke what was left of his heart. A deep sadness darkened her gaze and there were lines of weariness around her mouth. Lavender shadows colored the hollows of her cheeks and made circles underneath her eyes.

He let his lids flutter down and cursed himself. She looked like that because of him. There was no other reason and he knew it.

His mind skipped back to the moments before the car had come down the street. It *had* been a car, he was sure. A coupe. He struggled to recall more details but none came. Almost with relief, he knew that was all he could tell the police. He had absolutely

no proof that it'd been anything but an accident.
Maybe the driver had kept going because he hadn't
even known he'd hit something.

The argument sounded hollow, even to Conley's
doped-up senses.

He kept his eyes closed but the shot the doctor
had given him was working well and all the thoughts
Con usually managed to control now refused to stay
buried. The problems he'd managed to suppress for
months eddied around him like the snow outside.

It had all started with the notes.

They'd been arriving for several months, some by
regular mail, some by computer, one right after another. At first he'd been amused, then as they'd continued, he'd become annoyed. His answer had been
to ignore them, but lately even that had become impossible. Whoever had been harassing him had decided it was time to turn up the heat.

But *harassing* wasn't really the right word, he
thought groggily. Harassing implied something different, something angry and abusive. The neatly
typed letters and multiply-routed e-mails—all completely untraceable—were of a unique nature.
They'd been full of admiration for him, full of praise
for his accomplishments, for his successful business.
Then they'd turned personal. Comments about his
looks, remarks about his body. The author knew him
well, so well Conley had become increasingly uncomfortable, even though the tone of the notes had

never been threatening. Storing the letters in a safe at the office, he'd copied the e-mails to a file at home and passworded it so Lara couldn't read it.

The phone calls had started after that. There was never anyone on the line. As bizarre as it sounded, it seemed as if whoever called just wanted to hear his voice. He'd say hello over and over, then the caller would quietly hang up. Finally the flowers had started; red roses sent to him every Monday.

The last straw had come when his coat had been stolen during a business lunch. He'd dismissed the problem as inconsequential, telling Lara he'd misplaced it, but the keys to his office had been in the pocket. He'd immediately had all the locks changed, but it didn't seem to matter. A week later, someone got inside. Nothing had been taken, but he was positive someone had been there. Small things in his desk drawer had been rearranged and his chair had been left at a different angle. Worse, his computer had been accessed.

At that point, the problem took on a whole new meaning. Conley went to incredible lengths to maintain Harrison's proprietary secrets. Was someone trying to breech that wall? Knowing Matthew would die before he'd tell anyone, Conley had enlisted his help. Together he and his engineer had added extra security to their entire system, but for a couple of weeks afterward, Conley had made it a point to spend one night a week at the office, varying the nights. He'd set up camp in the room next to his own and waited, but no one had shown up. Finally he'd given up and picked up the phone to call the police.

Then he'd put it back down.

Harrison's *was* Conley Harrison. His investors were a nervous group and any hint, however remote, that something was amiss would send them flying faster than a covey of quails spooked by a retriever. Stalker, casual thief, corporate spy...they didn't care.

If this "accident" was in any way connected to the notes and his moneymen found out, Harrison's would be history, no matter how successful the company was. The fortune he'd made, the success he'd become...all of it would disappear. He'd be yesterday's news, another bad businessman who wasn't smart enough to hang on to what he'd made, his childhood poverty a mocking ghost that threatened to return.

Without the drugs swirling in his body, Conley knew he wouldn't have even allowed himself to think about any of this. He opened his eyes and looked at his wife. The horrific problems at work faded as he remembered her words that morning.

He'd known they were coming to this crisis but seemed incapable of stopping it. The long, cold silences, the angry accusations, the way she looked at him when she thought he didn't know. Everything had turned to shit and he didn't know how to avoid the inevitable. Conley let his eyes close again, the lids too heavy to hold up, his thoughts too onerous to consider anymore.

With Lara's pronouncement that morning, his future loomed before him. No career. No capital. No wife.

No life.

LARA SLIPPED BACK into the hospital room, the door closing behind her with a whisper. She hadn't wanted to leave, but with Conley asleep, she'd decided to run home and get him some clothes and give Ed a quick call to tell him what was going on. He'd been apoplectic when she'd refused his demands to bring Conley to Boulder, but Lara had persevered. "They're keeping an eye on him for a while. Basically, he's fine."

And he was. The doctor had already signed his release form. Despite being covered with bumps and bruises, some pretty nasty, Conley seemed all right.

But not exactly.

Placing the extra clothes she'd brought him in the bathroom, Lara came back and sat down, her eyes going to his still form. He appeared to be sleeping comfortably now, but before she'd left, he'd been turning restlessly, moaning from time to time. Lara had been shocked; Conley was the heaviest sleeper she knew. Was it pain that was bothering him or something more? She thought back to the look he'd sent her when Dr. Sorelli had said he'd called the police. What had that been all about? She'd wanted to ask, but in the end she'd said nothing because Conley wouldn't have answered her, anyway. He'd *have* to give answers to the two cops who'd already come by, though. Explaining that he was sleeping, Lara had asked them to return later and they'd agreed.

Too jittery to sit still, Lara opened the door and stepped into the corridor. She was halfway to the coffeepot at the nurse's station when Bess Mac-Dougal came out of the elevator. The older woman was clutching the stethoscope around her neck, her face wreathed in concern. Her gray hair was piled on top of her head in a haphazard bun, jeans and sneakers peeking out from beneath her white coat.

"Lara! I've been doing rounds and I just now picked up my messages and got yours! Is Conley all right? What happened?"

Just seeing Bess made Lara instantly feel better. Ed's third wife and the only one closer to his age than Lara's, Bess was a pediatrician and Lara's surrogate mother. She confided in Bess in a way she couldn't with Sandy, even as close as they were. Sandy was a good friend, but Bess was...something more.

"Your office told me where you were," Lara said. "I knew you'd come when you could."

"How is he?"

"He's fine," Lara answered, "at least physically…" They sat down on a nearby couch and Lara gave Bess the details. "He seems awfully nervous, though. I don't understand it."

"Well, good grief, child, he just got hit by a car. You'd be a tad nervous yourself!"

Lara nodded. "You're right. Things were so crazy this morning before he left I'm not thinking straight, I suppose…." She gave the older woman the rest of the story.

Without comment, Bess listened until Lara ran out of words. "Sandy thinks I'm an idiot," she concluded. With a troubled frown, she looked up at Bess. "Do you think I'm making a mistake?"

"Oh, Lord, Lara…I don't know." Bess reached into her pocket and pulled out an orange sucker. She offered it to Lara then stuck it in her mouth when Lara turned it down. "Relationships aren't exactly my strong point, you know. Ask your father if you don't believe me…."

Something more than her usual self-depreciating humor echoed in Bess's voice. Any other time Lara would have asked the other woman about it, but right now, her concern about Conley overrode everything else.

"I just don't know what to do," Lara said. "The last time we got to this point, I let him talk me out of it. When things slipped back into the same old routine, the pain was twice as bad.''

Bess patted her on the knee. "It always is the second time around."

"I can't go through that again. And I'm tired of trying. I have to protect myself."

"Well, you've already made your decision, honey, so stick with it and see what happens. That's all any of us can do. Young or old—" She started to say more, then her beeper went off. Grabbing the device and looking at it, Bess jumped up. "Oh, Lord, I've got to run! I've got a sweetie on the fourth floor who needs me. A bad case of flu—" She gave Lara a quick hug then flew down the hall toward the stairs. Wishing they could have talked more, Lara watched her leave. Bess would have been good for Ed, Lara thought for the ten millionth time. If they'd stuck together, he'd be a different man.

Turning around, Lara headed back to Conley's room, her emotions more tangled than ever. When she cracked open the door, her confusion only grew.

Conley was sitting up in bed.

With his rumpled hair and unshaven jaw, he looked vulnerable, defenseless...and sexy, Lara realized with a pang. Conley had always been one of the most handsome men she'd ever known, but he'd gotten more so as he'd aged. His eyes, forever dark and intense, now held shadows in them that drew her even closer. The few threads of silver that gleamed in the hair at his temples only added to his attraction. In one of those strange twists that couldn't be explained, the further apart they'd grown, the more appealing he'd become.

He lifted a hand to his forehead and touched his bandage. Then he threw off the sheets and started to get out of bed. Moving his right leg too quickly, he paled immediately, a sharp curse following the movement as he fell back against the pillows with a groan and pulled up the covers once more.

Lara couldn't help herself; she hurried into the room and to the side of the bed. "Are you all right? Do you want me to call the nurse?"

Before he could answer, the door squeaked open again. Lara and Conley both turned at the sound, but under his sheets, Conley immediately tensed, his whole body going taut and rigid. She glanced down at him in surprise then faced the two men who stood in the doorway. The two cops who'd stopped by earlier looked back at her.

"So you finally woke up, eh, Mr. Harrison?" The taller of the two, Officer Margulies, Lara recalled, walked to Conley's bed and held out his hand. He introduced himself and then turned to the shorter man beside him. The other one, Officer Fields, nodded at Conley.

"We came by earlier, but you were asleep. Your wife suggested we come back later."

Conley's mouth went tight. "She didn't tell me you had come."

"I didn't have a chance yet." Lara sent an apologetic smile to the officers, then a puzzled look to Conley. He was always short with his words, but he was rarely downright rude. "I was going to—"

"Doesn't matter, doesn't matter," Margulies dismissed her apology with a breezy wave of his hand. "We just wanted to talk to you about what happened, see if we can't track down the son of a gun who put you here, that's all." His smile was friendly enough, but behind his demeanor, Lara caught an edge of determination. He pulled out a notebook and pen as a wave of tension rose from Conley's bed. Lara was pretty sure the cops couldn't tell, but she could. If he'd been able, Conley would have sprung from the bed and raced down the hall to get away from the men.

"There's nothing to talk about," he said. "I'm sure it was an accident. The guy just didn't see me—"

"So it was a male driver?"

Conley tightened his mouth. "I couldn't tell for sure. I just meant the *driver*. Whoever he—or she— was, they couldn't see me. The snow was too bad and I was crossing the street against the light."

The cop wrote something. "Car, van, truck?"

"It was a car," Conley said, almost grudgingly. "A coupe, I think."

Margulies looked up. "Didn't get a plate number by any chance, did you?"

Conley shook his head.

"Color?"

"I don't know."

"Make?"

"No idea."

Lara stood by in silence. She wasn't surprised by Conley's answers; he'd been focused on their argument and wouldn't remember the details of the car. But why was he so nervous?

The other officer, who had said nothing up to this point, went to the opposite side of the room to lean against the wall. He spoke with his arms crossed, his face closed. "You own Harrison's, right?"

"That's right." Conley's voice sounded even tighter than it had before.

"Can't you give us any details at all about the car that hit you? Any damage on it, for example? A broken headlight maybe?" Margulies tapped his pen against his notebook. "This isn't much to work with."

"I've told you everything I can."

Fields spoke again, and despite her initial impressions, Lara realized he was the one in charge. "You have any enemies, Mr. Harrison?"

"Everyone has enemies, don't they?"

The two cops looked at him and so did Lara. After a second, Conley shrugged. "None that would want to run over me," he said finally. "At least none that I know of."

Slapping his notebook closed, Margulies shook his head. "Well, I guess that's it, unless you can think of—"

"Any problems at work?" Fields spoke as if the other man hadn't. Then he shot a glance in Lara's direction. "Any problems at home?"

"Everything's fine." Conley spoke quickly and Lara jerked her head in his direction. He smiled at her for the benefit of the watching policemen, but his eyes warned her not to call him on the lie.

Lara smiled back automatically. He was tighter than a watch spring, she thought in amazement. What on earth was wrong with him?

"I'd like to get home, though." He looked at the cops. "If that's all you need…"

"No problem," Margulies said, sending a nod in Lara's direction. "But you give us a call when you're feeling better and maybe we'll be able to do a little more. In the meantime, take care of yourself."

The door closed behind them with a swish, and Lara turned immediately to Conley. "What's going on?" she demanded without preamble. "You acted as if they were here to arrest you, for God's sake!"

"Nothing's going on." His demeanor sharp once more, he eased to the side of the bed with a grimace and stood up, an audible groan escaping before he could stop it.

Her first thought was to help him but this time she stayed where she was. "Conley, come on! I know you! I know you're hiding—"

Turning sharply, he cursed at her. "Dammit, Lara, I said nothing was going on. Would you believe me for once? Cut me some slack, for God's sake. I'm in pain here!"

When he came out of the bathroom a few moments later, he was dressed in the clothes she'd brought him. "Let's get out of here," he said without looking at her. "I want to go home."

CONLEY BROODED all the way home and Lara let him. It was pointless to try to get him to talk so she didn't even make the effort.

They drove through the snow-locked town in silence, the beauty of the frozen landscape nonexistent to them both. The only thing Lara could think about were the two cops and their questions. At Mesa, she frequently dealt with the police about the various cases they were handling. Margulies and Fields were good but it would have taken better to pry anything out of Conley.

And he clearly had something to hide.

As she turned down their street and eased into the driveway, it hit Lara. Maybe Conley *did* have something to hide…but not from them. She'd been in the room, too. Maybe his reluctance to elaborate had more to do with her presence than theirs.

The idea upset her, but there was nothing she could do about it. If she had any sense, from now on she'd close her mind to thoughts like those. Their marriage was over. She'd declared it dead with her request. The only thing left to do was bury it. Getting hurt and wondering about what could have been made no difference now.

She pulled the SUV into the garage and parked, but by the time she got to the other side of the vehicle to help Conley out, he'd already managed to open his door and slide from the seat. Pale and clearly in pain, he stood stiffly as she rounded the truck's fender.

"I would have helped you." She stopped, her hand on the cold metal. "Couldn't you have waited?"

"It's okay," he said from behind gritted teeth.

Always silent, always tough.

"Fine." She turned around and abandoned him where he was. If that was what he wanted, she could play by those rules, she fumed. Let him make his own damn way inside.

She unlocked the door and went into the house. She'd left the thermostat up that morning when she'd rushed to the hospital and a comforting warmth wrapped itself around her. The place felt like home. Except one ingredient was missing—the essential one—and that was, as Sandy had so aptly noted, love.

A few moments after she entered, the door squeaked again and Conley stepped inside. One look at his face and the thoughts she'd just had fled Lara's mind. Conley looked horrible, all his weight on his good left leg. She rushed to where he wobbled.

"Put your arm around my shoulder," she commanded. "You need some help."

"I don't—"

"Oh, for God's sakes, Conley! You're white as a sheet and just about as strong. Let me help you get into bed!"

He started to say something, then obviously thought better of it. Lifting his arm, he draped it over her shoulder.

Her reaction was instantaneous.

It'd been months since Conley had touched her, even the most casual of brushes. When they passed each other in the hall, they both went to great lengths to avoid contact. Now the whole length of his body was pressed up against hers, the warmth of his arms and legs heating her too sensitive skin, his chest tucked against her shoulder in a perfect fit. Memories of other times they'd walked this way, with her snuggled under his arm, his cologne filling her senses, suddenly flooded her. She could even feel his heart beating, she thought with alarm. His pulse was pounding a rhythm so fast and powerful, it had to be painful.

Then she realized it wasn't his pulse she was feeling. It was hers. And it *was* painful. Each beat spoke to her. *This is what it used to be like. This is what you used to have.*

She wondered for a second if he were experiencing some of the same conflicted emotions, then Lara gave herself a mental shake. What was she thinking? Of course, he wasn't.

He brought their progress to a halt and looked down at her. She lifted her gaze to his, his mouth so close to her forehead she could feel his warm breath when he spoke.

"Am I too heavy?"

"I—I think I can manage."

"What about the stairs?"

"Oh, my God..." Lara looked up at him. "I didn't even think about the stairs! There's no way you can go up there." The master suite was on the second floor. "You'll have to take the guest room."

His expression shifted minutely, then she understood.

"I'll move out," she said stiffly. "It won't take but a few minutes to get my things."

"Don't." He tilted his head toward the den. "Just put me in there. I'll sleep on the couch for a couple of days. As soon as the swelling goes down, I'll be fine with the stairs."

Without any argument, she nodded, and together
they made their way into the paneled room off the
kitchen. Lara eased him down onto the couch where
he settled with a heavy sigh. "You'll have to get
my stuff from upstairs," he said. "I need my brief-
case and my cell phone. There's a file on the chair
beside the bed, too. Bring it and—"

Lara stared at him in amazement. "Conley, what
you *need* is to rest! You can't work right now."

"I can't just sit here," he said in a tight voice.
"I'll go nuts."

"Then here—" she handed him the remote
"—watch a little TV. Do nothing for a change. Relax. That's what normal people do sometimes, you
know."

He started to reply but the telephone rang. Lara
crossed the room to answer it, and Theresa Marchante replied to her cool hello.

"Lara, is Conley there? I stopped by the hospital
and they told me he'd checked out."

"We got home a little while ago, Theresa. Would
you like to talk to him?"

"I'm afraid I have to. It's about the Baku situation...."

Without another word, Lara handed her husband
the phone then stepped out of the room. He was
going to work, with or without her help, so she
might as well leave him to it.

In the kitchen Lara started dinner, her mind hopping from one thing to another. Her thoughts landed, as she knew they would, back on Conley's behavior at the hospital. She opened the refrigerator and pulled out a bunch of onions to chop for the soup. He hadn't wanted to talk to the police, that much had been obvious. If her presence in the room had been the main factor, why?

Her fertile imagination had Lara coming up with more answers than she needed. The knife flashed as she listed them in her mind, but all the variations centered on one thing: the *Other Problem*.

Conley was having an affair.

Lara didn't know who the woman was and she didn't want to know, but she recognized the signs; in her business, she had learned them all. Through the years, though, she'd studied Conley as well and *that* was how she'd finally figured it out. He'd been hiding something from her for months now. Not to mention the nights he didn't come home. Or the times he raced to pick up the phone when they were both at home. And then there was the note, of course. The classic giveaway.

It was so clichéd, she'd wanted to throw up. On her way to the cleaners, she'd found a crumpled e-mail in one of his pockets. The message was clear, the point so personal and graphic, Lara's guts had been turned inside out. She'd gone home and searched their computer for more. She'd found an encrypted file, but hadn't been able to get past his security password. She was sure it held other e-mails.

She'd asked him point-blank if he was having an affair. He'd looked at her as if she'd sprouted horns then denied it—just as she'd known he would. That was when she'd moved out of the master bedroom.

A sound from the doorway brought her head up. She wondered how long he'd been standing there and watching her.

Their eyes connected over the kitchen table. "I think I need one of those pills Sorelli gave us. Do you have them?"

Lara nodded and wiped her hands on her apron. "They're in my purse. I'll get them for you."

She handed him the medicine and a glass of water a few seconds later. When he finished, he set the glass on the counter with a sigh. He looked worn-out.

She spoke without thinking. "Why don't you go back into the den and rest? I'll bring you your soup on a tray."

"You don't mind?" He ran a hand through his dark hair, leaving it spiked and wavy. "Waiting on me like this?"

"You can't very well do it yourself, can you?"

"No, but it's been a long time since you did anything like that."

"It's been a long time since you've been around so that I could."

Without a word, he turned around and went back into the den. Angry at herself for the pettiness, Lara returned to the sink.

An hour later, when she walked into the den with a wooden tray in her hands, Conley was asleep. Sprawled on the couch, he had a pillow tucked under his swollen knee and another one behind his head. In his restlessness, he'd already managed to throw off the afghan. It lay in a brightly colored pile at the foot of the sofa.

Lara put the tray on a nearby table and picked up the wool throw. Fluffing it out, she bent over to put it across his sleeping form, but it was too short; it barely covered his torso and the top part of his legs. Stretching it as far as the yarn would allow, she bent to her knees and tucked it in around him, then she stopped and looked at his bruised face.

Even in rest, Conley looked fierce and anxious, tension etching its way across his features. She reached out and gently smoothed a lock of dark hair that had escaped to curl over his brow. Long and silky, it was softer than she remembered. He was such a handsome man, she thought with a catch in her throat. Lean and hungry-looking, he was the type women glanced at then imagined in bed.

Her hand drifted lower, down to the edge of his jaw. A line of steel that never bent. His chin was dark with the shadow of his stubble, his skin felt warm, as warm as the rest of his body had been as she'd helped him inside. She let her touch linger for a moment, her eyes on the pulse at the bottom of his throat.

How many times had she kissed him in that spot?

How many times had he done the same to her?

For one crazy minute she thought about pressing her lips against his neck, then she came to her senses.

What was she doing? She'd told this man she wanted to end their marriage. She'd told him she wanted a divorce. She'd told herself she didn't love him anymore.

She'd told the truth.

Hadn't she?

CHAPTER FOUR

CONLEY HUNG UP the phone and started rearranging the papers in the file spread over his mahogany desk. It was busywork and nothing more, and with an angry curse, he stood and limped to the window that covered one wall of his office. In the crystal-blue distance, the Rocky Mountains glistened, their towering peaks blanketed in a thick layer of pristine snow, dotted with patches of green firs. Filled with a sense of doom, he stared out at the stunning view.

He'd gotten the first call the day after his accident. A second one had come the day after that. By the end of the week, it was clear his mishap hadn't escaped the notice of his investors. Suspicious and wary, it was almost as if they'd been told about the other incidents. With no options left, he'd flown to Houston that weekend and met the primaries in an elegant hotel. The gracious surroundings had done nothing to smooth their worried brows. To say they hadn't been happy was more than an understatement.

The shit had hit the fan.

They'd given him an ultimatum: Get security and

get it immediately. Call the police. Call the FBI. Call whoever it takes, but have the stalker found and stopped. And by the way, make damn sure no one hears about this, either. No one.

Conley shook his head. He couldn't deny their logic. The tech market was shaky enough on a good day; publicity as potentially bad as this could put a spike right through the heart of Harrison's. The whole company would go straight down the tubes. This morning—a week since his accident—he'd brought Matthew Oakley in and discussed the situation, explaining the nervous investors and their desire for security. Matthew had reacted just as Conley had known he would.

"This makes my point, Con," he'd said. "We need to move on the glass chip. I'm telling you, it's the best way for us to get on top. The money guys will forget about everything when they hear about this idea."

Standing beside Conley's desk, Matthew had worn a familiar expression—one of stubborn persistence. Quiet and self-effacing, the gifted designer understood the world of computer chips better than anyone Conley had ever known. But he was also invisible. Light-brown hair, nondescript eyes, average height and weight. When he walked into a room, no one ever saw Matthew. Even fewer listened when he talked. And so he was dismissed.

But not by Conley. He'd recognized Matthew's intelligence instantly.

Matthew put his hands on the desk. "Let me run with it, Con. We can't wait any longer. Somebody else will jump in there."

They'd had this discussion too many times to count. Matthew had designed a chip—on his own— that he wanted Harrison's to sell. But Conley wasn't willing to go forward. There had been problems with the preliminary run and even more had been discovered in the beta testing phase. If Harrison's delivered a product before the bugs had been worked out, the harm the company could suffer would be greater than missing the market completely.

"I can't do that, Matthew." Conley had shook his head. "Not now. Not yet. It's not ready and neither is the company. You've still got some problems with that chip and I'm not putting Harrison's name on it until those are solved."

The expression on Matthew's face had said it all. Anger, then resentment, then acceptance. "Okay," he'd sighed. "You're the boss. You know best."

Right, Conley thought now.

His company *and* his marriage were two trains on parallel tracks, each heading toward the edge of the canyon with no bridge in sight. *I'm the boss,* he thought. *And I know…shit.*

A knock sounded on his office door. Turning

painfully, his leg still sore, Conley called out and the door opened.

Theresa stood on the threshold, a notebook in her hand, her strong, distinctive perfume preceding her. She rented space downstairs, and in fact, that was how they'd met. Right after Conley had moved the company into the bigger offices several years ago, they'd literally run into each other in the hallway. When he'd learned she was an attorney they'd started talking and the relationship had followed.

"I just received the new contracts for the London deal. Is this a good time to go over them or would you rather wait until later?"

He motioned for her to come in, and she did so, closing the door behind her. Walking briskly to the conference table at one end of his office, she opened the file and spread out the papers. Conley stayed where he was, staring out the window.

After a few minutes, he realized she was waiting. "I'm sorry, Theresa," he said, shaking his head. "I've got a lot of my mind—"

"It's okay." She looked as if she were debating something. Finally, she spoke. "It's Lara, isn't it? She told me about the divorce, Conley. I don't know what to say except I'm sorry...."

Conley didn't bother to hide his surprise. "She told you?"

"Yes. When I called her about the accident, she explained."

Conley fell silent. Lara wasn't the kind of woman who shared personal things with people, excepting Sandy, of course. Her job called for that kind of discretion but it was her nature, as well. Then it dawned on him. She'd told Theresa so she could get a referral.

"Did you tell her who to call?"

"What do you mean?"

"Did you give her the name of an attorney?"

For once, Theresa looked flustered. "No— I—I didn't do that. She didn't ask. I—"

"It doesn't matter." He turned back to the window and stared out at the mountains in the distance. Their frozen peaks looked as cold and hard as his heart felt at the moment. "I think we'd better review those contracts later if you don't mind."

She murmured something he didn't quite catch and a few minutes later the door opened then closed. He stayed where he was for a little bit longer, then he reached for the phone. There was no sense in putting off his decision. This was a problem that had to be resolved…and there was only one firm for a thousand miles that could handle it.

THERESA CLOSED the door softly, but stayed where she was, her fingers wrapped around the door knob. Poor Conley. He didn't look well. Still pale and shaky from his accident, he shouldn't have been at work. He should have been at home, sipping hot tea in front of the fireplace, taking it easy after that horrible accident. He should have been relaxing. He should have someone taking care of things for him.

Someone who loved him as he deserved.

Her hand tightened involuntarily, the cold metal hard beneath her touch.

If he'd been her husband, she wouldn't have let him leave the house.

Forcing her fingers to relax, she released the doorknob and started down the hall toward the back stairs, her shoulders stiff with anger. Lara Harrison didn't deserve him and she never had. She didn't know the first thing about taking care of a man. All she cared about was herself. Anyone who'd ever met her knew how true that was. She was just like her father. Self-centered and completely oblivious to those around her.

Her heels clattering on the metal stairs, Theresa reached her office and slammed the door behind her. Dropping the files on her desk, she crossed the room and stood beside the window. Her view was the same as Conley's. She'd planned it that way from the very beginning. When she looked out at the mountains she saw exactly what he did.

The symbolism had appealed to her.

Closing her eyes against the startling beauty of the mountains, Theresa allowed herself a tiny smile. Her mother had always told her one day her luck would change and she'd been right. Theresa had grown up on a ranch in South Texas, a hardscrabble place where she and her mom, the cook and maid on the spread, had lived in a run-down shack that froze in the winter and baked in the summers.

Her whole life had felt like a struggle that never ended, one catastrophe after another. Her father was someone she never knew. The fight for grades and a scholarship. Then law school on no funds and a dishwashing job. Nothing had been easy for Theresa. Then she'd met Conley Harrison and everything had fallen into place. And that's when she'd understood. Conley was the key to her happiness. It sounded corny, but Theresa didn't care. She recognized the truth when it made itself known. For years, she'd been waiting for someone to make her life right. Conley was that person.

Because she saw everything as Conley did. Not just the view, either. His business, his way of life, even what he ate. Everything about them was the same, even their hard childhoods. They were two halves of one whole, and someday soon he'd realize that.

Lara would, too.

"WE NEED TO make sure we're clear on this." Tapping the file on his desk with one burly finger, Ed looked past Lara to where her stepbrother sat. Larry Journay—Ed's son by wife number three—nodded in agreement, which was exactly what he always did and what Ed expected him to do. The new client Ed was referring to, an accountant who thought his business partner was cheating him, was someone Larry would handle. "I don't want this guy going nuts if we find out the truth. Call the Denver police and make sure he doesn't have any priors. I'm not sure I trust what he's telling us so far."

Ed turned to Lara. Beneath a pair of beer-colored eyebrows, his green eyes burned with their usual intensity. "Has he sent in the retainer yet? If he hasn't, we might want to wait...."

Lara blinked and tried to focus. She'd been listening, but most of her attention was back at the house, not on Ed's latest potential catastrophe. The day after Conley's accident, work had intruded before he'd even dressed, Theresa visiting him with some papers needing his signature. Lara had wanted to talk to him about the divorce, to pin him down if she could, but he'd left in a hurry. He'd phoned later from the office and told her he was going to have to take a call in the middle of the night from Baku so he was just going to sleep there, on his couch. Then he'd flown to Houston for the weekend. A meeting, he'd said.

Right.

A week had passed since the accident, but she still hadn't been able to corner him long enough to talk about the problem. All she'd done was worry over the point Sandy had made. What *would* Lara do if Conley refused to give her a divorce?

"Lara?" Ed's voice boomed with impatience. "Have we gotten this guy's money or what?"

She answered automatically. "No. He said he was sending a check, but nothing's come in yet."

Ed made a sound of impatience, then continued his instructions until Stephanie, Larry's wife, came into the office and interrupted them. Her eyes fell on Lara, her voice subdued.

"Con's on line one. Shall I put him through to your office?" Normally bouncy and cheerful, Stephanie didn't wait for Lara's answer. "I can put him off," she offered. "If you don't want to talk to him...."

Ed had told everyone at their office Lara and Conley were divorcing, and they'd all been treating her as if someone had died.

Lara stood up. "I'll take it in there, Steph. Put him through."

Back at her desk, Lara took a deep breath, then picked up the phone. Conley's tense voice answered her own edgy hello.

"I need to see you," he said without preamble. "Do you have some time available this afternoon?"

Lara stiffened, Sandy's warning flashing through her mind like an out of control strobe light.

"I might," she hedged. "Is there something important we need to talk about?"

"It's not an issue to discuss over the phone."

"If this is about the divorce—"

"It isn't about the divorce, Lara." He spoke as quietly as ever, but behind the words, Lara detected something she'd never heard in Conley's voice. Ever. She told herself she was imagining things, then he spoke again and she was sure she was right. What she heard was fear.

Before she could question him, he said, "It's something else, a problem. I want you to bring Ed, as well. Come at three. I'll be free by then."

She said all right, but he'd already hung up, so she did the same, staring at the phone as if it could answer all her questions. She must have been mistaken. Conley afraid? It made no sense, none whatsoever. Whatever his faults might be, he was the toughest man she'd ever known. He'd left home at sixteen and joined the military as soon as he could. Afterward, holding down three jobs, he'd made his way through college and had still sent money home. He'd been on his own forever. Nothing could scare Conley Harrison.

But he'd definitely sounded frightened.

She wanted to give the idea more thought but she pulled herself together and went back to Ed's office. It wasn't worth facing his ire if she missed the rest of the meeting. She slipped inside and took her seat, and for the next hour they continued to discuss their current clients. The firm was respected in circles that counted. In fact, they had a waiting list because Ed kept the number of cases very limited. They only had three at the moment: a senator's wife who was scared of her about-to-be-divorced husband, the eleven-year-old daughter of a corporate raider who was under a kidnapping threat, and a Wall Street firm that thought someone was about to blackmail their CEO. If Mesa took the accountant, he'd be number four and that would be it. They never handled more than four cases at a time.

At long last, Ed finished up. Larry left the room, but Lara stayed where she was. Ed looked over his half glasses at her, his eyebrows lifted.

"Conley wants a meeting," she said. "With the two of us this afternoon. At his place."

"A meeting? How much time will it take? I have to be at the bank before five and I'm taking Bess out tonight. What does he want?"

He was taking Bess out? Lara wondered briefly what that was all about, then she put aside the question. She'd call Bess later and find out. If Conley was lying and he *did* want to fight the divorce, then Lara had more important things to worry about than what her father and Bess were up to.

"I don't know what he wants, Ed. Something about the divorce, I guess. What else could it be?"

"Then why does he need me?"

"I have no idea."

As Lara spoke, an indescribable weariness came

over her. Her life felt as if it were melting under the
onslaught of heated emotions and disappointments.
Ed stared at her and started to speak, but all at once
Lara gathered her papers and stood. She didn't want
to hear what he had to say, no matter what it was.
She turned and walked out of his office.

She couldn't handle anything more.

LATE THAT AFTERNOON, Conley limped around his
office with a restless energy, the cord of his headset
dragging along behind him. His leg was feeling better, but it still hurt some. He grimaced against the
pain and concentrated on his phone call.

"Have you checked on the dip switches on lines
two and four? Those com lines have to be open and
clear or there might be a timing problem. If all the
buses are trying to use the same path, the data's
gonna cross and everything will be scrambled."

He waited for the translator to relay his question
and cursed silently. He should be there in person!
How could you fix a computer without seeing what
in the hell was going on? It wasn't just the data that
was getting scrambled, he was sure. There was no
way someone who didn't know what they were doing could follow his directions.

Looking at his watch, he cursed again. Right now,
Lara and Ed were probably walking into the building, and he hadn't had a moment to think since he'd
called her early this morning. He'd wanted to or-

ganize his thoughts, get his facts lined up just so, and he hadn't had the chance.

Along with his phone problem, he'd been too busy staring at the damn roses sitting on his desk. Ellen, his secretary, had brought them in sometime midmorning. When he'd questioned her, she'd told him they'd been delivered by a courier. As always, Conley had her tracking down the florist but he was sure the people at the shop would say the same thing each florist did. The flowers had been ordered over the phone and paid for with cash mailed in advance. Sorry, they had no record of the sender.

He usually sent the bouquets immediately to the retirement home down the road, unable to stand the sight of their bloodred petals but he'd kept them this time to show Ed and Lara. The one word note lay on his desk, the four letters blinking up at him almost evilly.

Soon...

With a start, he realized the translator was talking again. He'd completely lost track. Interrupting the woman, he stopped her in midword.

"Look," he said, "I'm not going to solve this problem like this, okay? I can't come myself, but I'll send someone. Tell them—"

At the other end of the line, his Azeri customer started to scream. Obviously he knew more English than Conley had assumed. "No," the man cried.

"Not someone. You. Must be you. Other person, no!"

With promises he knew might be empty, Con soothed the man as much as he could, hanging up a few minutes later. He was ripping off his headset when a tap sounded on his door. The door opened and Theresa stood on the threshold, Lara and Ed right behind her.

Lara nodded toward Conley then her eyes went straight to the roses. She lifted her puzzled gaze to his as Theresa spoke. "How gorgeous! What wonderful flowers." Turning to Ed and Lara, the lawyer gestured to them with a wave of her hand. "I was walking through the lobby when they arrived so we all came up together. I bent their ears about my vacation and..."

Her voice drifted off. Pulling his eyes from Lara's, Conley realized Theresa was waiting for him to say something.

A stiff second passed, then Lara broke the silence. "And we appreciate the escort." With a reassuring smile in the other woman's direction, she stepped past Theresa and into Conley's office. Ed entered behind her and took a seat on Conley's sofa. "I want to hear more about your trip to San Francisco, too," Lara said in a friendly way. "It sounds as if you had a really good time. Maybe we can talk some more later?"

Clearly dismissed, there was nothing else Theresa

could do but smile. "I'd love to tell you about it. And I have some photos." She glanced down at her watch. "I've got an appointment on the other side of town with another client, but I'll dig them up and we'll have lunch next week."

"That sounds great." Lara then looked at Conley. No one else would have noticed, but he saw the strain behind her expression, the effort it was taking for her to make the smallest of conversation. Theresa waited a moment more, then she quietly closed the door, leaving the three of them alone.

His wife's mask fell away as the door clicked shut. All at once she looked even more weary and Conley's chest went tight. He didn't know how she was going to react to his news, but what he had to say wasn't going to help matters, that was damn sure.

Conley crossed his office but stopped short of his desk. Taking one of the chairs in front of the sofa instead, he waved Lara toward the couch. She stayed where she was, her hands gripping the back of the chair beside him.

"What's this all about, Conley?" Every muscle in her body was tense. With her sleek blond hair pulled back and her deep hazel eyes staring into his, she looked like a coiled cat, ready to spring and run away. "If this is about the—"

"I have a problem," he interrupted bluntly. "A

very big problem. And I need some help figuring out what to do.''

LARA STARED AT Conley, her heart in her throat as it had been ever since he'd called earlier. She'd thought about it all day, unable to imagine what he would want if not to talk about the divorce. Now as he spoke, she was dumbfounded. She'd never heard him admit to even having a *problem,* much less ask for help resolving it. When faced with a issue, he simply fixed it. End of story.

''A problem?'' She looked at Ed uneasily before returning her gaze to Conley's. ''What kind of problem?''

''It's with my investors. They're worried about the company and they think we need some help with our security. I'm not sure I agree with them, but they're right about one thing. If this gets out, Harrison's will be in trouble.''

'''This?''' With one word, as usual, Ed went to the heart of it all. ''You wanna be a little more specific there, son?''

Conley gave Lara a look. She'd been momentarily relieved, but now she remembered the way he'd stared at her at the hospital when the two cops had interviewed him. A cold chill, unexplainable but definitely real, rippled down her back.

Without saying anything he stood and grabbed a piece of paper off his desk. Tossing it to the low table in front of the sofa, he waited for them to read it.

Lara studied it. "'Soon?' What does that mean?"

"I have no idea." He tilted his head toward his desk. "It came with the flowers. The flowers that have been coming once a week for quite a while now. Along with notes and e-mails and phone calls." He shook his head with an impatient jerk. "I don't have a damn clue what any of it means. Some-one got into my office, too. I've been trying to catch them, but they never come when I'm here. It's creepier than hell. Changed the locks—doesn't even matter. They access the burglar alarm and walk right in. I've been blowing it off but I can't do that any-more. Not now." His eyes went hard. "My investors found out. They think the accident might be related to my problem and they're scared someone will leak the story. If that happens, Harrison's is as good as dead."

The words washed over Lara, almost meaningless in their unexpectedness, but one thing stood out. She instantly remembered the sheet of crumpled com-puter paper she'd found in his pocket. Then she re-membered how intimate it had been. How she'd as-sumed it meant he was having an affair... It didn't seem possible a stalker would write something like that. "I don't think I understand."

"I don't understand it, either." He pursed his mouth into a grim line. "All I can tell you is this—

someone's been bothering me for months. They seem determined to…do something but I don't know what. If the accident is connected to it…'' His eyes swept to Ed then they came back to Lara's face. Once again, something dark shimmered in their depths, something she didn't want to name.

Ed broke in. ''Well, if someone's getting into your office that easily, it's got to be someone inside. Have you considered—''

Conley swung his head around. ''I've considered everyone and everything, but I keep coming up blank. It might be corporate espionage or it might be something personal. Whatever they want, I can't ignore them any longer.'' Conley shook his head in defeat. ''I need some help. I need *your* help.''

''Give us more details.'' Ed pulled a notebook from the inside pocket of his jacket. ''When exactly did it start? What was the first thing that happened?''

Lara listened as Conley began to outline the incidents. It was almost too much for her to take in. Why had he kept this to himself? Why hadn't he told her? They weren't close anymore, but this was something so big…

She couldn't help herself. The words came out on their own. ''Why didn't you tell me about this, Conley? Why have you kept it a secret?''

He looked uncomfortable with her question, but he answered her. ''I didn't think it meant anything at first. When the situation got more serious, I decided not to bother you."

"'Not to bother...'" Repeating his excuse, Lara broke off in amazement. "Good grief, Conley, I could have helped you. We could have been working on this sooner and it might not have gotten this bad—"

"I assumed you wouldn't want to get involved."

His blunt answer silenced her completely. Not that there was anything else she *could* have said, she thought blankly. He'd summed up their situation perfectly, as always.

Ed broke the stalemate. "Mesa can handle this. Stalkers aren't that unusual. We've done them before."

"I know you can handle the situation." Conley turned to his father-in-law. "The problem is keeping it quiet. No one can find out about this, Ed. Absolutely no one. I'm on really shaky ground here."

"We're discreet, Con, you know that."

Conley listened, then with an uncharacteristically agitated move, he raised his hands and threaded them through his thick, dark hair. "They want me to have bodyguards, for Christ's sake! How can that be discreet?"

His stinging words still causing her pain, Lara spoke sharply. "What's more important, Conley? Your life or your business? Can't you see what's happening here—"

"Dammit to hell, Lara, this isn't my fault, okay? I didn't plan on having—"

"Hey!" Ed's booming voice stopped them both. "This isn't divorce court, okay? I know you two aren't seeing things eye-to-eye but this isn't the time or the place. We've got to solve this problem first, then you can scream at each other in some damn lawyer's office."

Conley nodded immediately, his customary cool returning. "You're right, Ed. Of course. We need to concentrate on the matter at hand."

Crossing her arms, Lara sat down without saying a word, a seething storm of emotions threatening to overwhelm her. She was angry at Conley, mad as she could be. Mixed in with her exasperation was something else, she realized suddenly. Something she wouldn't have expected, considering everything. She was worried about him, too. He was in danger.

But why in the hell did she even care?

Ed began to speak again, his standard discussions with a client. Lara listened, an air of unreality settling over her. After a while, under control once more, she told herself it wasn't that big a deal. The firm could handle Conley's case without her, and the divorce could proceed.

"We'll work out a plan, Conley. It won't be that difficult to come up with something." Ed stood, reaching for his coat and gloves. "We'll set up some kind of scenario, and I promise you, no one will

wonder why we're around. In the meantime, we'll
need copies of all the notes and anything else you
think is significant. And of course you should notify
the police. They'll be the ones in charge of catching
the bad guy. We'll be the ones in charge of keeping
you safe while they do their thing.''

"I've already talked to them. They're aware of
what's going on,'' Conley answered. "But I'm not
worried about my safety. I'm worried about my
business.''

Lara opened her mouth then snapped it shut. What
was it going to take for her to understand? Conley
didn't care about anything but Harrison's. The time
had come for her to accept that.

THE RIDE HOME seemed longer than it should have.
Lara stared at the passing scenery and tried to keep
her mind clear, but for some reason all she could
think about was when she and Conley had first gotten married. Things had been so different then! He'd
never been one to say "I love you," never been one
to be romantic with flowers or candy, but she'd always known he cared and cared deeply. When that
had changed, she couldn't exactly say. But somewhere in the past seven years, a subtle shift had
taken place, like the movement of the earth's crust
over time. What had been straight, was now
crooked. What had been whole, was now cracked.

Today another tremor had occurred and the damage was even greater.

A stalker had taken over Conley's life. And Lara hadn't even known.

Ed reached over and adjusted the heater, his voice breaking into her thoughts as if he could read her mind. "You really didn't know a thing about this, Lara? You didn't have a clue?"

"I'm as surprised as you are. He hadn't said a word. Conley doesn't share things with me, Ed. He hasn't for a long time."

"Was he acting differently? Quieter, more remote?"

"I guess if I thought about it hard enough, I'd say he's been more withdrawn but I would have attributed it to our problems. I had no idea this was going on."

Lara watched the mountains pass in silence. They were almost to the edge of Red Feather before she spoke again, her voice quiet and subdued. "I do know one thing." She glanced across the seat. "He's having an affair."

The car jerked to one side of the road, Ed overcorrecting it with a yank on the steering wheel. "What! Are you nuts? Conley wouldn't—"

"Oh, yes, he would. And he is." Lara felt her jaw go tight. "It's been going on for quite some time. I've asked him about it but he denied everything."

"I don't believe that," Ed said. "Conley isn't that kind of man."

"I didn't think he was, either," she said bitterly. "But the proof's there. I've seen it." In halting words, she told her father about the note and the phone calls.

Ed turned to her in amazement. "Lara, get a grip, for God's sake. He wasn't having an affair. The note came from the stalker!"

"That's what I thought, too, the minute Conley told us what was going on, but..."

"But what?"

She put aside the doubts that had been plaguing her since they'd left the office. She couldn't contemplate what it would mean if she were wrong about the affair.

"The note I read was a personal one," she said. "From a woman. Trust me, Ed, she made it more than clear the two of them had been intimate. This was *not* something a stalker would write." Staring at the passing scenery, Lara spoke. "It doesn't matter anyway. The relationship we had is gone. Conley's different and so am I."

"Well, you're going to have put all that aside." She felt her father's gaze and turned to meet it. "You're going to have to work this case, Lara. I need you, and so does Conley."

"You've got tons of men who can do the job, and Conley's never needed me for anything." Lara was shaking her head before Ed could finish. "I'm not having anything to do with this one, Ed. I can't—"

"Can't means won't." Ed twisted the steering wheel and the silver Cadillac, his pride and joy, shot into Lara's driveway with a screech. Cutting off the engine, he looked at her sternly. "You don't have a choice, Lara. It's *your* job. You *will* work it and that's that."

"No, I won't." She glared at him from across the soft leather seats. "We shouldn't even be taking the damn thing, if you ask me. It would put us over our limit."

"We'll dump the accountant. You said yourself he hasn't sent in the check like he should have."

Childishly, Lara stared out the window and refused to meet her father's eyes.

"You *will* work this case," he repeated.

She swung her head around, her hands in fists at her side. "You can fire me if you like, but I'm *not* taking this on, Ed. And it's incredibly unfair of you to ask." She crossed her arms. "What would I even do for Conley? He doesn't need a bodyguard as much as he needs a baby-sitter. That's what his investors want."

"Yes, but—"

"When he goes out, when he's in the office…someone has to be with him 24/7," Lara continued, uninterrupted and unfazed by Ed's response. "And whoever it is, they've got to be good. Someone no one will notice or Conley will be in even more trouble.''

"I was going to say that."

"I know his investors. They're hard men, Ed. They'll want the best."

"That's exactly right."

"You're going to have to find the perfect person."

"That's exactly right."

His repetition registered, and Lara finally understood. "Oh, no…" She held up her hands as if she could physically ward off his suggestion. "No way. Uh-uh. Ed, I am not—"

"You have to, Lara. You're the only one who can be around him that much and not raise any suspicions. We could set up a fake security review. You could tell everyone we're doing it at Con's request—even put an extra guy at the office so you could catch a break sometimes. If you don't want to do that, then we'll come up with another plan. As long as it's reasonable, his employees will accept the explanation, whatever it is.'' He paused. "It's perfect and you know it."

She swallowed hard. "It's *not* perfect and I'm *not* going to do this. Don't ask me to. Please, Ed."

He stared at her in the early-afternoon gloom. Outside the warm confines of the car, it started to snow again. She wanted to cry, she wanted to scream, she wanted to do anything but what he was about to ask her to do.

"No one on earth would give your presence another thought. The setup's too great to ignore." Ed stared at her, his fingers tapping the steering wheel. "You're his wife," he said quietly. "And you're going to have to act like it, whether you want to or not."

CHAPTER FIVE

CONLEY MADE IT a point to get home early that night. He felt strange walking into the house before eight, but he wanted to talk to Lara some more. To see if she and Ed had discussed any kind of plan. Obviously surprised by his arrival, she came down the hall from the bedroom where she slept and met him in the kitchen.

Her appearance made him stop and stare. Holding a bottle of cleaning fluid, she had on a pair of old sweatpants and a T-shirt two sizes too big. With her hair pulled back and her face free of makeup, it was clear she'd been cleaning house. She always cleaned when she was upset.

"You're early." Her hazel eyes glinted with suspicion.

Still in his coat and gloves, he stood in the center of the kitchen like an uninvited stranger. "I wanted to talk to you. About the problem."

"There's nothing to discuss right now." Her gaze left his then came back. "Ed made some suggestions on the way home, but they aren't workable. He needs to consider the situation a little longer."

Conley nodded. "I understand. But I'd still like your take on it." He hesitated. "You're sharp about things like this, Lara. You have good instincts. I think I made a mistake not telling you about this sooner."

A shocked expression crossed her face before she closed it once again. Conley shrugged out of his coat. "I'd like to discuss it with you over dinner."

She blinked—as if she hadn't quite heard him correctly—then nodded reluctantly. "All right. It'll be ready in half an hour."

"I'll go upstairs and change."

Feeling her eyes on his back, Conley made his way stiffly up the stairs, turning right at the top to go into the master suite. A little while later, when he came back down in jeans and a sweater, his hair still wet from his shower, she'd set the table and was pouring herself a glass of wine. Without saying anything to her, he retrieved a second glass from the cabinet and poured one for himself. In the first years of their marriage, this had been a ritual. Every evening before dinner, they'd talked about their day, a bottle open between them, the tribulations and successes growing more or less important as they shared everything with each other.

Conley couldn't remember the last time they'd done that.

He took his drink and walked to the window beside the kitchen table. In the snow outside, a perfect square of light fell from where he stood, his silhouette exactly centered in the yellow patch. Without turning, he spoke. "Tell me what Ed thinks. What were his preliminary suggestions?"

In the reflection of the glass before him, Conley watched his wife. She put down the spoon she'd been using to stir the pasta and paused at the stove without moving. Finally, she turned, her eyes on Conley's back. "He has some ideas but none that will work."

Conley pivoted and they faced each other across the room. Just as they had when she'd told him she wanted a divorce.

"Why not? What's wrong with them?"

An expression Conley couldn't read crossed her face, then she answered him. "He wants to put me on the case. He thinks I'd be best for the job because no one would suspect anything out of the ordinary if we're seen together. For the office, we'd come up with some kind of excuse—a security check, for example."

The approach instantly appealed to him. "A security check...that you would handle... I would never have thought of that idea myself, but it might be a good one."

"No." Lara's answer—and her tone—told him she wouldn't be dissuaded. "It's a very bad idea and I told him so. I won't do it."

"Why not?"

"I don't do field work anymore, Conley. And you know why."

"That was more than a year ago, Lara. And what happened wasn't your fault."

"I'm aware of the facts," she said evenly. "But I made the decision not to work on-site again, and I'm sticking by it." She stared at him a moment more—as if to make sure he understood her point—then she returned to her task, the sauce on the front burner suddenly needing her total attention.

Conley looked into his glass of merlot. A year or so prior, Lara had been assigned to protect the wife and five-year-old daughter of a man scheduled to testify in a federal suit. There had been no threats, but the prosecutors wanted to be careful. On the day of the trial, Lara had driven to the Boulder family mansion to take the woman and her daughter to court. With no warning whatsoever, the wife had been gunned down by a long-range rifle while getting into the car. Lara had pulled her weapon but she was too late. The woman died. The little girl had been unharmed, but traumatized beyond belief. As far as Conley knew, the child still didn't leave the family estate.

Lara's career as a field agent had ended that day. She'd worked in the office ever since.

"This isn't the same thing, Lara."

"You're right." She continued to stir. "Your situation is totally different. But I'm still not going to do it.''

"Why not?"

She turned then to look at him, her eyes flashing. "I've told you why."

"No." He shook his head. "You gave me an excuse. You didn't tell me why."

A warm blush darkened her cheeks—from anger or something else—Conley wasn't sure.

"I would think the reason would be obvious without me spelling it out, but clearly it's not." Her jaw tightened noticeably. "I just asked you for a divorce. We're in the process of dissolving this marriage. Hanging around you constantly and pretending to be your loving, supportive wife while carrying out an investigation would be a stretch for me right now."

"I understand but—"

She lifted her hand and stopped him. "You don't understand anything, Conley, or we wouldn't be having this conversation. I *can't* act as if everything is all right between us. I wouldn't be able to convince a soul we're the couple we used to be."

"You convinced the cops at the hospital."

His answer took her back. "I—I had to. I wasn't sure what was going on—"

"And I'm not sure, either. But together we can figure it out. Your father is right about this."

"No, he's not. And neither are you." Her voice turned heated. "I can't pretend to love you anymore,

Conley. It's way past the time where I could convince anyone that we're a couple, much less a loving one."

Her words cut straight to the bone. His fingers tightened on his wineglass.

She bit her lip, her eyes dark and unhappy. "Love is something that has to flow both ways, Conley. I can't sustain our marriage all by myself. It's impossible to love someone who never loves you back."

The only sound in the kitchen was the sauce softly bubbling on the range. Conley spoke, his words balancing on a tightrope of tension. "How can you think that about—"

She interrupted him, the strain in her voice notching upward with a jerk. "It's not what I think, Conley. It's what I know. You haven't loved me in a very long time and I feel the same way. I just don't love you anymore."

DINNER WAS AWKWARD. Conley ate but tasted little. From across the table, Lara dined with an equal amount of disinterest. It seemed impossible, he thought later, as he moved into the den, that seven years of marriage could be over so completely, so utterly. When the phone rang later that evening, he answered it almost eagerly.

Ed spoke quickly as always, his questions coming with staccato beat. "Did you and Lara have a chance to talk? Did she tell you my plan? Whaddaya think?''

"She told me,'' Conley replied. ''But it's not going to work, Ed. She's totally against the idea.''

"I'll convince her,'' the older man said confidently. ''Lemme talk to her.''

Conley shook his head but went and found Lara. The conversation droned on for over an hour, her voice traveling down the hallway and into the den on occasion, the words heated and quick. Occupied with the contracts for three new projects, Conley tried not to listen. At eleven, he rose awkwardly from his desk in the den and made his way to the stairs. His leg was much better but the injury still made itself known when he sat for a long time.

With his hand on the railing, he started up...then he stopped.

From the hallway, beyond the stairs, light spilled through the open door into Lara's bedroom. He didn't want to notice but he couldn't help himself. He dropped his fingers from the newel post and stepped into the hall. He could hear a radio playing something soft and low, and as he made his way closer, he noticed something else. Her perfume. Like a shadow he couldn't see, the scent drifted toward him. Freesias and white roses. She had it mixed specially.

He told himself he shouldn't go on, but Conley couldn't stop. He walked down the carpeted passage and when he drew even with the door, he took a deep breath. The perfume hit him with a heady intensity and the memory of all the times he'd smelled it on her skin, warm and sweet, came to him in a rush. Almost dizzy, he put his hands on either side of the door and held on.

The bedroom was empty.

But just beyond the room, in the adjoining bath, a sudden movement caught his eye. He focused without thinking, then realized what he was seeing.

Wrapped in a towel, Lara stood before the steamed-up mirror. Her hair hung around her face in wet ribbons of silk, her hand a blur as she combed the strands. She'd obviously just stepped out of the shower, the swell of her breasts gleaming above the towel's knot, her slender throat shining as well, still moist from the spray of perfume. For a second, she tugged at the comb, then she reached out and swiped a hand across the foggy glass, clearing a small patch. And then she saw him.

Conley didn't breathe, didn't move, didn't think. All he did was stare at his wife.

She held his gaze for a heartbeat, then she leaned over and slowly closed the door.

"YOU DON'T HAVE A CHOICE. You have to do it."

Lara was alone in her SUV, driving to Conley's office, but the memory of Sandy's voice filled the truck's cabin. They'd just shared breakfast, some-

thing they tried to do at least once a month. Lara
had explained that Harrison's had a "security issue"
that Mesa might look into, but she'd kept the details
to herself. Even though Matthew would probably be
told everything, Lara wasn't about to compromise
security by discussing the issue in public. Sandy
didn't need to know too much in order to have—
and express—an opinion on the issue, however.

"You're going to handle it, though, right?" she'd
asked confidently.

"No, I'm not," Lara had replied. She tried to
change the subject. "How's things at home? Has
Matthew painted the nursery yet?"

An odd expression skipped over Sandy's face. It
came and went quickly, then she'd reached over and
taken a scoop of Lara's hash browns onto her own
fork. "Don't think you can distract me. It won't
work." She chewed and stared at Lara. "He's your
husband. You aren't going to leave the man hanging
out there all alone. You've got to help him,
c'mon..."

"If we take the case, Mesa will provide whatever
Conley needs. He won't be 'hanging out there all
alone,' I can assure you of that."

"But you should be in charge of the operation."
The fork returned for more. "He's your husband."

Lara answered impatiently. "I'm not the right
person for the job, Sandy, and I've told Ed that. In

fact, I told him he could fire me if he wanted to but I'm not working on Conley's case."

"You don't mean that."

Lara pushed her plate toward her friend to make her continued raiding easier. She wasn't hungry anyway. Her stomach had been in knots ever since Conley had revealed his problem and Ed had outlined his plan. "I do mean it. It's impossible for me to be around Conley right now. Even asking me is unreasonable."

Sandy chewed for a while, then put down her fork. For a moment she was quiet, then she leaned forward, her eyes focused on Lara's face. "What are you afraid of?" she asked. "That you'll screw up or that you'll do a good job?"

Lara's hand froze, her mug of coffee halfway to her mouth. Slowly she put it back down. "What does that mean?"

"You know what it means." Sandy's gaze was steady. "If you mess this up, you'll take the blame, whether you deserve it or not. Just like last time. If you handle the job perfectly—which you will—you'll have to act like his loving wife...and you just might do that job too well."

"I don't know what you're talking about," Lara said stiffly.

"Give it up, Lara. You know damn well what I mean." Sandy leaned even closer, her arms braced on the table. "You're afraid you'll fall in love all over again."

Lara made a scoffing sound. "That's ridiculous."

"Is it?"

"Of course, it is."

"Then why not help him out?"

Lara had stared across the table with a blank look. She didn't have an answer other than the one she'd already given. And the next thing Sandy would want to know was if Lara had asked Conley whether or not he'd give her a hard time with the divorce. Lara had no more of an answer for that question than she had the first, because she'd been too scared to confront him.

She'd escaped Sandy by mumbling about a meeting she was late for, making her way out of the restaurant and into her vehicle.

But the questions echoed in Lara's mind. Ed had pushed her all week, too, finally telling her she had to see Conley to firm up the plan today. She felt as if she were under fire from seventeen different directions. She turned down Sixth Street and made her way to Harrison's.

Pulling up outside the building, she parked just as Theresa walked out of the front door. Lara sat still, killing time, her mind wandering as she watched the attorney go down the street. When she'd first read the note she'd found in Conley's jacket, Lara had thought of Theresa Marchante. The woman was single, gorgeous, smart. If Lara had been Theresa and worked closely with a man like Conley, she'd have been tempted. But he was married. And Lara would have never looked twice at a married man.

Did Theresa feel the same way?

It didn't really matter, Lara had decided. Theresa wasn't Conley's kind of woman. He liked blondes and Theresa had dark hair. Even more importantly, Conley was attracted to women who had a certain kind of attitude. Lara had always thought of it as a steely softness. Theresa was not that way. She had the strong part down, but if she had any softness to her, she kept it well hidden.

Lara headed for his office. Why did it even matter? Who Conley was sleeping with wasn't really important. She wanted to divorce Conley because their marriage was empty and he didn't seem to care any longer. She didn't love him; what did it matter who did? With that thought, the realization of what she could do suddenly came to her. There *was* a way she could accomplish her goal *and* make everyone happy.

She would get what she wanted. And Conley would be safe. Even Ed couldn't complain... because he wouldn't know the real reason behind her efforts.

Digging her phone from her purse, she called Ed and told him her decision. Obviously believing his powers of persuasion had changed her mind, he gave his approval so quickly she almost had second thoughts.

A few minutes later, when she walked inside his office and saw her husband, Lara had second, third...and fourth thoughts. He met her at the door and her ability to think clearly fled. He had on his usual attire—jeans and a sweater—but all at once she was flooded with memories of better times between them. Her reaction was the last thing she expected.

She wondered if her response had anything to do with seeing him last night in the bathroom mirror. That had been unexpected, too. She'd spent an hour in bed thinking about the look in his eyes. A very long hour. Finally she'd decided it had meant nothing and had drifted off into a restless sleep. Great sex was one thing but a marriage needed more than that.

She put her feelings aside and walked into his office. "I'm here to discuss your situation," she said calmly. "I think I know what we need to do."

CONLEY LET Lara's words wash over him, but his mind was on the night before. The image of her wrapped in a towel haunted him. All he'd wanted was to step inside the steamy bathroom and pull her into his arms, but that wasn't possible and he was a fool to even think about it. She'd made herself more than clear about that subject when she'd moved out of their bedroom months before.

He blinked and tried to focus. "I'm glad you've

come to a decision. I think someone was in my office again last night. Things had been rearranged...my favorite pen's missing.''

She frowned. ''Did you call the police?''

''I have a call into Fields but I haven't heard back from him yet.''

''Do they know anything else about the vehicle that hit you?''

''Margulies said they had a lead. Something about a stolen car. He said he'd call me when he knew more.''

Nodding at this information, Lara sat down in one of the chairs in front of his desk. ''I'll phone them as soon as I finish here and tell them what we're going to do.''

''And that will be...?''

''We'll start the protection today, but we'll tell everyone you've hired Mesa to perform a routine security review. On-site evaluations are SOP for companies like yours, and no one would be suspicious seeing an agent in the office—or me for that matter since I work for Mesa, as well. At the same time, though, we'll be covering you 24/7.''

He crossed his arms and nodded. Taking a breath, Lara continued. She seemed nervous to Conley, but he put the thought aside.

''We'll begin with a sweep of your office tonight. We'll probably check the house, too, just to make sure no one's bugging anything.'' She paused. ''We're very thorough, Conley. Mesa always develops a meticulous plan, but in this case, we'll be going even further. No one will suspect we're protecting you so your moneymen should be happy as well.''

Conley made his way around his desk to take the chair next to Lara's. ''What's your part in this?''

She looked at him squarely, her hazel gaze as clear as the brook that ran behind their house in the spring. ''If I need to come into the office, we'll explain that I'm working on part of the review. Primarily someone else will be with you when you're here. I'd like to use Jake Berger. He's Mesa's best man.'' She waited a moment. ''When you're out of the office I'll be with you...as your wife.''

Conley felt his pulse jump. Had she changed her mind about the divorce, too? He doubted it; Lara was as steady as a rock. Once she'd made a decision, that was usually it.

''I'm surprised,'' he said carefully. ''When we talked about this the other night, you seemed determined it wouldn't work.''

She crossed her legs, a swish of wool and silk accompanying the movement. ''I looked at the situation a little closer.''

He nodded, then before he could say more, she continued.

''I'll handle the job, but I want something from you in return.''

He waited for her to continue.

''When this is all over—when the police find whoever is doing this to you—I want the divorce. No delays. No discussions.''

The same stab of pain that had accompanied her first demand came back. He imagined this was what a heart attack felt like.

He looked past her, to the mountains, then after a while, he brought his gaze back. There was only one answer she'd take, and judging from the determination on her face, he'd better give it to her, whether he wanted to or not.

"If that's what you want, then that's what we'll do." The words were stones in his mouth.

She nodded quickly, as if afraid he'd change his mind. "I'll need your schedule for next week. All the functions, business meetings, whatever you might have scheduled."

"I'll have Ellen prepare one for you. She can fax it to you this afternoon."

"Good. You might want to explain to her that Mesa's doing a review so she can spread the word. Also, if you have any traveling to do, you need to put that on hold. At least for a while."

"All right. Anything else?"

"Yes. Stephanie will call you later. She'll ask you all sorts of questions. They're very personal but completely confidential. We'll need to build a file on you and develop our plan, but it's also standard procedure for security checks. We'll prepare a contract for you to sign. It'll outline everything we're doing regarding the review but it won't mention the guard work." She paused. "That's it, I guess."

She stood up, but Conley stayed where he was. If he didn't move, if he didn't acknowledge their relationship had changed, would things go back to how they'd once been? He realized instantly how silly that thought was. It was over. Their life together meant nothing anymore. Like a clock, their marriage had been winding down for years, and now it was about to stop. Completely.

He raised his gaze to Lara's and was shocked to see that she was crying. Or was she? She turned away, surreptitiously brushing at one eye. It happened so fast, he barely caught the movement, but all at once—with the literal blink of an eye—things were different. His breath stopped and his chest grew tight as he thought about what her tears meant.

Did she still love him? Was there a chance?

He reached out, but not seeing him, Lara had already stepped away. His fingers touched air and he dropped his hand. But the thought wouldn't leave.

What if there was a chance? Would he take it? *Could* he take it?

She moved toward the door with fluid grace, her back ramrod straight, her shoulders proud. Conley watched with fascination, myriad thoughts bombarding him from every side. Giving Lara whatever she wanted was something he'd always done without thinking. He'd wanted to.

But was this right? Even if she didn't love him anymore, was this how it was going to end? Regardless of how she felt, Lara was the only woman he'd ever loved. The only woman he'd ever really wanted. He'd been incredulous when she'd accused him of having an affair.

But he couldn't deny that he hadn't been putting any effort into their marriage. Until she'd stood in the middle of the kitchen and told him he'd already lost her, he hadn't truly comprehended how much she meant to him.

If he let her go without a fight, he wasn't the man he'd always thought he was. He would be the person *she* thought he'd become.

Oblivious to his revelation, Lara stopped at the door. "We'll go over the details of the plan with you after it's done."

Her words lingered in the still office air, and all at once, it felt as though even the walls were holding their breath. Conley was sure this was something she said to every client, but to his ears the statement took on a whole new meaning. The plan. Yes, he thought with sudden resolve, that was it. The plan.

She would work out a plan to protect him.

He would work out a plan to seduce her.

CHAPTER SIX

THERESA MOVED AWAY from the heater vent, her breath caught in her throat. She'd learned a long time ago it was easy to eavesdrop on conversations being held in Conley's office. She tried not to listen—a man needed his privacy—but most of the time she gave in and indulged herself. The words weren't important to her, she simply wanted the warmth of his voice. She craved it. The weekends were unbearable when she couldn't hear him; on occasion she had to give in and call him at home. She'd wrap herself in his coat and wait for him to pick up the phone. When he spoke, she'd hang up and quickly abandon the pay phone, his "hello" a stingy taste that would have to last her until Monday.

She made her way to her desk and sat down. It was true! They were actually getting a divorce! She'd halfway thought Conley might fight it, but she'd just heard him agree to Lara's every demand.

Opening the center drawer of her desk, Theresa took out the pen she'd taken from Conley's desk. She wasn't afraid of getting caught; she could say he'd left it on the conference table if questioned. Since stealing his coat, she'd spent a lot of time in his office. He'd changed his alarm code, but Ellen had put the information on her computer, and Theresa knew the secretary's password. One weekend a while back, Theresa had needed some information and the secretary had given her the password so Theresa could look up the document herself.

The keys had been an added bonus—she'd become addicted to sneaking in to the office late at night. When Conley had had the locks changed, she'd gone nuts until she managed to get his new keys and have them copied, as well.

But she wasn't really worried about anyone discovering her. She always covered her tracks. Lara and the police could investigate all they wanted; they'd never find out about Theresa. And there was no way they could connect her to that car accident. She would never hurt Conley; she just wanted to love him.

Bringing the pen to her nose, she inhaled deeply. The lingering scent of his cologne came to her and she had to close her eyes to fight a wave of longing.

Divorce! She couldn't believe her luck.

She tucked the pen into the pocket of her slacks and wrapped her fingers around it. It made her feel good to have it nearby. During the day, she'd be able to put her hand down there and touch it, knowing *his* hand had been on it, too.

And now he was going to be free.

Theresa smiled. She'd had a plan in place, of course. She always did. But this was much better, much cleaner. With Lara out of the picture, she and Conley could make a life together. If, for some reason, things didn't go as she thought, she could always go back to the original scheme. The bodyguards and security meant nothing to her.

She squeezed the pen, the smooth surface of the Mont Blanc cool against her fevered touch.

Soon. It would all be over soon.

And Conley would belong to her.

LARA LEFT Conley's office and headed for the shooting range on the outskirts of Boulder. She'd agreed earlier that week to meet Ed for an hour's worth of practice, but she'd rather forget about it now. Her legs felt weak and her pulse was ringing in her ears. She wondered if she was coming down with something but by the time she got on the interstate she knew she wasn't sick.

She was crazy.

Agreeing to handle Conley's case—even for the reasons she had—was nuts, plain and simple. She'd been in such a state coming out of his office she'd run right into Matthew obviously on his way to see Conley. The quiet engineer had worn a look of complete surprise as she'd apologized then pushed away from him and bolted down the hallway. Now her panic blossomed and grew until it seemed as if it took up all the oxygen in the car. She couldn't breathe. Going back on her word was not typical for her—she *never* did it, in fact—but this was different. Conley would just *have* to give her the divorce.

She'd call Ed right now and tell him she'd changed her mind. She couldn't do the job.

Her eyes on the road, Lara picked up her cell phone. Then she put it down. She couldn't back out. Not now. Breaking her promise would be wrong, and besides, she'd look like a fool. Conley would think she wasn't serious about the divorce.

Lara wrapped her fingers around the steering wheel and murmured another curse. All she wanted was to get away from Con. Why was that so complicated?

Twenty minutes later, she pulled into the parking lot at the range. She found Ed inside, his ear protectors clamped tightly over his ears, his eyes trained on a moving target coming at him quickly. She let him finish his round, then stepped to his side as he emptied the chamber of his weapon and reached for the shredded silhouette. With as few words as possible, she explained the meeting with Conley, leaving out the details of their agreement.

Ed looked at her with a speculative gaze. "Why'd you change your mind? Last time we talked, you threatened to quit before you'd handle this."

"You convinced me," was all she said.

Replacing his target with a new one, he turned to her. "You don't let anyone convince you of anything. You're just like me. You changed your mind for some reason."

"And that reason isn't important." Pulling her own weapon out of her purse, Lara headed for the cubicle beside Ed's. "Con's secretary is going to fax us his schedule. As soon as I get it, I'll start the file. I want Jake to take care of Conley when he's at work. He can handle the review situation better than anyone. I'll handle all duties outside the office."

Her father looked pained. Jake Berger was his best man, a young ex-Marine whose brain was as sharp as his body. Ed started to protest, but Lara reached for her ear protectors and popped the sides down, speaking as she did so. "How was your dinner with Bess? Is she doing all right?"

Ed squirmed under her gaze, a sudden detail on his pistol requiring intense scrutiny. "She's fine," he said scratching at a spot on the barrel of the gun. "She said to tell you hello."

"Are you and Bess—"

"We had dinner. That's it."

His answer was even more brusque than usual but it accomplished Lara's goal. He wanted to get away from her, his own questions forgotten. He repositioned his ear protectors over his ears and turned to the target, punching the button at his side to send it back down the alley.

Like father, like daughter.

She only wished she could handle Conley as easily.

CONLEY GAVE Ellen his Palm Pilot and had her print out the electronic calendar. With a hard copy in hand, he went over the details of his life for the next month. Nothing needed to be changed. He had enough events and scattered meetings to keep Lara by his side for a year.

Conley drew a star beside two of the items on the schedule, a business dinner next week and a professional meeting the following month. He'd never been scared of the nutcase who was forcing his hand, but he'd have to be twice as vigilant now that Lara was working the case. She'd do everything by the book—it was how she operated—and he couldn't let her get hurt defending him. His goal was to bring her back to him, but he had to keep her safe, too.

"This schedule looks fine," he said to Ellen a few minutes later. "Fax it to my wife's office with a note telling her the two starred events are very important. We'll be coordinating my meetings, etcetera, with her for a while. Mesa's going to do a standard security review for us."

With a curious look, Ellen took the paper from his outstretched hand. Conley then made a point of explaining. "You might want to pass the news on," he said casually when he finished. "So everyone will know." She nodded and a few moments later, he heard the drone of the fax machine.

His plan was going forward.

LARA SPENT the rest of the day wishing she was anywhere but the office. Her nerves were completely frazzled and every little thing seemed to irritate her. Late that afternoon, when Stephanie handed her the fax from Conley's office, Lara took one look at it, then grabbed her coat. "I've got to get out of here," she said. "Call me at home if you need me, otherwise, consider me out till Monday."

But once she made it to the rambling Victorian, Lara felt even more on edge. With nothing better to do, she called the police department and checked on the stolen car. Margulies confirmed the lead Conley had mentioned, but told her little else. "The department got a call late on the evening your husband was hit. Came from the apartments out west of town…a woman who runs a delivery service called in and said her car had been taken. We're trying to track it down." He promised to call Lara when they found out more.

She piddled around after that, accomplishing nothing until it was time for her to go to bed. Conley didn't come home until almost midnight; all she could do was lie there and listen and wonder where he'd been. How would Jake handle Conley's "work-

ing late?'' She'd find out soon enough but thinking
about it was almost too much to bear. She got up,
checked the house, and made sure Conley had armed
the alarm then she went back to bed, her heart
heavy.

When she stumbled into the kitchen the next
morning, Conley was sitting at the table, reading the
newspaper. He usually got up early on Saturday and
went into his office before she was out of bed. Seeing him sipping his coffee was such a surprise, she
squeaked to a stop, the rubber soles of her house
shoes complaining about her abruptness. She felt her
heart roll into a tight, protective ball, then wondered
why she even cared.

He nodded in her direction and she did the same
to him. A few moments later, with coffee mug in
hand, she headed out of the room. She'd get dressed
and spend the day at her office if he was going to
be home. She wasn't up for more torture than necessary.

Then she remembered. If he wasn't at work, she
had to be with him. All day. Every day.

She closed her eyes, drew a deep breath, then
turned and spoke. She chose the words carefully
with just the right touch of professional distance. ''I
need to know what your plans are for today, Conley.
Are you going into the office or what?''

''I'm not sure yet.'' He lowered the paper. ''I'll
probably go in later, but I was thinking about stop-

ping at the nursery first. I think the deer are getting into the backyard again. I may need some repellant. It's not supposed to freeze tonight, is it?''

She blinked. In any other kitchen in any other house on any other day, his pronouncement wouldn't have meant a thing, but this was Conley. Once upon a time, he'd been an avid gardener, but he hadn't been in the backyard for the past five years. She didn't understand what was going on, but she knew how she had to respond.

"I can pick that up for you next week," Lara said carefully, ignoring his question. "Why don't you let me take you directly to the office?"

"I wanted to stop at the bookstore first."

"The bookstore?"

"I ordered a technical manual. Ellen told me it came in last week."

Two errands, Lara told herself. That's all. It didn't mean anything. Did it?

"All right. I'll get dressed and we can leave in a bit." She turned and started out of the room, but his voice stopped her.

"Did you get my fax yesterday?"

Lara thought of the crumpled page still sitting on the seat of her SUV. "Yes."

"The two starred events—I hope you don't have a problem with either one of them."

Trapped, all Lara could do was nod. She'd already been wondering how she could convince Jake to go with him. "Why would I have a problem with them?" she hedged.

"The dinner next Friday won't be anything, but the professional meeting next month is fairly important. A lot of my backers will be there and some potential clients, too."

The rest of his explanation went unsaid, but Lara understood. Her presence was paramount to reassure his financial people and she was the one who should be with him at the dinner, not Jake. She was his wife. "I'll be there," she said.

He caught her gaze and held it. "Good. I'm counting on it."

She felt a sudden quiver of unease. Black and intense, his eyes drilled her with a special kind of force. All at once, she wondered if he knew more about this situation than he was letting on. First the errands and now this...his behavior didn't add up. Something was going on that she wasn't getting. "Are you expecting something to happen?" she asked suddenly.

"No," he said. "But you can't be too careful. It's a public event, very well attended. If I wished someone harm, I might make a move then. It'd be easy to escape in a crowd like that."

His observation was astute, and *that* stung, too. She should have already considered that possibility. With any other client, she would have. "I wonder if we need extra men,'' she said. ''Maybe I should call Ed and ask—''

''That's not necessary.'' Conley cut her off, folded the paper with precision and stood. The morning light glinted in his dark hair. ''Let's keep it simple. I don't need anyone—'' again, he gave her the look ''—but you.''

She swallowed hard, then left to get dressed. She'd remember his words later.

CONLEY WANDERED up and down the aisles of the bookstore with Lara trailing behind him. Spending a carefree Saturday had been his goal—they'd shared hundreds of days like this when they'd first married and he'd seized on the memory of those times, somehow thinking it might bring them closer.

But he couldn't have been more wrong.

Lara had been distant and quiet ever since they'd left the house. She'd insisted on driving and before they'd entered the bookstore she'd searched the street with her eyes, her body tense and ready to spring. Underneath her jacket, she wore her gun. She was anxious and uneasy.

If Conley had been a man who lied to himself he might have blamed *her* actions for *his* feelings of apprehension but he couldn't. From the moment they'd driven out of the driveway, he'd felt uncomfortable, too. And he didn't know why.

Lifting his head, Conley stared around the store.

A mother and two small children were in the reading corner, and an older lady stood by the cookbooks. Two teenagers were giggling over a magazine. Other than that, the store was empty, but his feeling persisted.

At his side, Lara spoke quietly. "What is it?"

Conley tightened his jaw. She didn't miss a thing, did she? "It's nothing," he hedged. "Someone walking over my grave, I guess...."

She started to say something then she stopped, and a few minutes later, they left the store, footsteps crunching on a snow-packed sidewalk. Before they'd gotten halfway down the block, Conley felt his anxiety take another leap, and suddenly he couldn't shake the feeling that someone was following them. Slowing to a halt, he pretended to gaze into the window of a small jewelry shop. The reflection of the street revealed nothing, but all at once, Lara moved close to his side and tucked her hand under his arm. She smiled up at him and his heart tumbled.

"We need to get out of here." Her voice was tight. "It's not a good idea to stand around window-shopping, okay? We need to move along."

It took him a second to understand what she was doing. He nodded, then put his hand over hers and smiled, too, staring into her eyes before he brushed his lips over her brow and whispered. "I think someone's following us. I wanted to stop and see if I was right.''

Her reaction was so muted he immediately knew she'd felt the same way, probably long before he did. She gave him a level stare, nothing betraying the emotions he'd guessed at. "What makes you think we're being followed?"

"I'm not sure," he said. "Not anything specific. I just felt weird. Like someone was watching me."

She looked thoughtful, then stepped to one side. "Walk behind me," she instructed. "Just a little bit...like you're looking in the window."

He did as she instructed, and Lara turned parallel to the street. A second later he understood what she was doing, and a flood of disbelief came over him. She was covering his body with her own. Without thinking any further, he grabbed her arm and wrapped it around his waist, pulling her to his side as he draped his other arm over her shoulder.

She laughed, a forced sound, and tried to jerk away, but he wouldn't let her. A second later they found themselves in front of the Suburban. She headed to his side of the vehicle first, but he pulled on her playfully and directed her the other way where he opened the door and helped her in. A moment later, he entered the vehicle from the passenger door, slamming it behind him with a thud.

"What in the hell do you think you're doing?" Her eyes blazing, Lara starting speaking before he could get out a word. Her anger burned from across the seats of the SUV. "If you pull another stunt like that, this deal is off! I can't protect you if you're going to act like an idiot."

Conley's own temper exploded. "I'm not going to let you put yourself in danger for me, Lara. That's not how this is going to work."

"What do you think bodyguards do?" she asked hotly. "It's my job, Conley. I have to keep you safe. That's what I signed on for. It's the price I'm willing to pay to get away from you so let me do it, for God's sakes."

Her angry words hovered between them in the tight confines of the vehicle, and Conley realized suddenly he was holding his breath. He let it go, his eyes still on his wife's.

In the quiet that followed, Lara spoke with a catch. "Just let me do my job, Con.... We'll both get through this somehow. Then you can go your way and I'll go mine."

FROM THE FRONT SEAT of her rental car, Theresa watched the green Suburban pull away from the snowy curb. Moaning out loud, she gritted her teeth and stared with heated disbelief. She couldn't believe what she'd just seen. He'd kissed her! He'd actually leaned over and kissed his wife. How could he...how could he do that?

Didn't he know she loved him? Hadn't the flowers told him so? The notes? The phone calls? What about the divorce? Lara was supposed to be protecting him, that was it. Nothing more.

Theresa held on to the steering wheel so hard her fingers began to cramp. Loosening them when she realized what she was doing, she let out a curse. Clearly she was going to have to step up her program. This couldn't be allowed to continue. She searched her brain for a way to get around this latest development, but nothing came to her. Nothing.

She'd have to think harder.

LARA STARED IN the mirror Sunday night and thought about the day before. Saturday had been such a disaster she still couldn't believe it. After the fight in the truck, she'd refused to stop at the nursery. Instead, she'd taken Conley straight to the office and dropped him off, handing him over to Jake whom she'd called. Conley hadn't come back to the house until after midnight and for the first time in years she was actually grateful for his absence.

She swiped a brush through her hair, then turned and headed for the kitchen. Being beside Conley, in the car, at the bookstore, walking down the street, had set her on edge.

She grabbed a cold drink from the refrigerator and went back to her room, fuming as she walked down the hall. More than his precious company was on the line here. Her professional life was being tested as well. If anyone knew how much her past had hurt her, it was Conley. When Margaret Atwater had been shot before Lara's eyes, she'd sworn she'd never again work in the field. Never. She couldn't handle it.

And now here she was, doing it again.

And to make things even worse, Conley was involved.

She took a deep swallow of soda and put the can against her forehead. The cold metal did nothing to clear her thoughts. She had reacted more strongly to his touch than she should have, but she'd been on edge from the minute they'd left the house. Once on the street, her uneasiness had only grown, especially when they'd left the bookstore. But Lara knew the drill. She had it down. She'd continued as if nothing was happening until Conley had made them stop.

Conley… God, his hand on her arm. His eyes on her face. The chaste kiss he'd planted on her brow. She'd experienced them all a thousand times, but out there on that snowy sidewalk, she'd thought she was going to lose control. The intensity of his attention was more than enough to send her spinning.

She opened her eyes, her gaze falling to the crumpled fax he'd sent her on Friday. The dinner party he had scheduled next week was going to be at Red Feather's nicest restaurant, the Black Bear Chalet. She'd have to dress up. He would wear a suit. The place would be full of business associates who would have to be convinced that they were deeply in love. It'd be difficult but not as big a trial as the professional organization he wanted to attend next month. That would be at the local ski resort. Fifteen miles outside of town, the Royal Mountain Inn clung to the edge of the range, every window looking out to a mountainous wonderland. It was a gorgeous place, set in the most romantic scenery Lara had ever encountered.

They'd been married in the resort's chapel.

Had held a party in the dining room.

Had spent their honeymoon in one of its suites.

Lara closed her eyes and moaned.

CHAPTER SEVEN

FRIDAY EVENING AS Conley straightened his tie in the mirror of his office bathroom he thought about the evening ahead. Yes, it would be a business dinner and yes, Lara would only be there because she had to be, but this was a chance he didn't want to screw up. Last Saturday had been a disaster; he didn't want a repeat of that. He wanted to make her see how good it could be for them again, how much she meant to him.

Turning away from the mirror, Conley walked back into his office to find Matthew standing beside his desk with a folder in his hand. The engineer glanced up in surprise as Conley entered the room, his hand still on his tie.

"Hey, Con, I didn't know you were still here."

"Yeah, I'm here. I was just about to leave, though. You and Sandy are going to the Black Bear, aren't you? For the dinner?"

"We'll be there. Sandy wouldn't miss a meal like that for anything. I'm going to go pick her up in a few minutes." He dropped the folder he'd been holding onto Conley's desk. "I wanted to bring you the revised schematics for the glass chip. I've been working on it some more in my spare time. I may have solved the connector problem.''

"That's good, Matt. But you don't have to do that, you know. We've got plenty of time—"

"It's okay," Matthew interrupted. "I needed something else to concentrate on. Things are tense at home. Sandy's always on my ass about something. You know how it is…."

Conley nodded, but he didn't know. Lara wasn't the kind of woman who nagged. Even with things as bad as they'd gotten, she'd never given him a hard time. She'd simply backed off and waited.

"How's the Mesa thing going? I've seen the guy around the office."

Ellen had spread the word that Mesa was doing a routine security check. Conley felt uncomfortable keeping Matthew in the dark about Jake and Lara's other role, especially when Matthew knew about the stalker anyway, but Lara had been insistent and he'd understood her point of view.

"It's coming along," he said in a noncommittal voice. "Probably take a while to analyze the whole thing."

"You think they'll figure out the stalker's identity?"

"That's not really why they're here. They're just checking to make sure we've got our bases covered." Remembering his earlier thoughts, Conley locked his desk and shut off his computer. "The police will find the bad guy, at least they should."

"Maybe so, but Lara's not the kind of person to sit on the sidelines."

Conley looked up in surprise. "What do you mean?"

Matthew shrugged as if to minimize his words. "She's sharp. She won't be happy just analyzing our security. She'll want to get to the bottom of what's going on. Track down who's sending those flowers. Study those notes…I bet she figures it out and fast."

Conley acknowledged Matthew's comment with a vague murmur then he diverted the engineer's attention, returning the conversation to the new chip. They discussed the problem a few minutes more, then Matthew left, closing the door behind him. Conley stood with his back to the darkened window, the cold Colorado night stretching out behind him in an endless vista.

Matthew was right, he thought. Hiring Mesa had sounded like a good idea at the time, but things were turning out differently than he'd planned. Saturday had proven that. Conley was going to have to do better. Jake Berger knocked on the door a few moments later and together they left, Conley still in deep thought.

LARA SNAPPED the clasp of her pearls behind her neck then grabbed her black heels from the shelf.

She'd picked out the most severe suit she had hanging in her closet. She didn't want Conley getting any ideas that this dinner was anything other than business. For both of them. She wasn't quite sure why she felt the need to so strongly impress that on her husband, but she was sure Sandy could analyze the situation and come up with something ridiculous. Such as *Lara* seeing the night out as something else. Or that she *wished* it was something else. Lara made a scoffing sound and reached for the scarf that matched her suit, though in the end, her outfit didn't matter. All it had to do was hide her gun.

She adjusted the shoulder harness of her weapon under her jacket, then reached for a tube of lipstick. The first one she picked up was bright red and that's what went on her lips. A quick fluff of her hair and she was ready to go.

Once in the car, she used the speed dial to call the office. Ed had been out all week. He'd gone to Santa Fe to a security convention but had come in late that afternoon after Lara had left. If she didn't contact him now and give him an update, he'd call her later; she might as well do it and get it behind her.

He answered the phone with a gruff hello.

Lara spoke quickly, her report short and to the point.

"And the file?"

"It's complete. I have it with me. I thought I

might run it over to you when we finish tonight. Every component of Conley's life—minute by minute. All his personal codes and a diary of everything that's happened so far, along with Mesa's plan on how to handle this. Stephanie did a great job getting the nitpicky stuff together so fast.'' She gave him some more details, then she said, ''Look, I'm on my way to the restaurant now. I'll see you later this evening.''

''Not so fast,'' he demanded. ''You gave me the details, but I want more. How are you feeling about all this?''

His question was so incongruent Lara blinked in confusion. Then she thought. He'd taken Bess out for dinner two weeks ago. He'd just come back from Santa Fe. There was no place on earth Bess loved more than Santa Fe. She'd actually insisted that she and Ed marry at the edge of Frijoles Canyon north of the city.

''You took Bess to Santa Fe, didn't you?'' Lara asked slowly. ''You ol' dog, you...''

''What on earth makes you think—''

''Forget the act,'' she said. ''You never ask me how I feel about anything, much less a job. You've been with Bess and she took you down a notch, didn't she? And she told you you shouldn't have made me do this.''

Before her father could reply, Lara went on, her

voice suddenly weary. "She was right, Ed. To tell
you the truth, this is hard. Really hard."

"I'm sorry, Lara." He sounded genuinely con-
trite—before his voice turned hard. "But if you
want to back out, you can't. You're in it for the
duration."

"I understand," she said, "and I wouldn't back
out even if you said it was okay."

"Why?"

"Let's just say I have a stake in it now."

He waited for more but she stayed silent.

"A stake?" he finally said. "Does Conley have
one in it, too? Besides the obvious, that is?"

She blew off his question and hurriedly hung up
as she pulled into the lot across the street from the
restaurant. It was hard to leave the Explorer. To say
she was dreading the evening didn't begin to cover
it. As if someone knew she needed a bit more time,
her cell phone rang again. She answered it almost
gratefully.

"Mrs. Harrison? This is Rick Margulies. I have
some information on the car that might have hit your
husband."

A coolness entered the vehicle that had nothing
to do with the outside temperature. Lara gripped the
phone. "Tell me about it."

"A patrol unit found a vehicle abandoned in a
rough part of town. We're pretty sure it's the right

car so we've had it towed to the lab in Denver. We've asked them to run some tests on it.''

"Blood analysis?"

"Exactly. Found some on the fender. If it's a match, we'll know we've got the right one.''

"And the owner?"

"She's out of town again but as soon as she gets back, we're going to talk to her. She reported it stolen late Monday night but we didn't get the paperwork until just the other day. Whoever took the car used it just to run down Mr. Harrison then ditched it. Prelim work makes me think they wiped it down afterward, too.''

They spoke a few more minutes, the officer assuring Lara he'd call her back as soon as he knew more.   She forced herself to abandon the sanctuary of the SUV and headed toward the restaurant.

ONCE INSIDE, Lara's anxiety only grew. The smoky bar off the side of the dining room was crowded, a pack of people milling about, some of whom Lara knew, others strangers. Any kind of attempt to keep Conley secure was laughable. She looked around for Sandy but her friend was nowhere to be seen.

Wading into the crowd, Lara managed to spot the head and shoulders of Jake Berger. He stood near to the bar where he towered over everyone else, Conley the only one close in height. An expert in security, Jake was fitting in well at the office. He hadn't appeared to mind going off-site with Conley—delivering him to the inn—but he'd already told Lara he had a date for tonight and he didn't want to be late. When he saw her approach the isolated spot where he and Conley were waiting, his face cleared with obvious relief. She sent her gaze around the room one more time, then nodded and Jake melted into the crowd.

Standing by himself at the end of the bar, Conley had been expecting her, of course, but probably not like this—materializing by his side, without any warning. For one unguarded second, his eyes held hers. In the anonymity of the crowded room, she felt as if only the two of them were present. Her stomach tumbled as she wondered about his look, then she told herself she was thinking too hard, analyzing the situation too much.

A heartbeat later, he reached out and gathered her into his arms.

Lara stiffened and pulled back immediately. Before she could say anything, he bent his head to hers and lightly kissed her.

She knew his touch as well as her own, but it'd been a long time since she'd felt it. She'd always melted under his attentions, and when they'd stopped she'd forced herself to forget the way they'd made her feel.

She remembered quickly.

The realization had Lara putting her hands on

We'd like to send you **2 FREE** books and a surprise gift to introduce you to Harlequin Superromance®. Accept our special offer today and

Indulge in a Harlequin Moment!

HOW TO QUALIFY:

1. With a coin, carefully scratch off the silver area on the card at right to see what we have for you—**2 FREE BOOKS** and a **FREE GIFT**—ALL YOURS! ALL FREE!

2. Send back the card and you'll receive two brand-new Harlequin Superromance® books. These books have a cover price of $4.99 each in the U.S. and $5.99 each Canada, but they are yours to keep absolutely free!

3. There's no catch. You're under no obligation to buy anything. We charge nothing—ZERO—for your first shipment and you don't have to make any minimum number purchases—not even one!

4. The fact is, thousands of readers enjoy receiving books by mail from the Harlequin Reader Service®. They enjoy the convenience of home delivery… they like getting the best new novels at discount prices, BEFORE they're available in stores…and they love their *Heart to Heart* subscriber newsletter featuring autho news, horoscopes, recipes, book reviews and much more!

5. We hope that after receiving your free books you'll want to remain a subscriber. But the choice is yours—to continue or cancel, any time at all. So why not take u up on our invitation with no risk of any kind. You'll be glad you did!

SPECIAL FREE GIFT

We can't tell you what it is…but we're sure you'll like it! A FREE gift just for giving the Harlequin Reader Service® a try!

Visit us online at
www.eHarlequin.com

The **2 FREE BOOKS** we send you will be selected from **HARLEQUIN SUPERROMANCE**®, the series that brings you provocative, passionate, contemporary stories that celebrate life and love.

Books received may vary.

Scratch off the silver area to see what the Harlequin Reader Service has for you.

HARLEQUIN®
Makes any time special™

YES!

I have scratched off the silver area above. Please send me the **2 FREE** books and gift for which I qualify. I understand I am under no obligation to purchase any books, as explained on the back and on the opposite page.

336 HDL DH4Q   135 HDL DH4P

FIRST NAME   LAST NAME

ADDRESS

APT.#   CITY

STATE/PROV.   ZIP/POSTAL CODE

Offer limited to one per household and not valid to current Harlequin Superromance® subscribers. All orders subject to approval.

THE HARLEQUIN READER SERVICE®—Here's how it works:

Accepting your 2 free books and gift places you under no obligation to buy anything. You may keep the books and gift and return the shipping statement marked "cancel." If you do not cancel, about a month later we'll send you 6 additional books and bill you just $4.05 each in the U.S., or $4.46 each in Canada, plus 25¢ shipping & handling per book and applicable tax if any.* That's the complete price and — compared to cover prices of $4.99 each in the U.S. and $5.99 each in Canada — it quite a bargain! You may cancel at any time, but if you choose to continue, every month we'll send you 6 more books, which you may either purchase at the discount price or return to us and cancel your subscription.

*Terms and prices subject to change without notice. Sales tax applicable in N.Y. Canadian residents will be charged applicable provincial taxes and GST.

If offer card is missing write to: Harlequin Reader Service, 3010 Walden Ave., P.O. Box 1867, Buffalo NY 14240-1867

DETACH AND MAIL CARD TODAY!

BUSINESS REPLY MAIL

FIRST-CLASS MAIL   PERMIT NO. 717-003   BUFFALO, NY

POSTAGE WILL BE PAID BY ADDRESSEE

HARLEQUIN READER SERVICE
3010 WALDEN AVE
PO BOX 1867
BUFFALO NY 14240-9952

NO POSTAGE
NECESSARY
IF MAILED
IN THE
UNITED STATES

Con's chest and pushing him away. He pulled back
but he didn't drop his arms. Surrounded by the
crowd, there was nothing Lara could do except look
into his eyes. They were so dark and full of mystery
they took away her breath.

"What do you think you're doing?" she growled,
the words barely audible to Conley, much less the
people standing a few feet from them. "This is way
over the top, Con. I'm warning you..."

"You're warning me? That's not how this is supposed to go, Lara." He shook his head, his lips
inches from her own, a devastating smile lifting their
corners for all to see.

Her fingers curled against his chest. "You know
what I mean—"

He leaned closer and rubbed his hands on her
arms, brushing his mouth against her temple, speaking into her ear as if she couldn't hear him. "I know
exactly what you mean," he said. "But we have a
deal. You're supposed to act like my wife in public.
Remember?"

She smiled and nodded, pulling back from him
slightly. "That's true. But not like this! This is too
much, Conley! I'm not going to—"

"Well, lookie here, would you?" A booming
voice suddenly sounded at Lara's side. "Is that the
lovely bride of Conley Harrison I see or are my poor
old eyes deceiving me?"

Lara used the opportunity to pull away from Conley. As she did so, the man who'd spoken stepped up and pumped her hand, a wide grin splitting his face. "I thought that was you, honey! Good to see you again. Haven't seen you in years!"

A real character, Malcom Stanger had invested pots of Texas oil money in Harrison's when no one else would even listen to Con. Lara smiled at the attractive older man with more enthusiasm than was needed.

"Malcom...how great to see you again." She squeezed his hand and smiled, but on the inside she was seething. What on earth did Conley think he was doing? And why was he doing it?

Even more importantly, why was her heart pounding the way it was? She'd thought she was past this point. She felt sick with confusion and anxiety.

Oblivious to her distress, the oil man beamed at Lara and started a fascinating conversation about the last time he'd been to Africa. Beside him, his wife smiled indulgently, the story one she'd obviously heard before. Two more couples joined them, along with Matt, Sandy and Theresa. Introductions were made, but all Lara could think of was Conley. He'd managed to move close to her again and had draped his forearm over her shoulders as if it belonged there, the heavy weight a constant reminder that something was wrong.

The wealthy investor finished his reminiscences and Lara managed to squirm from beneath Conley's arm. She shot another glance around the room, then looked back at her husband. "It's awfully crowded here. Do you think we should take our table now?"

Conley's dark eyes hadn't cooled. If anything, he looked even more intense. But he nodded, and tucking her hand into the crook of his arm, he led her into the restaurant, the others following behind them.

LARA THOUGHT dinner would never end.

Seated at a large table in the back of the dining room, Conley was so attentive, so considerate toward her, she wanted to scream. *It's an act,* she thought. *He doesn't really love me! Not one bit.*

The only one who understood was Sandy. Seated across the table, she had delivered a stream of concerned looks in Lara's direction throughout the entire dinner.

By the time everyone had ordered dessert and coffee, it was all Lara could do to stay alert and watch the room for possible trouble. When Conley finally suggested they move back to the bar for aperitifs, Sandy made a beeline for Lara's side.

"You'd better work on your act." She whispered in Lara's ear as they headed for the bar. "It's pretty obvious you aren't appreciating Conley's attentions."

"I'm not." Lara seethed inside as she sent a gracious smile toward one of Conley's investors.

Sandy raised one eyebrow. ''Well, you can't say the same for him. He certainly seems to be enjoying himself.''

Lara didn't get a chance to respond. Conley came up and took her arm with a loving look, drawing her to his side. For the next hour, she sat beside on him on a banquette in the bar, his fingers occasionally brushing the hair at the nape of her neck, his hand on her knee more than once. She distanced herself by scanning the room for possible trouble, and by the time the evening ended she was ready to run out the door.

But she couldn't.

They had to walk out together, the charade an unending torture as the group said their goodbyes on the front steps of the restaurant. In the cold night air, Conley waved goodbye to everyone, then knit Lara's fingers inside his own and led her to the parking lot. Lara tried to pull her hand away but he brought it to his mouth and brushed his lips over her knuckles. ''Your hands are cold,'' he murmured. ''Where are your gloves?''

She yanked her hand from his and mindful of their exposure, continued to walk swiftly through the parked vehicles. ''This is outrageous, Conley.'' She glanced over at him. He was keeping pace with her easily, his long legs making one stride for every two of hers. ''I told you before I wasn't going to put up with this kind of foolishness. While I'm with you, we can act like a married couple but that doesn't mean one that just got back from their honeymoon! I don't know what you think you're doing, but I don't appreciate it!''

His expression was blank, hiding any true emotion. "I don't know what you're talking about, Lara. All I was doing was playing my part—"

His denial was still in the air when Lara heard something. She went still then pivoted and grabbed his lapel. "Stop!" she whispered. "Right here. Don't move.''

He covered her hand with his—an automatic response—and looked down at her with a puzzled expression. "What the—"

"Shhh…" She put a finger to her lips and pulled him downward. Crouching behind a white Lexus, she spoke urgently. "There's someone over there. By the Explorer.''

He started to stand and she jerked him back down. "No!" Their eyes met. "I'll go see what's going on." She reached inside her purse and jerked out her cell phone, handing it to Conley. "Go back to the restaurant and call Ed and the police. Tell them I want backup." Slipping her hand inside her jacket, she removed her weapon then, still crouched, she eased forward.

Conley pulled her back.

"Don't do it, Lara." His voice was almost frantic.

"Give me the gun and let me go. You stay here and call."

"Are you nuts?" She hissed. "Let me go, Conley! This is my job."

"I'm not going to cower back here like some little kid. I'm your husband, for God's sake. Now give me the damn gun."

She didn't bother to answer him. She simply turned and ran. Too swift for him to do anything about it. Another second and she was over an aisle. One more dash and she closed in on their SUV. Peeking around the front fender of a black Mercedes parked next to her Explorer, she heard something behind her. Conley was three vehicles back. With a curse, she motioned him down. He was too tall...anyone could see him over the cars. He crouched lower on the snowy tarmac and made his way toward her.

He reached her side as the rear window of the Explorer exploded.

A shower of glass hit the surrounding cars and the Explorer's alarm started to scream. Lara jumped up, no longer trying to hide. A figure in black, a tire iron raised over his head, was poised by the back of her SUV.

"Drop it!" she called. "Drop the iron and move away from the vehicle!"

The person jerked around at the sound of Lara's

voice. Barely illuminated by a dim streetlight, he froze.

Lara gripped her weapon and started forward slowly. "Put it down. Right now. And step away."

She could see puffs of frost coming from the gaping hole of the ski mask the thief wore. Whoever he was, he was breathing hard.

"Put it down," she repeated one more time.

He seemed to hesitate, then he pulled his arm back and let go of the tire iron with a scream. It flew through the night with deadly accuracy. Lara ducked but she was almost too late. The iron missed her head by mere inches, hitting the side mirror of a BMW, then the door itself, setting off that car's alarm as well.

Something stung Lara's face. She brushed at her skin and popped back up. But she wasn't fast enough. The figure in black was already bounding away, something square and dark in his hand. Recognizing her laptop computer, Lara ran after him, her pistol held out before her. "Stop," she screamed. "Stop now."

She pounded through the lot as quickly as she could, but by the time she reached the street, the figure was long gone. Panting and frantic, Lara searched both ways, her hair flying into her eyes, her breath rasping so loud she could hear it over the shrieking car alarms.

Despite their noise Lara suddenly heard something behind her. Her heart jumped into her throat, and she pivoted, her gun out and aimed before she realized it was Conley. She dropped the barrel of the weapon and cursed, grabbing his arm and pulling him toward her. His momentum carried them both into the street and toward the lighted awning of the restaurant. She had him inside five seconds later.

He was safe.

But whoever had broken into her vehicle now had Lara's laptop computer.

And all her confidential notes on Conley's case.

CHAPTER EIGHT

MARGULIES AND Fields arrived shortly after Ed. The three men grilled Lara on the person in black.

"He was medium height," she said, "about five foot nine or maybe eleven. His head was almost to the top of the Explorer. Medium build. He had on a ski mask." She shook her head despondently. "I couldn't see anything else."

"Are you sure it was a man?"

She looked at Fields and shook her head again. "No. I'm not sure. Not at all. I don't think he was in great shape, though."

"What do you mean?" Fields asked.

"He was breathing hard. I could see his breath. He was either out of shape or scared."

"Did he say anything?"

She turned to answer Margulies's question. "Not that I could understand. He screamed when he threw the iron but it was just a sound." She shivered without thinking. "An angry sound."

"High-pitched or low?"

"Neither, really, but on the low side if I had to choose one."

"Which hand held the tire iron?"

"His left," she said after a second. "He threw it with his left hand. He had good aim, too. He almost got me."

The cop nodded and scribbled something in his notebook. "We picked it up," he said. "Doubt we'll get any prints, but you never know. These are criminals we're dealing with, not rocket scientists..."

"The car—"

"We're dusting it, too. But with the snow, it's damn near impossible. The footprints were already covered, too." Margulies made a few more notes, then nodded. "We'll be in touch."

Watching the men leave, Lara dabbed at her temple again with a wadded cocktail napkin. It came away bloody. A flying piece of glass from the Beemer's side mirror had caught her just above the eye. She hadn't realized she'd been hurt until they'd come inside the restaurant and Conley had seen the blood. Glancing across the room, she inadvertently caught Conley's eye. They'd been screaming at each other inside the bar when Ed and the police had first arrived, Conley upset at her for pursuing the thief. She'd defended her actions the best she could, but she was more upset with herself for leaving the computer in the car than anything else. Conley scowled at her then returned to his conversation.

Malcom Stanger and the other investors had already left, thank God, but Matthew and Sandy were

still here. Right after Lara and Conley had run inside, Theresa had joined the group as well, coming
back into the bar from the rest room. Everyone understood that someone had broken into Lara's car
and she'd chased them, but that was it.

"Did you see anything after the guy got away?"
Perched on the bar stool next to Lara, Ed spoke. His
hair standing on end, he wore a sweater and an old
pair of golf pants that didn't match. He'd been at
Bess's and had obviously left her place in a hurry.
"Did you hear a car start or maybe a motorcycle?
He had to get away somehow. Doubt that he ran..."

Lara thought for a moment. "I didn't hear anything unusual, but I wasn't listening, either," she
said. "All I could think about was getting Conley
inside. I didn't stop to consider anything else."

As she spoke, Ed's expression changed to disgust.
"What in the hell were you doing with your laptop
in your car anyway, Lara? Good God Almighty—"

She held up her hand, her embarrassment stinging
as much as her forehead. "All right! Enough! I
know it wasn't the smartest thing in the world to
do, but I had to leave it out there. I wanted to come
see you after dinner to give you the report and I
couldn't very well bring it in here." She looked
down at the floor then back up at her father, defeat
in her voice over her mistake. "The file was encrypted, but it's got everything on it about the case,

Ed. Everything. We'll have to change our plans completely.''

Her father compressed his lips and nodded, clearly unhappy with her stupidity but trying his best not to show it any more than he already had. Lara was too grateful—and too surprised—to say anything else. A second later, drawn by something she couldn't define, she turned her eyes back across the room. Theresa was touching Conley's arm in a solicitous gesture, her face concerned as she nodded in Lara's direction and obviously asked about her. Conley answered Theresa's question then sent Lara another frown. A moment later, he headed Lara's way. She cursed under her breath.

When he reached her side, however, Conley spoke to Ed, his angry voice too low for anyone else but them to hear. "Ed, look, this is not acceptable. You're going to have to get someone else to handle the case, think up another plan. Lara's not—"

"She's the best I've got, Con." Ed's green eyes turned flinty. "This wasn't her fault."

Lara stared at her father in shock. He was defending her?

"God, I know that. That's not what I meant at all." Conley's voice changed. "I *know* she's the best. But I don't want her doing this. When I thought it was a simple stalker, the risks were acceptable. But not now. I won't have her hurt because of me—"

Lara spoke from behind clenched teeth, her temple throbbing. "You don't need to worry about me, Conley. I'm perfectly capable of taking care of myself...and of you, too." She glared at him. "I'm not backing down. I signed on for this job even though I didn't want it. I'm not going to dump it now just because the going's getting tough!"

"I won't let you do this, Lara!"

"You won't let me?" She jumped from the barstool and moved closer to him, her face right in his. "We had a deal, Conley. A deal's a dea—"

"I don't give a damn. This deal's off. Definitely off."

Lara started to reply, then all at once she realized the room had gone silent. Everyone in the bar—from Theresa to her father—were listening and watching, their eyes filled with the same fascination held by rubberneckers at a wreck. Abashed by the attention, she took a step back from Conley and lifted her chin, nonetheless.

"No deal," he said quietly, his eyes boring into hers. "All bets are off."

No one in the room but Lara could hear him and if they had, they wouldn't have understood what he was saying anyway. But she did.

"You have a signed contract with Mesa." She spoke softly as well, but her mouth was so dry she was surprised she could speak at all. "And a verbal one with me. We *will* provide you what we promised and you *will* uphold your end of that contract. Whether you like it or not.'' Her gaze burning, she turned around and walked out of the bar.

THERESA TURNED BACK to the bar and fussed with the napkin under her drink. It was hard to hide her elation but she had to. No one could know how she felt about what had just happened. She lifted her head and stared at herself in the mirror behind the bar. Her face wore a concerned look, slightly nervous. She adjusted her expression, wrinkling her brow a tad more. There, she thought. Perfect. A friend of the family, faintly embarrassed, somewhat worried. Perfect.

She'd come into the bar just as Lara had pulled Conley back into the building. Disheveled and out of breath, they'd told Theresa what had happened. A few seconds later the police and Ed Bentley had arrive.

Theresa's eyes shifted to the scene behind her. The door was still swinging from Lara's hasty departure, and Conley, poor Conley, looked shell-shocked.

And who wouldn't, Theresa thought indignantly. The whole evening had been horrible for him...and her, too. If Theresa hadn't given the situation some serious thought, she would have been beside herself. But after she'd seen Conley and Lara shopping last weekend, she'd done nothing but think about his actions. She'd even driven up Mount Barton north of Red Feather to get away from all distractions so she could consider the situation more clearly. At the top of the mountain, she'd stepped outside her car, sat down on a ledge and slowly, bit by bit, she'd put the puzzle pieces together and gotten the whole picture.

Conley wasn't in love with his wife. No way. It was all a game. He was doing exactly what Theresa would have done! It was an act and a damn good one, she had to admit. He was convincing that witch he loved her then when he had her where he wanted her, he'd tell her the truth. That he was leaving her. That he loved Theresa. That Lara would get nothing. She'd be too devastated by his reversal to fight, and he'd get out easy.

It was perfect, really. Theresa couldn't have done better herself. A tiny smile crossed her face before she realized what she was doing. She immediately wiped away the look.

They were soul mates, she and Conley.

She sipped her bourbon with satisfaction and checked the mirror one more time. The cops were leaving now, Lara's father trailing along behind them, Conley walking out as well. Matthew Oakley and his sniveling wife Sandy had already left. Theresa took another swallow, the liquor easing down her throat with velvety smoothness.

She didn't consider herself a violent person, oh

no. But she couldn't help thinking that it was too bad the damn tire iron hadn't cracked Lara Harrison's skull. It would have made things so much easier.

CONLEY SEETHED all the way home but there was nothing he could do or say. He didn't want to get into another fight with Lara, especially in front of Ed who had offered to drive them home. The police had towed the Explorer.

Dropping them at the front door, Ed called Conley back when he started to get out. "You take care of her," Ed said gruffly. He tilted his head to the house into which Lara had already disappeared. "She's pretty upset."

"She'll be fine," Conley said. "But that's all the more reason you need to listen to me, Ed. I don't want Lara on this case anymore. I didn't think about it long enough. I—I made a mistake. I shouldn't have—"

"It's too late, Con. She's a dog with a bone." Ed pursed his mouth and hitched a thumb in the direction they'd come. "You heard her back there. She's not going to leave this alone. If anything, she'll dig in even more."

"I don't want her getting hurt."

"Neither do I...but that's the way this kind of work goes." Ed stared at him in a curious way. "Surely you thought of this before? Lara's job has always been different—sitting behind a desk is not her style. Until that Atwater fiasco, this was all she did. It's what all bodyguards do."

Conley's jaw clenched. He had to force himself to loosen it. "I *knew* that and I was glad when she stopped going out after the other case...but dammit to hell, I didn't really *understand*. Not until tonight. That's why it's so important you get her off this case. I don't want her injured and I especially don't want that to happen while she's protecting me. It's not right. You have to convince her—"

Ed interrupted him. "No one convinces Lara of anything. You should know that by now."

"But this is getting serious."

Ed looked at him through the open window of the Cadillac. "It's always been serious. You just didn't know *how* much so."

The window glided up, and Ed drove off into the darkness, snow crunching under the tires. Conley stood on the sidewalk and watched the Caddy leave, the cold air penetrating his overcoat.

All he'd wanted was to get close to Lara again. As stupid as it sounded now, he hadn't actually considered the danger. Sure, it'd crossed his mind after he'd been hit, but he hadn't been convinced that was anything more than an accident. Then last weekend, he'd been anxious when he thought they were being followed. But this... He shook his head, his breath clouding before him. An inch more to the left and that tire iron could have seriously injured Lara. The thought made Conley's skin crawl.

He turned and started up the sidewalk but he caught movement in his peripheral vision. Without thinking, he tensed, his hands fisted at his side. Then he realized what he'd seen. Someone had been at the window…in Lara's bedroom. The heavy satin draperies twitched again, a sliver of light falling out and hitting the snow. Finally, the light went off, but he could still feel her eyes on him. He couldn't have been on the sidewalk for more than two seconds after Ed had driven off, but she had been waiting. Watching. Guarding.

But she didn't *care*.

This was her job, just as she'd said inside the bar tonight. They had a contract and she was going to fulfill her part. Whether he wanted her to or not. Whether it put her in danger or not.

He reached the door and went inside. What on earth had he done?

LARA LET THE DRAPES fall as she heard the front door open then close. The beep-beep-beep of the security system told her Conley had armed the perimeter and she finally relaxed. Before they'd gotten into the car, she'd told Ed to detain Conley. The minute they'd arrived, she'd raced around and checked the whole house, gun drawn. Everything was fine, of course. The alarm had still been set; no one had been inside.

As Lara slipped out of her shoes then began to undo her top, a knock sounded on her bedroom door. Bracing herself, she crossed the room and opened the door, one hand holding her blouse together. Conley stood on the threshold. His dinner jacket was already off, and he was unbuttoning his shirt and pulling his tie askew. There were shadows in his eyes and his jaw was blue with stubble. They looked at each other through the open door.

"I want to talk to you," he said ominously.

She started to close the bedroom door. "Not tonight. I think we did enough 'communicating' before dinner, don't you?"

In a flash, his hand came out and stopped the door. "We *are* going to talk. And now."

Lara moistened her lips with the tip of her tongue. "There's nothing more to say, Conley. I'm staying on the case and if you think you can intimidate me into giving it up, you're highly mistaken."

His eyes narrowed into slits of anger. "What the hell are you talking about—"

"The kissing, the touching, the total charade... We had a deal. And you're sticking by it."

"You've got it all wrong, Lara. More wrong than you could even know. I want you off this thing because I didn't realize it was going to be this dangerous. I don't want—"

"I didn't think it was going to be like this, either." She tightened her grip on the edge of the door. "But I have a job to do so that doesn't matter now."

"It matters to me."

"I'm sure it does," she said. "You're the one who's the target. And the stakes went up tonight."

"What do you mean?"

With a sigh, Lara moved into the room and sat down heavily on the edge of her bed. It was past midnight, her head throbbed, and someone had tried to break open her head with a tire iron. The assault of Conley's lips earlier in the evening had been the worst part, though. Her mouth could still feel his.

And dammit, she'd enjoyed every second.

He followed her into the bedroom and she put aside her thoughts to look up at him. "Whoever took my computer now has access to all the information we had about you. Once they break the encryption they'll know all your appointments, your entire schedule. They'll know where you're going to be every minute of the day for the next two months. At that point, they'll know you better than you know yourself." She paused, her neck tight, her whole body tense. "We're going to have to do something about that."

"There's nothing we can do—"

"Yes, there is." She spoke patiently, as if to a child. "First, you're going to have to redo your schedule. Completely. Everything you had planned, you're going to have to unplan."

"I can't do that."

"You have to."

"I'm not in charge of the world, Lara. I can't wave a wand and get everyone's life to revolve around mine."

"I'm not suggesting that. I'm suggesting the opposite, in fact. For a change. You're going to have to accommodate...do the best you can."

"I don't see how that's possible. Especially the Royal Mountain meeting. People are coming from Europe for that. One guy's even flying in from Dubai. And I have to be there."

For one long moment, they glared at each other in the dim light. An impasse. Then Conley's eyes shifted. Downward.

Lara followed his gaze and realized what she'd done. Sitting down on the bed, she'd let her hands fall. Her blouse was half open, the lace cups of her bra the only thing keeping his gaze from her bare breasts. Feeling ridiculous, she gathered the edges of the silky fabric in her hands and brought them back together, her face growing warm. It wasn't as if he hadn't seen her breasts before, but the sudden heat in his eyes was unexpected, something she hadn't seen in a very long time.

Before she could recover, Conley came to where she sat and kneeled down. He put one hand on her knees then reached out with the other and took her chin between his fingers, lifting her gaze to his level. She blinked in surprise. His eyes burned, burned with an emotion she didn't understand.

He spoke softly. "Look, Lara...I know you don't love me anymore. You've made that perfectly obvious. But I'm not going to let you get injured for me. That's *not* how this is going to work."

"In this kind of job, that possibility is something I have to live with. It comes with the territory."

"I'm aware of that fact *now* but I've never been in this position before. And I don't want you hurt because of me."

"I've already been hurt, Conley. By you. Why do you care now?"

His jaw went hard. "You know what I mean. I don't want anything bad to happen to you, Lara. Things might not be right between us but that doesn't mean I don't love—"

She was shaking her head even before he finished. "Don't say that," she whispered. "Not at this point. It's too late."

"But it's the truth."

"Well, you have a funny way of showing it. Never being here. Putting your job first. Putting me last..." She couldn't bring herself to list the final reason, then she knew she had to. "Not to mention the fact that you're having an affair and have been for months."

He looked into her eyes. "I told you once already, Lara. I am *not* having an affair. That's not something I would even consider. We're married." He said the last sentence as if it explained everything.

"I read a note she sent you, Conley. It was more than clear you two have been sleeping together."

"That came from the nut who's stalking me."

"How do you know? You don't even know what note I'm talking about—"

"It doesn't matter. I'm not having an affair so anything like that had to have come from the stalker. End of story."

He spoke so plainly, Lara suddenly held her breath. Ever since she'd learned about the stalker, she *had* been having misgivings, and they'd been growing. What if Conley was telling the truth? What if she'd been confused? Until this very minute Lara hadn't accepted how much she'd come to doubt herself but now she had to face the possibility that she'd been wrong. The prospect terrified her.

Because if Conley hadn't fallen in love with another woman, then he'd fallen *out* of love with her. The empty looks of the women her father had left began to haunt her.

Lara looked away, her composure failing as the reality of the situation proved too much to ignore. He wasn't having an affair and never had. The sad truth made her aching heart even more sore.

"It doesn't matter, Conley," she said. "We've

gotten too far away from where we're supposed to be. We're two separate people now...we aren't a family...we aren't even a couple. I'm not going to let that pain drag out forever. Not this time."

She pushed his hands away from her knees and stood up slowly. He rose as well, his gaze filled with confusion as he looked down at her.

"We're just two people living in one house," she said quietly. "A real marriage is more than that."

CHAPTER NINE

THE WEEKEND was torture. Lara took Conley into the office and left him with Jake on Saturday *and* on Sunday, but in between their hours apart, they had seconds together—seconds in which each of them did their best to avoid the other. If she was in the kitchen and he walked in, she'd get up and leave. If he came into the den while she was there, he'd turn around and disappear. They weren't in the same room for more than a minute, but it didn't seem to matter. A suffocating tension hovered between them, unanswered questions and unresolved issues filling the thick silence.

Worst of all Lara kept remembering the kiss. The way Conley's lips had heated hers…the taste of his mouth…the feel of his hands. Had her life depended upon it, she couldn't have gotten the images out of her mind. Monday didn't come fast enough for her.

Still the situation didn't get any better.

Lara dropped Conley off at his office, then drove straight to the police station. Margulies had instructed her to come in first thing that morning to finish the paperwork on the incident, but when she got there, he was at home with a sick child. Only Fields was available. Walking to the back of the station where the officer's cubicle was located, Lara found herself wishing the situation was reversed. She felt comfortable with Margulies; something about this other, more intense, cop bothered her. As she found his desk and shook his hand in greeting, she decided it was his eyes that disturbed her. They swept over her in a judgmental way, instantly instilling a false sense of guilt. It was probably something he cultivated, she thought, sitting down in the chair he indicated. A trick he used to his advantage.

She dealt with her discomfort by asking a question. "Did the lab finish their tests on the stolen car?"

"Yes, they did. The report was sitting on my desk when I came in this morning." He paused. "The blood on the fender matches your husband's."

A sick feeling rose inside Lara at the image, her throat closing off.

"The owner said the car was stolen while she was supposed to be picking up something early that morning—she owns a delivery service. When she discovered the vehicle was gone, she walked to a service station, called her brother, and got him to bring her his car so she could finish her run. She told him to call us, then left for Denver, but he's just a kid and he got sidetracked. She supports them both and she couldn't jeopardize her rush jobs to stop and call us herself. She phoned the station late that night when she found out he'd forgotten." Fields flipped to the front of the report he held and shuffled through some of the papers. "Woman by the name of Nanci Thompson. Owns Thompson Messenger Service. Name ring a bell?"

Lara started to say no, then stopped. The name did sound familiar, but she couldn't place it. Red Feather was so small, she could know the woman from anywhere. She told the cop that, then said, "Maybe it'll come to me later."

Nodding, he reached inside his desk drawer and pulled out another thick file. Once more, they went over the details from Friday night, Fields's questions short and to the point, Lara's answers the same as they'd been that night. Half an hour later, when he got to the end of his form, the cop looked up at Lara, then slowly pushed the papers to one side. He didn't say anything and Lara simply waited. She might not like Fields but she was accustomed to dealing with men and their silences.

Finally he broke the silence. "Mrs. Harrison, you seem like a savvy woman. So tell me something... Tell me why there's so much tension between you and your husband."

Lara gave him a level gaze. "I'm not sure I understand what you're asking, Officer Fields."

"Oh, I think you are very sure," he said. "The first time I saw you two at the hospital you did a good job of covering it up, but last night pretty much gave away the secret. There's trouble in paradise, isn't there?''

Lara thought for a moment. She didn't like lying, but spilling her guts to a cop like Fields was the last thing she wanted to do. ''That's a very personal question,'' she countered. ''Why would you want to know something like that?''

''Please answer the question, Mrs. Harrison.''

She wasn't going to win this one, Lara thought. She might as well tell him what he wanted to know and get it over with. ''Conley and I have our ups and downs,'' she said with reluctance. ''Like any married couple.''

''But you're guarding him, aren't you? Through Mesa.''

''Yes. I explained the details earlier to Officer Margulies—I assumed he had passed them on.''

''He did. But tell me again.''

''Mesa's supposedly conducting a security review for Conley but we're actually using the opportunity to cover him because of the stalker. I'm in charge of the case.''

He leaned back in his chair and seemed to consider her answer as he tucked his hands behind his neck. ''Why do I have the impression it's not something you volunteered for?''

She wanted to protest once more, but the effort would be pointless. ''The job isn't an easy one,'' she admitted. "This situation is very difficult. My husband's under a lot of pressure."

"And so are you." Again the look. This time it held speculation. "Safeguarding your husband is not something just any woman could handle. That's gotta be a tough one." He waited. "Especially if the marriage isn't what it used to be."

"You're making a big leap, Officer." Lara kept her voice calm, her expression matching it. "We had words after a very upsetting incident.... I would think it'd be natural for anyone to be edgy after something like that."

"I'm a cop, Mrs. Harrison. And I've been one for twenty years. When your husband lied to me in the hospital, it was very obvious. A little digging, and I backed up my suspicions." He waited for her to meet his eyes. "You've asked him for a divorce, haven't you?"

Lara wondered if he'd talked to someone or made a good guess, then she decided it didn't really matter, either way. He knew the truth. "Yes," she said quietly. "I have asked Conley for a divorce. But I don't see what that has to do with the case...."

He waited a second before speaking and she got the impression he was trying to make her nervous. It was working.

"Someone tried to run him over," the cop said. "He's being stalked and watched. Now this latest problem... Divorces put a lot of stress and strain on people. They go a little nuts sometimes, especially when it looks like they might not get what they want.''

Lara started to speak but he held up a hand.

"Thing is...I can see how you might hire someone to do your husband harm, but why would you stalk him, too? Just to spook him?'' He shook his head. "Doesn't make sense. You'd do one or the other, not both...."

His words shocked her, which she immediately suspected was exactly what he wanted. "You honestly think I could be behind all this? That's ridiculous!''

She didn't bother to defend or even address the suggestion—it was so obviously crazy. She went directly to logic, something the cop would understand. "Even if I was trying to kill him, why on earth would I hire someone to break into my car and steal my own computer? To what end?''

"You tell me.''

They stared at each other across the expanse of the metal desk, Lara in a state of stunned confusion, Fields calm and collected. When she didn't answer, he spoke again. His tone was conversational, as if they were sharing a cup of coffee at Starbucks and discussing a soap opera instead of her life.

"I could have it all wrong, of course. Maybe even backward. It'd be a pretty slick plan, I do have to admit...''

Lara's mouth went dry, a feeling of sick realization washing over her that Fields was *finally* getting to the real point of his conversation. He'd maneuvered her straight into a corner from which she couldn't escape.

"Wh-what do you mean?"

"What if your husband didn't want a divorce...but he did want out? What if he planned all this—the accident, the stalking, the tire iron—to get you involved?" He leaned toward her. "It'd be pretty tragic, wouldn't it? The man's loyal wife dies while trying to protect him? What a shame..."

Without even stopping to think, Lara answered, her defense as natural as breathing. "That's ludicrous!" she said, "and completely wrong. Conley isn't that kind of man. We may have our differences, but he'd never do anything like that. Never."

"Are you sure?"

"I'm positive. Conley doesn't have a manipulative bone in his body. If he wants something, he goes for it. Outright. He doesn't believe in hidden agendas."

But the second the words left Lara's mouth, she remembered Conley's expression in the hospital, the mystery in his eyes, the way he'd looked past her. And what about the errands a few weekends ago, when she'd thought someone was following them? He'd acted so strange then, so out of character. From the moment they'd made their deal, she'd felt as if there was more going on than she realized.

But not this.

It couldn't be this.

While Lara sat in stunned silence, Fields began to speak in a neutral voice, rising as he did so and holding out his hand. "All right then. Thank you for stopping by. We'll be in touch."

She was at the end of the hall when Lara turned around. Leaning against his cubicle wall, Fields nodded at her. Lara nodded back then pushed through the door and left the building.

CONLEY'S GLOVE hit the ball with more force than was necessary. It bounced off the leather with a startling whack then sailed straight out of bounds. Matthew whooped and their regular Monday night handball game was over.

Cursing soundly, Conley pulled off his protective glasses and threw them after the ball. It wasn't often Matthew could beat him at handball. In fact, it damn near never happened, but that outcome had been inevitable today. Still slightly sore from the accident, Conley wasn't at his best. And his mind definitely wasn't on the game. It wasn't on anything but Lara.

Matthew pounded him on the back, his glee at winning too obvious to hide. Despite his quiet nature, he was fiercely competitive and losing to Conley always put him in a horrible mood, regardless of how often it happened. They'd been on the same baseball team in college, Conley barely winning the pitcher's spot over Matthew.

"Good game," Conley said, holding out his hand. "But the next one's mine."

"I'm sure it probably will be." Matthew shook Conley's hand, then wiped his face and tried to temper his gloating. "You had a pretty rough weekend. That's the only reason I got to you...."

Conley nodded as they exited the handball court, then sat down heavily on a nearby bench. "To put it mildly," he answered. "And I don't see them getting any better, either."

"The police haven't found out who broke into the Explorer?"

Conley spoke guardedly. "Not really."

"But they know about the stalker?"

"They know." Conley shook his head, a wash of anger coming over him that he couldn't hold in. He was still upset over Lara's actions in the parking lot but he couldn't very well go into that with Matthew. He thought fast, transferring his frustration to a point that made some sense. "I don't know what in hell they're doing about any of it, though. I can't see any progress being made, that's for sure."

Matthew made a sound of understanding. Snapping his mouth shut, Conley stood and headed for the showers, Matthew trailing behind. What was the point of even thinking about the situation? Lara was going to do what she wanted to, regardless of how he felt.

Half an hour later, both men emerged from the locker room. From his easy chair in the club's waiting room, Jake jumped up. Lara's entry into the men's facility had obviously presented a problem so under the guise of wanting to get a game in himself, Jake had "hitched a ride" with Conley and Matthew. He and another agent had then rented the court next to Conley's. Falling in step with Conley and Matthew, the men headed for the snowy parking lot. Matthew stopped by a dark-blue Lexus, the sides and tops dusted with a thin layer of snow. It looked like powdered sugar against the perfect navy paint.

Conley halted, Matthew's expression turning sour as Con whistled at the expensive sedan. "That's some ride, Matt. When did you buy that?"

"Last week. I had to," Matthew said in a defensive tone. "Sandy's been driving me nuts for months. She wanted a new car so I finally gave in...as if I had a choice."

Conley nodded as if he appreciated the dilemma, but walking off with Jake and the other guard a few minutes later, he could only wish he had the same problem. When he was younger, he'd thought new cars and diamond rings were all it took to keep a marriage going. His parents had fought endlessly over money. Not the extra kind that bought luxuries but the necessary kind that bought bread and rent.

If they'd had money, he'd always thought, everyone would have been happy. Now he knew better. It took more than that. A helluva lot more.

He just wasn't sure what *it* was.

SATURDAY MORNING dawned clear and bright. When Lara opened her bedroom drapes, the Colorado sunshine hurt her eyes with its brilliance. Once again, she'd been up half the night thinking about her conversation with Fields. He'd said a lot of things that had bothered her but one thing kept coming back. Why would she—or anyone—stalk Conley *and* be trying to kill him at the same time? That kind of action didn't make a lot of sense, as Fields had pointed out, and Lara hadn't been able to get the question out of her mind. Even crazy people had motivations, she told herself, looking out the window. They just weren't understood by the rest of the world. She'd have to think about it some more, she decided. Something would come to her, she was sure.

A Steller's jay landed on the feeder outside the window, his startling azure feathers catching her gaze. On another day, in a different time, Lara would have welcomed the perfect weather. She and Conley were supposed to be on the slopes west of town at 1:00 p.m. He'd given her his revised schedule on Friday and casually pointed out the obligation, as he called it.

"I go up every so often," he'd said. "When Bess asks me." He'd refused to say more when Lara had pressed him. "It wasn't on the original schedule because she didn't call me until Wednesday but no one knows we'll be doing this," he'd told her. "We'll be safe, believe me. Just wear something warm."

She'd started to point out that someone out there knew everything about him, but she'd kept her mouth closed. It hurt too much to realize there was so much about him *she* no longer knew. He helped Bess out? Doing what? Lara had always assumed he'd been going to work whenever he left the house on the weekends. What was he doing? And why hadn't Bess told her about this?

The ache of being excluded from Conley's life was a honed knife that twisted sharply inside Lara's heart. She reminded herself that although he wouldn't have told her if she had inquired, she had stopped asking. Which had come first?

Turning away from her bedroom window, Lara went into her bathroom and dressed. The rest of the morning she spent catching up on the paperwork she'd neglected since taking on Conley's case. Regardless of how deeply she immersed herself in her work, however, she stayed aware of his every move. The kiss he'd given her at the restaurant had flipped some kind of switch inside her head and no matter what he did or where he was, her thoughts were filled with Conley. She also suspected their recent conversation had had just as much to do with her newfound sensitivity as his kiss. Conley hadn't been having an affair and she believed him now. Their problems were theirs and theirs alone.

She could hear him walking around in the house, talking on the phone, sending a fax. When she got up from her desk at noon and went into the kitchen, he was standing by the window looking out into the backyard.

"We'll need to leave in thirty minutes," she said.

"I know."

He didn't move from the window, then a few seconds later, he spoke again, so quietly she could barely hear him. "There's a fox in the backyard. Come look..."

She walked on silent feet to his side and peered out the window. Sure enough, a small red fox stood near one of their pine trees, his coat glistening in the sun, his tail a thick brush that pointed straight out. As she watched, he swiveled his head and stared directly at them.

"He's gorgeous," she whispered. "Look at that fur! Can you believe it?"

Conley murmured his agreement, then looked down at Lara. Whatever he'd been about to say was never spoken. He simply gazed at her, his eyes connecting with hers in a way that stopped her breath. As she struggled to regain it, she realized they were standing so close together she could see where he'd nicked himself, shaving that morning. He had a spot under his chin that he never could get without the blade going too close. She reached up and touched his face, her finger brushing his skin.

"You cut yourself," she whispered.

He kept his eyes on hers but took her fingers, closing his fist over her hand. His touch warmed her, bringing a lump to her throat. She didn't want to experience the attraction she felt; it hurt too much. She was only reacting to him now because it had been too long. His kiss, as manufactured as it was, had awakened desires she thought dead and buried.

"It's just a scratch," he said in a husky voice.

"You should put something on it."

The words meant nothing to either one of them, but they had to say something. If they fell silent, who knew what would happen? For a very long second, they stayed that way—frozen by their emotions, trapped by their past—then finally, Conley spoke. His words were unexpected.

"I'm sorry," he said. "I'm sorry I've created all these problems for you, Lara. I never meant for this to happen."

She wasn't sure what he was saying. Was he talking about his stalker or their marriage?

"Lots of things happen we don't plan on," she said. "But they happen for a reason. We might not know what it is, but it's there."

"Destiny?" His voice was mocking.

"Maybe," she said self-consciously. "Don't you believe in it?"

"Once upon a time, I did…but not anymore."

"Why not?"

"I learned better," he said. "We make our own way, Lara. The choices are ours. We decide how the game's going to be played."

Still holding her hand, he started to pull her closer, his intentions clear. She resisted and shook her head.

"Conley…no…please. Last time this happened, you promised me things would be different but they haven't been. We spent a few months getting closer then we drifted apart all over again…and it hurt even more. I have to take care of myself." She took a deep breath. "I can't keep falling in and out of love with you."

He started to reply but she put her fingers over his lips and stilled his words. "I've been hurting too much and for too long. And you haven't seen it. You were too busy working, too busy building your business and tending to your own life. I need someone who can be there for me—when I need him—not just when it's convenient."

"But I didn't know—"

"I know you didn't. And that's the really sad part. You didn't know and I wasn't able to tell you. I used the excuse of believing you were having an affair to push you even farther away. And the pain only grew…then grew some more. Now it's too big for either of us to overcome.'' She shook her head, a deep sadness coming over her. ''I'm sorry, Conley, but I have to protect myself. There may not have been another woman…but you haven't belonged to me for a very long time.''

AN HOUR LATER they pulled up to Royal Mountain. Lara had insisted on driving them to the ski resort. The road was too dangerous, she explained, the sides too steep. She'd done a course in survival driving, especially in snow. If anything unexpected happened, she was trained to deal with the situation. She could handle it—Conley couldn't.

He climbed out of the vehicle and tightened his jaw. There seemed to be a lot of things in his life he couldn't handle these days. The business, his stalker, the incident at the restaurant. All those things mattered, but not as much as Lara. The more she pulled away from him the more he wanted her back. In the kitchen, right before they'd left, he'd seen a spark in her eyes that gave him hope but it'd disappeared a second later. She didn't trust him and nothing he could do or say would make her come back to him.

He couldn't decide which was worse—the agony of understanding the problem or the hell of not knowing how to fix it.

He stepped to the rear of the SUV and pulled their

skis from the rack on the top of the roof. Lara
reached inside and grabbed their boots. Shading her
eyes with one hand, she looked up the mountain. He
followed her gaze. It was already getting crowded
on the upper slopes. They were faster and steeper,
and most of the people who came to Red Mountain
wanted to experience that danger and speed.

"We aren't going up there." Interpreting her
look, he tilted his head toward the higher runs then
turned back into the truck and retrieved his goggles.
Using them to point with, he indicated the beginner
slope. "That's our destination today."

Lara's eyes rounded, their hazel depths turning
green in the bright sunshine. "Are you kidding?
You haven't skied anything but black diamond since
I've known you!"

"Not today," he countered. "Today it's the
bunny slope."

He tossed his skis to his shoulder and headed off.
Behind him, a puzzled Lara followed.

CHAPTER TEN

LARA STUDIED the area as Conley walked away. She saw families, snowboarders, skiers of all ages but nothing that worried her. Continuing her scan, she started forward wondering just what in the heck was going on, when she spotted Bess. The pediatrician was standing in the snow near the edge of the beginner's slope. An older man stood right beside her, and with a start, Lara realized it was Ed. He leaned down to catch something Bess said, then to Lara's amazement, he laughed heartily and kissed her on the cheek. Bess swatted at him playfully and he continued the game, grabbing her and pulling her into his arms as she fought him halfheartedly. At that point, Lara realized they were surrounded by children. Her confusion grew as Conley joined them. Feeling as if she were watching a movie, Lara stared as Bess and Ed greeted Conley and the children started to yell. Lara hurried to catch up, her curiosity growing with each step.

Beset by a half-dozen kids, Conley bent down and started to help them strap on their equipment. Most of it was new and shiny, the skis waxed to perfection, their boots free from scuffs. Their clothing was just the opposite, though. Mismatched jackets and gloves that were too big. Jeans that had holes in them, hats with the same. As Lara reached the little group, she looked up at Bess with questions in her eyes. The doctor shook her head slightly as if to say don't ask.

Baffled but silent, Lara went to Conley's side and knelt in the snow to help. A few of the children edged closer to Conley—they wanted him, not her—but one little girl, a beauty with brown eyes and silvery blond hair, allowed Lara to tighten her toe binding and then the heel, her hand against Lara's shoulder as she steadied herself.

"Thank you," she said shyly as Lara straightened up.

"You're very welcome," Lara countered. "I hope you enjoy your skiing."

The little girl's eyes lit up. "I hope so, too." She dropped her voice to a whisper and leaned closer to Lara. "But I'm kinda scared. I've never done this before…."

Lara patted her on shoulder. "You'll have a great time. Just remember…everybody falls down! You just have to get up and try it again."

The child nodded seriously, then she scooted over to the others, maneuvering closer and closer to Con. A second later, she was by his side. Slipping her hand inside his, she glanced back at Lara and smiled, giving her a little wave.

A few moments later, organizing the children into a semblance of order, Ed and Conley led them to the towline. Bess came to Lara's side and the two women watched as the men shepherded the group up the tiny slope.

Lara turned to Bess. "What on earth is going on here?"

The older woman angled her head toward the ski rope. "They're patients," she said. "Kids who've come to the clinic." She looked down at her feet then raised her face to the mountains. For a moment she was quiet, then she spoke again. "Red Feather's a gorgeous place to live, but there's a lot here that isn't so pretty. These kids come from families that are barely hanging on, Lara. There's not always enough money in the budget for food, much less for fun. When I can, I load them all up and bring them out here for a treat. It seems like the least I can do."

Lara wasn't surprised that Bess would be involved in something like this. When her patients had no insurance or money, she didn't charge for her services, her medical center the only one in town that took everyone, regardless. Lara wasn't even that surprised to see Ed. It was pretty clear the two of them were getting together once more, and knowing Ed, he'd do whatever it took to win Bess over.

But what was Conley's role in the whole event?

"He's been helping out for quite some time." Bess glanced sideways at Lara as she answered the unspoken question. "I called him one day after I treated a very bright little boy. He was nine, and he was sick as a dog. I think it was some bug, I don't even remember now. Anyway this kid was throwing up and had a fever like you wouldn't believe but he couldn't take his eyes off the computer on my desk. He asked me if I had access to the Internet. He had a little report due the next day and all he wanted was to do some research. There's only one machine at the library and needless to say, he didn't have a system at home."

"So you called Conley," Lara said.

Bess confirmed Lara's guess. "I called him. An hour later, the kid had a complete system. Three days later, the library had a dozen more."

A swell of emotion threatened Lara's heart. Conley had been raised in a home that had less than nothing. It made sense he'd want to help. But it hurt that he hadn't even bothered to tell her and let her share this with him.

She inclined her head toward the slopes. Her voice was thick. "How did that translate to this?"

"He stopped by the clinic one evening shortly after that incident and we started talking," Bess said. "He told me about his childhood and I told him about theirs.... After that he started helping. More computers. Supplies for the clinic. I mentioned our Saturday get-togethers and he just showed up one weekend. With every piece of ski equipment you can imagine and some you can't. Boots, bindings, poles…the whole enchilada, as they say."

All Lara could do was nod.

"You didn't know about any of this, Lara?"

"I had no idea." She could feel Bess's curious gaze on her profile, but Lara said nothing more. What *could* she say?

Sensing Lara's discomfort, Bess sidestepped the issue. "Well, your father's been coming for quite a while, too." The older woman grinned. "I told him if he wanted to hang around me, he had to come here to do it. Next thing I knew, he was strapping on some skis and going up the bunny slope with the best of them. The kids adore him. They call him Grampa Ed."

Lara felt her eyes go wide. "Grampa Ed! Are you kidding?"

"Absolutely not." Bess beamed. "Isn't it a hoot? Who woulda thought…"

"Not me," Lara muttered. "Never me."

She turned her eyes back to the ski run. The kids were screaming with excitement, Ed and Conley picking them up when they fell and dusting them off to try again. The little angel she'd helped waved proudly in Lara's direction then promptly fell over. Laughing, she reached out for her ski poles, then she tipped into the snow once more, her tattered blue jacket a flash of color against the blinding white drifts.

Conley skied to the little girl's side. He picked her up and set her back on her feet, pushing her gently to slide down the hill. Looking up, he shaded his face with one hand and sought out Lara.

Their eyes met across the slope.

THEY DROVE HOME in silence. Lara didn't know what to say to Conley and he obviously had nothing to say to her. She'd asked him about his involvement with Bess's patients and why he'd never mentioned it to her, but he'd answered in monosyllables and looked out the window, his mind somewhere else. As always.

Lara carefully negotiated the treacherous road and told herself it didn't matter. In the growing gloom, she had enough to think about. The road was deadly, the turns sharp, the drop-offs steep. One slip of the wheel and the newly repaired Explorer would go off the side of the mountain and never be found. The smallest accident could end up being deadly. By the time they got off the mountain and back into town, she was nervous, anxious and ready to get back to the house.

Instead Conley asked her to drive to the office.

"I'll only be a minute," he said. "I forgot some papers I want to go over this evening."

She nodded and swung the SUV down Sixth

Street. A few moments later they parked in front of Harrison's, the downtown area quiet, the shadows emerging. Dark came quickly in the mountains; the sun had fallen in the short time it'd taken them to get here from the lodge.

Conley started out of the vehicle, but Lara grabbed his arm. "Not so fast," she said. "I'm coming, too."

"I'll only be a second—"

"That's all it takes."

In the dim cab of the vehicle he opened his mouth, then he shut it. "All right," he said. "Come with me."

They left the truck at the same time, Lara walking quickly to keep up with his long stride. The downstairs vestibule was vacant as they entered, their footsteps echoing on the cold tile floor. The empty building was creepy to Lara, tomblike and dark. She felt as if it were listening to them, watching them. They climbed the stairs and reached Conley's office, Lara taking a deep breath as Conley unlocked the door. He reached for the light switch and she reached for her holster. The reassuring heft of her weapon did little to make her feel better.

Then Conley cursed.

Lara tensed, her right hand clenching the pistol's grip. "What's wrong?"

"The power's off," he answered. He flipped the switch up and down and looked out the window at the end of the hallway. "Must be a problem in the whole damn neighborhood. Nothing's on."

Power outages weren't unusual in Red Feather, especially during the winter, but Lara kept her hand on her gun as she pushed ahead of Conley to step inside the office and look around. Everything seemed fine. She walked to the window to look down the street, Conley coming in behind her. He was right. She saw now what she hadn't before— the whole block, for as far as she could see, was dark. Lara relaxed slightly, her shoulders easing.

Then Conley moved closer to her.

His breathing was even and measured, but Lara couldn't say the same for hers. Inside her chest, her heart thudded heavily, knocking against her ribs. Just as it had happened that morning in the kitchen, she could feel his power, sense his presence, even without physically touching him. He was too close. Too warm.

The conversation they'd had before they'd left for the slopes had been painful and sad. The raw words should have pushed them farther apart than before, but all afternoon they'd seemed even more connected than ever.

She didn't understand what was happening. It scared her.

Lara turned slowly and looked up at her husband. "Did you get your papers?"

He ignored her question. Putting his hands on her

shoulders, Conley stared at Lara. He didn't speak, didn't move, didn't do a thing. But he didn't have to. She could read in his eyes that he felt the growing bond between them as plainly as she did.

For a very long time, he simply looked at her, then finally, she could take it no more. She started to back away but her legs wouldn't listen to the command her brain sent out. As she puzzled over this newest development, Conley bent down and kissed her.

His action shocked her, but her reaction stunned her even more.

Her fingers curled into his sweater and she pulled him closer without even thinking twice. His chest was hard against her own, his arms wrapping around her with almost viselike strength. He smelled like snow, clean and cold and pure. He tasted even better.

Conley didn't hesitate. He drew her to him, his hands gliding over her shoulders then down the curve of her back. This kiss was different from what had taken place at the restaurant last week. This one was real.

And Lara found herself craving more. They'd been apart for so long she hadn't realized until now how much their lack of intimacy had really hurt. She'd longed for this and had not even understood how badly. As strange as it sounded, she'd known all day this was going to happen.

Conley made a sound in the back of his throat, a familiar groan that Lara recognized immediately. He wanted her. He wanted her as much as she wanted him. How many times since they had met and fallen in love had she heard him telegraph his desire like that? A thousand? Two thousand? Too many to count. In the past, during happier times, that very sound had made her weak with desire.

It did the same to her now.

His hands slipped inside the coat she still wore, to the sweater beneath it. He lifted the bottom of the garment and eased his hands beneath the wool. His touch was warm and smooth and all Lara wanted was to feel more. As if he could read her mind, he deepened his kiss and traced a path to the small of her back. And in the silent, darkened office, over-whelmed by her memories, Lara suddenly remembered why she'd fallen in love with this man.

He was smart and kind and sexy beyond belief. He loved small children and they loved him. His generosity knew no limits. He was her husband and even though he'd hurt her deeply, she'd loved him. With shock, she found herself wondering if she could once more.

Then the lights came on.

GASPING, Lara pulled away from Conley's embrace, the illumination as startling and disruptive as a bucket of springwater. She looked as dazed as he felt, her hazel eyes widening in surprise, her tousled hair mussed and standing on end. She started to step back, away from him, but he reached out and took her arm.

"Don't," he said. "Lara, please..."

She shook off his hand. "This isn't right, Conley. I can't—"

"Not right?" His voice was incredulous. "We're married, for God's sake! What's not right about it?"

She pushed a hand through her hair, tangling the strands even more. "We're divorcing, dammit! Didn't anything I say to you this morning register? Kissing each other like this—" She held out her hand and searched for the right words, her expression revealing the answers she couldn't. *Hurts too much. Makes me want you too much. Brings us too close together again...*

"It—it's not right, that's all," she finished lamely.

He shook his head and reached for her again, but she moved back. She didn't want him touching her.

He'd been thinking all day about their conversation that morning. He wanted to tell her how much he loved her and what she meant to him, but the words wouldn't come. He wasn't the kind of man who knew how to express himself that way and the sinking feeling suddenly came over him that words were what Lara needed.

He stared at her and wondered what on earth he

could say. Lara didn't give him the chance to decide. She turned and walked away. Away from his touch. Away from his arms.

THERESA HEARD the door shut a few minutes later.

When the slamming sound marked the Harrisons' departure, she let the breath out of her lungs slowly, a dizzy rush accompanying the release. She'd left Royal Mountain earlier after following the two of them out there then growing sick of seeing what was happening. She'd come back to the office to bury herself in work, then the power had gone out. Disgusted with her life and everything in it, Theresa had been about to leave when she'd heard their voices.

She scurried across her office to the window in one corner of the receptionist's area. Pressing down the slats of the miniblinds with a nervous finger, Theresa peered down at the street and watched Conley and Lara get into her SUV.

After the incident at the bar, Theresa had been sure she'd seen the last of Lara. But she'd stuck around. And things weren't getting any better. In fact, this afternoon out at the ski slope, Lara's eyes had followed Conley's as closely as Theresa's. She hadn't even needed the binoculars she'd brought to see the connection between the two of them.

Theresa had wanted to tear down the slope from the lodge and kill Lara Harrison with her own bare

hands. Conley, too, for that matter. He wasn't helping things at all, acting this way. He didn't even
seem to care that Theresa loved him so much. The
flowers and cards had meant nothing to him. They'd
been ignored just as much as the demented attempts
on his life while he wooed his stupid wife.

The whole situation was driving Theresa crazy.

As had the silence from Con's office. She knew
what it meant. She'd heard the exhalations, the tiny
moans. Closing her eyes for just a second she imagined herself in Conley's arms, his mouth on hers
instead of Lara's. She touched her lips with her
thumb, brushing the tender skin. Then slowly, she
opened her eyes.

From her vantage point she couldn't hear the engine but a cloud of vapor puffed out of the Explorer's tailpipe, signaling its start. The vehicle
pulled away from the curb a second later, the tire
tracks visible for only a moment before the snow
covered them once again.

She tapped the glass with her fingertips, drawing
a line in the condensation, an idea coming to her.
With a little luck and some timing, she might be
able to pull it off. She would wait and watch, just
as she had been doing, and sooner or later an opportunity would present itself. If she managed it just
right, she'd come out looking great.

And best of all…Conley would be hers.

ON MONDAY MORNING, Lara dropped Conley at his office then headed straight down Sixth Street. Saturday, on the way to the slopes, she'd told Conley about her visit to the police department, leaving out Fields's suppositions, which had continued to haunt her. Something didn't add up. Ignoring the mess between herself and her husband, she concentrated on the vow she'd made leaving the station the week before. She was going to figure out what was happening and she should start from the beginning. She headed for Red Feather's hospital.

The emergency room was busier that morning than it had been the day Conley had been brought in. The snowy roads had caused a three-car pileup and the town's two ambulances had both been called into action. Sitting down in a corner of the bustling room, Lara picked up a magazine and waited for things to grow calm.

After a while, when it looked as if everyone had been bandaged and medicated and sent on their way, she got up and approached the desk. The nurse was the same one who'd been on duty the day of Conley's accident.

Lara smiled at the woman. She wore a bright floral pantsuit, similar to the smock she'd had on that day, her blond hair pulled back in the same severe fashion. Noting her name tag, Lara greeted her.

"Mrs. Whicker? I'm Lara Harrison." She held

out her hand. "I'm sure you don't remember me, but my husband was brought in—"

"Three weeks ago on Monday," the nurse supplied, taking Lara's hand briefly then dropping it. "He was the one hit by a car. Clipped him on the knee. Dr. Sorelli gave him five stitches, observed him for a while then sent him on his way."

Lara shook her head. "That's amazing. How can you remember that?"

"I have a photographic memory. It's a curse sometimes." Dropping her gaze, she fussed with some papers on the desk, her eyes refusing to meet Lara's.

The woman's attitude immediately confirmed Lara's suspicions. She put her elbows on the counter and leaned closer, waiting for the woman to look up before she spoke. "Do you remember me coming to the desk? I told you I was Mrs. Harrison and you seemed surprised."

The nurse wanted to lie; Lara could see it in her face. Reluctantly, she nodded. "I remember, yes."

"I've been wondering about that day. You were confused when I introduced myself." Lara shrugged and smiled in a self-deprecating way. "I know it's silly and probably not important at all, but I've been curious about that. Why did you think the other woman with my husband was his wife?"

The nurse fiddled with her folder of papers, and Lara wasn't sure she was even going to answer. Finally the woman sighed and looked up, dropping her file to the top of the desk in obvious resignation. "Look, you seem like a really nice person. I don't want to get into the middle of anything that's going to be touchy...."

An invisible hand went around Lara's throat. "It's all right, Mrs. Whicker," she said in a calm way. "You can tell me."

"I could lose my job for talking about patients."

Lara kept her eyes on the nurse's. "I promise you that won't happen because of me," she said. "But I need to know what happened that day. It's important."

The nurse pursed her lips and looked past Lara. After a moment her gaze returned. Pity softened her voice as she began. "The woman that was with him...the attorney."

Lara nodded. "Ms. Marchante?"

"Yes, that was her." She hesitated then continued. "She had her arm around your husband's shoulders when they came in and she was hovering around him. He wasn't paying the slightest bit of attention to her, but she was all over him."

"She was worried—"

"Yes, that's what I thought at first, too. I had them go to the back and then I paged the doctor. He was on the other side of the hospital so it took him a few minutes to get here. That's when she came back out here and..."

Lara's heart thumped erratically. "And what?"

The nurse took a deep breath. "She told me I'd better get the goddamn doctor here or she'd come across the desk and I'd be sorry. Those were her very words." The nurse picked at an invisible thread on the cuff of her blouse, then she lifted her gaze to Lara's. "I'm accustomed to people who are upset, Mrs. Harrison, people who are ill and worried. I tried to calm her down but she wouldn't listen to me. Her emotions only escalated and the cursing did, too. I wanted to call security but instead, I put my hand on her arm and addressed her calmly—just as I'm speaking to you—and I called her by name…at least what I thought was her name at the time. The transformation was instantaneous. She backed off immediately and acted like a different person. It was…an unusual reaction, to say the least. I—I didn't understand until you came in a few minutes later."

Lara swallowed. She didn't want to ask the question, but the words came out anyway. "What did you call her?"

The nurse met Lara's eyes once more. "I called her Mrs. Harrison. And she never corrected me. She let me think she was his wife until you walked in the door."

CHAPTER ELEVEN

LARA PUZZLED over the nurse's words the rest of the morning. By lunch time she couldn't stand it any longer. She picked up the phone and called Theresa's office to make an appointment with her. All she got was a recording, a mechanical voice that said the attorney would be out until Friday. Lara started to dial Conley's number then she put the receiver back down, something telling her another approach might be better.

The next day, after she got to work, Lara headed straight for Ed's office and recounted the incident.

"What do you think it means?" He frowned, tapping a pen against the top of his desk.

"I'm not sure," Lara replied. "But I know one way to find out. I'm going to ask Theresa the minute she gets back."

He sat up straight. "Call that guy Fields and tell him. Then you leave it alone."

"I'm not sure I want to do that."

"I don't give a rat's ass if you're sure or not." He glared at her. "I'm sure enough for both of us. Call him. Then drop it."

Lara nodded and left his office but she didn't phone the cop. The following day she thought about the scenario some more, Fields's question echoing in her mind. *Thing is…I can see how you might hire someone to do your husband harm, but why would you stalk him, too?*

Jake brought Conley home at seven that night. He grabbed a sandwich and headed straight for the den where, hunched over a huge file, he ate and read, muttering as he flipped the pages over and back. Passing by the doorway once, then again, Lara studied him surreptitiously. The third time she went by the opening, he looked up at her with an inquisitive expression, his dark eyes sending a shiver down her back. She ignored it and spoke without preamble, her decision fast and impulsive.

"Do you think Theresa Marchante could be the woman stalking you?"

Conley leaned back in his chair. He wasn't surprised by her question and she realized belatedly that was the reason behind her abruptness. She'd been trying for a reaction.

"No," he said immediately. "I don't think it's Theresa. I wondered about her at first, then I decided it couldn't be her. Why do you ask?"

Explaining the incident at the hospital, Lara put her hands on either side of the doorway.

"She was upset, worried about me. Maybe the

nurse just managed to calm her down. And don't forget Theresa brought me to the hospital. I don't think she would have been able to run me down, ditch the car, then come back and rescue me."

"Are you sure? How long were you out?"

"I don't know," he admitted.

"They found the car not that far from the office, down by the railroad tracks. She might have had the time to take it there and come back." Lara tapped the edge of the door frame with one finger, her mind twirling. "Was Theresa more upset than necessary that day?"

Conley shrugged. "I don't know how upset she was. I was pretty out of it myself."

"Well, what makes you think it couldn't be her? You obviously decided that some time ago."

"It's not her style," he said. "If she was interested in me, she'd make the first move and see what would happen. I've seen her do that before—it's how she operates. She doesn't hesitate."

"But she works for you. You're not her boss, but you're probably the closest thing she has to it. You're definitely an authority figure to her," Lara persisted. "Are you sure she'd act the same way with you that she would with someone else?"

His eyes went dark, his voice pointed. "No, I'm not sure, Lara. I'm not sure about anything connected with women anymore."

CONLEY SHUT THE LIGHT off in the den and went into the hallway to go upstairs. Without thinking, he glanced down the corridor first. Ever since that night when he'd seen Lara after her shower, she had kept the door closed. But he always looked to see if the light was on. He wasn't sure why he looked. Even if she was up, he'd go upstairs, by himself. His tread heavy, he thought about her question as he climbed the stairs and headed for his bedroom.

Theresa Marchante, a stalker?

She was an attorney, a well-educated, confident woman. She could have any man she wanted.

Pining after a married man just didn't make sense.

"YOU'RE GOING TO Royal Mountain tomorrow night, aren't you?" Over the telephone line on Thursday morning, Sandy's voice held a hint of panic. She didn't wait for Lara's answer. "I don't have a thing to wear. I'm big as a house and Matthew got really upset when I threatened to buy something new."

With the phone propped against her ear, Lara half listened to Sandy's complaint. She couldn't concentrate on anything but Conley. Seated in a spare office at Harrison's, she'd told Ellen she was helping Jake with some figures for the security report but she was actually going through Conley's long-distance phone bill, searching for any clue. The police had already requested the statements and examined them, too. She was probably wasting her time but she had to do something.

"Wear that black outfit," she said with distraction. "You know, the knit thingie with the expandable waist."

"It's expanded all it can. Another inch and the poor thing's gonna explode. Just like me."

Sandy's voice ended with such a pitiful note, Lara stopped what she was doing and focused on her friend. "How about the blue dress, then?" she suggested. "The color matches your eyes and brings out the highlights in your hair. It's nice."

"I don't know," Sandy whined. "If I weren't so fat things would be different. *Everything* would be different...." Her voice drifted off.

They'd talked several times already this week and Sandy had complained about everything in her life, but especially about Matthew. He wasn't ambitious enough, he didn't try to do his best, his hair was thinning. Nothing about the poor guy satisfied her anymore.

But it never had.

If Sandy hadn't been such a great friend who'd been sympathetic to all of Lara's problems, Lara would have grown thoroughly tired of the complaints. Sandy had never been happy, and as Lara mused about it now she realized suddenly the Oakleys' marriage had never been as good as hers and

Conley's. Abruptly Lara caught herself, the importance of what she'd just thought hitting her hard.

Luckily, Sandy groused again, leaving Lara no more time to think about the revelation. "I've worn that dress a thousand times. Everyone has seen it. I've had it cleaned so many times it's getting shiny."

"That dress is beautiful and so are you. You looked wonderful in it at the restaurant the other night. And it goes great with your new car," she teased.

"Oh, the Lexus…" Sandy perked up, at last, Lara thought with relief. "It is gorgeous, isn't it?"

"It's spectacular. And Matthew's a sweetheart for buying it for you. You should be thanking him instead of giving him a rough time."

"He should have bought it last year," Sandy said sharply. "He got a raise then, but did I get anything? No…" She started to complain again, and Lara's attention drifted to the window. Downstairs, a small red car was parking by the curb. A white magnetic sign decorated the door on the passenger side.

Thompson Messenger Service.

As Lara watched, the door opened on the driver's side and a tiny blonde tumbled from the seat, a Christina Aguilera-look-alike. She had on a green parka and her arms were full of legal-size envelopes and a small box. She scurried to the front door of the building and disappeared from sight.

Sandy's complaining still filled the line, but Lara cut her off unceremoniously. "I gotta go, Sandy. I'll see you Friday." Belatedly softening her rudeness, she added, "And don't worry. You'll look radiant no matter what you wear. Pregnant women always glow!"

RUNNING DOWNSTAIRS, Lara caught the messenger as she ran up the steps in the opposite direction, a bundle of energy and purpose. No wonder she was so skinny, Lara thought. If she maintained this rate all day, it was a surprise she wasn't smaller.

"Are you Nanci Thompson?" Lara puffed.

The woman nodded but kept up her pace. "That's me," she said, taking the steps at a record pace. "What can I do for you?"

Lara introduced herself. "I talked to the police last week. They told me your car was the one used to run down my husband."

The woman grimaced. "Jeez-Louise...I'm *so* sorry. I feel real bad your husband got hit with it, even though, of course, I had nothing to do with that." She held the small box up she still carried. "I'm kinda embarrassed to even go up to his office, to tell ya the truth. But a delivery's a delivery. I gotta give him this."

"You bring him a lot of boxes?"

The woman nodded, a birdlike gesture reinforced by the blond tufts of her hair which stood straight up. "If he gets anything, he gets it from me—I cover all of Red Feather, but mainly downtown. I make the run down to Denver once a day, sometimes twice. People call and I go."

"The police know you do work for him?"

"Sure thing."

Lara held the door open and thought about what that meant. Fields had known Nanci Thompson came to the office. He'd simply wanted to see what Lara had to say about her. Lara followed the courier into the reception area where Ellen greeted Nanci then signed for the box. The delivery woman made a smart turn and practically ran back to the door, Lara right behind, peppering her with questions as they went downstairs where the other woman shoved legal envelopes under Theresa's door. Nanci Thompson's answers all seemed reasonable, nothing out of the ordinary.

"The place you went to make a pickup the morning the car was stolen..." Lara said as they headed for the lobby once more. "Was it a normal stop for you?"

"Never been there before," Nanci said, shaking her head. "Big waste of time, too. Nobody was around. Nobody. And I got up early just to go!"

On the street once more, she bid Lara a quick goodbye then grabbed another two packages from her car and ran to the office building next door. Two minutes later, she came outside and jumped back in her vehicle, racing off without a backward glance. In the cold, sparkling sunshine, Lara stood on the sidewalk and watched the little car disappear.

Fields *had* to have realized what was going on, Lara decided. Surely he could see that someone had phoned Nanci Thompson and set up a fake delivery simply to get her car. They'd needed a vehicle—an untraceable vehicle—to run down Conley. Fields must have held this information back so he could judge Lara's reaction. But what connection did the delivery woman have to everything that had been going on?

It wasn't until late that night, as she drifted off to sleep, that Lara got her answer. She sat up in bed and flipped on the light, the truth hitting her fast.

Nanci Thompson didn't carry a purse or even a fanny pack. She always left her car with her arms full of packages and envelopes. The keys remained in the ignition, the engine running.

Anyone who knew her or used her services would be aware of that fact. Anyone at Harrison's. Anyone in the building. Anyone...including Theresa Marchante.

ON FRIDAY MORNING, Lara and Conley argued about how to get him to Royal Mountain Lodge that night. He was on his cell phone, Jake driving him to a meeting in Grand Falls, the next town west of

Red Feather. Lara had gotten stuck in her office in Boulder at a meeting she couldn't cancel.

"Let Jake take me," Conley insisted. "You're going to be in Boulder all day. By the time you get back here, get dressed, drive downtown and pick me up, it'll be late. Jake and I can go to the lodge in his car. We might not even make it back to the office before it's time to be there anyway. You can meet us at Royal Mountain and take over for him at that point, just like you did at the Black Bear. We'll come back together. That worked out fine last time."

Except for the fact that someone had broken into her SUV and almost struck her down with a tire iron. Lara started to point out that fact but it wasn't truly relevant. And Conley was right as well. Letting Jake take him to the lodge made more sense.

Lara wasn't happy with the arrangement, though. Something about the whole evening was bothering her. It didn't feel right. She started to try to explain this to Conley then stopped herself. He wouldn't accept her vague feelings as a good reason to stay away, and frankly she didn't understand what they meant herself. Maybe everything she was learning was making her nervous. She still hadn't had an opportunity to talk to Theresa. Despite the message saying she was returning that day, the attorney was not answering her phone. Lara had driven by her house, too, but it'd been empty and dark.

"All right." Her fingers cramping on the phone she held it so tightly, Lara finally gave in. "Jake can drive you up there but I'll be right behind you guys. I'll leave Boulder early. Look for me around six."

Conley gave his usual monosyllabic reply and rang off, then Lara did the same, turning to look out her office window. It faced the north and she could see Royal Mountain on a clear day. This morning, though, storm clouds were gathering. They hung with a heaviness over the top of the mountain. But just seeing the summit was enough to remind her of the previous Saturday. The image of Conley skiing with those kids had stayed persistently in her mind since then. When she wasn't worrying about his safety, she thought about him and that afternoon. When she wasn't thinking about that, the memory of his kiss was there.

She returned to her meeting and forced herself to concentrate until lunch. Grabbing a sandwich with Ed and Larry, she stayed another hour, then announced she had to leave. The clouds that had been drifting above the mountains had made their way down to Boulder. More snow was imminent and Lara didn't want to get caught between here and Red Feather in the Explorer. Without any warning at all, the heater had gone out yesterday. She'd take Conley's Suburban to Royal Mountain tonight.

By the time she got home, she was cussing. Cold and uncomfortable in the small SUV, she felt as if she'd been tossed from Boulder to Red Feather. The wind had definitely picked up and an early dusk was slipping over the house, the windows reflecting the clouds coming off the nearby mountains. It was only five but it felt like midnight, the first of the snow hitting her as she scurried inside.

She checked in with Jake. He and Conley were already back from Grand Falls and were planning to leave the office shortly. She gave the bodyguard some last-minute warnings about the weather, then drew a hot bath. An hour later she was ready to leave. This time she wore her navy suit, her only concession to the evening a shimmering ivory blouse beneath the jacket and a string of pearls around her neck. In between the blouse and form-fitting jacket, she slipped on her shoulder harness and drew it tight. Five minutes later she was out the door.

And wishing she could go right back in.

The wind was howling, its bite so cold she could feel it straight through her good gray coat. She started to turn around and get her down-filled parka but she kept going. The parka would look ridiculous over her suit and she was running late as it was. Vanity won out. Making a dash to the garage, Lara jumped into the Suburban and backed out of the driveway.

LARA WENT STRAIGHT to Sixth and turned right at Red Feather's only light. The road to Royal Mountain led only to the resort yet the city managers usually kept it clear, their snowplows working overtime if necessary. It wasn't good for business if tourists disappeared off the side of the mountain while trying to reach the lodge.

Tonight, though, the plows couldn't keep up.

Taking the turn slowly, Lara gripped the steering wheel of the big SUV and peered through the windshield. She could barely see the tracks of the plows, the snow coming down so hard, the parallel impressions had already begun to disappear. The wind was so strong it was forcing the slim metal poles that marked the edge of the road to graze the tops of the snowbanks.

A chill passed through Lara that had nothing to do with the temperature outside. She'd lived in the mountains most of her life but weather like this made her wary. She knew how destructive it could be. She took her eyes off the road for a second and sent a fearful glance toward the clock. Jake and Conley should be at the lodge by now. She thought about calling them to check but taking her hands off the wheel was not an option.

And neither was pulling over. The shoulder had completely vanished in the near whiteout conditions. She wouldn't know how far to go and anyone coming up on her wouldn't be able to stop.

Making a conscious effort to relax, Lara eased the

muscles in her shoulders and rotated her neck slightly. Although it was dangerous, the road was only ten miles in length. She'd get to the lodge sooner or later. And others would be making the trip as well. There was no reason to get worked up about driving. She tried to calm down but it was a pointless exercise.

She rounded a blind corner, the road dropping to a single lane as the sharp turn twisted into the side of the peak. She'd heard once that ten men had lost their lives blasting the original route through the pass in the 1850s. For a second, a flash of headlights split the darkness behind her and then was gone, swallowed by the snowy night. The sight reassured her—at least she wasn't completely alone.

When she took the next curve, the big SUV seemed to hesitate then it lurched forward, sliding slightly on an unexpected patch of ice. She fought the wheel and in a second she had the Suburban under control but not her pulse. It continued to pound and there was nothing she could do about it.

Without taking her eyes from the road, she hit a button to her left and rolled down the window. She couldn't see as well as she wanted, but she might be able to listen for traffic ahead of her. The vehicle filled instantly with frigid air and something else.

The whine of a snowmobile.

Lara could hardly believe what she was hearing— who on earth would be out in this?—but there was no mistaking the sound. The throaty hum of the vehicle's engine was too distinctive to be taken for anything else. As she strained to identify the snowmobile's location, the sound died. For a moment she wondered if she had imagined it, then her high beams reflected off something at the side of the road within the trees. Within seconds she'd passed the spot.

Whoever was out there must know what they were doing, although Lara couldn't imagine what it must be. She rolled up the window and continued on, feeling as though she were wrapped in a blanket of darkness.

A second later, a shot ripped into the SUV with a roar of noise and light, the windshield shattering instantly. Jerking backward, Lara shrieked and raised her hands in an automatic gesture of protection. She realized immediately what she'd done and her training kicked in…but it came a second too late, her foot pressing down on the brake before she could stop herself.

The SUV began to spin. She grabbed the wheel and turned into the skid, but the big truck couldn't respond. Ice, black and slick, covered the road. There wasn't a vehicle—or driver—in the world that could have competed with its treacherous smoothness.

She spun once. Then spun again.

In the middle of the second turn, the back tires

flew off the edge of the road with a stomach-dropping lurch. For a moment, the SUV tottered, the front end on the pavement, the rear in the air. Lara stomped on the gas pedal but with no purchase for the rear tires, her action made no difference.

The SUV seemed to shiver, a ripple of movement going through the metal that almost felt human. Through the broken windshield, snow swirled into the cabin, a deadly cold chill coming with every flake. She knew she should do something, but what? How could one stop the inevitable?

A second later, the vehicle sighed softly. Then it slipped over the edge and slid backward down the mountain.

CHAPTER TWELVE

THE FOREST was quiet and cold.

Holding her coat tight against her body, Theresa peered over the edge of the cliff, fright and anticipation coursing through her. In the darkness there was little to see, but she knew she was in the right place. A jagged path of broken undergrowth and snapped-off tree trunks gave testimony to that. The evidence was rapidly being covered by snow, and within minutes it wouldn't even be visible. Just like the side of the road, two feet away from where she stood. A second before, it had been scraped clean, all the way down to the pavement, but a frosting of white had already begun to dust it. The edge of the blacktop looked half-eaten, as if something had taken a bite from its rim then left the rest to rot. A monster, Theresa might had thought if she didn't know better.

But she had seen the Suburban go over.

Her pulse was pounding. She wasn't prepared for this, the opportunity she'd dreamed about coming much quicker than she'd ever imagined. She lifted

her hands to her mouth and called out. "Hello out
there. Anybody hear me? Hellooo?"

Her words were swallowed instantly by the
blowing spirals of snow and wind. She rubbed her
palms together, then tried again. "Hellooo? Hel-
looo-oh?"

Nothing but silence.

She didn't hesitate a second longer, plunging into
the thicket of pines and undergrowth. The low-
hanging branches snatched at her hair, the snow
piled on their limbs falling into the tops of her boots.
It soon soaked her feet. She hardly noticed. All she
could think about was getting to Conley.

She loved him. She had to rescue him. She had
to make him hers.

Slipping and sliding down the incline, Theresa
crashed through the trees, following the track the
Suburban had taken. It wasn't a difficult task. The
broken branches and overturned rocks were as good
as signposts, even with the snow covering them rapidly. In less than a minute, she saw the outline of
the SUV.

Sucking in her breath, Theresa uttered a quick
prayer. It looked as if the vehicle had landed on its
side, on a ledge, not too far down the side of the
slope. Five feet of overhang and little more was the
only thing that had stopped the SUV from tumbling
even farther. She couldn't see much more than the
outline of the truck, but one thing was obvious. The

sides and roof were badly damaged, the paint scratched and scarred by the tumble. It would have been a helluva ride down. She swallowed a rise of nausea and headed toward the twisted wreck, stumbling in snow that now reached her knees.

She approached the vehicle from the rear, then gingerly picked her way to the passenger's side. Scared her weight might cause the truck to move, Theresa hesitated before touching it. With one hand brushing the frame for balance, she edged toward the shattered window, her throat going tight with fear.

CONLEY TURNED TO Jake for what seemed like the tenth time in the past five minutes. "Try her again," he said sharply. "She never turns that damn phone off. And she's never late. There must be something wrong." He glanced down at his watch again. It was long past the time Lara had promised she would be at Royal Mountain.

Jake pulled out his cell phone and pressed the Redial button, but Conley couldn't listen to what happened next. His attention was taken by a well-dressed man with silver hair and a gold Rolex. One of his investors from New York. Conley shook the man's hand and pretended to listen to his monologue about his flight to Colorado, but the whole time Con was really struggling to hear Jake above the noise in the elegant dining room.

Conley nodded at the man standing before him, then he gripped his elbow and leaned forward. "I gotta hear more about this, Bob," he said over the din. "You grab me after dinner and we'll share a bottle and talk again, okay?"

The investor smiled his agreement and mercifully moved off, Conley pivoting to stare at Jake before the other man had taken two steps. Jake shook his head, a regretful look on his face.

"Nothing," he said. "Just like before. All I get is her recording. The phone's been turned off, Conley. Do you want me to leave another message?"

Conley shook his head, and muttering a curse, he moved toward the nearest window and took a deep swallow of his drink. The Jack Daniel's burned as it went down his throat but the storm outside registered more. The weather had worsened in the past hour. Where was she? What was she doing? He had told himself he was acting paranoid, but Conley couldn't lose the feeling that something bad had happened. He could sense that she was in trouble. Despite the fact that she'd denied their growing closeness at the office the other day, he and Lara shared a tie that was only growing stronger. He didn't know why, but his plan to draw her closer was working, almost in spite of his own ineptness.

As Conley watched, the wind moved suddenly, sending a small avalanche of snow down to the cedar deck that outlined the lodge. In the summer months, the wooden expanse was covered with chairs and tables but all that decorated the platform right now was ice and snow. It looked slick and cold and dangerous.

Conley stared a moment longer, then he threw back his drink and slammed the tumbler to a nearby table. "To hell with it," he said to no one but himself. "I've had enough."

With a startled Jake struggling to catch up, Conley rushed from the room, issuing instructions at the same rate of speed. "Call Ed," he told Jake. "Tell him Lara's missing. Then get the police and tell them the same thing. I want Fields up here now. I'm going to look for Lara."

"You can't do that, Con! God, Ed'll kill me and then he'll fire me—"

"I'll take care of Ed," Conley answered grimly. "You do what I tell you to do or you'll be wishing Ed was your only problem...."

Jake argued some more but Con ignored him. They were at the front of the lodge now and he grabbed his coat and ran out the door, leaving the younger man behind.

He didn't know where he was going or even what he was doing but Conley did know one thing.

He had to find Lara.

SHE NEVER LOST consciousness.

Lara had felt every bump, seen every spin, heard every crash. The SUV had slid backward, knocking down trees and hitting rocks. She'd braced herself, the inflated air bag popping and hissing uselessly as it exploded then deflated. When the Suburban finally stopped, it did so with a bone-jarring suddenness. The sounds of the wreck seemed to go on, though, the vehicle moaning and creaking for another few minutes before that, too, finally stopped.

It was quiet now. So quiet she could hear her heartbeat.

She lay still within the mangled remains of the SUV and took inventory, moving her fingers and legs, each one responding, albeit painfully. A trickle of blood inched down from one eyebrow, but incredibly Lara didn't seem to be hurt beyond scratches and bruises that tomorrow would no doubt be spectacular. Her brain was foggy, though, and she felt slightly nauseous from the smell of the air bag. In her confusion, she thought she heard something. The scrape of a fingernail against metal? The slide of a glove against a fender? Was she hallucinating?

A moment later she had her answer.

A dark form appeared at the shattered window across from Lara. She sucked in her breath, the cool air painful as it went into her lungs. She couldn't see the person's face, but Lara didn't have to. She would have recognized Theresa Marchante's expensive perfume anywhere.

"Theresa?" Lara said hoarsely. "Is that...is that you?"

The other woman didn't speak for a moment and Lara had enough time to envision a thousand bloody deaths. Theresa pulling out a gun. Theresa stabbing her. Theresa pushing the Suburban until it tumbled farther down the mountain... When her panic cleared and logic returned, Lara realized how silly she was being. The attorney didn't have to do any of those things if she wanted to get rid of Lara. All she had to do was walk back to the top of the road and pretend she knew nothing. The SUV—and Lara's frozen body if she couldn't crawl out— wouldn't be found until spring. No one would ever know about the shot-out windshield. No one would ever know it wasn't an accident.

If she wanted to get rid of Lara...

"Lara?" Theresa finally spoke, her voice incredulous. "Lara? My God, is that you? I saw the Suburban and I thought—"

Relief flooded Lara at Theresa's obvious surprise. The woman wasn't faking her reaction; she was shocked to see Lara, totally unprepared. Unless she'd been hiding her skills as a world-famous actress, Theresa couldn't have caused this accident.

"It's me," Lara croaked.

"Oh, God, I assumed it was—" Theresa started to say something then stopped for the second time.

After a pause, she seemed to gather herself. "Are you hurt? Can you move?"

"I—I'm all right." Lara began to pull herself up then she stopped. "I don't think I can get out, though. Not without some help."

"I saw your lights in front of me and recognized the Suburban then all at once you were gone. What on earth happened?"

"I hit a patch of ice." It wasn't a lie, Lara reasoned. She *had* hit the ice—after the windshield had been shot out.

"Oh, God…I'll call someone right now. I have my phone in my pocket."

Lara started to answer when another cry broke the silence of the night.

Her heart jumped into her throat, a sweep of relief coming with it. It was Conley. And he was calling for her.

Lara hit the horn to show Conley where they were, but the only sound that emerged was that of her fist beating the cracked casing. The horn was dead. She called out, her first attempt feeble, her next one louder. "Down here, Conley! I'm down here." She looked at Theresa. "Call him," she said. "Tell him where we are."

Theresa took a second too long and Lara's earlier suspicions bloomed into panic.

"Theresa? Are you down there? Hellooo?" Conley's cry echoed eerily in the snow filled night, the noise strangely muffled but sounding nearby.

"Theresa…" Lara's voice held alarm. "Answer him for God's sake. Let him know we're here!" Not waiting for a reply, Lara tried again herself. It was probably useless—she didn't think he could hear her—but she had to try. "Conley! We're down here!"

As if she'd been asleep and suddenly woken, Theresa added her own cries to Lara's. A moment later, she heard something crashing through the underbrush and then Conley's curse, a flash of light accompanying the movement and the noise.

"God Almighty! What the hell…"

Theresa spoke before Lara could. "I found her! I—I was coming up to the Lodge for the meeting and I saw the Suburban go over the side! It was terrible. I followed the track down here and I was just trying to call the police."

Conley's face appeared where Theresa's had been a moment before, the sweep of his flashlight blinding Lara with its illumination. An emotion too deep to name swamped her at the sight of him, and she cried out and held her hand toward him. He reached down and grasped her fingers tightly, his touch making her feel a thousand times better. "Are you okay?"

"I'm fine," she said. "Shaken up and bruised but okay other than that."

The flashlight was powerful, light filling the cabin and beyond to reveal his puzzled face and the mangled condition of the SUV. "What the hell happened?"

She shot a look over his shoulder into the darkness. She couldn't see Theresa but she knew she was still there. "I hit some ice," she said.

"Ice! For God's sake, Lara, you know how to drive in stuff like that! What the—"

She jerked his hand with a hard, quick movement, and puzzled, he broke off. She shook her head and he caught on.

"Jake called the police. Fields is on his way."

"How did you know I was here?"

"I started getting worried when you were late. I decided to go look for you then when I came down the mountain I saw Theresa's car. I stopped because of it." He eased closer to the window. "Let's save the questions for later. We need to get you out of there."

Lara nodded. Her seat belt was stuck but with Conley's help they got it undone and two minutes later he was pulling her out of the wreckage and into his arms.

She didn't struggle. The warmth of his body was more than welcome, the strength in his arms a refuge she craved. She clung to him and told herself it was comfort that anyone would want after such an ordeal...but she knew better.

She was falling in love with Conley.

Again.

This was not what she wanted. But Lara had the sudden feeling this might be one of those things she couldn't control. Conley's expression seemed to confirm that. Shrugging off his gray overcoat and draping it around her, he clutched the lapels close to her, looking as if he wanted to hold her forever. A thousand words traveled between them, all unspoken. Lara didn't know how to respond, but mindful of Theresa's presence, she pulled away from Conley, a stuttered thanks falling from her lips.

"I think the police are here." Theresa nodded toward the upper slope. "I see lights."

Conley turned to Lara. "Can you walk?"

She nodded and the three of them started up the uneven slope, Conley supporting Lara with an arm around her waist. She didn't actually need the help, but she wasn't about to tell him that right now. It seemed so right to have him close. And she didn't give a damn about feeling that way, either. Not with the sounds of the tumbling SUV still ringing in her ears. Not with the fright of seeing Theresa's face...

The snow had finally stopped falling but it was still difficult to slog through the drifts. By the time they reached the top, Lara was out of breath and hurting, a distinct pain originating from the vicinity of her ribs.

Fields met them at the top, a black hooded parka

obscuring his features, the flashing red lights of his car painting them all. He flipped the hood back and took them in with a sweeping glance. "You found her...."

Conley tilted his head toward the wreck. "She slid off. The Suburban's down there."

"I'll call an ambulance."

Lara spoke up. "No, no... That's not necessary. I'm fine—"

"I'm sure you are, but indulge me." The cop looked at her with his usual intensity and Lara got the message; her opinion in this matter was not important to him. He would do it by the book. He indicated his vehicle with a tilt of his head. "We'll sit in my Jeep until they get here. You can tell me what happened."

Conley nodded but Theresa held back. "Do you need me? I'd like to go on unless you want me to stay..."

"We'll be fine here, Ms. Marchante," Fields said. He nodded toward a cop in a uniform, someone Lara didn't recognize. "Why don't you give your statement to Officer Lewis then you can be on your way? I'll call you later if we need to talk to you."

Through the haze of what had happened, Lara registered surprise that Fields would release the attorney. On the other hand, why wouldn't he? As far as she knew, Lara was the only one suspicious of Theresa at this point.

Two seconds after that they were inside Fields's vehicle, Lara and Conley together in the back, the cop in the front. He'd left the truck running, the heat pouring out of all the vents. A thermos appeared from underneath his seat, and he poured a cup of something black and hot and handed it to her. The coffee was steaming and strong and she drank it down. When she finished she looked up.

The cop lifted one eyebrow and waited.

"Someone shot out my windshield," Lara said without preamble. "I braked too hard and went into a spin. There was ice on the road and the Suburban went over."

"Shot out the window— Dammit to hell, Lara! You didn't tell me that!" Conley turned and stared at her, his voice cold and upset in contrast to the warmth and comfort of the car. "Why didn't you say something earlier? Who in the hell would do something like that? What—"

Fields took out a notebook and pen, his manner calm as he interrupted Conley's tirade. "Start from when you left your house."

Lara did as the cop instructed. Ten minutes later she was done and the ambulance was there, a huge tow truck waiting behind it.

Fields clicked his pen shut and stuck it in his coat pocket. Rolling down his window, he called to one of the uniformed officers, his instructions brusque as he told the man to get some people onto the upper slope to search for a snowmobile. When he finished, he turned back to Lara.

"So who wants *you* dead?"

Lara caught the emphasis and understood the meaning. *Her*...as opposed to Conley. She shook her head. "I was driving Conley's vehicle—"

"And that's the *only* thing we know for sure." Fields stared at her. "We don't know who shot out the windshield and we don't know who they were after. But you were driving this time..." He shrugged. "It's something to consider."

Lara thought about the possibility a bit more seriously. "I don't know who was 'supposed' to be in the SUV." She sent her gaze to Conley's, her thinking taking a different tack. "But Theresa Marchante arrived awfully fast—just as she did when you were hurt."

"She was on her way to the meeting at the lodge," Conley said.

Fields turned to Lara. "She saw the vehicle go over?"

"That's what she told me," Lara said. "But the shot came from the front. She was behind me."

"Or so she said."

Lara nodded. "I saw lights behind me but I guess that doesn't necessarily mean it was her."

"Would she have had the time to take the snowmobile ahead of you, shoot, then get her car back down here and 'find' you?" Conley looked at Lara.

"How much time lapsed from when you went over to when she got there?"

Lara shook her head. "I don't know. I lost track...ten, fifteen minutes? Maybe more. I can't say for sure." She clutched the thermos cup. "But aren't we jumping the gun here? Why would she want to do anything to *me?* Why would she want to hurt me?"

"If she's stalking your husband, she'd want you out of the way, Mrs. Harrison." Fields's voice was flat, totally without emotion. "You're in her place. She would want to get rid of you. She has more of a motive to kill you than him...."

"But follow through with the logic," Lara replied. "If that's the case, then why would she try to run over Conley?"

Fields looked at Conley then sent his gaze back to Lara's. "That's a very good question, and I'd like to know the answer to that one myself."

CHAPTER THIRTEEN

ED ARRIVED at the scene just as Lara was climbing into the ambulance. In the darkness, Lara couldn't tell for sure but her father's face seemed to pale as he rushed to her side.

"Are you all right?" Not waiting for an answer, he forged ahead. "What in the hell happened here, Lara? I thought you had a wreck but then—"

"I'm fine, Ed," she interrupted. "Just some cuts and bruises."

"Well, what did you—"

"It's complicated...Conley can tell you after I leave. Right now I have to go to the hospital and let them check me out."

"I'm coming with you." Standing beside her father, Conley looked at Lara with a determined expression. There would be no argument, it said. Turning to Ed, he spoke quickly but just as firmly. "I'll call you after we get things settled and give you the details then."

Ed argued with them both for another few minutes—trying to get them to at least go to the hospital in Boulder—then finally he realized he was beaten. Nodding unhappily he watched as Conley and Lara entered the waiting ambulance. The snow had stopped but the white van eased down the mountain slowly. Con reached over and took Lara's hands between his own, warming them as he rubbed them softly. She was grateful but at the same time, frightened. His touch made her feel as if she were in the Suburban all over again—only this time her emotions were the ones tumbling down the mountain. This slide felt as inexorable as that one had. There seemed to be nothing she could do to stop her betrayal of herself.

Within fifteen minutes they were at the hospital's emergency room, an eerie reenactment of Conley's accident.

Dr. Sorelli eyed Lara with curiosity.

"I had a wreck," was all she said.

Keeping up a steady chatter that curiously relaxed her, the doctor made short work of examining Lara.

"You're very lucky," he said when he finished. Washing his hands at the sink, he shook them off then turned to her. "Go home and take it easy for a day or two. You'll be sore. If you feel anything besides that, call me."

They phoned Ed on the way home, then twenty minutes later, Conley led Lara inside the house, a solicitous hand wrapped around her elbow. She quickly sat down at the kitchen table—as much to get away from his touch as to rest.

She looked up at Conley. "What are we going to do about Theresa?"

His eyes were steady as they met hers. "*We* aren't going to do a damn thing. The police will take care of it." He took a step toward her. "Do you understand me, Lara? I don't want you confronting Theresa. If she's the one behind this—"

"Then she has to be stopped."

"But not by you." He stared at her for a few more seconds, then he shook his head, almost as if in disbelief. "Do you really think she's behind what happened tonight?"

"I don't know," Lara said truthfully. "At first I was terrified when I saw her stick her head in the window. I just assumed she'd done it—how else could she have found me?" She pursed her lips and frowned. "But later I wasn't so sure..."

"Why not?"

"She was shocked to see me and she wasn't faking the reaction—she couldn't have been."

"Have you linked her to the stolen car? For sure?"

"She uses the same service. I saw Nanci Thompson put envelopes under her door." Lara stayed silent a bit then she spoke again. "It's hard for me to believe she would be doing any of this...but in a way, I can understand it, too."

Conley looked at her with curiosity. "Why?"

To Lara the answer was obvious. Her husband

was a rich and handsome man. Everything about
him spoke of power and grace. Any woman would
take a second, maybe a third look, at Conley. He
had to be very attractive to Theresa. His assessment
of the attorney's willingness to go after anyone she
wanted made no difference—unless it served to increase Lara's suspicions. Sometimes when you
wanted something *too* much, your usual tactics
failed you. You had to find another way.

"Let's just say I can see it from a woman's perspective."

Conley seemed to accept her reply. And quietness
filled the kitchen, a weariness coming with it that
suddenly swamped Lara.

After a while he looked down at her, his eyes
holding a concern she wasn't sure she wanted to see.

"Are you okay?" he asked. "Really okay?"

"I will be." She paused for a moment to gather
her thoughts but she kept getting distracted. He'd
dressed carefully for the meeting at the lodge,
choosing a black suit and charcoal shirt with a tie
that matched. He looked like the compelling, successful man that he was.

But his gaze didn't match his appearance. His
eyes were too probing, too intense. Ironically Lara
was reminded of the man he'd been when they'd
first married—the one who could arouse her with a
single touch, with the briefest of caresses. Remem-

bering the kisses they'd shared recently, she responded immediately.

And this distracted her most of all.

He kneeled before her, his eyes searching hers. Then he spoke. "I was worried about you, Lara. When you didn't come to the lodge, I knew something had happened." He paused. *"I knew."*

As he spoke, a lock of his dark hair fell across his forehead. It made him look younger and more vulnerable, a trait she'd seldom seen in Conley. She resisted an urge to smooth the curl back, and the effort that was required was more than she would have expected.

She tried to brush off his implication. "I'm usually on time. You just—"

"It was more than that." He interrupted her, his intensity reaching out and ensnaring her. "You know what I'm talking about."

Lara sat perfectly still and said nothing.

"It's happening all over again, Lara. We're coming together. Just like before, like it should have been all along. No matter what, you can't deny that. And whether you like it or not, it's the truth." He reached out and put his arms on either side of her legs, trapping her in the chair. Through the fabric of her skirt, torn and ripped from the accident, she felt the heat of his touch warming her thighs.

She stared at a spot over his head. He was confirming what she'd already suspected. They were falling in love with each other again. But she couldn't accept it. She was too *scared* to accept it.

Because these feelings wouldn't last. They'd come together in crisis then drift apart again. The result would be fatal, the cumulative effect of a second failure too much for her to handle. She couldn't subject herself to that agony. Not again. She had to protect herself.

"I don't know what you're talking about." The lie fell easily from her lips.

"Yes, you do," he said. "You feel it, just like I do."

Her throat grew tight, her throat and something else, the emotions that made her want him—and hate him at the very same time. "It's late, Con. I'm tired and sore. I need to go to bed."

His fingers tightened against her hips, and she thought for a moment he might argue, then pick her up and carry her off to his bed. The image lingered in her brain longer than it should, imprinting itself like a tattoo. She waited, her breath coming in short, swift bursts, then he nodded once and moved away. She rose from the kitchen chair and made her way down the hall to her bedroom, feeling his heated gaze on her back until she closed the door behind her. Soundly.

She went to sleep thinking of his touch and of his eyes. But she dreamed about tumbling vehicles and screaming metal, dark figures and strong perfume.

She woke in the middle of the night, her moans filling the room as she jerked her eyes open. A shadow moved at the door and her pulse jumped before she realized it was Conley.

He spoke from the doorway. "Are you all right? I heard you call out—"

In the darkness, she answered him. "It's okay. I—I'm fine."

He waited for a second—for a lifetime—then he slowly turned and left the room, gently closing the door behind him.

Lara expelled the breath she'd been holding and lay in the dark.

She wished he would return but the door stayed shut.

CONLEY AND ED SAT at the kitchen table in the early-morning light, steaming mugs of black coffee before them.

"She had nightmares last night," Conley said, tilting his head down the hall to Lara's room. "I checked on her twice. She was moaning and crying out."

"I can't imagine what it felt like going down that mountain." Ed massaged his temples then looked at Conley with a face full of distress. "Not to mention having the damn windshield blown out a second before."

Conley nodded. "I phoned the station the minute

I got up but Fields didn't have anything yet. They're still looking for the snowmobile. He called Theresa on the pretext of wanting to ask her more questions. Said she was quite cordial and that she'd do anything she could to help."

Ed's expression didn't change. "You think she's the one trying to kill you...and Lara?"

"I don't know, Ed. Lara thinks it's possible, but the idea doesn't make any sense to me. Then why should it? I don't understand why anyone would want to kill either one of us."

"This has turned into more than just stalking."

Conley looked up at the man's pronouncement. His words held a fear Con would never have expected from Ed Bentley. But he was getting older, and his daughter had never been in danger like this before. She'd been a bodyguard, sure, but Ed picked his cases carefully. Cheating wives, con artist boyfriends, partners who embezzled funds...he chose cases with little or no potential for violence, especially after the Atwater murder last year.

Ed spoke bluntly. "I'm scared, Con. Lara is all I've got. I never really appreciated her as much as I should have, but seeing Bess again... Well, let's just say she's opened my eyes. I'm beginning to realize what a jerk I've been all these years. I missed out on a lot because I cared for nobody but myself. Lara's safety..." He let his words drop and reached for his mug, avoiding Con's eyes.

All Con could do was nod. When he'd seen the tangled remains of the Suburban last night, he'd felt as if all the blood had left his body. He'd faced plenty of risky situations while he'd been in the Marines, but nothing like this.

The older man held his mug but he didn't drink. Abruptly, the coffee sloshing toward to the rim, he put the cup back on the table and jerked his gaze to Conley. "I think we need to reassess the situation."

"I agree," Conley said. "In fact, I've been thinking about that myself. I'd like her off the case, but as you said, that's not going to happen. The next best thing would be to hire some guards—for her. She won't like that, though."

Ed looked out the window to Conley's left, his gaze distant and unfocused. He appeared to not have heard the suggestion, but Conley knew better. Ed was thinking about what he wanted to say and how to say it. Gruff and presumptuous with most people, he tread a finer line with Conley. He always had, and Con suspected it was because he knew he had to.

"Guards aren't the answer." He spoke as if he'd been thinking about the problem for a long time. "After you and Lara left last night, I talked with Fields. He thinks the best thing would be for the two of you to disappear for a while. He needs some room to work on this—some room and some time. As long as you're here, you're going to be in danger and in his way.'' He drew a deep breath. "You and Lara should get out of Red Feather, Conley. At least for a little while. Until this settles down."

Conley didn't have to think about the idea for long. He knew the solution was perfect. Not only would it offer protection for Lara, but getting her away would help Conley achieve his goal, too. He couldn't believe he hadn't thought of the approach himself, but if he suggested it, Lara would never go for it. Coming from her father—*and* Fields—this idea held much more weight.

Conley started to offer his agreement, but Ed held up his hand. "I know, I know…you don't want to leave the business, but you might have to—"

Conley interrupted the older man, holding up his own hand to stop his argument. "Wait a minute! That's not what I was going to say. I don't mind leaving. In fact, I think that's an excellent idea. We *should* get out of here—it makes a lot of sense."

Ed was too worried to be surprised by Conley's immediate acquiescence. "How about the fishing camp?" he offered. "It's quiet up there this time of year. No one in their right mind would bother you. I've got an office already set up—you could work from there."

The camp…Conley hadn't thought of the cabin in years. Two hours north of Red Feather, it could hardly be called a fishing camp. Ed had had the place built in a useless attempt to entertain one of his wives, Conley couldn't remember which. It was a jewel of a home, one bedroom with a huge fireplace, slate floors, views of the mountain from every direction. Perched on the edge of Hannah Lake, the road going up was often impassable this time of year.

"That's a great idea," Conley said. "I like it. It's a perfect solution, in fact."

"The hell it is."

Both men turned abruptly. Lara stood in the doorway, wrapped in a chenille robe. The right side of her face bore a dark purple bruise and the expression underneath it was just as angry.

"We aren't going to that cabin." She shook her head, her blond hair tumbling around her shoulders. "No way. Forget about it. It's not even an option so you can drop that idea right now."

LARA STARED defiantly at her husband and her father. Their voices had carried to her bedroom, and she'd gotten up and made her way gingerly down the hall…when she heard this outlandish proposal.

"I'm not going up there. It'll look like we're running away from this problem instead of facing it."

As soon as the words left her mouth, Lara wondered which problem she was actually referring to; the problem of someone coming after them or the state of their marriage. She and Conley had used the cabin a lot when they'd first married. It held memories she didn't want to revisit, especially right now. She felt unguarded and exposed, her nerves raw from being around Conley these past few weeks.

"Why do you give a damn what anybody thinks?" Ed asked abruptly. "It isn't your job to take care of this, anyway. I've already told you that once. You need to leave this one to the police."

Ignoring Conley, she sent her father a sharp look, her words even more pointed than her eyes. "Why? They haven't done squat as far as I can see. Whoever tried to run down Conley is still out there. Last night proved that if nothing else." She jabbed a finger toward her chest. "I'm the one who told them to look into Theresa and that was before last night. What have they done?"

"This isn't TV, Lara. You have no proof Theresa took that car. Give the poor guys some time to do their job—"

She glared at Ed, aware the whole time of Conley's steady gaze. "They've had their chance. Going to the cabin isn't going to make them work any faster."

"I disagree and so does Fields. This was *his* suggestion." Conley rose from the table and crossed the room to the coffeepot. Refilling his cup, he faced her again and spoke. "He told your dad he needs some time—and some room. If we leave, we won't be in his way and he and Margulies can concentrate on what's already taken place instead of having to deal with a new incident every time they turn around.''

He said nothing more and for a moment all Lara could think about was the fishing camp. That damn cabin had been built for one thing and one thing only. The luxury was complete, the isolation total. There wasn't even a television set. Long days of incredible stillness, even longer nights with nothing but the fireplace crackling. The prospect terrified her. How could she stay away from Conley under those conditions? She was wavering now and even the memory of the pain she'd gone through when they'd tried to reconcile and failed couldn't stop her from thinking of the possibilities the cabin presented.

She lifted her gaze to Ed and in his eyes she saw something that turned her inside out. All he wanted was to keep her safe. For once, he was thinking of someone besides himself and the fact that she was foremost in his mind rattled her even more.

"It's a good idea, Lara." His voice was quiet and sincere. "You should consider it before you dismiss it."

"I'll consider it," she said finally. "But that's it." Then she turned and left the room.

MONDAY MORNING had barely begun as Theresa watched the policeman walk down the street from her office and get into his unmarked patrol car.

She'd struggled to keep her emotions under control as he'd bombarded her with questions. Oh, he'd been slick, but she knew what he wanted. He thought she'd caused Lara Harrison's accident and he'd done his level best to trap Theresa into saying so.

But he'd failed.

And rightly so.

Turning away from the window, Theresa went to her desk. She'd answered all his questions with a quiet kind of dignity, her simmering indignation well hidden. What kind of fool did he think she was? Was he so stupid as to assume she'd do something like that? Something so blatant? She'd had nothing to do with that wreck but show up—at the wrong time, it seemed now.

She sat down and opened her desk drawer, pulling out the pen she'd stolen from Conley's office. Rubbing it against her cheek, she felt the coldness of the enamel, the smooth black surface no balm to her feelings. Nothing could make her feel better as she remembered Conley's eyes when he'd seen Lara inside the Suburban. With an angry cry, Theresa threw the pen against the wall. It hit the Sheetrock with a thud then tumbled to the carpet in two pieces.

When she'd rounded that fender and looked inside to see Lara Harrison, Theresa had thought for a moment she might faint, feeling as if it'd been her who'd crashed down that mountain instead of Lara, falling and falling until there was nowhere else to go.

She'd have to be flexible, something she'd managed throughout her life. For a second, she'd been tempted to handle the problem once and for all. Strangely enough, Lara had almost acted as if she'd sensed the same thing. Then Conley had shown up and Theresa had had to think fast. The plan had been a good one, she thought, telling him how she'd found Lara. How it was she—Theresa—who was there to save his precious wife. But he hadn't listened. He'd helped that little witch up the mountain and into the police car without a glance in Theresa's direction. He hadn't even said thank you.

She sat for a moment more, then she stood and went to pick up the pieces of the Mont Blanc. Theresa felt tears gather in the back of her throat. It wasn't Conley's fault. He was only doing what he thought he should. He *had* to ignore Theresa. He couldn't risk the chance that Lara might see the passion between the two of them. One look and she would know. She'd know how much Conley loved Theresa and how she lived for him. Lara would know they were meant for each other...and who could say how that witch would react?

Closing her fist over the broken pen, Theresa let the tears slide down her face unchecked.

CHAPTER FOURTEEN

SANDY WATCHED AS Lara put the last of her sweaters into her duffel bag and zipped it shut. Lara shot a sideways glance at her friend, a frustrating guilt coming over her as she lied. "We won't be gone that long. A week, maybe two at the most." She frowned at the very pregnant woman and shook a finger. "You'd better not have that baby while I'm away."

"I'm never going to have this baby." Sandy put a hand on her stomach and grimaced. "He's going to stay inside me for the rest of my life. I'll be 110 and still pregnant."

Lara sat down on the bed and patted Sandy's hand. "It just seems that way right now. You'll forget all the problems the minute you hold your baby."

Sandy didn't look convinced. "I hope so...but I still wish you didn't have to leave. Matthew and I just aren't getting along at all...."

"I'm sorry." Lara squeezed her friend's fingers. "I wish I didn't have to go, too. But I don't have a choice. Conley...really wants this trip and I—I had to say yes, Sandy. I didn't have a way out.''

This, at least, was the truth. Over the past week, Ed and Conley had worn her down with their insistence that Con and Lara get out of town. When Fields had called her and added his weight, Lara had felt overwhelmed. He was a good cop and smart, too. Jake was another factor in her decision. With Lara temporarily out of commission, the poor man had been on duty 24/7 and he was exhausted.

If Lara's hunch was correct, she could handle the situation better than Jake anyway. He didn't know the perp. She did. The more Lara thought about it, the more convinced she became Theresa was the one behind the flowers, the notes, the stalking. Everything Lara had heard—from the nurse at the hospital to Nanci Thompson's story to what had happened on the road to the lodge—made her believe this. Lara didn't yet understand why, but she knew she was right. Leaving was the last thing she wanted to do, though.

Sandy broke through Lara's thoughts, the other woman's voice filled with an unmistakable hunger. ''I just can't believe it. The two of you back together again! A romantic getaway like this. I'm so happy for you, Lara. So glad you were able to work everything out.''

Lara couldn't stand to see Sandy's look of longing, especially since the cover story was such an incredible lie. She stood up and escaped into the bathroom to gather her things. Sandy shuffled right behind her, continuing to babble about Lara and Conley's "reconciliation" and how wonderful it was.

Lara let her ramble. Finally Sandy ran out of steam, falling into an uncharacteristic silence.

Stuffing her bag with makeup and toiletries, Lara closed it in the silent room, the rasp of the zipper loud. "I'll call you after we get where we're going," she said when she finished. "We can talk about everything some more...but try not to worry. It's not good for the baby."

Sandy's face seemed to fall another inch, and Lara moved to where her friend leaned against the doorjamb. Her words sounded lame, even to her ears. "Things are going to be okay. You and Matthew will work it all out."

"But he's abandoning me, too. He's going to Denver at the end of the week. Something about a new supplier. I can't believe he's leaving with me so close to my due date."

"Maybe he doesn't have a choice," Lara countered.

"That's what he said when I asked him, but I still don't like the idea." Sandy's expression shifted and Lara read the fear that was suddenly revealed. This wasn't just worry.

"Denver's not that far away." Lara tried to reassure her. "He can be back in an hour."

"He can be...but *will* he?"

"Of course he would be! What are you saying?"

Sandy started to cry. "I—I don't know, Lara. I—I just don't feel right...and Matt says I'm acting crazy but he's the one who's acting weird. I—I'm afraid...."

A trickle of tears rolled down her cheeks, her gush of words ending as she swiped at her face.

"Your hormones are working overtime," Lara said, gently embracing her friend's shoulders. "And you're nervous, which is perfectly understandable. But Matthew will be there for you, I'm sure of that."

"I wish I was." Tears still swam in Sandy's eyes. "But I'm not sure of anything anymore, especially of Matt. He's cold and angry...and he won't have anything to do with me. We had a big fight the other night and he told me that I didn't appreciate him. It—it really bothered me." She lifted her guilty eyes. "Because I know he's right...."

Lara didn't know what to say. Anxious and nervous, Sandy was making too big a deal of the disagreement, just as she always did. "Matthew's worried about the baby, Sandy. He's as frightened as you are—as all new parents are."

"Do you think so? I—I never thought of that."

"Consider it from his perspective. He's never

been a father. Never had that kind of responsibility. Conley would be scared to death, I'm sure. And you know how men are when they get scared...they get angry then blame us!''

She sniffed. ''Maybe you're right.''

Lara reached over and brushed a kiss on her friend's forehead. ''He'll be okay and so will you. It's just a rough spot you have to get through. The baby will come, then the two of you will work things out, and it'll be just like it was before. You'll be crazy about each other and madly in love again.''

''Just like you and Conley, right?''

Lara smiled tightly and looked into her friend's hopeful eyes, the lie so big she almost choked. ''That's right, honey. Just like me and Conley...crazy about each other and madly in love again.''

SANDY LEFT a little after that, her eyes red, her nose dripping. With a sigh of relief, Lara closed the door behind her friend, the phone ringing as she threw the lock. She ran down the hall and picked up the receiver to hear Bess's voice.

''I hear you're leaving town.''

Feeling even worse than before, Lara deceived Bess just as she had Sandy, the cover story awkward and unbelievable—at least to Lara. If Ed had told the older woman anything different, she didn't say so. But when she didn't comment on the renewed

relationship, Lara immediately suspected Ed had
told Bess the truth.

"Be careful," the pediatrician said. "And call me
when you get back. I may need some help with a
little social event."

Lara started, her fingers gripping the phone, a
thousand ideas racing through her head, but one
standing out. Like a child, she crossed the fingers of
her other hand behind her back and made a wish.
"A social event? That wouldn't be a wedding,
would it?"

Bess suddenly sounded tentative. "How would
you feel about it, if it were?"

Lara answered quickly. "Nothing would make me
happier, Bess. I'd love to see you and Ed together
again. I always said you were the best thing that ever
happened to him and if I needed any more proof,
I've certainly had that lately."

"What do you mean?"

Lara explained her father's attitude after she went
off the road.

"He loves you, you silly goose," Bess exclaimed
when Lara finished. "Surely you didn't ever doubt
that."

"Of course not," Lara answered automatically.
"Then again...with Ed, who can be sure?"

They both laughed, but the message got across.
"Let's just say, *I* always knew the truth, even if you
didn't." Her voice turned serious. "You're the most

precious thing your father has, Lara. He's always felt that way, but some men don't understand love until they're about to lose it.''

They talked a bit more, then Lara glanced at her watch. It was time to go to the office and pick up Conley. They had a two-hour trip ahead of them. Two hours together in the car. Alone. After that, who knew how many hours. Alone. In the cabin. In the woods. She shook off the images and told Bess goodbye. Fifteen minutes later she pulled up at Conley's office and lightly tapped the horn.

Whether she wanted it or not, she was about to go on a second honeymoon.

CONLEY HEARD the sound of Lara's horn and glanced out the window. With both of their vehicles still in the shop, they'd rented a Range Rover for the trip.

Conley turned back to Matthew. They'd had a million details to go over that morning and Matthew had been distracted and angry. His attitude didn't inspire Conley's confidence. ''You've got my cell phone number and I'll have my laptop. If you need me, call or send an e-mail and I'll get back to you.''

Matthew nodded, a jerk of his head telling Conley he'd repeated himself once too often. ''I can handle it, Con, okay? Just leave, for God's sake!''

''Are you *sure* you're okay with this?''

Matthews stared at Conley, then unexpectedly

jumped to his feet. His desk chair rolled to the wall behind him and bounced against the paneling. "C'mon, Conley!" he said. "We've worked together for years and I know this business inside out, upside down. Sometimes you act like I'm some kind of idiot or something, like you don't even trust me!"

Conley held up his hand and stopped the flow of words. "Matthew...Matthew, I trust you," he protested. "It's just that with everything that's going on..." He stopped, the words drifting off. They'd decided to tell no one the truth about Lara's accident.

"It's the baby," Conley ad-libbed a second later. "I know you've got a lot on your mind and Sandy's going to need you. I'm worried that this is coming at a bad time for you, that's all."

"I'll handle it." Matthew's voice was tight but his expression eased slightly. "Don't worry. I'll take care of everything."

"I'm sure you can, Matt." Conley reached out and squeezed his friend's shoulder. "I didn't mean to imply you couldn't."

Matthew's gaze fell to his desk. "I—I'm sorry, Con. I'm under a lot of stress right now...I didn't mean to jump down your throat." The apology came out grudgingly, as if the engineer was forcing it. There was no emotion behind the words, nothing sincere in them at all.

"It's okay," Conley said. "I understand."

Matthew raised his face and their eyes connected across the office. Conley was startled at how empty and blank the other man's gaze was.

"I don't think you do," Matthew replied. "But that's all right. I'll see that the job gets done."

CONLEY BROODED as they traveled up the winding mountain roads and through the tiny burgs between Red Feather and the cabin. Lara sent him occasional looks but they didn't communicate, which was just as well. Sitting next to him in the Rover was bad enough. The strain and stress of being this close to him was about to overwhelm her. Her eyes kept going to his hands on the wheel, and all she could think about was the feel of them on her breasts that night at his office. And the warmth of his mouth. And the smell of his skin.

She stared out the window. The Colorado mountains glistened with snow, their cold, cruel beauty almost too much to take in. Beside the road, a river was encrusted by ice, its flow stopped until spring. She closed her eyes against the blueness of the sky just as Conley breached the silence.

"Have you noticed anything strange about Sandy lately?"

His question was unexpected, but Lara answered readily. It seemed innocent enough, an easy query that had nothing to do with the two of them. "She's unhappy but that's not really strange."

"How so?"

"She and Matthew aren't getting along...again. She thinks he might not even be there when she has the baby and she's scared."

Conley seemed thoughtful. "That might explain things."

"Things?"

She watched his profile as the line of his jaw tightened then flexed. This was what he'd been thinking about, she realized, during the trip. In the past few years she'd become an expert at reading the signs. It was all he gave her of what went on in his mind.

"Matthew jumped all over me this morning, which is pretty unusual for him. He must be nervous about the baby."

"That's what I told Sandy," Lara replied. "It's understandable, I guess." She turned and looked out the window again, but the beauty of the day didn't register. "Having a baby's a big event. It'd change everything."

Conley retreated into his usual silence and another hour went by. Shadows began to fall across the road, the afternoon sun blocked by the canyons they were driving through. The temperature dropped inside the vehicle as well and Lara reached over and turned up the heat. Conley said nothing more but Lara's nervousness only grew. She fidgeted against the leather, trapped by her own imagination. All she could think

about was the man sitting beside her. The last part
of the trip was torture, relief only arriving as Hannah
Lake Village came into view.

"Do you want to stop and get groceries?"

Lara tilted her head toward the rear of the vehicle
at Conley's question. "I have everything in the
back," she said. "I went shopping before I left Red
Feather. We should be completely stocked."

Passing the only store in the tiny town, Conley
nodded and kept going. Lara immediately realized
her mistake. If they'd stopped, she would have had
another half hour to compose herself. As they left
the grocery store behind, she realized how silly she
was being. If she hadn't prepared herself during the
two-hour drive or the week previous, another half
hour wasn't going to make any difference.

Five miles outside town, Conley turned into a
drive that was hidden between two towering pine
trees. Flanking the blacktop and extending to a point
that disappeared in the darkness, a tall fence—sixteen feet at least—added to the sense of isolation.
Conley eased the truck up to a small pole on the
driver's side then rolled down his window. Using
the lighted keypad, he punched in the code Ed had
given them, the gate creaking open in response a
moment later. The house was set back, perched on
a ridge that cut through the fifty-acre tract. The
Rover plowed up the snow-covered driveway, its
wide tires cutting an easy swath through the drifts.

Five hundred feet back, maybe less, from the main road, they stopped outside the beautiful little cabin, and Conley shut off the engine.

In the silence, Lara thought she could hear her anxiety going up a notch.

IT TOOK SIX TRIPS between them to bring in all the groceries Lara had packed. By the time they'd finished, dark had surrounded the cabin, the eerie stillness unbroken by the slightest sound. Conley stood on the porch and surveyed the pristine landscape. There wasn't a tree or rock or patch of ground that wasn't covered in white. Overhead, the sky was dotted with stars he couldn't see back home. There was absolutely no artificial light to be seen, except what came from the window behind him. They weren't that far from town but it felt as if they were the last people on earth.

He turned and looked toward the window. Lara had pulled the shade but he could see her shadow moving behind it, from countertop to refrigerator and back again. She was putting everything away. He wasn't quite sure why but she'd brought enough food to feed them for a month.

He put a hand against the stone column beside him and sighed. He wanted to keep Lara safe, but he also knew that coming to the cabin was his last chance to bring her closer to him. He'd done all he could do back home and she hadn't moved an inch.

Sure they'd kissed, but Lara had made herself clear; he'd hurt her too much in the past and she was determined not to let him do that again. He looked down at the wooden slats beneath his feet and brushed at a nail head with his boot. He couldn't blame her for the way she felt.

But, God, he wanted to change her mind...

LARA LOOKED UP as Conley opened the heavy front door and stepped inside. The strain between the two of them on the ride up had been bad, but once they'd arrived, it'd gotten even worse. He'd bumped into her once carrying the groceries inside and she'd reacted as if he'd stuck a hot poker against her skin. He'd looked at her curiously, then he'd reached out to steady her with a murmured, "Sorry..." She was acting like a fool, but every nerve felt raw and exposed. Everything was over between them—why didn't her body recognize that as clearly as her mind?

Moving toward the enormous fireplace at one end of the room, Conley stopped beside the set of brass tools on the hearth. "I think I'll start a fire."

"It—it's kinda late for that, isn't it?"

Her words held a nervousness that she couldn't hide. The fireplace was two-way. From the bedroom or the living room, the flames could be seen. It was all too cozy for her. "Ed's caretaker came out earlier and turned on the electricity—the heat's been on for hours."

"I still think it'd be nice," he said. "We've got plenty of time."

She didn't look at him as he spoke. He turned back to the fireplace and moved the brass shield, before stacking logs on top of the grate and stuffing kindling underneath. In a matter of moments, she could hear the flames and the room began to warm.

Apparently satisfied with his fire, Conley stepped into the kitchen where Lara was rearranging the groceries. She didn't want to move from the confines of the kitchen—the only other choices were the living room with its comfortable leather couches or the bedroom...with its single king-size bed, a situation they had not yet addressed. There was nothing to do but face the problem head-on. She turned with every intention of doing so and found Conley right behind her.

"I think we should—"

"I want to start—"

She stopped. "Go ahead."

"No, no...ladies first."

She spoke again, feeling so awkward and stilted she wanted to scream. "The bedroom...uh...the bed..."

He stated the obvious. "There's only one."

She nodded stiffly. "I'll take the couch. I'm

shorter and it'll be more comfortable for me. I can keep an eye on things that way, as well."

His gaze went to her holster. "Do you really think that's necessary up here? No one but Ed knows where we've gone."

"I feel better with it close."

They stared at each other.

"Is that…okay with you?" she asked finally. "If I take the couch?"

"No," he said. "It's not okay. None of this is okay with me."

"I—I'm sorry. Would you rather take the couch? I can do something different—" She fell silent as he reached out and cupped her cheek with one hand. The skin beneath his fingers turned warm, but he didn't answer. He leaned over and kissed her instead.

Which was, she decided later, the only answer she needed.

THE KISS LASTED forever, but it ended way too soon.

Lara blinked as Conley raised his head and looked down at her.

She made a noise in the back of her throat, a groan that had no meaning, and he leaned over once more. His lips were warm and soft. They seduced her, luring her even closer.

She couldn't help herself. Her hands went around his waist and then up his back. He wore a cashmere sweater, a gift from her too many years ago. The turtleneck was incredibly soft beneath her fingers, the muscles of his back ribbed and full of strength.

Their kiss deepened and Lara couldn't have stopped the inevitable had her life depended upon it. She wanted Conley as she'd never wanted him before. Their past no longer mattered and neither did their future.

CHAPTER FIFTEEN

THEY STUMBLED OUT of the kitchen and toward the living room, clothing scattering as their desire took control of their better judgment. If she'd been thinking logically, Lara would have known she was making a mistake. Sex with Conley would put her in a place she shouldn't be, a vulnerable, exposed place.

But her body craved his touch, her lips his mouth, her skin his hands.

He obliged her willingly, leading her to the couch before the fireplace and lowering her to the soft leather expanse. At first, the smooth upholstery was icy against her bare skin, then it warmed as Conley joined her. Running his palms up and down her legs and then her hips, he brought shivers with his caresses. Months had passed since they'd been together in the Caribbean, but that time hadn't been like this.

Lara didn't stop to ponder why.

She reached out for Conley and mimicked his movements, her fingers running over his skin, skipping down his arms and chest and legs. She'd desperately missed this contact and had longed for the intimacy, but the need to protect herself from him had been too strong. That need seemed distant at this moment, a distress she'd invented. In the morning light, she wouldn't understand but right now, it didn't matter. Only their touch was important.

Conley kissed her once more, his mouth working a slow path from her temple to her lips then lower to her throat. His tongue was a torch. It melted everything it touched but she didn't want him to stop. By the time he'd reached her stomach, heat seemed to be rising from his body, enveloping her. She lost herself in his kisses and his touch and the feel of his body against hers. But instead of being satisfied, she only wanted more. When he finally raised his head, all she could do was plead with her eyes.

He read her mind and granted her wish, entering her a moment later. She cried out and pulled him closer, their bodies falling into a rhythm they'd perfected through the years. She urged him on, her faint cries filling the fire-lit room as their world shrunk to the couch and their hands and the cadence of their love. They came together and forgot everything else.

SOMETIME IN the middle of the night, Lara felt Conley pick her up and carry her into the bedroom. Burying her head against his chest, she clung to him in sleep, unable—and unwilling—to acknowledge what had happened between them. She wanted to stay a while longer in the nebulous place she found herself, a place where she didn't have to figure out what to do next.

He understood, somehow sensing her need, but the knowledge didn't stop him from making love to her again. Silently he touched her, his heated caresses and persuasive mouth taking her back into the world of longing. This time they went slower, and Lara felt something give inside her, something she'd been holding for too long. She thought it might be her need to keep herself safe, but then the moment was gone. Conley dismissed it with his touch, taking over her very body and mind.

When she woke up the next morning, his side of the bed was empty. She reached a hand across the sheets and felt where Conley had been. The linens were still warm.

Rolling over on her back, Lara closed her eyes and tried to forestall the morning a little while longer. She had no idea what to say to her husband and no idea how to handle what had happened between them. She tried to tell herself that making love with Conley hadn't changed a thing between them.

But who was she kidding? Last night had changed *everything*.

Moaning in confusion, she pulled the down comforter up to her chin and screwed her eyes shut. A second later she heard Conley enter the room. He came to her side of the bed, then she heard a clink and smelled coffee. Opening one eye, she saw a thick stoneware mug on the nightstand beside her. From its depths, steam curled in a ribbon above the cup. She opened her other eye and found Conley standing at the edge of the bed.

She looked at him and he stared back. For what seemed like a long time, they stayed that way, then Conley broke the silence.

He nodded toward the mug. "I added one sugar and a spoonful of cream."

It was a simple thing, straightforward and uncomplicated but the fact that he remembered how she took her coffee suddenly meant more to Lara than it should. She recalled the day several weeks ago when she'd seen him on the slope with the kids, helping them ski. She remembered how he'd looked when he'd peered inside the wrecked Suburban. How she'd felt when he'd kissed her in his office.

She didn't want to acknowledge what these disparate thoughts meant. She reached for the coffee and put everything else aside. "Thank you," she said. "It's perfect."

Holding his own cup, he sat down on the edge of the mattress. He wore jeans and a pullover sweater, casual clothes that made her want him all over again. With her free hand, Lara clutched the comforter against her skin, suddenly aware of her lack of clothing. If Conley noticed her discomfort he kept it to himself.

They sipped their coffee in silence, each lost in thoughts they couldn't voice.

Lara could see the bottom of her mug when Conley spoke. "We'll need firewood soon." He tilted his head toward the window. "The bin's almost empty. I guess Ed didn't have any delivered last year."

"I don't think he even came up last year." She put her mug on the table.

Conley acknowledged her reply with a thoughtful look. "And neither did we."

"We didn't have time."

"*I* didn't have time," he corrected her. "If you'd suggested it, I wouldn't have come. Too much work," he added, almost as an afterthought. "Always too much work."

Lara didn't answer. What he had said was the truth.

"How did I get that way?"

His question threw her off guard. She glanced up from the sheets where she'd threaded her fingers. "Things happen," she said with a shrug.

"Not on their own," he replied, surprising her even more. "We didn't just 'drift' apart. We didn't just 'stop' talking." He reached across the tangled linens and took her fingers in his. "We didn't just 'quit' making love, Lara. We let other things—*I*—let other things become more important than the two of us." He lifted her chin with his other hand. "I'm not worth a damn at saying things like this, but the truth is the truth. I love you with all my heart, but I've been a rotten husband. I don't know why you put up with me as long as you have.''

The declaration *and* the apology shocked Lara but before she could say anything in reply, Conley leaned over and kissed her. His mouth was warm and tasted of coffee. Raising her hands with every intention of pushing him away, Lara found herself doing just the opposite. She pulled him closer.

He slipped his hands beneath the covers to find her bare skin. Easing his fingers over her waist then up to her ribs, he brushed her breasts with a gentle touch.

Lara forget everything else. Conley climbed back into the wide bed and the world slipped away one more time.

THE REST OF the week passed as if it were happening to someone else.

They slept late, made love, got out of bed only when they felt like it. Time passed in a fog of desire and passion. Conley seemed to not only understand her reaction to everything but to fuel it as well. Content with what was happening between them, he appeared unconcerned with the arrangement. Lara was astonished at his reaction but even more so at her own. How could she do this? She'd asked him for a divorce, for God's sake, and here they were acting as if they'd just married. It didn't make sense but she couldn't bring herself to end it.

She floated through the days and lived for the nights.

THE WEATHER TURNED unseasonably warm. Sitting in the breakfast nook Saturday morning a week later, Conley and Lara were enjoying the sunlight pouring through the windows when the shrill ring of Conley's cell phone interrupted their breakfast. It actually took a moment for him to realize what the noise was. Even after he recognized the sound, he ignored it.

When he stayed in his chair, Lara looked over at him with a curious expression. "Don't you want to get that?"

He shrugged. "Not particularly." He turned the page of a week-old newspaper. "It can't be that important."

Conley dismissing work? It didn't seem possible. The phone stopped ringing, then started all over again. Lara started to get up. "It could be Ed," she explained. "I've got to see—"

"I'll do it. You stay put." Following the recurring rings into the bedroom, Conley picked up the unit from the shelf in the closet where he'd put it and flipped it open. "Hello?"

Nothing but static. He thought he heard a voice but the sound cut in and out, then stopped completely. He wasn't surprised. They had to be miles from any towers and surrounded by the mountains as they were, they couldn't expect good reception. He hit the Caller ID button but it proved to be little help. Out of Area was all it said.

Slipping the phone in his pocket, Conley walked back to the breakfast table. "The line dropped. But it wasn't Ed." He explained the Caller ID message, then added, "Ed would call here anyway. He's the only one who has the number."

A few minutes later, the cell phone rang once more. This time, Matthew's voice broke through the scratchy connection. "…need to ask you…stuck in Denver…e-mail me…" Conley tried to answer him, but the line failed once more.

"I've got to see what the hell's wrong," he said with a look of apology. "He's in Denver talking to that supplier."

"Okay, but e-mail him. Don't call."

Conley nodded and went to boot his laptop computer, the disk drive chattering as it came to life. Whatever had been bothering Matthew when Conley had left, had apparently been resolved. They'd e-mailed back and forth several times, but nothing more had been necessary. Typing a note to the engineer, Conley hit the Send button then sat back and waited for a reply. Matthew had to have been waiting at the other end, wherever he was. His answer was long and involved, half of which made no sense at all to Conley, the other half being a convoluted explanation about a supplier who was threatening total disruption of the business unless Conley intervened. He answered the rambling message as best he could then sent the second message with an impatient click of the mouse. Not even waiting for a reply, he shut down the system.

He didn't want to think about business.

Through the open bedroom door, he watched Lara sitting in a bright sunbeam, which brought golden highlights to her hair. She'd taken to wearing his ancient bathrobe—the white one with the hood on it he'd had since college—and she was wrapped inside its considerable folds, the hood hanging off the back, the sleeves rolled up to her elbows. If he closed his eyes and concentrated he could almost smell her perfume.

Their interlude here had been wonderful, a replay of what their life had once been, a glimpse into what it could be again. Conley was too smart to think he'd changed her mind about the divorce, but too much in love to give up completely. What could he do to prove to Lara what her love meant to him?

He stood up slowly and went to Lara. He didn't have an answer, but he knew he would before they left.

He had to. His life depended on it.

THEY WERE STILL sitting an hour later, the brilliant sunshine too warm and inviting to abandon. Lara had moved from the table to the nearby couch. She was drifting into a dream, half awake, half asleep, when Conley's voice brought her back.

"I think I'll go get us some firewood." He tilted his head toward the wood bin at the side of the garage. "I used the last of the oak this morning."

She opened her eyes. He was leaning against the French door to the deck, his arms crossed, his dark hair gleaming. Behind him the sky was so blue it seemed like a set, an unreal backdrop to their unreal life.

She sat up, suddenly aware of how lulled by their isolation she'd become. "I'll go with you. I don't want you going into town without me."

"Who said anything about town?" He jerked his right thumb toward the woods behind the house. "There's tons of downed trees out there. I'll clean up for Ed and get some exercise, too. There's a saw in the garage. I already looked."

Lara started to protest. "I'm not sure that's a good idea, Conley."

"I can handle a saw—"

"That's not what I meant." She looked toward the forest and the land beyond. "There's fifty acres out there. The fence is good, but—"

He crossed the room to the sofa and took her hands. His grip felt warm and reassuring, his persuasive eyes sending a shiver over her body as their gazes met. "You're doing your job too well, Lara. It's safe—no one but Ed even knows we're here. I'll be fine." He grinned. "I'd be more likely to run into a bear than my stalker, believe me."

His reassurances made sense, but even beyond that, Lara suddenly felt the need for some time alone. Over the course of the past two weeks, she hadn't been able to think clearly. Eventually, they had to leave the cabin and face reality. She had to decide what she was going to do and she couldn't think straight with Conley nearby. She looked up once more, into his eyes, and saw that his light expression had left.

He felt the same way. He needed some space. He had some thinking to do as well.

She nodded slowly and ten minutes later Conley was stalking off into the trees, a heavy chain saw in one hand, a set of ear protectors in the other. She watched his tall form merge with the shadows of the thick pines, then half an hour later, the raucous cry of the chain saw interrupted the peace and quiet. Lying on the couch under a plaid woolen throw, Lara closed her eyes and let the mechanical drone fade into the background of her consciousness.

As much as she hated to admit it, Lara knew the barriers she'd put up had been broken, allowing the truth to come in. Sandy had been right all along. Lara had never stopped loving Conley. But did she still want to be married to him?

It was a sad question to ask, but she knew Harrison's meant everything to Conley. If they *were* to reconcile, it'd only be a matter of time until history replayed itself. Conley would start staying late at the office, he'd concentrate on the business, he'd put her in last place, just as he had before. She'd try to fill her empty time with something else, then they'd drift farther and farther apart. Did she really want to go through that painful process a third time? She'd never considered herself a stupid person, but if she allowed that kind of torture to take place again, she'd have to question her intelligence.

Half an hour later, she woke up abruptly, feeling anxious and distracted. The sun had gone behind some thick clouds to turn the day dark and gloomy. The saw was still going, but the noise was fainter. Conley had moved deeper into the woods from the sound of it. Pulling the hood of his robe over her head, Lara stepped outside to see if she could spot him.

Just before she reached the railing, she thought she heard something. Still sore from the accident, she turned awkwardly, her balance off, her movements strained.

A second later, the bullet slammed into her. Lara screamed and grabbed her shoulder as if she could halt the pain, but the motion was useless.

She tumbled over the railing of the deck and fell to the earth beneath.

CHAPTER SIXTEEN

THERESA RECOILED without thinking, her gasp piercing the cold gray silence. She was having a dream—a nightmare—but instead of waking up, she was mired in the horror. From her hiding place, a thicket of juniper covered in snow, she watched in disbelief. A hundred feet in front of her, on the wraparound porch of Ed Bentley's cabin, a figure in black crouched by the edge of the garage. He still had the rifle on his shoulder, a weapon she hadn't realized Matthew Oakley was carrying until he'd fired it a second before. Her eyes flew from him to the deck, then her heart stopped, a wash of rage surging into her throat.

Conley clutched his shoulder and staggered to the side of the deck. Too horrified to call out and too terrified to run, she realized her mistake a moment later. The person who'd been shot was too small to be Conley. It had to be Lara! God in Heaven, Matthew had just shot Lara!

Her mouth hanging open, Theresa held her breath as Lara stumbled again. She hit the railing hard. The cedar held for a second, the silvery wood shaking, then it gave way. Lara plummeted over the edge with an echoing cry and vanished.

The drop was at least ten feet, maybe more.

Matthew Oakley never even looked back.

Slipping around the corner of the house, the engineer continued on his mission, too determined to notice anything else. He'd been that way since they'd left Red Feather. Theresa had followed him every mile of the way, not sure exactly where they were going but sensing things were coming to a head. As she'd tailed Matthew, she had thought of all the things she would say to Conley when this was over, how she would tell him that she loved him, how they were meant to be together. How she'd come to save him from Matthew....

Forcing herself to wait until she was sure he wasn't returning, Theresa sprinted to the corner of the house, her breath coming out in puffs of cold air. She flattened herself against the rough stonework for just a second, then continuing to follow Matthew's path.

Matthew was the one behind everything that had happened. A few weeks after Fields had questioned her, Theresa had managed to connect the dots the policeman hadn't even seen. It had been an easy task for her because she knew more than the cop ever could.

Just to be sure, she'd used her key and entered Matthew's office the day before yesterday. She'd

found all the proof she'd needed, notes and plans
from Lara's computer, even diagrams the engineer
had made. Setting up a fake delivery, he'd stolen the
messenger's car and tried to run Conley down, but
when that had failed, he'd decided on a different
tactic. Scouting out the weekend homes close to the
resort, he'd found one with a snowmobile and another one stocked with a deer rifle. With the mistaken belief that Conley was driving the Suburban,
he'd shot out the window of the vehicle, then returned to the resort with no one the wiser. The incidents had gone unreported because the homes had
been unoccupied, a fact he'd counted upon. The police had searched the area, but the terrain was rough
and the homes scattered. They'd found nothing.

When he'd left the office that morning, Theresa
had had no idea where he was going, but something
had told her to follow him. By the time Matthew
had reached Hannah Lake Village, she'd figured it
out. Ed's cabin. Conley had used it once for a party
he'd given everyone at Harrison's and Theresa had
been invited as well.

From an isolated spot down the road, she'd
watched as Oakley pressed the buttons on the electronic gate. When it became obvious the code had
been changed, he'd removed the back of the box and
had quickly disarmed the unit, snipping some wires
then slipping inside the gate. After he'd disappeared

up the driveway, she'd sprinted to the opening and had made it inside with inches to spare. She'd glanced quickly at the security box. Harrison's logo had caught her eye. Matthew himself had probably designed the chip that regulated the gate....

Theresa even knew why Matthew was doing all this. She prepared all of Conley's legal papers; Harrison's was part of an irrevocable trust. If Conley died first, Lara could dispose of the business as she liked. If they were both gone, Matthew would be named trustee of Harrison's. He would be able to run the company as he saw fit. All he had to do was funnel the proceeds—subtracting his salary, of course—back into the trust, which named Ed as the beneficiary.

Oh, yes. Theresa had understood immediately. But that didn't mean she could stop him.

Her pulse ringing in her ears, Theresa made it to the end of the house then slowed her steps. A single piece of oak, slight but sharp, rested on the concrete where it'd fallen beside a bin built into the wall of the garage. She wrapped her fingers around the kindling and picked it up, hefting its weight in her hand. It was perfect. She took a deep breath and swallowed her fear, turning the corner with a scream in her throat.

Poised beside the crumpled body off the deck, Matthew didn't see Theresa until it was too late. She swooped down the patio stairs to his right and charged him, the wood held high above her. Using all her strength she aimed for his head, the air ringing with her scream.

But Matthew ducked.

Pivoting smoothly, he raised his rifle and shot her.

CONLEY HAD MADE his way deeper into the woods than he'd intended. Ed had taken advantage of his fifty acres by building the cabin on the highest point, which meant Conley was now at the lowest. But he'd found the perfect tree, a dead oak sprawled across a rocky expanse. The wood was covered in snow, yet aged just right. Cranking up the saw, he'd worked up a sweat and his reward was a pile of logs they'd never be able to completely use.

Leaving the chain saw for his second trip, Conley stacked his load onto the canvas tarp he'd brought. He started back toward the house, hauling the heavy burden over his shoulder. The path was a rough one and it went straight up. His legs would be screaming by the time he reached the house, but he didn't care. He welcomed anything that would take his mind off Lara and their situation. He'd left for that very reason, knowing the physical activity would at least give him another focus for his energy. He hadn't come up with a solution but he'd cleared his mind for a little while.

He was past the halfway point when he heard the gunshot.

Conley froze in midstride and listened, every hair on the back of his neck standing straight up. He'd been wearing ear protectors while using the saw earlier and he wasn't sure he'd actually heard a shot. Was he imagining the sound or was it real?

There were hunters around this time of year and backpackers, too. He told himself everything was okay, but a heartbeat later, he knew he was lying. Nothing was okay when gunfire was involved.

Dropping the load of logs, Conley broke into a run, his heart jumping into his throat and staying there. A quarter mile, maybe more, of dense trees and underbrush lay between him and the house. The distance suddenly seemed more like a hundred miles.

Closing his mind to how long it'd take, he pushed through the tangle, his legs pumping, his lungs screaming. His still-healing scars stretched and pulled, but Conley ignored their complaint. Blindly, he plunged through the brush, a searing sting on his right temple telling him at least one cedar limb had hit its mark. Blood trickled into his eyes, a cold wetness that meant nothing.

All he could think of was Lara.

Five minutes later, another realization came to him. He prayed he was imagining this, too, but a quick glance into the sky told him otherwise.

Something was on fire.

LARA WOKE TO the stink of acrid smoke, a sense of panic washing over her before she even knew why.

She gasped and rolled over, grabbing her shoulder and crying out as she hit a nearby wall. She was in total darkness. She remembered getting shot but nothing else. Scrabbling to get her bearings, she tried to sit up.

More pain was her only reward—she'd cracked her head on something. She raised her hands and found the low ceiling. It hovered a foot, maybe less, above her. She fell back, a wave of claustrophobia cutting off her air as she moved her legs and arms frantically, confirming what she feared.

She was in a box, the size and shape of a coffin.

And somewhere nearby a fire had started.

Terror replaced everything else, and she began to kick wildly, her screams a muffled sound that didn't escape her casket. A small line of light and cold air broke the darkness and she pushed even harder, her legs going numb with the effort, her whole body shrieking as she managed to open the crack a bit more. The silhouette of a hasp and hinge emerged from out of the inky blackness. Coughing, eyes tearing, she pushed once again, and saw the rest of her dilemma. A brass lock gleamed, the closed shackle catching a glint of firelight and sending it back to her, the snap and pop of a growing blaze coming with it.

She understood instantly, but the realization

brought no comfort. She was locked in the wood bin. And someone had set the house on fire.

CONLEY BROKE OUT of the woods at a dead sprint, his lungs at their bursting point. He felt as if he were in a nightmarish, never-ending marathon, but in truth, his chaotic dash through the forest had lasted ten minutes, maybe fifteen at the most. Not bad for a guy in his forties...but not good enough.

The orange glow of a fire lit the cabin at one end, the flames making their way toward the rest of the house, fanned by a growing breeze. He hadn't thought it possible, but from somewhere deep within, Conley summoned a reserve of energy and charged forward, unsure of what he'd find, but knowing it wouldn't be good.

Sudden gunfire confirmed his suspicions.

He veered to the left and then to the right, crouching to evade the shots. The gun sounded again and Conley felt something slip past his cheek. A millimeter closer and he would have been bleeding. The knowledge didn't slow his progress. If anything, he ran faster. Reaching the far edge of the holly that ringed the house, Conley lunged into the bushes, grateful for the cover they offered.

Grabbing the first weapon he could find—a rock the size of a brick—he scrambled to his feet and plowed through the greenery. The shots had come from near the garage so he headed in that direction.

Halfway there, Conley whirled around, the sound of a footstep behind him.

Matthew Oakley faced him, and he held a .22 bolt action rifle. The barrel was pointed at Conley's chest.

LARA TOLD HERSELF not to panic, but she was too late. Fear swept through her as fast as the flames that were growing outside. She screamed and beat her feet against the wooden lid of the bin. A second later she heard an echoing cry.

"Hellooo?" she shrieked. "Is someone out there? Can you hear me?" She kicked the top again and the muffled sound of another voice reached her through her frenzy.

Lara instantly stopped kicking, but couldn't hear anything above her pounding heart. She screamed again, and this time someone answered her. There was no mistaking the voice. It belonged to Theresa Marchante.

Lara's hopes died with the sound.

Theresa called again. "Lara? Lara? Is that you?"

Her voice was weak and she seemed confused. If she'd just shot Lara, why wouldn't she know it?

The lid of the bin lifted a quarter of an inch.

"Are you...are you in there?"

Lara didn't know what to do but if there was the slightest chance of survival, she had to take it. Clearly the attorney had lost her mind but there had to be something left, some shred of logic to which Lara could appeal.

She swallowed, her throat burning, her shoulder feeling as if the flames were already touching her. "Theresa, it's me...it's Lara," she said urgently. She put her fingers at the crack along the lid. "Please...please let me out. We'll talk, okay? I—I don't know why you shot me, but whatever it is, we can work it out. We—we'll get you help, I promise."

"Shoot you? I—I didn't shoot you," Theresa said. "It was Matthew! I—I saw him. I tried to stop him but he shot me, too!"

Lara recoiled in shocked disbelief. Matthew Oakley had shot her? The idea was so ludicrous Lara instantly rejected it. Theresa was clearly past the point of appeal. "Okay, okay," she said. "I—I believe you.... Can you get me out of there? The fire's getting closer—"

"I—I don't know. He thought...thought I was dead. He set the fire so no one would know.... I've got to find Conley...."

The attorney's voice seemed weaker and farther away. Lara squinted through the gap but all she could see was smoke. She coughed. "Please, Theresa—just unlock the bin and let me out! Break it if you can!" Crying out in frustration, she kicked against the lid but it didn't move. Her eyes burning, her lungs filling up, she called out again.

But Theresa didn't answer.

"WHAT'S GOING ON, MATT?" Conley spoke with a calmness he didn't feel while inside he was reeling. How in the hell had Matthew found them? How in the hell had he gotten inside the gate? Questions flashed through Conley's mind but he put them all aside. They didn't seem important with the barrel of a gun pointing at him. "What's with the rifle, buddy?"

Matthew Oakley stared at Conley with eyes that were already dead. "Drop the rock and turn around," he said. "Head for the garage."

Conley stood his ground. "Where's Lara?"

Matthew glared at Conley with a stony expression. "If you don't turn around right now, I'm going to shoot you, Con. If you don't believe me, you're going to die learning different." He raised the weapon and worked the bolt, pulling it back and sending a shell into the receiver. With another quick jerk, he pushed the bolt forward and put the shell in the barrel, the sound deadly. "Drop the rock and start walking."

Conley opened his fingers and let the rock slide out. But he didn't move. "Tell me where Lara is," he demanded. "Then I'll do whatever you want."

"I'm not telling you shit." Matthew lifted the gun with a menacing air. "And you're going to do whatever I want anyway. Now move."

His voice was as lifeless as his gaze. Raising his

hands, Conley slowly stepped backward, his eyes on his friend's face. "Okay, okay...but talk to me. Tell me what's wrong?"

"What's wrong?" Matthew jabbed the barrel of the rifle in Conley's direction. "You're what's wrong, you bastard. I'm sick and tired of living in your shadow. The whole world knows Harrison's but who knows me? Huh? No one, that's who."

Conley stopped. "What in the hell are you talking about?"

"The business," Matthew screamed suddenly. "Your perfect, precious business, that's what I'm talking about!" He hit Conley in the chest with the barrel of his weapon. "No one knows I'm the brains behind that operation and that's gonna change, by God! I'm sending your ass to hell and I'm taking charge."

Conley stared at the wild-eyed man before him.

"That's right," Matthew cried. "Look surprised. Act like you don't know what I'm talking about—"

"I don't—"

"The hell you don't! I've been trying two bloody years to get you to market my glass chip and all you've done is blackball it." He mimicked Conley's deep voice. "It's not ready, Matthew. It's got problems, Matthew. I'm not putting Harrison's name on it, Matthew...." He narrowed his eyes and shook his head, a dark lock of hair falling over his forehead. "I'm not taking that crap, anymore, Conley. I could make a fortune off that chip—for once I might even get Sandy off my ass—and I'm not waiting for your approval anymore. I'm taking over the business…after your unfortunate murder."

"They'll catch you." Conley kept his voice calm, his manner even. "You won't get away with this, Matthew."

"I'm in Denver, remember? I checked into the hotel last night and you just got e-mail from me that proves that fact."

"That proves nothing and you know it. You programed the system to send that note. The cops aren't stupid, Matt. They'll figure it out. They'll find the code."

"It's already gone," he said smugly. "I put in a self-destruct trap."

Conley started to argue some more, but Matthew silenced him, shaking his head. "None of that matters. The police are going to find out that Theresa was responsible for all this. She's been stalking you, you know, a convenient complication for me. She was crazy. She shot herself, but first she murdered you and set the house on fire." He wore a studied look of regret. "Oh, she shot your loving wife, too."

Conley went completely cold, a physical response that rippled through his body from his head to his toes. The knowledge that Theresa was the one who'd been stalking him barely registered. "What are you saying?"

"I've killed them both," Matthew said in a matter-of-fact voice. "They're in the garage." He raised the gun. "Let's go join them."

CONLEY HAD HEARD of people who'd said that they'd become so enraged their vision had changed, but he'd never believed them. Until now.

He stared at Matthew Oakley through a haze of crimson. He felt as if a curtain had suddenly come down between them.

All he could think of was Lara. With an enraged cry, he reached out and grabbed the end of the barrel, twisting the weapon up and over his shoulder. Matthew bellowed and held on, firing a second later. The shot went over Conley's head and into the pines behind him, the sound deafening.

Conley was taller, but Matthew possessed a strength that went past reason. They struggled over the weapon. Conley began to wrench the gun away, but Matthew refused to give up. Screaming with rage, he gripped the stock with both hands. Nothing, it seemed, would make him the loser.

Exhausted from his trek, out of his mind over Lara, Conley felt his hold loosening. His muscles burned and for a moment, his vision went dark. Blinking, he thought he was imagining things. Then he blinked again and realized he wasn't.

Theresa stood behind Matthew, a pair of pruning shears in her hands. She was bleeding profusely, a huge red stain on the front of her parka. Her eyes were glazed, and they burned with something Conley couldn't name. Love? Madness? A combination of both? She slowly smiled at him, her lips curving upward almost seductively. Then she raised the pruners and threw herself at Matthew.

He gasped as the point of the shears entered his back. Swaying, he looked down in horror and disbelief. Conley followed his widened eyes. Two sharp tips protruded from Matthew's chest. He lifted his gaze to Conley, his expression puzzled—then he fell to his knees, taking Conley with him.

CHAPTER SEVENTEEN

MATTHEW WAS DEAD by the time they hit the ground.

Struggling to his feet, Conley pushed off the engineer's body and then Theresa's, leaving them tangled where they fell. He threw Matthew's rifle into the bushes and bounded toward the garage, praying the whole time that he wasn't too late, that he could find Lara. As he raced across the deck at the back of the house, the windows began to pop, glass flying from the frames as the fire reached the inside of the cabin.

Skidding to a halt outside the open garage, Conley peered into the smoky interior. The flames and fumes were even thicker at this end of the house. He took a deep breath then charged forward. After making one quick circuit he was forced outside, coughing and sputtering. She wasn't there! Had Lara somehow escaped like Theresa?

He pulled his shirt over his mouth and reentered the burning garage, this time dropping to his knees and patting the cement. A few moments later, he crawled outside, heaving as the smoke reached his lungs. Despair and panic filled him. She wasn't there and he had no idea where to look.

Then he heard something. Something faint, something almost inaudible. A scratching sound coming from outside the garage.

Screaming Lara's name, Conley jumped to his feet and ran around the building, stumbling toward the storage area. The muted sound grew marginally louder, then he saw the lid of the wood bin bounce up a fraction. He skidded to a stop and pulled at the cover, Lara's voice answering his frenzied calls.

"Conley! Is that you? Can you hear me! Can you see me?" Her voice was hoarse and fading, the last of her energy taken up by her cries.

"I'm here, Lara, I'm here!" His frantic eyes landed on the lock. He grabbed the metal—already growing warm—and shook it uselessly. "I've got to get something to pry off the damn lock," he yelled. "I'll be right back—"

"No," she screamed. "No, Conley!" The high pitched sound of her panic tore at his heart. "Please, don't leave me—"

"I'll be right back, baby. I promise—"

With her terror filling his ears, he ran back into the garage. It was completely enveloped in smoke, dark flames already eating up the walls. He found his way to Ed's tool box by memory. The metal compartments seared the palms of his hands but Conley barely noticed. He grabbed the drawers and flung them open, slinging their contents across the metal floor. Snatching up a hammer, he flew back to the wood bin and began to batter at the door, yelling at Lara to cover her eyes.

She didn't reply.

Conley continued to pound. After a lifetime had passed, the lid began to give way. Ripping off the boards, he reached in and lifted Lara out, cradling her against his chest. Her eyes were closed, her face white behind the smudges. His horrified glance took in the robe she wore—his robe—and the bloody splotch on her shoulder.

With a scream of grief and anger, he stumbled backward, into the snow and away from the fire, his wife's still form protected in his arms.

WARMED BY A weak patch of sunshine, Lara sat in the wheelchair and waited for Conley to bring the Rover around. She'd spent three days in the Boulder hospital—Ed had been impossible to put off this time—and she was more than ready to go home. She still had a bit of a cough from the smoke she'd inhaled, but the gunshot wound had been minor, a hot line that had merely grazed her shoulder. And she'd suffered only minor injuries from the fall off the balcony.

Her emotions had suffered far more than her body. Lara had suspected Theresa's involvement but Matthew's betrayal had been a shock. The quiet, unassuming engineer had hidden his anger well. He and Theresa had both died, despite the medics' efforts.

Lara lifted her face to the sun but her thoughts stayed on the visit she'd gotten from Fields and Margulies following the attack. They'd searched the Oakley home and found out everything. He had known all along that Theresa was stalking Conley and he'd not only made it easier for her to get into Harrison's offices, he'd planted clues for her, leading her to the cabin to set her up for the murder. The only thing he hadn't counted on was how much she'd actually loved Conley. That had been his undoing.

The Rover pulled into the hospital's porte cochere and Conley hurried to Lara's side, interrupting her gloomy reflections. Helping her from the wheelchair, he guided her to the SUV as if she were blind, his hand on her elbow, his worried eyes dark beneath a furrowed brow. She finally realized what he was doing and she looked up at him in amazement.

"Conley, I'm okay. You don't have to treat me like I'm going to crack in two...."

He glared at her. "Lara, you were shot. Not to mention the fire!"

She held back her exasperation. "But I'm fine. Really..."

He ignored her protests and lifted her into the vehicle. Closing the door behind her, he hurried to the other side and pulled away from the curb. Traffic was light and they were back in Red Feather in under an hour.

Lara felt as if she should say something, but she didn't know what. A thin thread of cooperation was strung between them, so delicately balanced, she didn't want to upset it.

All she could think to discuss was Ed and Bess. They were getting married again, Ed confessing to Lara that the whole ordeal she and Conley had suffered had made the older couple realize life was short. Too short to waste. Conley made the appropriate comments as Lara brought up the wedding, but she knew his mind was elsewhere. Hers was as well, but she didn't want to go where it had landed. When the house came into view, she gave a silent sigh of relief. Conley helped her inside.

Before Lara could even make her way into the den, however, the doorbell rang. Conley sent her a look of warning, then shook his head. "It's probably Sandy. She must have seen us turn down the street...."

Lara felt her heart twist. "I have to see her, Conley."

After hesitating for a second, he went down the hall and opened the door. The murmur of Sandy's voice drifted down the hallway, along with a baby's cry. Sandy had had an emergency delivery the night Matthew had died.

A few minutes later, with a blue blanket draped over her shoulder, Sandy walked slowly into the kitchen. She paused in the doorway, then she met Lara's eyes and they both began to cry as they came together in the center of the room. The baby caught between them, they hugged tightly. Lara had no idea what to say or how to even begin, but Sandy saved her by speaking first.

"God, Lara, I'm so sorry…. I had no idea what Matthew was doing or I would have said something, I swear!" She wiped her eyes with her free hand, above her son's tiny head. "I—I didn't know he felt that way! Those last few days, he said what I told you…about how I didn't appreciate him…I had no idea…"

Lara shook her head and stopped her friend's apology with a finger to her lips. "You couldn't have done anything about this, Sandy. None of us knew."

"But I should have figured it out," Sandy cried. "That night your Explorer was broken into he left the bar and returned just as you guys came inside. When I asked where he'd been, he said he'd gone to the bathroom and why was I always keeping track of him! He got so angry I dropped the subject. I should have guessed, though. I heard you tell the cops the guy threw the tire iron with his left hand. And that his aim was good." She wiped her eyes with the edge of the baby's blanket. "And the night you were run off the road—he was supposed to pick me up and take me to the lodge but he never showed up until later." Her voice broke. "God, Lara, I just can't believe this...."

Lara hugged her friend. "You couldn't have stopped him even if you had figured it out, Sandy."

"Maybe so, but the truth is the truth. I nagged him constantly, and you know it. I was never happy with our relationship and complained about everything." She sniffed. "Even that damn car—he only bought it because I threw a fit." She dropped her head, her tears falling on her baby's blanket.

Lara reached out and squeezed her shoulder. "You *are not* responsible for any of this, Sandy. All you're responsible for now is this little baby." Leaning over, Lara brushed a finger over the infant's cheek. "He's what's important at this point. The past is done."

The healing words of forgiveness seemed to calm Sandy, if only for a little while. Sitting down in a chair at the kitchen table, Lara let her place the baby in her arms, then Sandy began to fix them tea. The ritual didn't help, though. The dark cloud of the past few days hung over them, and their conversation seemed strained. Closing the door behind Sandy when she said goodbye and left an hour later, Lara realized their friendship was over. Matthew had murdered it, just as surely as he had killed Theresa. Sandy was moving to Arizona to be closer to her family, and Lara would probably never see her or the baby again.

Lara shuffled back into the kitchen just as Conley entered the room from the den. He turned as she came into the room and raised one eyebrow. Lara shook her head and sat down at the table.

"I didn't know what to do," she said. "She feels responsible for what happened. I told her it wasn't her fault, but I didn't know what else to say."

"You did all you could." Conley's eyes went dark as he spoke.

Lara looked down and ran a finger along the edge of the place mat. The time had come for them to face the topic they'd each been avoiding. There was no easy way to approach it so she simply asked the first thing she thought of. "Did you find Theresa's mother?"

He nodded grimly. "She still lives on the ranch where Theresa grew up." He stared out the window, obviously recalling the painful conversation. "She was torn up, naturally. I told her I'd take care of everything."

"Theresa loved you," Lara said in the silence that followed. "I don't believe she would ever have hurt you...or even me. She just wanted to be close to you. The night Matthew shot out the car window and I crashed the car—she was so shocked when she saw me inside the SUV. Now I understand why. She'd expected you to be in there. She wanted to save you. The flowers, the notes, everything, even the nurse's comments about calling her Mrs. Harrison.'' Lara shook her head, her throat going tight. ''She only wanted to love you and have you love her back. Maybe she thought she could do that by rescuing you.''

Conley frowned. ''If that's true then why didn't she try to warn us after she figured out what Matt was doing?''

''I don't know. Maybe she didn't have time. Maybe she wanted to take advantage of the situation. If she'd rushed in and saved you at the last minute it would have served her purpose. She probably thought if she could do that then you'd love her for sure.'' Lara hesitated for a second, then added, ''If Matt had killed me…then it would have accomplished something more. You would have been free.''

An indefinable heaviness fell between them, the kitchen full of their emotions, swirling, it seemed to Lara, with all that had happened to the two of them.

Lara sat numbly, waiting for what, she didn't know. After a moment, Conley crossed the room and knelt beside her. ''So where does this leave us?'' he said, looking into her eyes.

All at once her thoughts flashed back to that day in the kitchen when everything had started. The day she'd asked Conley for a divorce. Only two months had gone by, but to Lara, a lifetime had passed with them.

"I'm not sure where it leaves us." The truth hurt but she had no other option. "I don't really know."

"Well, I've been thinking about it enough for both of us." Standing up, Conley hesitated and his expression shifted minutely. Lara couldn't read the change and she suddenly felt uneasy. Before she could question him, he continued, his next words sending her heart into a dive.

"And I have a confession to make before we continue."

"A confession?" She swallowed, her throat squeezed by a sudden, unnamed reaction. "To what?"

"I started this whole thing off by forcing Ed to take my case—"

She interrupted him, shaking her head. "You didn't force Ed into anything—"

"Oh, yes, I did. I could have found another company to handle the situation, maybe not as good as Mesa, but a different one, nonetheless. I didn't want to do that, though." He clenched his jaw stubbornly. "I wanted Mesa to take the case, and I wanted you to handle it. I knew when I asked that Ed would go along with me. But I wanted Mesa for one reason and one reason only. And it had nothing to do with keeping me safe or finding my stalker."

Lara stared at him.

"I was using the situation, Lara. Just like Matthew used Theresa."

He put his hands in his pockets. "I didn't know what else to do. I couldn't let you go without a fight, but I didn't know how to win you back. I thought I could manipulate the circumstances to bring us closer together. You had to be with me all the time. I thought I could make you fall in love with me again."

He looked down and met her shocked eyes. "Instead of making things work, I almost got you killed. I've been selfish and incredibly stupid, Lara. I only thought about what I wanted—which was you—and how I was going to go about getting you back. I know you'll never be able to forgive me and I understand completely." He paused, his voice hoarse when he spoke again. "Because I'll never be able to forgive myself."

He took a second to regain his composure as Lara waited in stunned silence. His gaze was dark and empty when it finally returned to hers. "I'll give you the divorce now if you want it. It's the least I can do."

LARA'S EYES ROUNDED. If Conley had harbored any lingering hopes that she'd refuse his offer, they disappeared as he stared at her. His future—his whole life—cracked into a thousand pieces and fell apart, leaving him with nothing but an empty hole and the prospect of an even emptier life. She was going to leave him. He'd have to give her the divorce, just as he'd promised.

She rose stiffly from the kitchen chair. "Is that really what you want?"

"No. It's not at all what I want. But I think it's time I forget about what *I* want and think about what *you* want. Thinking of myself is what got us where we are right now."

She moved to the door leading outside. Looking out at the driveway, she stood there, her hand on the doorknob. For a second he thought she was simply going to open the door and walk away, just as he'd done to her the day she'd asked him for the divorce. The thought of her doing that was so painful, Conley had to force himself to stand still and stay where he was. He wanted to run to her and pull her into his arms. He'd had no idea—none whatsoever—until this very second how hurtful he'd been to her that day…and others as well. How many times, he wondered, had she watched him leave or waited for him to come home? How could he have been so blind to what he'd had?

Once again, the silence built between them. It was stiff and hard, a wall that separated them. Their time at the cabin suddenly seemed as if it had never happened. Only the memory of her touch, of her mouth, of her body against his own, assured him that he hadn't made it up.

He waited for her to speak.

Finally, she turned and looked at him. "I'm not sure what I want anymore." Her confession was spoken softly, hesitantly. "All I know is what I *don't* want."

He braced himself. "Then tell me about that. Tell me what you don't want."

She gathered her thoughts and while he waited, Conley felt as if he were back at the fire, his own body locked inside the bin, the smoke and flames surrounding him.

"I don't want to feel as if I'm the only one who cares whether or not this marriage makes it," she said after a minute. "I don't want us to come together then drift apart again. I don't want to be like one of those women who waited for my father to love them, on his terms." She drew in a painful breath. "I don't want to be hurt again when it doesn't work out."

"Lara, I love you and I care about our marriage—I really do. I *promise* it wouldn't be that way this time—"

"You can make that promise, Conley, but you can't keep it." Tears gathered in her voice. "Without some kind of drastic change in our situation, we'll go right back to where we were before. You living your life and me living mine. We won't have a marriage or a real relationship. We'll drift apart and then we'll be right back where we are now."

She shook her head. "I don't want to try again, Conley. I *can't* try again. It hurts too much when we fail."

"But you don't know for sure that would hap—"

"You're right. I don't know the outcome for sure." She looked out at the driveway then back at him. "But there's one thing I *am* sure of—I'm sure I'm not going to let myself be put in that position again and there's only one way I can do that...." She lifted her gaze, her expression so raw and painful, he felt a burning stab of guilt.

"I'm sorry, Conley. But it's over. Our marriage is finished."

SHE SAT IN the kitchen while it grew dark outside. The mugs and plates from Sandy's visit still littered the table but Lara left them where they were. She had no energy. No energy to clean the table, no energy to do the dishes, no energy to heal her broken heart. Conley had been gone for hours. He'd told her she could reach him at the office if she needed him for anything. Then he'd closed the door and left.

Just as she'd wanted him to do.

She put her head down on the table and began to cry, her quiet sobs a lonely echo in the empty kitchen.

CHAPTER EIGHTEEN

THE WEDDING WAS huge with all their friends and business associates present. From across the elegant reception room at the Royal Mountain Lodge, Lara caught a glimpse of her father and new stepmother as they greeted their guests. Bess looked radiant and Ed was ecstatic. Lara took a glass of champagne from a passing waiter and lifted it in a silent toast when Bess saw her watching. The older woman smiled her acknowledgment then leaned over and said something to Ed. He looked in Lara's direction and blew her a kiss that she immediately returned with a flourish. In the weeks that had passed since the fire, they'd grown much closer. Ed seemed like a different person, softer somehow, more open.

Turning away from the happy couple, Lara felt a catch inside her chest. She was thrilled for her father and Bess, but a lingering sadness hung over her.

She missed Conley. Desperately.

Before the thought could gather strength, Bess appeared at Lara's side. Leaning over, she whispered in Lara's ear. "Let's find a quiet corner for a bit— I need a break before my smile slides off my face!"

Grateful for the timely distraction, Lara let Bess direct her to a padded couch near the wall. Sinking into the cushions, the older woman emitted a sigh and slipped off her high heels.

"I'm too old for this," she grumbled with a grin. "We should have eloped. I wanted to but your father had a cow when I suggested it."

"Well, I'm glad you didn't run off!" Lara eyed Bess appreciatively. She wore a filmy chiffon dress the exact shade of her eyes—periwinkle blue—and her gray hair was styled to perfection. A sapphire necklace—courtesy of Ed—gleamed around her throat. "The party's wonderful and you look absolutely fabulous. You deserve a celebration."

Bess raised an eyebrow. "This is a celebration? From the look on your face, I thought it was a wake!"

Lara started to smile, then found she couldn't. Instead, her eyes filled with tears. She turned her head abruptly so Bess wouldn't see.

But she wasn't quick enough. Bess reached around and gently pulled on Lara's chin. "Tell me," she said softly.

"This is your day, Bess," she protested. "I don't want to spoil it—"

"You're not going to spoil anything," Bess insisted, "and besides that, I asked. I want to know what's going on."

"There's nothing to tell." Lara held out her

hands. "It's all over. I haven't seen Conley since he walked out of the kitchen a month ago. The day I came home from the hospital. I guess he's leaving everything up to me." She paused and swallowed hard. "To contact a lawyer and do all that..."

"And have you?"

"Not yet." The excuse sounded lame, but it was the best she could do. "I—I just haven't had the time."

Bess called her on the lie immediately, just as Lara had known she would. "The time or the desire?"

Lara looked down into the flute she still held. Bubbles rimmed the edge of the crystal. "A little of each, I suppose."

"You still love him," Bess said in a matter-of-fact voice.

"I'm not sure." Lara's gaze stayed on the champagne. "But it doesn't matter, I can't leave myself open to that kind of pain again. I'm not that stupid."

"And this is better?" Bess pressed.

Lara shook her head.

"Well, what are you going to do about it?"

Lara had asked herself that same question a thousand times in the past month. A million times. When she let herself think of the alternatives—usually at 3:00 a.m. when she couldn't sleep and the sheets were tangled—her confusion only grew. She was stuck in an emotional quagmire—too stubborn to go backward and too scared to go forward.

"I don't know," she admitted. "I have absolutely no idea."

"He *does* love you. You do know that, don't you?"

Lara bit her bottom lip then released it. "He might have at one time, but now he just feels guilty. He thinks he's responsible for everything that happened. I don't want Conley sticking around because he feels like he should…to somehow make it up to me." She looked up. "That's even worse that it was before."

Bess considered Lara's words with a thoughtful expression, then she turned her head and looked at the crowd before them. Across the room, Ed was gesturing wildly to someone, punctuating a joke, no doubt.

When she felt Bess's sympathetic gaze once more, Lara spoke quietly. "I got exactly what I asked for, Bess, and there's nothing I can do about it but accept it."

BESS WENT BACK to her guests and Lara stood up. From a spot across the room, Conley watched as she headed for the opposite side of the salon. She disappeared through a set of double French doors then reappeared a second later, on the deck. It was May and still cool, but the weather had cooperated. A gorgeous, clear blue sky hovered over the mountains, the air so clean and pure he could almost taste it.

Conley followed Lara's path then stopped at the threshold. She stood twenty feet in front of him, at the railing. Seeing her there, he remembered the snowy night of her car wreck and how he had waited for her. He'd stared out at that very spot and had known in his heart that she was in trouble and needed him.

He wished desperately for that same kind of confidence now, but wishing didn't make it appear. He had no idea how she would react to what he'd done, no inkling of how she'd respond. He may have just committed the biggest mistake of his life, and if he had, he didn't know what he'd do. Because it was too late to go back. Even if the deal didn't go through, he'd become a different man during the past few weeks. There were angles and emotions, feelings and attitudes he wasn't quite familiar with yet.

He wasn't sure who he was, but he knew that other man—the one he'd been before—was gone.

There was no sense in waiting any longer. Conley started across the deck, and as his footsteps sounded against the wood, Lara turned swiftly.

Her smooth blond hair, one side tucked behind an ear, shimmered with her movement, the streaks catching light from the afternoon sun. She wore a

short sleeveless dress of deep emerald silk, something with a shine in it. The color was reflected in
her eyes, making them more green than hazel. Her
expression went from shock to something else, a
guarded look sweeping over her beautiful features.

He stopped two feet in front of her. "Hello,
Lara."

"Hello, Conley." She lifted a hand to her neck,
to the string of pearls she wore. "I—I didn't know
Bess and Ed had invited you."

"I wrangled an invitation. I wouldn't have missed
this for the world." His easy voice hid his nervousness as he tilted his head toward the reception room.
"I think it's going to take. Bess won't let him get
away this time."

Lara smiled without thinking. He could tell by the
way her mouth lifted. "You may be right," she said.
"And I hope that you are. He's a different man.
Bess has changed him."

"A good woman can do that."

Lara's eyes jumped to Conley's face before she
turned abruptly, giving him her back. He waited a
second, then he came to her side and gripped the
railing. He wanted to do this perfectly—wanted it
so much it hurt—but he didn't know how to proceed. Dammit to hell, he'd never known how to go
about things like this and that was what had gotten
him to the place he was in now. After a while,

he simply reached inside the pocket of his jacket and handed her the papers.

The blue-covered documents hung in the air between them, suspended by Conley's fingers.

Lara had never been the kind of woman who could hide her emotions. In that moment something flared in her eyes, and he felt his own hopes leap. Maybe...just maybe...he had a chance.

Her gaze still troubled, she lifted her hand and took the papers from him. Opening them up, she scanned the first sheet then shot him a shocked look. Immediately, she went back to the documents, flipping page over page until she'd reached the end. Then she raised her eyes.

"Are you crazy?" she asked.

Her reaction wasn't at all what he'd expected. Conley laughed out loud. "Probably so," he said. "But it seemed like the only solution. You said yourself something drastic had to change in our lives to convince you things could be different."

"But this—" she shook the papers "—this is *really* drastic."

"It's not a done deal yet," he said. "Harrison's is part of a trust. We both have to sign the documents to sell the company." He reached inside his jacket again, pulled out a pen and held it out to her. "Here. Go ahead. I've already signed them."

She didn't take the pen. "Why?" she asked

softly. "Why are you doing this, Conley? I don't understand. The business means everything to you."

"Not anymore."

"What changed?"

"I did," he said. "I nearly died when I pulled you out of that box, Lara. I thought you were dead and if you had been, I would have been more guilty of your murder than Matthew Oakley."

"That's not true—"

"It's the truth to me," he interrupted. "Even more importantly, though, I realized how I'd taken advantage of your love, how I'd let the marriage go and assumed you would carry the load. It wasn't fair and I didn't treat you right. I wanted to do something that would prove to you I'm a different man, that I've changed and so have my priorities. I contacted a broker in New York and put the business up for sale. Now I have a buyer. All we have to do is sign the papers." He took a painful pause. "I'll still give you the divorce if that's what you want. But it's not what *I* want. I love you, Lara. And I want another chance at showing you how much."

She looked into his eyes and that was all she needed. She didn't have to ask him if he was sure. She could tell by meeting his gaze that he'd asked himself that same question and had answered it as well. Nothing—absolutely nothing—meant more to him than her and in one single heartbeat she knew this was now the case.

She tore the legal papers in two and let the pieces flutter from her fingers to the sun-splashed deck.

"I love you, too, Conley. I always have and I always will." Her eyes filled with tears but this time they were happy ones. "Let's give forever another chance."

With a huge smile, he opened his arms and she walked into them.

Again.

The Shannon Sisters

A Trilogy by C.J. Carmichael
The stories of three sisters from Alberta whose lives and loves are as rocky—and grand—as the mountains they grew up in.

A *Second-Chance* Proposal
A murder, a bride-to-be left at the altar, a reunion. Is Cathleen Shannon willing to take a second chance on the man involved in these?

A *Convenient* Proposal
Kelly Shannon feels guilty about what she's done, and Mick Mizzoni feels that he's his brother's keeper—a volatile situation, but maybe one with a convenient way out!

A *Lasting* Proposal
Maureen Shannon doesn't want risks in her life anymore. Not after everything she's lived through. But Jake Hartman might be proposing a sure thing....

On sale starting February 2002

Available wherever Harlequin books are sold.

HARLEQUIN®
Makes any time special ®

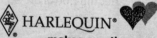

If you enjoyed what you just read,
then we've got an offer you can't resist!

Take 2 bestselling
love stories FREE!
Plus get a FREE surprise gift!

"YOU KNOW THERE HAVE BEEN NO OTHER MEN."

"I know only that no other man has had you. I doubt most men would dare for fear of freezing to death."

"You had no such fear."

"I, madam, have nothing to lose. You have my name, my fortune, and my future in your hands."

"Except for your name and a child, I want nothing from you, Mr. Ashford."

"Nothing?" he said as he took a step toward her. "Are you quite sure?"

She saw the controlled anger in him, the deliberate way he moved toward her.

"Is it only a child you want, Rachel, or is there more?" He traced the line of her throat with his finger, circled the hollow at her collarbone over and over again. "Tell me, Rachel."

"I want more," she whispered.

He lowered his mouth to hers slowly, tauntingly, his lips brushing hers, back and forth, over and over again. She could not raise her arms to draw his head closer, his grasp was so tight, and so she raised up on her tiptoes, straining toward him, reaching for him, reaching for more than a deeper kiss. Reaching for him.

"Say it again, Rachel." His tongue skimmed over her lips and barely dipped inside.

"I want more, Henry. I want to—"

Her arms were suddenly free, and she lifted them to encircle his neck, but she found nothing but air as he backed away, that familiar mockery slanting the mouth that never smiled.

"Then, madam, you must work for it."

MORE THAN JUST A NIGHT

"This is my kind of book . . . one you'll read again, and again, and again."
    —Bertrice Small, author of *A Moment in Time*

"High romance with just a twist of fantasy . . . love and adventure in this haunting story of a man lost and in search of home . . . and himself."
—Laura Kinsale, author of *The Shadow and the Star*

"With vivid characterizations and Connie Rinehold's flair, MORE THAN JUST A NIGHT is a compelling tale of romance and suspense."
    —Catherine Hart, author of *Tempest*

"I was captivated from the first page to the last by the powerful and compelling love story, and held spellbound by Ms. Rinehold's rich, expressive prose and depth of emotion. MORE THAN JUST A NIGHT is alive with all the raw passion and emotion of the West."
    —Kathe Robin for *Romantic Times*

CONNIE RINEHOLD

UNSPOKEN VOWS

A DELL BOOK

Published by
Dell Publishing
a division of
Bantam Doubleday Dell Publishing Group, Inc.
1540 Broadway
New York, New York 10036

The trademark Dell® is registered in the U.S. Patent and Trademark Office.

ISBN: 0-440-21358-4

Printed in the United States of America

Published simultaneously in Canada

February 1995

10 9 8 7 6 5 4 3 2 1

OPM

A dream is worth doing.

This book is dedicated to friends, family, and supporters who, in one way or another, have helped me to make my dreams become realities. To name but a few . . .

Booksellers everywhere including: Gerald and Jenny Ratcliff and staff at Bookrak; Mary Lou Boylan and Shawne Anderson of A Book Shop; Beth Anne Steckiel of Beth Anne's Books; Bobby McClane and Donna Young of Basically Books; Cenetta Williams, Carolyn Wilklow, Annie Oakley, and all my friends at Waldenbooks; Karen Patterson and everyone at B. Daltons—for caring.

Parents-in-law, Dorothy and Sam Rinehold—for reasons too numerous to list, and especially for the respect and support you have shown for my dream.

And in loving memory of my stepfather, Alfred "Mick" English, who accepted me as I was and never doubted that I could be so much more, and who taught me that family is a matter of spirit rather than blood.

With special thanks to:

The talented and blessedly honest participants in the Tuesday Night Insanity Sessions: Virginia Rifkin, Pamela Perry, Francie Stark, and Erica Winkler—for sticking around to hear the fat lady sing.

Diane Kirk, Anita Battershell, and the members of Rose Petals and Pearls—for understanding, appreciating, and remaining faithful to the lyrics of romance.

Sharon Lass Field—for setting the stage so beautifully with just the right details and historical facts.

Jo Lichtman of Yesterday's Garden for Rachel's hat—a heartfelt "Brava!" for a most exquisite prop that is a work of art in itself.

Jay Acton, Marjorie Braman, and Tina Moskow—for making the performance possible in the first place.

Prologue

"I had no choice." The whisper was faint, a litany repeated over and over, begging for absolution, performing the last rites of a life spent in hell. "No family . . . no choice . . . hopeless. . . ."

Rachel listened in anger and helplessness. She'd heard it before, from every girl who surrendered to the existence of a whore rather than taking her chances as a lone woman in a man's world. She'd heard it just yesterday from one of the newer inhabitants at Madam Roz's. Yesterday, before the house had exploded with angry shouts and screams of pain, a single gunshot, and finally shocked silence as people gathered in the doorway of Liddie's room. Then the only voice had been Roz's, ending the chaos as if it had never been.

"It's over. Drinks on the house and business as usual, gentlemen . . . ladies." Footsteps receded and doors closed against the nightmare in room 3. Within minutes, laughter could be heard behind one door. Bedropes creaked behind another.

Business as usual.

"It can't be worse than this, Rachel."

Liddie's breath shuddered in and out, and Rachel wished that she could breathe for both of them. "What can't, Liddie?"

"Hell."

"No, Liddie."

The voice became stronger, full of pride and dignity. "My name is Lydia Marie Bentley. Please, Rachel. Don't let them bury me without my name. It's all I have left."

The parlor clock chimed three, the hour when darkness was complete and loneliness mated with despair. Rachel swallowed and stared straight ahead, unable to look at what she could become—a frail and beaten young girl whose porcelain-doll features had been reduced to crude pottery, her delft-blue eyes dimmed as if the paint had been worn away by too much exposure to the harsher elements of life. She and Liddie bore no resemblance to one another, yet Rachel knew that if she remained in her mother's house, she would turn into just another body that housed an all-but-dead soul. All of "Madam's Girls" looked alike after a while.

Rachel swallowed the bile that rose in her throat. "I promise," she said firmly.

Liddie smiled as her eyes began to close. "Lydia Marie Bentley," she whispered. "It's a respectable name, Rachel. We were all respectable once."

"No, Li-Lydia Marie Bentley," Rachel whispered. "Some of us were never respectable."

Liddie grasped Rachel's hand, holding on it seemed, with the last remains of her strength. "You can be, Rachel. It's a good dream."

"Yes, Liddie," Rachel said dully as she felt a chill creeping through Liddie's fingers.

"Take the money I've saved. It's all planned out . . . letter written . . . a chance for you, Rachel. Promise me, Rachel . . . *please* . . . live it for both of us. Make me count for something."

"I promise, Liddie—for both of us." An ache spread through Rachel's hand as Liddie clasped it tighter still.

"I'll be watching, Rachel . . . watching you . . . happy . . . free. . . ." The last word faded on a final sigh, a soft shadow of life that lingered in the air. Liddie's hand squeezed once, her fingers like ice now, as she surrendered to whatever peace her soul might find.

And Rachel remained there, holding Liddie's hand, listening to the sounds of laughter and moans and the creak of bedropes behind closed doors.

"You wanted to see me, Mother?"

Roz narrowed her eyes at her daughter's form of address. It was bad for business. Rachel knew that. It made the customers edgy, reminding them of wives and daughters sewing in the parlor at home while they did some "sowing" of their own. Not that everyone in town didn't know Rachel was hers. Some of her older customers looked through Rachel as if she didn't exist, afraid that if they did look, they'd find a telltale resemblance to themselves. If they weren't too scared to count, or to remember which whore they'd had and when, they'd realize that Rachel had been conceived before Roz had set up shop. Still, the possibility of shared blood had been a kind of protection for Rachel, so Roz had let them wallow in their fear.

But that was changing. The town was growing. She saw new faces every day: miners heading for the mountains; men with money and dreams wanting to build em-

pires; cowboys and drifters looking for work, whiskey,
and women. More than one had asked for Rachel. She
was seventeen. The house had an empty room now.
There were better ways for Rachel to earn her keep than
doing the laundry and cooking the meals. Roz closed her
eyes, forcing herself to silence her thoughts.

Dear God, why don't you give us more choices?

Roz watched her daughter. There was a new defiance
about Rachel since she'd taken a knife and carved Liddie's name into the wooden cross marking the newly
filled grave. Foolishness. Whether Liddie wound up in
heaven or hell, the man in charge would know who, and
what, Lydia Marie Bentley had been.

"It's time, Rachel," Roz said. "No girl with your
looks can stay in this house and not work. It's trouble I
can't afford."

"I'll be leaving in the morning."

"I heard about the plans you and Liddie were making," Roz said harshly. If Rachel was surprised by Roz's
knowledge of Liddie's dream, she didn't show it. But
then whores and their daughters couldn't afford to show
anything but their bodies.

"Then I don't need to explain."

"I didn't think you were stupid enough to believe it
would work."

Rachel shrugged. "Liddie and I had planned to leave
in the spring, anyway." Her voice caught then, a little
snag in tone, a slight drop in volume. "Only a few
months more, and we would have been gone. Liddie
would have been able to live with her own name again."

"She was a brainless little idiot. It's a miracle she
survived as long as she did." Roz's mouth tightened.
"Damn her—"

Rachel swung away from the window, her fists
clenched at her sides, anger ignited in her eyes.

Roz saw it coming—the burst of temper Rachel so seldom displayed. She smiled, relieved to know her daughter wasn't above losing control once in a while. "You want to hit something, Rachel? Go ahead. I'll give you just one, so be sure you're fighting for yourself and not someone else." Roz stared up at her and waited.

Rachel curled her fingers into her palm and lowered her arm. Still, her expression did not change. No anger. No regret. Nothing.

"You're tough, and you've got sense. I'll give you that." Roz smiled. "You'd make a hell of a good whore, Rachel."

With stiff movements, Rachel stepped back until she was once again at the window, her back toward Roz. Only then did Roz see her react with a shudder, a drooping of shoulders. "Is that what you really want, Mother?" she asked, her voice a raw whisper.

"I stopped wanting anything a long time ago," Roz said wearily as she opened the bottom drawer in her desk and pulled out a leather bag filled with money. The sheriff had given it to her this morning—a reward for killing the man who had beaten Liddie. He'd brutalized more than one woman, regardless of her social class, or lack of one.

"You got someplace to go?" Roz asked as she weighed the bag in her hand.

"I'm going to reclaim Grandfather's homestead."

It felt strange to hear Rachel saying "Grandfather" as if it meant something and he had been a part of her life. Roz could barely remember the father and brothers who had gone hunting one day and never come back, leaving her alone in a cabin in the wilderness. She'd tried to make it on her own, but at fourteen she'd fallen victim to the first man who had come through her land.

At fourteen it was easy to believe whatever flatteries and promises she'd heard. It had been even easier to believe she was in love. But his promises had been empty and she had been left alone with a baby to feed. Once she'd come to town, it hadn't taken her long to figure out that the only way to protect herself was to give men what they wanted, on her terms.

Roz shoved her thoughts away. She couldn't afford to be soft, to remember anything past yesterday or to think beyond tomorrow. That's why Liddie had been killed and Rachel was leaving. "Any plans once you get there?"

"I'm going to build a life."

"Just like that? Don't you know that women aren't entitled to lives other than what men give us? Hell, we're not even real people."

"We have the vote."

Roz snorted. "In one little parcel of the world, we're allowed to vote because Esther Morris gave a tea party and backed opposing politicians into a corner they couldn't get out of. Our right to vote in Wyoming has been taken away once. It'll probably be taken away again."

"I'm not staying here, Mother."

"You know what it takes to run that place? The hands are retired outlaws and gunmen. Grace is old and she's shot enough men to have a reputation. The men don't mind taking orders from her, but they sure as hell won't take orders from you." Roz sighed when Rachel didn't respond. She thought of big, raw-boned Grace, the madam who had sold her the brothel and retired to manage Roz's land in the Big Horn Basin, preferring to work a place in the wilderness than to outlive her girls in a cathouse. "A looker like you will wind up on your back in the barn rather than on your knees in the garden."

"You and the other girls taught me to take care of myself," Rachel said.

"Lessons don't mean squat without experience, girl."

Rachel turned her head, and Roz saw the bitter twist to her mouth. What more could she say, knowing what Rachel had seen over the years? "You can't do it alone."

"I don't plan to do it alone."

Roz stared at her daughter in disbelief. "You won't find a husband, Rachel. There's not a man in the territory who'll want the daughter of Madam Roz for anything but a night's pleasure."

"I'll find a husband when I'm ready."

"What respectable man will have you? A beat-up cowhand? A drifter?" Roz asked harshly.

Rachel drew her shoulders back. "A respectable, *desperate* man," she said.

Inhaling sharply, Roz shook off the melancholy that seemed to fall over her more and more often. Regrets were as useless as an aging whore. All that mattered was having enough money, a tough hide, and more brains than the average male. Rachel had the brains, and she knew more about life than most of the women who found themselves alone, without the protection money or family could provide.

Maybe it was enough.

It didn't matter. Rachel's mind was made up, and if she had half as much sense as Roz thought she did, she'd never look back once she walked out the front door.

Sighing, Roz held out the pouch of money. "Here's the reward money—five thousand dollars collected from husbands and fathers of the women that piece of manure beat up over the years. It ought to keep you for a while." She smiled with a wry slant to her mouth. "This and the money Liddie had socked away. . . . Are you sure this is what you want to do?" she asked, hating herself for it. "This isn't such a bad way to live."

Rachel straightened her shoulders as she turned away from the window. "Maybe not, Mother. But I can't think of a worse way to die."

1

---·❦·---

"He's daft," a seaman shouted above the wind. His shipmate nodded. "Lost a few buttons, he has."

Ignoring the comments, Henry Ashford stood on the deck as the clipper heaved upward on another wall of water and balanced precariously on the crest before plunging into the trough. A cold wave broke over the decks and the wind hammered icy rain into his face. Heavy, flinty clouds rolled and clashed and shot jagged bolts of fire into a night that glowed with an unearthly yellow-gray light. Again the ship teetered on the peak of a wave and seemed about to escape the restraints of man and earth to take sail on the wind.

Freedom. The word had been drifting through his consciousness since he'd been exiled from England, taking him on flights of memory that reminded him of his own needs, the dreams he'd once had. And amid the fury of the midnight storm, he remembered the park surrounding his ancestral home, the serenity of ancient trees and the ducks floating on a pond, his mother strolling beside him in the meadow with her paint box and tablet in hand as they both planned the day's masterpiece. That had been freedom—to do as he wished for a little while each day, to see beauty, to create beauty, to share his visions with one who understood what drove him . . . until it had all been lost, snatched away when his mother betrayed her own children.

He had been searching for freedom and peace ever since, putting as much space as he could between himself and his brother, Luc, his only remaining connection to the past. Only distance weakened the hold they had on one another, the link that bound them through an accident of birth. And now, through an accident of fate, he was escaping *to* Luc rather than away from him.

Henry braced his booted feet wide apart on the pitching deck as he released his grip on the rail, standing free, pitting his strength against the elements.

"Get that fool below!" a voice shouted from the quarterdeck, and a sailor hastened to obey.

Henry stared at the crewman with a cold, dead gaze that stopped the man in his tracks. Slowly he removed the cap on his flask and took a long pull of brandy. He stared at the silver flask, seeing his replection as lightning illuminated one side of his face and left the other half in darkness. His ice-blue eyes blazed in the flash and held the light as his face faded into shadow once more. The wind brushed back his hair with a violent hand, tousling it about his head like a blackened halo. His cape billowed around him, the ends rising above him, dark wings on a tainted angel unfurling to ride the storm.

The seaman crossed himself as he shrank back and found a more urgent task to perform on the other side of the ship.

A corner of Henry's mouth slanted upward in a parody of a smile as he turned back to the sea. It appealed to him—the thought of becoming a part of the storm, becoming part of a power greater than he was instead of fighting it.

What would it be like, he wondered, to give himself up to the fury of the storm and be torn apart by the wind? What would it be like to be at the mercy of an unforgiving sea?

It would be no different from living.

He began to laugh, a mirthless sound that rose above the wind.

Fort Fetterman, Wyoming Territory

"She's crazy as a bedbug," one citizen of Fort Fetterman said. "Drove that old wagon of hers along the Oregon Trail and picked up all the leavin's the sodbusters left behind."

"Loony," another man agreed. "Lives in that there valley and puts up fine buildings. Not one of 'em a hog ranch," he said, disgusted. "Folks'd take her more serious if she had a hog ranch. It ain't natural. Ain't no men gonna go up there less'n she offers more'n dry goods and food."

"Ain't so," another man said. "Every yahoo in the country whut's got no other place to go is up there buyin' her goods. And mark my words, families lookin' to settle down will go to her cuz there *ain't* no hog ranch."

The first man snorted. "Indians and outlaws and useless old men. Onc't she gits her 'town' built, the gov'-ment will put walls around it and post sentries. She's loco, I tell ya."

The second man spat tobacco onto the dust of Fort Fetterman's thoroughfare. "Wish't I was that crazy . . . and that rich."

Another man, silent until now, spoke up. "You wish you had half the balls she does."

"She ain't got no balls," the first man said sullenly. "No brains neither. Whoever heard of a woman doin' whut she's done . . . ridin' the trails and pickin' up the leavin's from the wagon trains an' huntin' like an Injun and tannin' hides like a squaw? Balls ain't got nuthin' to do with it."

"How'd you know, Jasper? She's got the money. All you got is bunions on your butt."

The other man's eyes narrowed. "You been sneakin' up there and gettin' into her bloomers?"

"Now you know that her legs is locked together tight. I heard tell she thinks hers is gold-plated and no man'll git in less'n he's got a big stake an' a weddin' ring."

Little by little, Lucien Ashford, tenth Earl of Fairleigh, pieced together the life of Rachel Parrish, and the more complete the picture, the more intrigued he became. Stories had been circulating about the notorious Madam Roz's daughter since she'd had the gall to vote in the last election. He'd been fascinated by the tale that had reached Cheyenne of the way she had made her way to the ballot box among whispers and stares, her head held high as she spoke to a woman who was obviously torn between the instinct to give Rachel the cut direct and the training that insisted on politeness.

When he'd seen her advertisement on the same day that he had received Henry's wire from New York, an idea had taken root. The hope that at last he had found a way to save his brother had prompted him to explore the possibilities, no matter how far-fetched they seemed. Henry had been wandering for years, trying to lose himself, to forget who and what he was. Luc knew that Henry was dangerously close to succeeding.

Luc felt desperation warring with apathy more every day as Henry's journey brought him closer to Wyoming. And at times darkness overcame him, descending over his mind, swallowing his emotions. Henry's darkness. Henry's nightmares. It was always there now, a shadow haunting him, warning him that the light he had always seen in his brother was slowly fading, that Henry's wit and brilliance and talent and the very essence of the man himself would be lost. Henry had been fighting for survival for far too long. So long that he'd forgotten that one had to live life in order to survive it.

Again he read the advertisement, studied the legal documents he'd had drawn up, and reviewed all he had learned of Miss Rachel Parrish—a woman of uncommon courage and purpose. A woman whose determination to build herself a future was as strong as Henry's determination to destroy his. By planning and executing his deception, Luc knew that he was risking all that he and Henry shared—friendship, respect, trust . . . love. Yet, if his plan worked—*if* he could present Henry with a good wife, a decent home, and enough incentive to ensure that he'd want to keep them both—Henry himself might be saved. Still, Luc knew that his brother would not easily forgive his machinations. It was a case of damned if he did and damned if he didn't. He could live with Henry's anger far more easily than he could live without his brother.

He folded the papers very carefully and slipped them into an oilskin pouch. Yes, Rachel Parrish did indeed seem the answer to his dilemma. By not sending Henry the funds he'd requested, he'd managed to slow his brother's progress from England to Cheyenne. If all went well and Miss Parrish lived up to Luc's expectations, Henry's fate would be sealed by the time he arrived.

In two weeks he would meet her and make his final decision.

Big Horn Basin, Wyoming Territory

"Gal, you ain't got the sense of a moth," Cletus said, the cold wind snatching his voice from the air. "You think Gracie cares whut's on her marker?"

Rachel looked up at him through the flying snow of an early-spring storm, her gaze distant, as she remembered another time, another grave, then bent to her work once more, carving a name onto the crosspiece of a wooden marker. Grace was gone, lost to age—as lost as Rachel felt.

Her hands had long since become stiff and blistered from her efforts, the flesh chafed and tight from the bite of the wind. Her heart felt like a stone in her chest as she breathed through the woolen scarf tied around the lower half of her face.

Phoenix stood above and behind her, shielding her from the worst of the wind, keeping his silence as she worked. He'd wanted to do the carving, but Rachel knew that it had to come from her—this last small gesture of recognition that Grace Ellen James had touched at least one life in a profound way.

"Make her stop, Phoenix. It's loco fer her to keep doin' this," Cletus shouted.

"She'll stop when she's finished, old man."

Phoenix's voice touched her as it always had, calming her with the musical lilt of an accent, supporting her with its steadiness and depth. Rachel turned back to her work and painstakingly carved as she consulted a piece of paper she'd anchored with a rock for the proper curve of the last letter.

A strong hand gripped her elbow, urged her to stand. Her knees seemed to be frozen as she labored to straighten them. But the hand was there, holding her upright, keeping her steady. She smiled up at Phoenix, though she knew he couldn't see it through the scarf. "Thank you," she whispered.

He wrapped an arm around her waist to lead her back to the house.

Cletus sighed in relief as he trudged beside them, his small, wiry body leaning into the wind. "I'll be goin' back to my place. Rain will have supper ready." Before he veered off to the right, he lowered his head and spoke into Rachel's ear. "You goin' t'tell 'im?"

Reluctant to answer, Rachel kept her gaze fixed on the ground. To tell Phoenix what she had done was to make it official, to relinquish a part of her life that was precious to her. To tell him was to bring closer the day when he would leave her. "Yes, I'm going to tell him," she said firmly.

Cletus nodded and turned away to find the warmth of his own cabin and the Indian woman who had simply appeared in the valley one day and moved in with him.

Despite the wind and murky light, Rachel raised her head, needing to see the boundaries of her home. Mountains rose around the basin, shrouded in thick, gray light and flying snow, yet in her heart she saw the meadows as they would be a month from now, vivid with wildflowers growing randomly among rich grasses nourished by streams and rivers, a sky so blue and clear it hurt the eyes. For six years this small valley tucked into the Big Horn Mountains had been her sanctuary, her dream of the future.

Phoenix pushed open the heavy wooden door and waited for her to step into the house set against the sheltering fold of a mountain. With stiff fingers, she unwrapped the scarf and fumbled with the buttons of her coat.

Silently Phoenix brushed her hands away and slipped the buttons free. Since he'd come to the basin five years ago, he'd performed a thousand different tasks for her: planting seeds in the vegetable garden, salting meat, helping her decide how much to charge for the food they had grown and the gloves and shirts she'd made throughout the winter to sell to cowhands and hunters and cavalry men. She knew nothing about him except that he wore his guns like a shootist and spoke like a scholar. In spite of her curiosity, she hadn't asked about his past. Here in the basin, nothing mattered except surviving today and building for tomorrow.

"I received an answer to my advertisement for a husband," she said quietly.

"When?"

"The day before Grace died." Rachel stared into the past, to see Grace, still so close, still vividly alive in her memories. To her last breath, Grace had been adamant that Rachel follow through with the plan conceived by Rachel and Lydia, and supported by the motley group of misfits at the small settlement. She would find a husband, and they would all build respectability as surely and as carefully as they were building a town. It had held them together, had seemed to give them purpose.

"Is this one like the others?" Phoenix asked.

"No. He's from England—brother to an earl." Averting her face, she walked to the brand-new cookstove and checked the water in the kettle. Even as she said it she had a sense of unreality about such a man being interested in what she had to offer. "Grace was pleased."

"And you're not," Phoenix stated.

She paused in grinding the coffee to hide the sudden tremble of her hands. "An aristocrat, Phoenix? What would such a man want with me?"

"He's a second son, Rachel," Phoenix said. "Such men have few prospects beyond what their families choose to dole out to them. Unless they seek their own fortunes, their futures hold little freedom. The easiest way to become independent is to make a good marriage.''

Rachel gave a short, harsh laugh. "A good marriage? Me? I am a good prospect for the minister from Laramie who knew about me and wanted to cleanse my soul and hold me up as an example of his power to redeem the 'worst of Satan's daughters.' Or for the miner who went from camp to camp looking for his pot of gold. According to them the daughter of Madam Roz deserves no better.''

"I only have to look at you, Rachel, to know what you deserve from life.''

"Few people get what they deserve, Phoenix.'' Warmth touched her back as Phoenix moved closer, grasped her shoulders gently, and turned her to face him. His pale-blue eyes seemed to see all the way through her. For all the harsh planes of his face, she had seen only gentleness and a soul-deep sadness that were as much a part of him as the silence and mystery that surrounded him.

"Most people get exactly what they deserve,'' he said softly, his voice distant. "Few have the courage to believe that they deserve more than they already have. Even fewer have the strength to hope.'' He released her, pulled a freshly baked loaf of bread from a wooden box, and selected a knife from the hooks set into the wall above the sideboard. "You know what you want, Rachel. You know how to hope. Your destiny will be fulfilled.''

Rachel smiled. *Destiny.* She liked the sound of it, the promise of it, just as she liked the peace that Phoenix's presence always brought. She had never felt more at ease with another human being than she felt with him. She had never imagined that a man could actually make her feel safe, protected, or that a man could be her friend, enjoying her company without desiring her body.

Darkness intruded through the windows, encroaching on the firelight that cast wavering spears of light on the smooth planked walls of the new house Phoenix and Cletus had built. She thought how much like home it felt—*he felt*—with the easy companionship that required no words and produced no awkward sense of right or wrong. Among other people, they could not be friends without judgment. For months she'd struggled against the impulse that had returned over and over again to tempt her with its simplicity and perfection. But Phoenix was near and she saw temptation so clearly in the firelight.

"Phoenix," she whispered. He looked up at her as if he knew what she wanted. "I don't have to look any further. You're here . . . you're not a stranger. We could both have the dream." It had become that to her—The Dream—a distant someday that she envisioned yet couldn't grasp. How perfect it would be to share it with him—a man who would require nothing from her but simple friendship.

"Your dream, Rachel, not mine. I have no place in it."

"And a stranger does?"

"He will be a stranger only until you decide that you want him to be more."

"Yes—a business partner. A convenience, as I will no doubt be to him." She took a deep breath and plunged headlong into impulse with a note of longing that clogged her throat. "I don't want to be with a stranger, impersonal, a matter of . . . business."

"It isn't always so," he said.

"I've never seen it any other way. I've never known men to want it any other way." Rachel swallowed. "I want to believe that life is more than—" Unable to voice her dread, she shook her head.

"Business?"

She nodded. "You know how to dream, Phoenix. We share that."

"What you are asking—is it not a matter of convenience?"

"No, I—"

"You're afraid and I am safe." He bent his head again and wrapped the remainder of the loaf in a piece of muslin. "It wouldn't be sharing, Rachel. Together neither one of us would have life as it should be."

"I don't know how it should be."

"You'll know when your soul feels the touch of a lover's hand."

The pain in his voice hurt her, shamed her. "You have felt it," she said, wanting to ask more, yet knowing she couldn't. Here, where misfits and wanderers sought refuge from the past, memories belonged to the ones who held them, and secrets were shared willingly or not at all.

"Yes. And I'll not compromise that—not even for you."

The truth was there, in his calm, even voice. It had always been there in the way he watched and listened and waited . . . always waited. "We cannot bring peace to one another, Rachel. You would slowly die and I would live on in emptiness," he said as he put away the knife and walked toward the door, to leave her as he did every evening, to return to the bunkhouse.

"What do you want from life, Phoenix?" she asked, accepting that she could not be his future.

He opened the door and paused, his back to her. "Just that—life," he said in a rough whisper. "And at the end of it, a peaceful death."

The door closed behind him and Rachel wondered if
her heart would ever know a portion of what she sensed
Phoenix had lost.

Purposely she made a racket as she set the table for
her own meal, drowning out the silence that magnified
Grace's absence.

Her hands gripped the edge of the wooden counter,
and she stared out the window, seeing the mountains she
loved ringing the Big Horn Basin like a fence, enclosing
her in a world that seemed far distant from the one she
had left behind. "I'm so frightened," she whispered.

But there was no one to hear her.

Fort Fetterman—Wyoming Territory

Luc stood in the doorway of the saloon cum dining
room, allowing his eyes to adjust to the indoor light
hazed with the combined smoke of cigars and kerosene.
Few people were scattered about the long, narrow
room—a pair of drunkards at the bar, a group of ranch
hands playing poker at a table, and sitting alone in another corner was a hard-faced man nursing a shot of
whiskey as he sprawled in his chair, observing those
around him without any apparent interest. Yet Luc felt
as if he were being studied very thoroughly. He hoped
so. He'd like to think that Miss Parrish had the sense to
bring adequate protection when meeting with a stranger.
The last thing Henry needed was a wife as reckless as
he was.

Luc saw her sitting alone at a table in a far corner,
looking neither right nor left, as if she hadn't noticed his
appearance and the whispers of curiosity that marked
him as a stranger. Her dark-blue gown was that of a lady
of quality and appropriate to the occasion. Not a hint of
her background was visible from the discreet dip of her
lace-trimmed neckline to the way she sat with her hands

folded primly on the table. Only the stiffness of her posture and the dull glaze of her eyes betrayed her effort to ignore her surroundings and the sidelong glances the two drunks cast her way.

He stood in the entrance a moment longer, taking stock of his manner and attire, satisfying himself that he hadn't lost his ability to impersonate his brother. Then, schooling his expression to cynicism and aristocratic disdain, he swaggered over to her table.

"Miss Parrish? May I join you?"

"That depends on who you are," she said coolly.

A corner of Luc's mouth slanted upward in an imitation of a smile that was uniquely Henry's. "I am Henry Ashford, at your service." From the far corner, he heard the scrape of a chair and glanced over at the man who sat alone. He had shifted, sitting up and blatantly fixing his gaze on Luc, his eyes hooded, his mouth grim. Luc smiled slightly, pleased to have his suspicions confirmed. Rachel had indeed brought a protector.

"Please sit down, Mr. Ashford," Rachel said.

Removing his cape with a flourish, he propped his cane against the wall and accepted her invitation. The cane and cape were dramatic flairs that Henry employed when it suited him to flaunt his position. Luc thought it would add to the image of respectability and class—both attributes he thought would impress Rachel. During his investigations, Luc had learned a great deal about what would impress Miss Rachel Parrish, and he felt a mixture of pity for her predicament and awe for the way she had chosen to deal with it.

"Are you applying for the position, Mr. Ashford?" she said briskly as she squarely met his gaze.

"I am fascinated by your proposal, Miss Parrish," he said, beginning to enjoy his deception.

"It's quite straightforward, sir," she said as she smoothed her napkin over her lap, though they had yet to be waited on. From the way their table was being avoided by the serving woman, he judged that they would starve if he didn't take matters into his own hands. He lifted his hand and, with a smile that often melted the most frigid disdain, beckoned a plump, middle-aged woman whose face reminded him of a road over which many prospectors had traveled.

Flushing, the barmaid approached as if she were about to face a pox victim.

"Wine to begin, I think," he said, exaggerating his accent. "In precisely twenty minutes, you may bring us the specialty of the house."

"No wine," the woman stated. "Whiskey, water, or coffee—take your pick."

Following his lead, Rachel nodded imperiously and said, "Water would be fine."

With a "humph" the barmaid raised her painted-on eyebrows at Luc.

"Coffee," he ordered, then sat back and stared at Rachel, waiting for her next move.

"Why are you here, Mr. Ashford? I hardly expected—"

"Someone with charm, wit, and a dashing figure?"

"And humility."

"Humility is not one of the finer attributes of the aristocracy, Miss Parrish, even those of us born too late to inherit the title."

"How many times are you removed from a title?" she asked.

"Once. I am first in line for an earldom if my brother should—God forbid—meet an early demise."

"Then why?"

Lucien sighed and affected just the right amounts of boredom and embarrassment. "I have met with some . . . social reverses in England, which demanded that I seek a more hospitable climate. Since my brother, the Earl of Fairleigh, is in excellent health . . .'' With a small shrug, he spread his hands. ''I find the idea of making my own mark in a new world refreshing.''

''You don't need me for that.''

''I'm ambitious, Miss Parrish, but not foolish. Why not take whatever opportunities come my way? By the same token, you can benefit from my talents.''

''Such as?'' she asked.

Luc had to think a moment. Henry's talents were somewhat obscure. ''I am resourceful, strong, a seasoned veteran of the military, I have impeccable lineage, a modest fortune that will be wholly mine within a few years, and I am desperate. That in itself can be a virtue. Surely you know that?''

''Why would I know such a thing?'' Her hands disappeared beneath the table and he imagined that she was wringing them.

''Because you have been desperate for most of your life.''

Her gaze widened as she started, then brought herself under rigid control. ''You know,'' she said with no effort to dissemble.

Luc admired that even as it alarmed him. ''Never give yourself away, Miss Parrish. I could have simply been guessing to draw you out.''

''You weren't.''

''No.''

She crumpled her napkin on the table. ''Then there is no point in continuing with this—''

''No?'' he asked as he examined his nails.

''Don't mock me, Mr.—''

''Henry.'' He reached into his pocket, pulled out the packet of documents, and gave them to her. ''I would not mock the woman who now holds my future in her

hands.'' He leaned back in his chair. "I have prepared
an agreement, which we will both sign . . . after you have
read it, of course.''

Abruptly she dropped her gaze as her face colored.

"Miss Parrish," Luc said softly, gently. "Can your
menacing friend in the corner read?''

Her head jerked up. "Yes," she said, again making
no effort to dissemble.

"Then perhaps you would ask him to join us and give his
counsel on the details of our rather strange covenant.''

She inhaled sharply and glanced over at the man.
Without a word being said, he pushed his chair back and
sauntered over to their table.

Luc stood to meet him and extended his hand. "Henry
Ashford at your service, sir.''

The man nodded slightly, his eyes seeming to burn
through Luc's flesh and bone to see what lay beneath.
"Phoenix," he said, and then looked at Rachel. "Are
you all right?''

Rachel relaxed as she smiled up at him. "Yes. I
need . . . there are some papers I'd like you to read with
me.''

Phoenix hooked a chair with his foot and sat down to
read the papers, leafing through them once, then starting
over again, asking questions of Luc in such a way that
they also explained the contents of the agreement to Rachel.

The barmaid plunked down plates heaped with stew
and heavy dark bread and stomped away.

Tucking in to his meal, Luc listened to Rachel and
her protector discuss the papers, and answered questions
only when they were directed at him. It was interesting
to witness the relationship between Rachel and Phoenix,
their ease with one another, their mutual respect, and the
kind of silent understanding that existed only between
the best of friends. It reminded him of times past with

Henry, of the way their thoughts and actions had harmonized, the way each of them gave first consideration
to the other.

Suddenly the food seemed to lose its flavor, and Luc's
mood dipped into darker regions. If he went through
with his plan, things would not never again be the same
between himself and his brother. Henry would surely
view Luc's actions as a betrayal of the worst sort, a
betrayal that would rob him of the control he valued so
highly.

But then again, Luc thought, with Miss Rachel Parrish
by his side, perhaps Henry would discover for the first
time in his life that fate could be exactly what he made
of it, rather than what was forced upon him.

Gradually Luc noticed the silence—no rustling of
parchment, no low murmured voices at the table. Rachel
was eating her meal, yet he had the impression that she
neither tasted nor enjoyed the rich stew. Phoenix looked
up from the last page and regarded Luc with a probing
stare.

Though he'd had no idea of what Phoenix looked like
until now, he'd certainly heard enough about the man
who seemed to have no past nor any plans for anything
beyond the next moment. And he'd learned enough to
know that above all others, Rachel trusted this man. If
Phoenix did not like the transaction in question, then
Rachel would most likely walk away.

Smiling slightly, Luc gazed back at him, unflinching,
careful to keep all expression from his face. "Any questions?" he asked.

"They are Rachel's to ask," Phoenix said.

Setting down her fork, Rachel again lowered her
hands to her lap. "It seems that I will benefit from these
terms more than you. Compared to this, I have little to
offer."

Luc knew then that he was doing the right thing. That
Rachel was the right woman. Few others he had known
would choose honesty and fairness over the opportunity
for exploitation. He arched a brow at her. ''On the contrary, Miss Parrish, I admire your resourcefulness and I
am fully prepared to take advantage of it.''

''I now pronounce you man and wife.'' The justice of
the peace counted the money Luc handed over to him
nodded, and walked away.

Luc stood beside Rachel, admiring her composure and
straight-backed dignity in the face of the disdain the justice barely managed to conceal. Still, with Phoenix
flanking her on one side and Luc on the other, the man
exercised enough discretion to protect himself from their
combined wrath should he overstep the bounds of courtesy.

For the sake of appearances, Luc leaned over Rachel
and kissed each corner of her mouth, gently, reverently
It was a provocative mouth, though unresponsive and
cool. He couldn't help but wonder what it would be like
to experience her response, to feel her passion, and for
the briefest moment was tempted to tell her the truth of
his deception and ask her to stay with him.

She would make a most exceptional countess.

But he knew it could not be. A woman like her deserved so much more than a title and a husband whose
desires were trapped inside his mind by an impassive
body. In spite of her containment, or perhaps because of
it, Luc sensed that she needed a man of passion and
ambition to remind her that there was more to life than
mere survival. A man like Henry, who had forgotten
how to need anything at all.

Rachel Parrish Ashford was a woman worth wanting

Luc remained where he was, allowing Rachel privacy
as she walked outside with her noble protector to bid

him farewell. After they had concluded their initial meeting the night before, Phoenix had announced his intention to ride back to Rachel's home to oversee the spring planting.

It was a relief really. If anyone was to see through his impersonation of Henry, it would be Phoenix. Of course Luc had no doubt that Rachel wouldn't be fooled for long once she met Henry. Luc was counting on Rachel's serenity and beauty to fascinate and lure Henry into accepting the marriage. Luc was counting on her good sense and Henry's desperation to keep them both from walking away . . . in separate directions.

He would know soon enough.

Within the hour, he and Rachel would begin the journey to Cheyenne, and within days of their arrival, Henry would appear. He sensed his brother's fury and frustration more keenly every day. He'd planned it all so carefully—the delays to slow Henry's progress, the masquerade and marriage, the persuasions he'd employed to convince Rachel to accompany him back to the civilization that had shunned her. It was ironic really that he, who never gambled unless he could afford to lose, would take such a risk with his brother's future.

But then, to not take the risk was to accept that his brother had no future.

Luc stared down at the marriage papers, his vision blurring until the names seemed to merge: Henry Percival Sinclair Ashford and Rachel Parrish. For better or worse, Henry was married.

The vows were spoken. Henry's fate was sealed.

2

H enry had been in brawls with more refinement than the town of Cheyenne.

Hell on Wheels—the description given to a town where vagabonds and kings rubbed elbows as they fashioned a new realm from the dust of the plains. It was obvious from the shabby buildings, falsely fronted with elegant facades, to the shanties and tent dwellings scattered about, that in the beginning, the citizens had no faith in the immortality of their settlement. A settlement that had been nurtured on the promise of wheels and tracks, but could have easily been removed or left behind if the promise was broken.

He grimaced at the pall of black smoke shrouding the train station. The promise had been honored. Mercantile establishments were being built in a more permanent fashion, and on Carey Avenue, merchant princes and emperors of finance had raised mansions of fine wood and stone. A variety house, from which he could hear the words to a bawdy song, displayed an age-yellowed advertisement for the performance of *Trovatore*. A majestic new opera house occupied one corner, while citizens caroused across the street in saloons, brothels, and a roller-skating rink.

Every man wore at least one revolver and some even sported whips. Lethally sharp knives were tucked into belts, and rifles and shotguns were carried as if they were appendages, grown in answer to the ruthlessness of the environs. And with the arrival of every train, more men with guns and knives stepped down wearing their reputations strapped to their hips as whispers circulated about more hell arriving on the wheels of progress.

Henry tucked a worn leather folder under his arm— the only baggage he had brought with him from England—and watched it all with fascination and morbid curiosity. For the first time in years, he felt excitement and a sense of challenge. Vagabonds and kings and a civilization too new to have its rules engraved in the kind of stone-hard tradition that had bound and gagged him all his life. How ironic that his journey should end in such a place.

Henry stepped around a fresh pile of horse manure and approached the threshold of what was reputed to be an oasis of refinement in the Territory of Wyoming.

More than likely, the description of the Cheyenne Club was as pretentious as the other "civilized" structures he'd seen. It wouldn't surprise him at all if he found livestock drinking from the punch bowl.

He paused inside the entrance to the Cheyenne Club, adjusting to the shock of the hushed atmosphere after the cacophony outside. Standing to one side of what appeared to be the main gathering room, he allowed his eyes to adjust to the softer light and tasteful decor that was a reasonably acceptable facsimile of its British counterparts. The pigs, dogs, and cattle that roamed freely in the streets outside were absent, though some of the illustrious members carried the scent of stockyards on their black-and-white "Hereford" suits. Some wore working clothes and their boots were adorned with spurs that bore no resemblance to those worn in the fashionable circles of English society. Most continued to wear their hats—large-crowned affairs with their wide brims either turned jauntily up on one side or tilted downward over hooded eyes as they sat alone and in small groups playing cards, reading, and discussing business. Geisler champagne, brandy, and Old Tom gin flowed at the snap of callused fingers or the nod of an aristocratic head.

One by one, each head turned toward Henry. The hush became absolute silence as they stared at him, nudged one another with their elbows, or rolled their eyes in his direction. Inevitably, their gazes shot from Henry to a man sitting at one of the tables.

Henry sighed as the combined weight of melancholy and anger that he'd been carrying seemed to drift away on the cloud of cigar smoke the man blew in his direction.

"You're late," Lucien Ashford, the Earl of Fairleigh, said as he glanced up from his cards and arched a brow. Suddenly the others in the room began speaking in low tones to one another as they stole furtive glances at the Ashford brothers.

"Unavoidable since I had no funds with which to travel," Henry said in a deceptively mild voice.

"Yet you are here in spite of your penury." Luc deftly shuffled the cards and spread them out on the table, then flipped one and ran his hand along the row, gathering them up as if they were attached to his palm by a string.

"You knew I would come, Luc." Henry bit out the words, then clamped his mouth shut. He couldn't ignore the other players who sat around the table, their gazes

following Luc's vulgar showmanship as he dealt the
cards, their hearing no doubt tuned to the conversation.
Many things about Luc had changed, but not the inbred
arrogant assumption that the presence of an Ashford rendered all others insignificant. The presence of *two* Ashfords rendered them invisible. But discounting servants
was one thing; addressing private family concerns in
front of strangers quite another. In spite of their dress
and various degrees of breeding, these men sat as equals
with Luc, and they each had an aura of power and success that could not be mistaken.

The earl nodded to his companions and tossed money
into the center of the table. Four men watched the earl's
face for signs that he was bluffing and met his amused
stare. "Gentlemen? At this point in this barbaric game
I believe it is customary to raise, call, or fold."

Henry stood by silently while his brother played out
the hand. At heart, Luc was bourgeois to the core, a
throwback to their distant ancestor who had been, in fact,
a merchant. Those tendencies cropped up from time to
time to embarrass the Ashford family, though one would
have expected it to have been bred out of them by now.

Most of the Ashfords were hopeless wastrels, like
himself.

Luc played out the hand and methodically stacked his
winnings in piles according to denomination. The other
players threw down their cards and, one by one, left the
table.

Henry laid his folder on the table and sat down in one
of the velvet-upholstered chairs. "A creative way to
shore up the family consequence," he said, and mentally
calculated the sum of the coins stacked in front of Luc.
"Impressive. One would think that money was self-
propagating in this . . . *place.*"

Luc's hands stilled as his gaze swept over Henry from
foot to head, before settling on his face, a steady burn

that seemed to sear away all pretense. Though he knew what Luc would see, Henry didn't flinch under his brother's shrewd regard. His clothing was threadbare and soiled, but the cravat was tied just so, the high boots polished to a brilliant shine. His hair hadn't been touched by a barber's scissors in several months, yet it was brushed to perfection. His folder of paper and charcoal and paint was cleaner than he was—a fact Luc had no doubt noticed.

"Good Lord, Henry, you smell. Don't tell me you rode in the cattle car."

Henry gazed at Luc without expression. "*Your* cattle car, to be exact," he said. "I convinced the trainmaster that I was entitled to ride with the rest of the Ashford stock . . . speaking of which—what are your cows doing here?"

"Taking up residence on my new ranch."

"I was afraid of that."

"They are highly profitable, Henry."

"Now there's a civilized concept." Henry shifted impatiently, wishing he had a drink to ease the passage of a request he did not want to make. He hadn't asked anyone, not even Luc, for aid since he was in leading strings. It had always been the other way around. He'd been the stronger one when they were growing up together, the one more able to see things done. The one who took blame and punishment alike for their misdeeds. Because of Luc's poor health he'd had no choice but to be his brother's protector, to aid Luc in the lie that he was fit to hold what was most important to him— the title and responsibilities of Fairleigh. It had been easier to help Luc get what he wanted rather than pursue his own goals. Goals he knew he could not reach.

He swallowed, tasting grit and bitter gall that he was now forced to such a pass.

"A bottle of Red Dog whiskey, I think." Lucien nodded to an attendant stationed discreetly in a corner. Moments later, a bottle and two glasses were placed on the table, the attendant duly ignored as he poured a measure for each man, then shrank back into his corner. "Now, pray tell me how you have come to be in Wyoming with only that folder for luggage."

Swirling the liquid in his glass, Henry lifted it to his nose and sniffed. The congestion caused by dust and stench immediately cleared. "Claremont," he said.

Luc gave an imperceptible start at one of the most influential names in England. "The old duke? Did he lighten your pockets at the races?"

"I killed the heir apparent." Henry tossed down his drink and grimaced at the barely distilled fire that burned into his gullet and recoiled up into his head.

Luc choked on a swallow of whiskey. "Charlie? You *killed* the old man's grandson?"

"A duel, in a manner of speaking."

"In this day and age? Bloody hell."

"Exactly. I am now a wanted man." Henry refilled both glasses. "It's fortunate that my money is tied up with yours or I doubt I'd ever see it again."

"I don't like our family name being linked with criminal activities. Couldn't you have settled your squabble with Charlie some other way?"

"Certainly I could have. I deloped. Charlie didn't. Caught me in the shoulder. I went after him."

Luc sat back in the overstuffed chair and stretched out his long legs. "Well, that explains the abominable ache I had in my shoulder. Who removed the bullet?"

"The ship's surgeon was competent, though rather ham-handed with a knife," Henry said, irritated by Luc's deliberate reminder that their bond extended beyond blood to the spirit itself, a spirit that they shared in times of extreme distress or stimulation.

He emptied his glass. At least he could find comfort in knowing that their shared curse was limited to sensation and emotion. "I've noticed that your cough has been absent for some time now."

"The climate is agreeable. I seem to be quite free of the malady unless I overexert—or indulge in too many of these," Luc said as he stubbed out his cigar.

"And I gather that you have taken up with a lady who has a fondness for lavender?"

Luc started and gave Henry a sharp look. "Wherever did you get that idea?"

"The odor has drifted through my mind at the oddest moments. You must have some feeling for her if I am catching her scent."

"Actually, she is quite extraordinary," Luc said, his expression both wary and bemused. He plucked a fresh cigar from his pocket and rolled it between his fingers as he abruptly diverted the subject to more weighty matters. "Charlie deserved a beating, Henry, but did you have to kill him?"

"I didn't lay a hand on him. He saw me coming and backed away. In his usual lumbering fashion, Charlie tripped over a blade of grass, cracked his head on a tree, and broke his neck."

Lucien sighed as he stared into his glass. "Poor bumbling fool. He fell into a basket of lilies at Lady Morton's ball three seasons ago. Would've made a shambles of the dukedom. Did he leave a widow?"

"With child . . . God knows how he managed without spraining his cock."

"Well, then all is not lost. Pray it's a boy. The duke might forget you in time."

"Not until he's bare bones in the family crypt."

"Then something must be done."

"Ah, you begin to see, Luc." Henry relaxed back in his chair, his anger diluted by bad whiskey and high

hopes that the sudden and hated dependence on his
brother would soon come to an end. It was galling to
beg for what was his. "How long will it take you to get
my money out of England?"

Luc breathed deeply and sighed. "I would ask the
measure of your desperation, but the odor surrounding
you is answer enough."

Henry examined his nails. "Had you received my
wire from New York requesting funds, you would know
the measure of my desperation."

"I received it."

Bile rose in Henry's throat, and he struggled to keep
his voice even, casual. "Then you *knew*."

"Until now I knew little beyond what my steward
included in his message to me—that you were in dire
straits. The wireless is a marvel, but limited in its ca-
pacity for information."

"Tell me, Luc, just when did Hawkins inform you of
my 'dire straits'?"

"Before your ship cleared the Thames."

"I see." There was no way Luc's steward would
know of Henry's activities so quickly unless he was
watching him, as if he were a wayward child incapable
of managing his own affairs. He forced his hands to
maintain their relaxed drape over the arms of the chair,
struggled to keep his voice calm, to control the anger
and sense of betrayal he felt. Never would Henry allow
Luc—or anyone else—to see him bleed. If he had his
way, no one would ever know that he had any blood to
let.

"And still you did nothing, Luc."

"I'm told poverty builds character."

"So, in addition to being the caretaker of my *estate,*
you have now appointed yourself to oversee my moral
evolution. How very noble of you."

Luc smiled, only a slight lift of the corners of his mouth as if sadness weighted down his amusement. "We are not the same for all that we share, Henry. Aside from your years in the army, you have insisted upon squandering your time, your money, and your mind. I won't allow it to continue."

Henry stared at his brother and wondered why he recognized him, why he still looked so familiar when his behavior was decidedly *not* Luc's. "I don't like the sound of that, Luc."

"I don't like administering the affairs of my grown brother. I certainly don't need the additional burden, and I am damn tired of suffering the effects of your misadventures."

"Then it will be my pleasure to relieve you of your burden."

"In due time, Henry. First you must convince me that you are capable of administering your own affairs."

"Conditions, Luc?" The words tasted so old and bitter in Henry's mouth he could barely spit them out. He ground his teeth together to keep from saying more, from believing that the worst had happened and Luc had stepped fully into their father's shoes. How many times had he listened to conditions and demands? How many times had he been forced to compromise with no alternatives?

"Not conditions, but expectations."

Henry's hands clenched over the arms of the chair. "I have no expectations of myself. Why should you?"

"Because, Henry, everyone must have a purpose in life, a goal to work toward."

"I'm rich, Luc. Should I find myself in need of a purpose or goal, I'll purchase one."

"Don't be obtuse, Henry. What do you want from life?"

"What is mine," Henry said with quiet force. "And what do you want from me, Luc? My soul I fear has long since cocked up its toes."

"Then it is time for a resurrection."

"Is that what you're asking for, Luc? My soul?"

"I am asking for your cooperation, and your trust, Henry." Luc smiled grimly, and in that grimness Henry saw the desperation that he would spare his brother at any price.

Even his soul.

He sighed. "You have it, Luc, or I would not be here now." Henry poured himself another draught of whiskey and emptied his glass in one swallow, feeling the fire, feeling it fuel the one that already burned inside him. "But why do I have the feeling that I do not have *your* trust?"

"I trust you with my life." He looked up, meeting Henry's gaze. "I do not, however, trust you with *your* life."

"Is there a difference?" Henry asked bitterly.

"Oh yes, there is a difference. Yours is infinitely more valuable to me."

"Damn it, Luc! It is my life, and how I choose to live it is none of your affair."

"Was it not my affair when I felt the impact of the bullet? Or when I felt your pain and the fire when the 'competent' ship's surgeon cauterized the wound?" Luc pinned him with a stare that had been frozen by generations of Ashford power. "I will not permit you to tease death so ambitiously again, Henry."

"And just what exactly will you *permit*? What tricks must I perform to please the new Earl of Fairleigh?"

"This is a good country, Henry, where a man is not judged so much by his birth or name as by his deeds. Here opportunity is available for anyone who would take it—"

"Ah, so I am to be allowed the opportunity to live down my name?"

Luc smiled fleetingly, and Henry wondered at the irony he saw in Luc's expression. "It is a proud name, Henry, and one that deserves more honor than our father gave it."

"Don't tell me that you are proposing that *I* join you in redeeming the family honor?"

"Not even I would go so far. I am merely proposing an agreement between us—a business transaction if you will." Luc rose and snapped his fingers at the steward awaiting his pleasure. The man nodded as Luc inquired whether the room adjoining his had been readied for Henry's use and ordered a bath.

"What have you done, Luc?"

"In anticipation of your arrival, I have taken the liberty of placing an order with my tailor on your behalf." Pushing back his chair, Luc rose. "We can discuss the steps I've taken to ensure your future while you bathe and change into fresh clothing."

"We will settle matters now."

"Matters are settled, Henry."

Henry heard the conviction in Luc's voice. The earl had control and would not be swayed. The choice Luc spoke of was really no choice at all. "God damn you, Luc."

"You never did have a sporting nature, Henry."

"You want sport, Luc?" Henry picked up the deck of cards and shuffled them. "My estate against the future you envision for me on a single cut of the cards."

"You have gambled enough with your life, Henry." He reached into his pocket and pulled out a packet of documents. "Your fate has already been decided. You will either accept it or you will not. Your choice." He unfolded the papers and set them in front of Henry. "I suggest you read these very carefully and give them due

consideration, for they represent the only opportunity I
am willing to give you.''

Henry glanced at the papers on the table between
them. The top sheet was a yellowed newspaper clip-
ping—an advertisement from the looks of it. The print
was small beneath a bold headline, as if the subscriber
had wanted to attract attention, yet had been reluctant to
make the details any more public than was necessary.
The headline was enough to make his blood run cold.
He lowered his gaze and focused on the fine print:

LANDED HEIRESS SEEKS REFINED HUSBAND
*Respectability, education, strength, resourcefulness,
and a genial nature required. Skills will be appreciated. Send details of qualifications, morals, and family
to Box 3, Fort Fetterman.*

Caught between laughter at such an absurdity and the
fury of knowing Luc would even consider such a thing,
Henry crumpled the paper in his hand and glanced up
at his brother. ''Your sense of humor has failed you,
Luc.''

Luc shook his head and walked away, his steps as he
climbed the stairs firm and controlled, his back straight
and shoulders stiff.

Henry tossed the crumpled paper on top of the others
that he refused to read and stood abruptly, his chair
crashing to the floor behind him. Closing his eyes, he
concentrated hard, trying to feel what Luc felt, but there
was nothing—no pain, no anger, only a void where his
brother had always been. And he knew then that by turning his back on Henry, Luc had made an unspoken vow
that would not be broken.

3

He had to do something about the whore's tongue, Henry thought as he watched her lounge back against the wall, thrust her sagging breasts out at him, and tilt her head while she again licked her lips. That tongue kept popping out, as if she thought the sight of it was the key to a man's arousal, and therefore his patronage. As old as she was, perhaps it was the only part of her body that still provided decent service. Bile rose in his throat and his hand stilled. Whores were the same the world over—all of them showing the depravity of their lives in faces and bodies aged beyond their actual years, worn out from too much use, the skin sagging from increased layers of paint used to hide the marks of their profession. He glanced down at the sketch pad in his lap and studied the drawing he'd been laboring over for the past hour.

He had left the Cheyenne Club, escaping to the worst saloon the city had to offer, a place filled with drunkards and prostitutes, embodiments of the demons that haunted him with images both desperate and the profane. It was a place in which he was content to be a spectator, a chronicler of the ugliness that lurked beneath paint and plaster and false-fronted buildings. There were times when he needed to remember his nightmares, remind himself that he had the choice of being an observer rather than an unwilling participant.

Shooting a quick glance at the whore, he began sketching again. There was no help for it—that tongue was the woman's liveliest feature and would have to be featured prominently in her portrait.

He drained his glass and shuddered. Nasty stuff. Nevertheless, it was the only way to sufficiently blur the edges of the ugliness of his surroundings . . . and his thoughts. He lifted his hand, signaling the bartender to repeat his earlier order. As if he'd met with Prosperity itself, the man moved with alacrity, bringing Henry a fresh glass of whiskey.

"Same as before, sir?"

"Same as before," Henry said without looking up. "A drink for each man and bill it to the Earl of Fairleigh." It was a petty revenge, Henry knew, but he didn't give a bloody damn. All he wanted was his money. Luc could take his high-flown plans for Henry's future and feed them to the derelicts living in tents on the edge of town.

"What are you drawing?"

Henry stiffened. The scent of stale sweat, cheap perfume, and even cheaper sex was so strong he almost gagged. He moved his pencil more quickly over the paper. "Your likeness, madam," he said, distracted by a particular curve of her cheek, the way the bones seemed to be collapsing beneath folds of skin, as if she were disintegrating from the inside out.

"My name's Nellie. You don't have to draw me. You can have the real thing." The whore bent over his shoulder and gasped. "That ain't me."

"No?" Henry glanced up at her and arched his brow. The whore backed away, her eyes wide with horror.

As if she had never interrupted him, Henry returned his attention to the sketch pad. Actually, it was quite good. Especially the tongue. Obviously the woman had no appreciation for the subtleties and interpretations of fine art.

He drained his glass, then closed the custom-made folder containing his pad and chalks and rose. He'd had enough of slumming for one day, and his stomach was protesting the lack of solid food. It was time he sought out one of the finer eating establishments Cheyenne had to offer.

Henry stepped out of the saloon and breathed deeply, cleansing the odor of the whore from his nostrils. The streets had cleared of traffic and the ribbons of sunset color in the western sky were narrowing as the weight of darkness pressed the remaining light toward the horizon.

Suddenly he heard a husky, feminine voice speaking in low, soothing tones. Turning his head, he saw a woman, heavily cloaked for the time of year, kneeling in the alley over what appeared to be a sobbing child. Her clothes were dark but of obviously fine cut and cloth, yet she seemed unperturbed by the dirt and garbage strewn about her. As he watched, she lifted her skirts and tore a ruffle from her petticoat, baring a trim ankle and gracefully curved calf. Her shoes were odd leather-beaded affairs that resembled ballet slippers and her stockings were an opaque, nondescript color favored by serving women and housemaids. It was an odd combination to say the least—a lady's garb layered over the underpinnings of one of common birth and profession. More peculiar still was the simple calico sunbonnet on her head, obscuring her face from view.

Intrigued by the disparate impressions her appearance presented, he stepped into the alley . . . and saw blood-soaked linen piled on the ground next to her. "What the devil?" he said as he crouched down beside her.

A small, grubby boy sat up and stared at Henry through bleary eyes, his knees hugged to his chest, his feet bare, one of them bleeding profusely. The woman didn't look up, but continued to fold the ruffle into a thick pad, which she pressed to the wound.

"He cut it on a piece of broken glass," she said in a low, tranquil voice that stroked and soothed like the whisper of misty rain on summer leaves.

"Is he yours?" Henry asked, wondering at a woman who dressed so well, yet sent her child out into the street shoeless and clothed in filthy rags.

"No, he's not mine," she said, a mixture of sadness and anger in that simple statement.

"My ma works in there." The boy nodded toward the saloon. "I was waiting for her."

"I see." A whore's child, no doubt, Henry thought distastefully. "Do you wait out here for her every night?"

"No. I'm supposed to be home with my sister, but she's gettin' poked by a man tonight."

The woman's head jerked back, as if she'd been struck, yet in the next moment she bent to her task once more.

He had to admire her. Clearly she was a lady, judging from her articulate speech and her shock over the boy's crude comment, yet she maintained her composure in the face of so much blood and filth. No lady of his acquaintance would have stooped to aid a child of the streets, let alone destroyed a good petticoat to sop up his blood. He wished she would look up at him, let him see if there was as much grace and dignity in her countenance as there were in her movements, her voice.

"The cut is deep, and the bleeding won't stop," she said.

"He needs a physician. Is there one in the vicinity?"

"No doctor," the boy begged as he clutched at the woman's arm. "My ma says they're all butchers."

"There's no help for it, boy. That's a nasty gash and must be stitched up," Henry said firmly as he edged a little closer, pulled off his tie, and held it out to the woman. "Secure the pad on his foot with this. I will carry him if you will show me the way."

"My name's Benny, and I ain't goin' to no butcher."

She took the tie and, working quickly, did as Henry asked. "It's all right," she said to Benny. "I will see to it that the doctor takes very good care of you."

"But he'll hurt me."

"No," Henry said. "He'll only hurt your foot and since it's already hurt, you'll hardly notice."

The woman turned to him then, the grateful smile freezing on her lips as she met his gaze. She appeared to be shocked and chagrined at the same time.

"I'm sorry, I didn't realize it was you."

"Have we met?" Henry asked, knowing they hadn't. He would have remembered such a woman. He would have remembered such eyes—wide, and golden brown with a touch of summer in their depths. Never would he have forgotten a face so beautifully molded into high cheekbones and perfectly sculpted mouth and nose, nor the clear, fair skin that glowed with the kiss of the sun, as if she spent much of her time out of doors and her bonnet failed to shield her. In her aspect, he saw all the seasons, and imagined that she had sprung from the earth itself rather than from a mortal woman. He wondered if there were any colors on his palette that could do her justice.

She frowned at his question and her lips parted, but before she could reply, the boy yanked on her sleeve as he stared up at her. Immediately she turned back to him.

"Promise you won't leave me?"

"I promise," she said.

"You, too, mister. You promise, too."

Henry smiled at the boy's tenacity, the way he faced adults without being cowed. "I promise," he said solemnly, and bent to lift the child in his arms. "Madam, if you will kindly lead the way?"

Again the woman flinched, as if something he'd said had somehow hurt or insulted her. She rose to her feet and met his gaze steadily, her frown returning as she studied his features.

"You don't know me," she said, more a statement than a question.

"Not unless our paths crossed in England. I have only just arrived here to meet with my brother." He shifted his hold on the boy and breathed through his mouth to avoid the odor of the gutter clinging to the urchin. "I suggest we make haste to the surgeon's quarters."

She stared a moment longer, then nodded as if she had found the answer she sought. Her gaze dropped to the boy's foot, and she turned quickly, leading Henry down the street. "This way."

"Have our paths crossed?" Henry asked, pursuing the subject, wondering if he had indeed gone mad. The expression on her face when she had first looked up at him had been one of pleased recognition and those remarkable lips of hers had parted in a smile of greeting. How could he have encountered such a woman and not remembered? She was quite extraordinary with her lush countenance and serene manner. Her voice alone was enough to create carnal visions of midnight whispers behind the bedcurtains. He caught a subtle hint of lavender in the air and breathed deeply, trying to capture it more fully. All he smelled was the blood and grime of a whore's child.

"Your name is Ashford?"

"Henry Ashford." The boy's arms snaked around his neck and clung tightly, as if he wanted to remind Henry of his presence . . . and his odor.

"I have . . . met your brother, I think," she said as she adjusted the bandage.

"Ah, yes, Luc, my esteemed twin brother. We are often mistaken for one another. That would explain it." He heard her sigh and adjusted his pace to match hers as she walked more quickly toward a flight of stairs on the side of a two-story building. A crude wooden shingle was tacked to the clapboard siding announcing the office of a Dr. Holloway.

"Yes," she said finally. "That explains a great deal."

Curiously, the woman said no more—curious because women always sighed over Luc before embarking on delicate interrogations into his habits and interests while oblivious to Henry as anything more than a vessel of information. Luc, after all, was an earl. A wealthy, eligible earl. Regardless of their similarities, Henry ran a poor second. Because of their similarities, Henry was viewed as a curiosity rather than a likely candidate for marriage.

Thank God.

The wooden stairs creaked alarmingly as he followed the woman up to the second-story landing and waited for the doctor to answer her knock. She stepped aside as the door swung open.

A man dressed in dark pants and shirtsleeves took one look at the boy's foot and frowned. "Who's paying?"

"I am," the woman said without hesitation.

The doctor's eyebrows rose. "Coming down in the world, are you, girl? Wouldn't have thought you'd—"

"Think what you like, Doctor," she interrupted, "as long as you do so while you stop the bleeding and stitch up the cut."

Before the doctor could reply, Henry shouldered his way into the office and through an open door into the surgery. "I assume you have adequate credentials?" he asked, disliking both the man and his disrespect toward the lady. He walked over to read the framed certificate hanging on the wall.

"Oh, Mr. Ashford. Didn't see you clearly."

"Obviously not," Henry said, amused. Apparently Dr. Holloway knew Luc and mistook him for his brother. "Now that the pleasantries are out of the way, I suggest you put your training to use." He leaned over to set Benny down on the operatory table.

"No. Don't let him stitch me," the boy wailed as he tightened his hold on Henry's neck. "He don't like me."

"Like you or not, he will take good care of your foot. Is that not so, Doctor?"

The doctor snorted. "It's just Nellie's boy. The barber usually patches up his scrapes. I don't take care of whores or their brats."

With casual deliberation, Henry began to remove his gloves and flex his fingers. He'd been in a mood to strike something all day. The doctor would do nicely. "He is a child . . . an innocent human being, *Doctor.*"

The woman stepped forward. "He did not choose his mother, Dr. Holloway. You, on the other hand, did choose your profession." She pulled several coins from her bag and set them on the table next to the boy. "This should be adequate compensation for your skill."

"For that sum," Henry added, "I expect that you will exercise your skill with great care." Waiting until the woman had caressed the boy's cheek and reassured him that they would wait in the next room, Henry took her arm and guided her through the doorway.

"Thank you for your help, sir. I believe I can manage now."

Henry leaned his shoulder against the wall and examined his nails. "Can you carry the boy to his home?"

"I will manage."

"No doubt. But as you are an acquaintance of my brother, I'm afraid I cannot allow you to walk about in the dark, much less to a whore's hovel."

"I'll take him to his mother," she said stubbornly.

"Will she care for him or make him wait for her in the alley?"

Rachel turned her head away, as if she were ashamed of his assessment of Nellie's character.

"I thought not. We can't very well force the boy's mother to come out and take him home. Every prospective customer in the saloon will come down upon us in outrage. I will see him settled in bed after I escort you home."

"But his sister is—"

"Entertaining. I know." He pushed away from the wall and strolled around the office, examining the appointments for dust. "Whores beget whores, it seems, and this poor lad is left to the mercy and whims of others. It will give me great pleasure to rid whatever dwelling the boy calls home of one rutting pig and convince his sister to retire for the night."

She took a step backward, her expression stiff and blank.

The doctor opened the door and nodded. "All done. Now get the brat out of here."

Henry shouldered his way into the surgery. The boy sat on a high table, his face streaked with tears, though Henry had not heard a whimper come from him. He inspected the clean bandage wrapped around the boy's foot, then picked him up and silently carried him out of the office, standing aside at the door to wait for the woman. Looking neither right nor left, she swept past him and paused only when she reached the bottom of the outside stairs.

She smiled at the boy and brushed his hair away from his face. "Now tell us where you live."

"We will see you home first, Miss . . . ?" Henry said.

She ignored his bid for her name. "No, I'll go with you to make sure—"

"You will not. It will not be a fit place for you."

Her smile was an odd, sad little slant in her otherwise serene countenance. "It is not fit for him either, sir. And I want to instruct his sister in the care of his foot."

The boy's gaze swung from one to the other as he followed their argument, his forehead puckering in a frown. "He's right, ma'am. Our shack ain't no fit place for a lady. You let us see ya home first." He stared up at Henry and beamed with pride as Henry nodded with approval.

"It can be our secret, Benny," she said, her face hidden within the shadows of her bonnet.

Henry could only imagine the tender smile he heard in her voice as she again brushed the hair away from the boy's forehead. It irritated him to have that extraordinary face hidden from him, to know she was smiling and he could not see it. He shifted impatiently and chased the whimsy from his thoughts. "We will escort you home, madam, unless you have a penchant for making a spectacle of yourself in the street."

Her head jerked up, and her hand fell away from the boy. "Only as much as you have for making an ass of yourself, sir." She delivered the setdown softly, with the serenity that both fascinated and annoyed him.

Before he could reply she turned on her heel and walked away, her cloak billowing behind her as she turned a corner and disappeared from view.

"You didn't have to make her mad," the boy said.

Arching his brows, Henry looked down at Benny. "Do you know of a better method to get a woman out of the way?"

Benny scrunched up his face in thought. "My sister always goes off to pout when I make her mad. I guess all women are alike," he said sagely.

"A lesson you should not forget," Henry said as he stared in the direction she had gone. "Did she perhaps give you her name?"

"Naw. I just called her 'Lady.' "

Lady. Either a title of rank or a description of character. In Henry's experience, the former was seldom deserved and the latter was more often than not a means of separating a well-bred whore from a common one. Yet in this case the woman in question appeared to give definition to the word. In this case, he could almost believe that the word was more than an empty promise made by elegant clothing and cultivated manners—

"You gonna take me home, mister, or are we just gonna stay here an' make a spectacle of ourselves in the street?" Benny said, turning Henry's earlier words to the woman back on him.

Wiping all thoughts of the woman from his mind, Henry stepped off the wooden walk and concentrated on dodging the piles of animal droppings littering the dirt road.

"Shack" was too fine a description of the dirty canvas and rotting wood structure Benny pointed to as they came to the end of a narrow track on the edge of town. As he approached the upright slab of crude planks tied together with rope that served as a door, a man stepped out, still fastening the buttons on the front of his worn Levi's. Henry didn't look at him as he brushed past. His attention was focused on the girl standing just inside the doorway.

Henry handed over the boy in his arms. "Your brother needs attention," he said, wanting nothing more than to put this hole behind him: He lingered instead, making sure that Benny washed and went to bed on reasonably clean linens. And then he made sure that both Benny and his sister understood the details of tending to Benny's foot, drawing an appropriately grisly picture of the consequences if infection should set in. The boy's eyes widened with fear, and his sister muttered something about "not needing no cripple around"; yes, she would see to it that the wound was kept clean. Still, Henry lingered, watching as Benny's eyelids grew heavy, and his scrubbed-pink face softened in sleep, waiting until he was sure the rest was peaceful. He turned back to the sister.

"Does he have nightmares in his sleep?" he asked, not knowing why.

The girl started, then shrugged, her mouth twisted in a bitter smile. "He goes to sleep to get away from the nightmares."

Henry inhaled sharply at the acceptance in her voice—acceptance, he imagined, that waking nightmares were all life had to offer. And as he stared down at Benny, he wondered how long it would be before the nightmares haunted the boy even in sleep.

The girl sidled up to him and slipped a sleeve off her shoulder, baring one breast. "Two bits and I'll show you more, mister. Four bits and you can do whatever you want."

His gorge rose and his blood chilled in his veins. This was the nightmare—the stench of rancid food and stale semen, of discarded hope and decayed lives. He swallowed and held his breath as he turned toward the door, seeing it as if it were at the end of a long tunnel. Gagging, he slammed his open palm against the wood, pushed it open, and stumbled into the darkness.

For hours he wandered the streets and patronized the saloons, seeking forgetfulness in whatever spirits each establishment had to offer. Yet the more he drank, the more vivid the image of a child's blood and tears and the hopelessness that crouched in Benny's future, waiting to claim him. As he always did, he sketched what he saw and what he remembered, putting the nightmares on paper so that they might not linger in his mind.

He left the last saloon and stared down one side of the street and up the other. Shouts were directed at him from what appeared to be a respectable house if one didn't notice the ladies displaying their overblown charms from the upstairs windows. They beckoned to him, their eyes gleaming with avarice, their voices mingling with the bawling of cattle in the stockyards.

He drew a crude sketch of the house and its occupants, then snapped his book shut and walked toward the Cheyenne Club.

He'd had enough of cows and whores.

How could there be two such men?

Rachel paced the breadth and width of the sitting room in her hotel suite, denying her suspicions, reluctant to accept the obvious. Her arm wrapped around her midsection, tightly, as if she were trying to hold herself together. Twins. Henry Ashford and the Earl of Fairleigh were identical twins, exceptional in face and form with their dark hair and deep-blue eyes. How strange it had been to look into the face of the man she had married only to realize that she had never seen him before. It had been difficult to maintain her composure as she'd walked beside him, and even more difficult to remain silent about their connection. She'd wanted time to think before she acted. Except that she was too furious to think.

The man she'd met tonight was Henry Ashford, and he'd only arrived in the territory today. Yet the man with whom she'd exchanged vows two weeks ago had been living in Cheyenne for two years. The similarities between Henry and his brother were uncanny, their differences startling. One was warm and temperate in nature, the other as cold and biting as the Wyoming winter, each man as distinctive as two seasons within the same year.

She had run all the way back to the hotel, too agitated to linger, too horrified that her husband was not the gentle soul she'd thought him to be—that he was not the man with whom she had exchanged vows. That the man she'd met in the alley was her true husband she had little doubt. It explained the urgency with which she'd been coerced into coming to Cheyenne. It explained why her marriage had not been consummated. She took a deep breath and forced herself to sit in a chair by the fire, allow the changing patterns of light and color in the flames to soothe her.

She'd deliberately refrained from giving Henry Ashford her name, reasoning that if she were to participate, however unwillingly, in a game, then she would participate fully. But first, she had to learn its purpose. Only one thing was clear in her mind. Lucien Ashford, Earl of Fairleigh, had married her in his brother's name for reasons that eluded her.

Rachel didn't know whether to laugh or cry. She'd fretted over how the earl would receive her and the odd circumstances of her marriage to his brother. Now, under equally odd circumstances, it remained to be seen how she would receive the earl . . . *and* his brother.

4

It haunted Henry—the slightest scent of lavender wafting through the air, waking him each time he dozed off. The night was at its darkest hour, a time Henry preferred to sleep through, unless he was too far into his cups to notice it. God, he was tired. His muscles ached as if he'd been riding for days, and his mouth felt as if it was stuffed with dry leaves. He groaned as he opened his eyes and stretched muscles cramped from sleeping in a chair. Below, he heard footsteps, hushed voices, someone climbing the stairs.

It was about time Luc put in an appearance. Henry had arrived back at the Cheyenne Club to find that his room was locked and the key denied him on Luc's orders. The steward informed him that he was, however, welcome to await the earl's pleasure in Luc's room. He had ordered a bath only to be told that no expense could be incurred without the earl's permission. Even his new wardrobe was locked away, and he'd been forced to remain in clothing that smelled of blood and back alleys and the dried tears of a child.

With a muttered curse, he stretched his cramped limbs and, in a dozen steps, reached the small cabinet that housed Luc's supply of liquor. It had been a simple matter to rip the door off its hinges to get to the brandy.

A key turned in the lock. Henry grimaced as he heard a cough. Facing the door, he waited with a snifter of brandy in his hand as Luc walked in.

"In a town like this, it is not wise to stand in front of a window, Henry."

"The entire male population is either senseless with drink, sated with women, or shot to pieces by now." Henry held out the glass. "Drink."

Luc accepted the drink as his gaze caught on the broken door of the cabinet and then on Henry. "Good God, have you been shot or stabbed?"

"Neither," Henry said, smiling grimly as Luc instinctively examined his own torso for pain.

"What have you done, Henry?"

"What do you think, Luc? I have been rescuing innocents from the jaws of evil." From the corner of his eye Henry saw Luc riffling through his sketch pad. "Close it, Luc. Now." It angered him to see Luc so casually leafing through all that Henry had left of his life, as if he had the right to deny him even that if he chose. Their father had taken great satisfaction in methodically stripping Henry's soul, leaving him without pride or dignity or purpose. But he had been an innocent child then, believing that fathers were gods. He had been helpless and therefore trusting in a strength and power greater than his.

He would not allow it to happen again.

"You never minded sharing your art with me before."

"Before what, Luc? Before you denied me my own assets? Before I was reduced to breaking and entering?"

Henry nodded at the broken cabinet. "Before you became the Earl of Fairleigh, setting my estates in order and administering justice for my sins?" He stopped short of accusing Luc of severing their filial bonds. He did not want to believe it had gone that far—not yet. It was that last shred of trust in Luc that kept him from yielding to the fury that was a constant pounding in his veins.

Luc stared down at the drawing of the whore in the saloon, then flipped the page to the sketch he had rendered from memory of a street urchin lying in the alley, his clothes and face streaked with grime. Without comment, Luc turned away to sit in one of the chairs that flanked the fireplace, removed an oilskin-wrapped packet from his pocket, and tossed it on the table at his side. "You'll want to look these over."

"I will not answer that advertisement, Luc."

Luc rested his head on the back of the chair, his hands gripping the arms as if he were bracing himself. "But you *have* answered it, Henry. Your wedding occurred two weeks ago." Luc held up a sheet of parchment elaborately bordered in scrollwork.

Henry stared at the document—a marriage certificate with his name scrawled at the bottom. "A prank, Luc?" He and Luc had indulged in many over the years, each more elaborate than the last as they grew older.

"No, not a prank," Luc said. "Arranged marriages have been an honored tradition since the beginning of time. This is no different."

"No different?" Henry spoke softly, repressing his anger, refusing to show that he was affected enough by Luc's actions to feel anger. "Luc, I wasn't there," he said patiently, though he knew . . . *he knew*.

"The minister might not agree. He saw you . . . and that is your signature, is it not?" Luc smiled. "After all these years I haven't lost my touch."

"You've lost your bloody mind!"

"Calm down, Henry. I haven't the energy for it."

"Of course not. Even God had to rest after six days. You've been at it for more than a bloody month." Henry read the certificate again. Her name was Rachel Parrish. Correction: Rachel Ashford. What kind of woman has to advertise for a husband?

"An extraordinary woman, Henry," Luc answered as if he had heard the thought. "A good match, I'd say. The Ashfords need new blood."

Henry tossed the papers onto the table. He felt cold inside, too cold even for anger. "You took the vows, Luc. *You* keep them."

"No, Henry, you will honor all your vows." Luc's voice took on a hard edge Henry recognized. How many times had his father spoken in just such a way, letting Henry know that anything he could say or do would be less than significant?

"I repeat, Luc. I have spoken no vows." Henry waited for the inevitable reminder of the pledge he had made to Luc over fourteen years ago. It had come up from time to time, and more frequently since Luc had assumed the title.

"No, if I remember correctly, you nodded your head. Nonetheless, you promised to do what I could not."

"What you *would* not, you mean."

"You're splitting hairs, Henry. Fairleigh needs an heir. You agreed to provide one."

"Dammit, Luc, I was eighteen and you were dying. I would have said anything to—"

"Exactly," Luc said, raising his head and arching his brows as he looked at Henry.

"You lived, Luc."

"I don't recall that being a condition to your vow."

Henry glanced sharply at Luc, at his broad shoulders and the bronzed flesh on his face that no longer defined only bone. Nothing in Luc's countenance showed evidence of the lung disease that robbed him of breath and threatened his life. For the first time in Henry's memory Luc looked healthy and fit, as if he might live to see his dotage.

"This place has had a miraculous effect on your health. Have your own sons."

"And risk passing on my affliction to an innocent child? No, I will not marry and procreate. You know that, Henry. And I can't remain here forever," Luc said. "One day I must go back to England and its damnable climate."

Again Henry felt the presence of demons hovering over him. Demons of fear and rage and weakness. The hackles rose on Henry's neck at the subtle warning. Grievances were forgotten in that moment as Henry focused on the way Luc stared at him without blinking, his expression intense, apprehensive. It had always been this way—the instant casting aside of all concerns save those centered around Luc. It defied reason and required no explanation. Luc was his connection to life, to the remnants of his own humanity.

"Are you so anxious to die, Luc?"

"Hardly. If I were, I would have done so long ago. I would, however, enjoy the luxury of choosing how I live."

"So you try to force a life I do not choose onto me." Brandy splashed onto the table as Henry filled his glass and drained it. It had always worked before—drowning the demons in whiskey, rendering them useless with his own insensibility. "Let the name die out, Luc. It deserves to die."

"No," Luc said. "It deserves what we can bring to it. You and I, Henry, have the power to right wrongs. We will deserve to feel pride again."

"All that from an arbitrary transfer of seed from one receptacle to another?" Henry said, forcing lightness into his tone and a mocking smile to his expression. An ache began in his neck and his head suddenly felt heavy with the burden of a fraternity he did not want to share. So much bound him and Luc together—their shared past and family tradition, a love and trust that even now he couldn't deny. But now it seemed as much a curse as a blessing.

"As arbitrary as your promise to me, Henry," Luc said with a trace of impatience.

"So you will hold me to a promise capriciously made."

Luc shook his head. "I will hold you to a promise sincerely made."

"No, Luc. Not even for you."

"No, not for me . . . but you will do it for yourself."

Henry snorted as he paced the room, fighting the urge to shout out the old childhood dare of "You can't make me." Fighting it because he knew that Luc had the power to do just that. Betrayal such as he had never felt twisted in his chest and churned in his stomach. He had learned to fight his father. He did not know how to fight Luc. That was the source of his fear—fighting Luc and, perhaps, discovering that he was instead fighting himself.

"Make your threats, Luc, and let's have done with this farce."

"Very well, Henry." Luc rose and walked over to the bed, his voice weary, his footsteps heavy. "Either you accept this marriage or you will be cut off. Your estate will be held in trust until such time as I deem you responsible enough to assume control."

"How do you plan to do that, Luc? I haven't lost my touch either. I can present myself as the Earl of Fairleigh as easily as you wed a complete stranger in my name."

"You can try, Henry. But how do you propose to do that in your present state? Can your wardrobe uphold the masquerade? I have not been idle tonight. You will find that every merchant and shopkeeper in Cheyenne knows of your existence, and your poverty. All my accounts have been settled and closed.''

Luc lowered himself to the side of the bed without his usual grace, and his hands hung limply between his outspread knees as his body jerked with a spate of coughing. Henry might have accused Luc of fakery if he did not feel the suggestion of spasms in his own chest and throat, feel the exhaustion and sense of defeat that drifted over him—sensations like shadows crossing over his own. It was the most insidious of curses, and it was the strongest of bonds.

With the calm of the vanquished, he refreshed Luc's drink and handed it to him. ''You would be tired,'' he muttered, as if he were speaking to himself. ''I can't argue with you when you're tired.''

After sipping his drink, Luc stretched out on the bed. ''Then I am extremely tired, Henry, and not feeling at all well.'' He added a second pillow beneath his head and crossed his feet at the ankles.

Distaste twisted Henry's mouth. ''First Red Dog whiskey and now you occupy the bed with your boots on. I suppose you ride a horse all over the territory rather than taking a carriage. Next, you'll be wearing those Levi's and a red kerchief around your neck.''

''A wagon, actually, and if you'd noticed, most of the men wear a black silk kerchief. It is most effective in keeping the dust out of one's mouth.''

''Good Lord. A wagon and black silk—spurious compromises on gentility to say the least.''

''Practical compromises, Henry. Your bride has a need for supplies, which she was going to purchase at Fort Fetterman. You convinced her that they could be obtained in Cheyenne just as easily. It was a rather long

and difficult journey in which the necessities of survival
outweighs the need for gentility.''

His bride. Survival. The words were a whisper in Henry's mind, an urging that became more insistent with
every echo. Either he stepped willingly into Luc's trap
or fell into another, less hospitable one of his own making. His future had been narrowed down to a choice that
was no choice at all.

''Pray tell me, Luc, where is *my bride*?''

''She is at the Inter Ocean Hotel where you left her
for some much-needed rest. I have arranged for luncheon
to be served in her suite tomorrow so we can all become
acquainted in privacy.''

''How kind of me. Tell me, have I consummated the
union?''

''Of course not. You're much too chivalrous to take
premature liberties with a gentle soul such as Rachel.''

Henry slumped into the nearest chair, then looked at
Luc. ''Just how well do I know this''—he angled his
head to glance at the papers on the table—''this Rachel
Parrish?''

''Ashford. Rachel Ashford,'' Luc corrected him.
''Your interest was piqued when you observed her at a
. . . public event. You inquired as to her identity, and
after finding her two weeks ago, you dined with her at
Fetterman, and married her the next day, then traveled
with her back to Cheyenne. Mr. and Mrs. Henry Ashford
arrived here less than two days ago. Surely you remember?''

Henry closed his eyes and rubbed his temples. ''My
memory fails me, Luc. Pray refresh it.''

''You know her well enough to admire her grace and
carriage and her courage. You also know that she inspires a certain amount of lust—''

''Lust,'' Henry said through gritted teeth. ''For a
woman who advertises and sells herself. You know better, Luc.''

"Exactly what the refined and proper young women of England do to acquire a name."

"And what is she—a farmer's daughter?"

"She is, as the advertisement states, a landed heiress, an orphan who is surprisingly well spoken," Luc said as he closed his eyes. "Her clothing is refined and she smells—"

"Like lavender," Henry said without realizing it.

His eyes opened again and Luc turned his head to stare at Henry, a calm, searching stare that held no surprise at the observation. "Yes, like lavender. You have no misgivings about presenting her to your brother for whom you hold some affection."

"A weakness I will strive to eliminate," Henry said, knowing that his best efforts would not be good enough. Luc had always been his weakness . . . and his strength. He'd never been able to find a way to separate the two.

Picking up the papers, Henry crushed them in his fist, as if he could crush their significance. Control was slipping away from him. He didn't care. This was Luc, who knew him so well, who had seen him lose control before. Luc, who had betrayed his trust, and arranged Henry's life to suit his own purposes.

He heard it then, the soft thud of Luc's glass falling onto the floor, accompanied by the wheezing snore that spoke eloquently of weariness and tension and Luc's tenuous hold on mortality. Henry stared at the remaining swallow of liquor in his own snifter, comparing the changing patterns of light and color to the vagaries of fate. Holding the glass high in salute, he muttered a toast to the silence and the darkness.

"To the brothers Ashford, separated yet inseparable, two shadows for one soul."

He set the glass down on the table without drinking and straightened out the documents Luc was so determined that he read. The night was almost spent and his eyes were blurred from too much drink and too little rest.

And as dawn crept between the panels of velvet draping the windows in thin sheets of light, Henry sat sprawled in the chair, his head against the back, his gaze blindly fixed on the last embers of the fire in the grate. The documents lay scattered on the floor around Henry's feet where he'd dropped them after reading just enough to understand that he was "hog-tied and branded," as they said in this primitive wasteland. He tossed the marriage certificate onto the pile. Luc had thought of everything: an allowance for the five-year term of the contract with Rachel Parrish, the release of his inheritance upon completion of the term, a temporary home in a place called the Big Horn Basin, and the comfort of an unfamiliar but willing wife in his bed.

He had no money of his own, no future beyond that outlined by Luc, no choice but to comply in all things. No negotiation, no alternatives.

For the moment.

The first gunshot of the day echoed from the fringes of town. Life began early on the frontier and ended late, as if its inhabitants knew that their time might end without warning.

Luc awakened as he always did—quickly and completely—and left the bed, his boots still on his feet and his clothes wrinkled. He grimaced as he stripped off his shirt and poured water from a pitcher. "Ring for service, will you, Henry?"

"Your wish is my command," Henry said mildly, and rose from the chair to pull the bell rope, his movements slow and calculated, his manner cavalier.

"Yes, it is," Luc said without pausing from soaping his face.

"Be careful what you wish for, Luc. It might come back to haunt you."

"Have done, Henry," Luc said gruffly. "If you choose to hate me, then do so in silence."

Jamming his hands into his pockets, Henry turned away. Hate. The word hung between them in the room, a curse that had plagued the family for most of Henry's life. He waited for it to surface, to claim and hold him within deadly claws. But all he felt was sadness creeping over him, into him, a sense of isolation and . . . nonexistence. Hate? It would be easier to hate Luc, but even now, he couldn't seem to get the hang of it. To hate Luc would also mean the destruction of all that was right in the world. The best he could do was hate Luc's actions and the goodness in him that made Henry feel like a mere shadow in comparison.

"I had no choice, Henry."

Henry heard his voice as if it came from another place, another being. "You could have given me what is rightfully mine. Mine, Luc. I bled enough for it."

Dropping his razor into the basin of soapy water, Luc picked up a length of fine linen and wiped his face clean of shaving soap. "You bled too much, Henry. You have forgotten how to live."

"Well, I'll certainly remember that I have been consigned to the Ashford stable of breeding stock."

"If you had read the documents, Henry, you would have seen that it is only for five years—more only if you wish it to be. You can bloody well go hang after that if you wish. Until then, you will live quietly in the country and provide Fairleigh with an heir."

"I see." Once again Henry was in control, his body chilled by the familiar sensation of being only half alive, only half a human being, relentlessly pursued and torn apart piece by piece by the demons that screamed across the plains like the wind and left only dust and emptiness in their wake.

"What do you see, Henry?"

Henry inhaled the fragrance of the stale brandy in his snifter, hoping it would drown the fury that was all the more overpowering in its impotence. "I see . . ." he said softly, musingly, as if he were speaking of a dream too ugly to be given a strong voice. He took a sip, only a sip, because the words on his tongue rendered the drink bitter and acid. "I see that you have made me the whore."

5

Whores beget whores . . .

The words Henry Ashford had spoken had echoed through Rachel's dreams all night. The bitterness she'd heard in his voice and the cold anger she'd seen in his eyes haunted her yet. Now she understood why the earl had requested that she not speak of the past again . . . to anyone. It hadn't been a request at all but a subtle warning. She had taken a husband in good faith, and now she feared that she had made an unspoken vow to live a lie.

Rachel stood at the window and watched two elegantly dressed men stroll from shop to shop. One was her husband, the other an earl, both born to rank and privilege and taught to always expect the best. A prostitute's daughter could hardly be considered the best. She knew too much, had seen too much to be pure in mind as such men expected.

She had thought her new husband extraordinary in the way he had shown her admiration and respect on their journey from Fort Fetterman even though he knew of her background. He'd assured her that her ancestry didn't matter. *Ancestry.* Such an elegant word, she'd thought then, a word that seemed dipped in gold. A word that couldn't possibly apply to a woman who could not trace her lineage beyond a house of pleasure and a grandfather who had disappeared into the wilderness before she'd even been conceived.

The man she had met tonight was harsh on the subject of whores and their children, yet he had taken care of Benny and been solicitous of her safety. It seemed unlikely that Henry Ashford would know who his wife was . . . what she was. How ironic that her ancestry didn't matter to an earl, yet she suspected that it would matter a great deal to his brother . . . that if he knew about her past, he would paint her with the same garish colors that decorated Madam Roz's house.

Rachel gazed down at the hustle and bustle of the street. In the past hour, she'd seen more familiar faces than she cared to think about. Memories were long in the territories and gossip was always squeezed dry before it was forgotten. Laramie and her mother's house might as well be next door.

Why had she agreed to come to Cheyenne where drifters, gunslingers, and even the town drunk received more respect than she? Why hadn't she asked Phoenix to accompany her and her husband to Cheyenne rather than encouraging him to return to the Big Horns?

The two men stood across the street, their hats shading their faces. Both were tall, broad of shoulder, lean of hip, and dressed in the latest European fashion. One appeared relaxed and calm, the other militant, his arms stiff at his sides, his fists clenched.

What was her husband really like? she wondered. Was he as angry and bitter as he'd appeared to be last night? Was he a participant in the scheme that had brought her here, or was he, too, a victim of the earl's intrigue?

Anxiety brought her heart into her throat, increased the dampness of her palms. She shouldn't have done it, shouldn't have stepped so blithely into an arrangement with a stranger. A man she had liked instantly. She should have remembered what her mother had often told her "girls"—that men were usually agreeable when their bellies were full and their passions well satisfied.

The earl had certainly eaten well, having ordered all manner of food prepared for their journey, and his power was unmistakable in the way others hastened to do his bidding. As to the other, her mother had also counseled that there was more than one way to satisfy a man's cock, for it was the pole from which his pride waved, and could be stroked with words and deeds as well as a woman's body.

She'd dared to hope that the man she'd married was easily satisfied with words. It had been a relief when he'd announced that he would not exercise his conjugal rights just yet. Though she had no fear of the act, she thought men's naked bodies to be rather grotesque and doubted she would find pleasure in sweaty gropings and animal grunts. Still, as a result of her own explorations, she knew that the body could feel such pleasure. Since meeting Henry Ashford the night before, she'd had more than one stray thought on the matter. Oddly enough, while his brother's body held no appeal for her, she was fascinated by the way Henry carried himself with a languid swagger that called attention to the fineness of his frame.

It frightened her to think he might give her pleasure, that he might—as the girls had told her—have the power to control the responses of her body.

She stared as the men headed for yet another shop at a leisurely pace, their heads down as they watched for potholes and animal droppings while the less-refined pedestrians sloshed through whatever lay in their paths. A buckboard careened around a corner and passed within a hair's breadth of them, spitting up dust and rocks as it bounced over a hole.

One of the men whirled around, his cane raised, his feet planted firmly apart, as if he had sensed danger and was prepared to meet it. The wagon disappeared from view. The man's stance was arrogant, indignant, and she imagined that in England the hapless driver would have lost his head for such an infraction.

That, of course, had to be Henry—a man who obviously took his pride very seriously.

The men disappeared from view as they entered the hotel. The time for second thoughts had come to an end.

She whirled around as she heard the rap on the door, a soft sound at odds with the sudden pounding of her heart. As she took a step toward the door, she wiped her palms on her skirt, then looked down in horror at the small streak of moisture on the bronze-colored velvet. It struck her then, the reality of what she had done. All that she had wanted and worked for—a respectable husband, and an opportunity for a normal life—had knocked on her door. Yet, now that she had them, she didn't know what to do with them.

She heard the muted sound of feet shifting in the hall, a cough, a murmur of deep, male voices. Meticulously, she adjusted the folds of her skirt and took the remaining steps toward an uncertain future.

Trapped.

The hallway of the Inter Ocean seemed to be getting narrower by the second as Henry stood with Luc outside the door to Rachel's suite. Sounds of patrons coming and going, their laughter and whispers muted behind the closed doors of their rooms seemed both intimate and remote, other lives brushing past him without noticing his existence. He'd always found it comforting—that distance, the sense of unreality it fostered, as if he were the dream, untouched, insensate, unassailable. Now it simply felt like loneliness.

This wasn't happening. He wasn't about to meet the woman whose life had suddenly become an extension of his. Damn it! He had made a career of avoiding extensions of any kind beyond the inanimate objects he considered to be the necessities to good living and self-indulgence.

His life had suddenly become *our* lives. He had come to Luc for help and had been handed responsibility. The idea knotted his stomach. If he were even remotely familiar with the concept, he bloody well wouldn't have needed Luc to pry him out of this mess in the first place.

With a vague awareness, he heard a soft, even voice call out for them to wait a moment.

He'd gladly wait forever.

Luc whispered in his ear, "She is unique, Henry. You will never be bored."

The doorknob turned and the slight sound was a roaring in Henry's ears. All because the heir to the Claremont Duchy was a bumbling popinjay. "If Charlie wasn't already dead, I'd kill him for this," Henry muttered.

The door opened. He turned his head and stared.

The sun streamed in from the window across the sitting room, surrounding her with an aura of light that picked out glints of rich auburn and gold in her light-brown hair. Her eyes were wide, golden brown with a touch of summer in their depths. This time, she wore no bonnet, no cape to conceal graceful curves that were pure in line and symmetry. He *had* smelled lavender in that alley last night.

Bloody hell.

"Mrs. Ashford, I assume?" Luc said, breaking the silence . . . and the spell. "I am Lucien, your brother-in-law."

The chill increased as she stared at one brother, then the other, and stepped back. "Please come in."

Henry sauntered into the sitting room and turned to watch her, his mind captured by the play of light on her dress and in her hair. Her expression was enigmatic as Luc made some comment designed to charm. Luc's expression was bemused as she walked past him without the appropriate simper. It intrigued Henry—her lack of response to his brother, her coolness of manner that chilled slowly from the inside out rather than freezing him in a blatant attitude of displeasure.

She approached Henry and extended her hand in a gesture that would intimidate Queen Victoria herself. "Mr. Ashford. I am Rachel . . . your wife."

Luc stilled, his mouth open as if he would speak if only he knew what to say.

Finding entertainment in Luc's bewilderment, Henry bowed over her hand. "Did you not call your husband by his given name during your journey here?"

"No." She met Luc's gaze. "I addressed your brother as 'Henry.' "

"Ah yes, I remember now. Yesterday you called *me* an ass."

Luc recovered quickly. "I suspect mischief here."

"And what might that be, Luc?" Henry asked.

Rachel strolled toward the settee and spread her skirts around her as she sat down and folded her hands in her lap. "The mischief is yours. Please sit down, sirs, and tell me which of you is my legal husband." She studied Henry and Luc without further comment.

Henry stood still beneath her regard, studying her in turn. She looked young and innocent, yet the wisdom and knowledge in her eyes was ancient as man himself. Her serenity was palpable, touching him, irritating him.

His mother had been serene once.

Sighing, Luc bowed gallantly before Rachel. "I apologize for the deception, Rachel."

"Am I the only one deceived?" she asked.

Ignoring his reluctant admiration for her composure and obvious intelligence, Henry lowered himself into a chair and stretched out his legs in a negligent sprawl. This was Luc's coil; let him straighten it out, if he could.

Luc settled in a chair facing her. "Does it matter? The marriage is legal."

"I believed that my groom felt a certain enthusiasm for the contract. I did not wish to enter into an agreement on anything but equal terms."

"If you're so damned discriminating, why did you advertise for a husband?" Henry asked.

"For reasons that are important to me," she replied. "But I am beginning to wonder if yours are based on a whim."

"My brother is more subject to whimsy than I," Henry shot back.

"Leave me out of this, if you please," Luc said.

Henry snorted. "An admirable sentiment, Luc, but a little late."

"Enough said, Henry."

"I've said precious little on the subject of *my* marriage." Henry crossed his feet at the ankles. "Fortunately, my bride appears to have more scruples about such things than you. Since she has no wish to abide by an unequal arrangement, your schemes are for naught. All that remains is for us to file for an annulment."

"No," Rachel said as she favored him with a direct, challenging glare. "I may not have wished it under such circumstances, but I will honor our contract."

Henry's gaze jerked to Rachel. "Honor, madam? You have upheld my belief that females have no grasp of the concept."

Luc brought his fist down on the upholstered arm of the chair and spoke in a low voice. "Enough, Henry. You chose the course that brought you here, and I, for one, feel that you have arrived at an auspicious destination."

Henry snorted. "A marriage made in hell—auspicious indeed." His gut tightened with the need to fight Luc, but he refused to give in to it. It had all been said last night with the same result. He folded his hands over his midsection and extended his sprawl, knowing it showed disrespect. From beneath lowered eyelids, he watched Rachel. "I take it, *Mrs. Ashford,* that you are willing to live in hell. The question is: What do you gain by doing so?"

He had to admire the way she didn't flinch under attack, the way she paused, as if she were giving the subject due consideration before responding. Luc was right. Rachel was quite unique . . . and thoroughly annoying.

"I gain the protection of your name—"

"Didn't Luc tell you? My name is coupled with scandal."

"I gain," she continued as if he hadn't interrupted her, "five years of your time."

"Ah, sentence has been pronounced. Do I serve at hard labor?"

"And I will have children."

He didn't like the sound of her voice, the soft borders of it as she spoke of children. "*A* child, madam. My brother requires only one. Is that not so, Luc?"

The earl merely nodded.

"Are you aware that, as heir to the title, the child's interests would be in England?" Henry asked.

"The earl has made it clear in the documents that our child will inherit, but will not have to assume responsibility until he reaches his majority. The only conditions are that my . . . our . . . son will be tutored by a man chosen by the earl, that he and I will visit England at least twice, and that he will attend an eastern university."

"The Fairleigh sons have always attended Oxford," Henry said.

"Perhaps it is time for the Fairleigh sons to learn new ways, Henry," Luc said. "There is much to be learned in this country, and my man will see to it that the child has a good understanding of our society."

"And you agreed to this, knowing that your son will someday leave the country?"

"It is customary for a son to pursue his own life when he is of age," Rachel replied.

"Is it?" Henry said musingly. "How extraordinary that I have not been accorded that particular privilege."

She tilted her head slightly, her brow puckered, as if she were sorting her thoughts, drawing conclusions. Her scrutiny unsettled him, and he imagined that he had somehow revealed himself to her, that his functions were being analyzed and catalogued.

"You have been accorded the privilege of a new life, Henry," Luc said. "Consider the agreement with Rachel a deed on that life."

"An agreement which I have not signed, Luc."

"You signed them, Henry," Luc said, a hard edge to his voice.

"As I exchanged marriage vows, Luc? In absentia?"

"Most people are not as discerning as Rachel, and they are easily led to believe what they are told and what they see. You would find it impossible to prove your signature is not authentic."

"I can prove that I was on the train—"

"Perhaps, but not that you didn't sign a proxy." Luc rose and walked to the window. "Did I mention that your signature is on a document stating that you will forfeit all rights to your estates and inheritances should you fail to abide by the terms agreed upon? Everything you own will pass to Rachel's offspring whether you are the sire or not."

Henry waited for rage, despair, any emotion that he knew he should feel under such circumstances . . . such betrayal. Yet he felt nothing but the same defeat and emptiness he'd experienced when in the grip of his father's power over him. An emptiness in which even pain could not breed. He had been stripped of himself before. It was simple enough not to show it, to remain outside of himself until life was once again welcome to him.

Rachel observed the change in Henry, the sloughing away of all expression, and perhaps the emotion behind it. She'd seen it before, in the girls who used blessed numbness to make the unthinkable more bearable. She had done it herself in those early years of being hidden in the attic before the locked door and deep shadows became a haven rather than a prison.

Somehow, she didn't think that Henry had been so fortunate in finding substance in the darkness. His blankness was too complete, his voice too flat and cold.

Henry leaned his head back and closed his eyes. "Then it is settled," he said in the same tone he might use when choosing a suit of clothes. "You have won."

The earl inhaled sharply as his gaze shot to Henry. His mouth tightened as if he were fighting pain. "The matter has been settled for some time, Henry. The marriage stands." He cleared his throat and dipped a hand into his pocket to retrieve a package as he took a seat beside Rachel on the settee. "I beg your forgiveness, Rachel, for my trickery. I hope that this will convince you that I had the best of intentions in my plotting." He held out a lacquered box inlaid with ivory and jade. "This belonged to our mother and though it came to me upon her death, I believe she would be pleased that it will be worn by Henry's bride."

Henry's eyes opened then and he watched them from beneath his lashes, his face still devoid of expression but for a slight tilt to a corner of his mouth.

She focused her gaze on the box, unable to face the man who had been tricked into accepting her as his wife. Luc may have been the perpetrator, but she'd become a willing accomplice the moment she'd insisted that he honor the contracts even though Henry hadn't been the one to sign the marriage certificate. That she had done so knowing that he was not aware of her past compounded her guilt and her apprehension. She had no doubt that he was not a man to forgive easily—much less forget—either her part in his brother's plot or the truth of her origins should he discover it.

A large, strong hand took hers and pressed it for a moment, and she felt the cool surface of the ornate box that had the look of age and tradition. Just then the only gift she was conscious of was that of the earl's reassurance and warmth.

"Won't you open it, Rachel?" Luc said softly.

Mechanically, her fingers worked the clasp on the box and flipped open the hinged lid. "Hinges are such a luxury. I seldom see them," she babbled as she kept her attention fixed on the small gold rectangles that held the box together.

"There you have it, Luc. I told you jewelry was mundane. You could have made her happy with a few pieces of hardware," Henry said with sarcasm.

"Enough of your skewed wit, Henry. Your bride is a woman of rare refinement and grace. These particular pieces shall suit her well," Luc said pointedly.

Refinement and grace. Rare. Those words cleared her mind of anxiety and gave Rachel the impression that his remarks were directed at her rather than Henry, as if he knew what troubled her and sought to allay her apprehension.

"Jewelry?" she asked, looking at the contents of the box for the first time. Five strands of creamy pearls lay in a circle on a bed of black velvet, and in the center of the choker an oval ruby was surrounded by diamonds. She'd seen pearls before, paste beads draped around the necks and in the hair of her mother's girls—beads whose coating of gloss chipped off to reveal something else. But these . . .

Her hand shook as she traced the slightly irregular surface of the pearls. There was a richness to their ivory color, a depth to their luster that denied the presence of paint and manufactured origin. Hesitantly she raised her gaze to Luc's. "They're beautiful. I didn't expect . . ." She shook her head.

"What did you expect, Mrs. Ashford," Henry said, maintaining his bored tone, "paste beads?"

The question stung. His attitude rankled. "I expected nothing, *Mr. Ashford,* but a simple business arrangement. The circumstances hardly warrant such a gift."

"The circumstances," Henry replied bitingly, "are neither here nor there. You are an Ashford bride and as such entitled to all the *necessary accouterments*"—he nodded toward Luc, mocking his brother's earlier statement—"of a lady."

"From what I have seen," Luc said evenly, "Rachel needs no accouterments to prove that she is a lady."

The box slipped from her grasp and tumbled onto her lap, spilling the pearl choker into the folds of her dress. "I do not need them, sir, nor will I accept a family heirloom."

"You were not to take my remark seriously," Luc said, amused. "You may not need jewels, but you are entitled to them."

"Perhaps she would prefer another hundred prime Herefords and a good bull," Henry said.

Rachel dipped her head as she retrieved the necklace from the folds of her skirt and arranged it in the box.

"Forget the bull, Luc. She has already acquired two . . . with pedigrees."

Rachel held the box, her fingers clenched tightly around it as she struggled to hold on to her composure, to control the chill that shivered through her at Henry's implication.

Sighing with exaggerated patience, the earl took the box from her and pulled a tiny gold chain that lifted the false bottom to reveal another velvet-cushioned layer.

Rachel caught her breath at the exquisite ring set into a hollow of the velvet bed. The band was rich gold, burnished by time and fashioned into a cutwork lace pattern so fine and intricate, she wondered at the skill of hands and brilliance of mind that could create such delicate beauty. And worked into the design were small rubies and diamonds that, oddly, made her think of teardrops and blood—

"Our mother's wedding ring," Luc said softly.

"How appropriate," Henry said. "It marked her bondage and now my own."

Rachel lowered the false bottom and closed the lid of the box, then held it out to Luc. Henry snorted. "Take the damn jewels, Rachel. Luc wants you to have them."

Imitating the earl's earlier actions, she placed the box in his hand and closed his fingers over the top, then glanced at Henry. "That's the point, isn't it, Mr. Ashford? The jewels belong to your brother and so does the sentiment." She smiled at the earl. "I thank you for both, sir, but I cannot accept them."

With a bemused smile, Luc slipped the box back into his pocket. "Will you at least call me Luc?"

"Yes," she said simply.

A sharp rap on the door preceded an impatient voice. "Grub!"

"Charming. Does that mean beans and bacon?" Henry said as he finally opened his eyes and raised his head.

"The food here is excellent," Luc replied as he opened the door.

As Luc ushered the waiter in and directed the placement of dishes, Rachel watched the brothers, noted the identical deep-brown shade in their hair, the same dark blue of their eyes, the matching perfection of their well-defined mouths, lean cheeks, and straight noses. For all his negligent demeanor, Henry was stiff and impatient, with that mocking twist to his mouth and grim look in his eyes, while his twin seemed to have a perpetual twinkle in his eyes, an ease of movement that displayed the comfort he felt in his own skin.

She imagined that she was looking at two sides of the same man, one bright, the other dark. Yet, in spite of his anger and acerbic manner, she saw something in him that was familiar. It was his distance, the quality of separation, as if he had concealed himself in the darkness . . . as she had been concealed in the attic at Madam Roz's, away from danger, yet knowing the threat was always there, in the light.

She had escaped by indulging in dreams that lured her with the promise of a different life in a place where she belonged. And by candlelight, she prepared for that future by reviewing all that she learned during the day from the other girls, by teaching herself how to live in the outside world.

She wondered if her husband had dreams—if he could see them in the darkness of his mind.

His gaze raked over her then, his eyes like emeralds in dim light. She forced herself to remain still, to stare back at him without blinking. She'd met Indians and a mountain cat in the same way, knowing that a single blink could blind one to sudden attack. She'd made peace with the Indians and she'd been forced to shoot the cat.

She had the feeling that Henry Ashford knew nothing of peace.

6

Silence . . . another form of darkness where the shadow of unspoken thoughts gathered to taunt and torment, offering Henry no peace.

He was alone with Rachel . . . his wife.

He'd been vaguely aware of Luc explaining that he must go to what passed for a wine cellar to choose a more amiable vintage. It had been easy to concentrate on his hunger with Luc and the servant speaking in the background, with teasing odors of food wafting through the air as Luc lifted covers to inspect each dish. But now the plates were covered again and the scent of lavender drifted about him in vaporous tendrils drawing his attention to the woman sitting across from him, sharpening the curiosity he wished to deny.

He wanted to turn from her, but she would not release him from her calm regard that held him trapped like an animal blinded by light. And so he continued to watch her, matching her stillness, her unblinking stare. He fo-

cused on her fingers laced together in her lap, as if she
held his fate beneath the dome of her hands, warming it
so that it could be molded more easily to suit her purpose. He saw it then, a ring on the fourth finger of her
left hand, a plain, wide band that was already losing the
gold leaf that covered cheap tin.

For that she had forsaken rubies and diamonds.

"You refused the ring. Why?" he asked, surprising
himself with the sound of his voice.

Her gaze lowered, following the path of his. "Because
it was offered by the wrong man."

"Sentiment, Mrs. Ashford? I would not have thought
it of you."

"Some things, I suppose, deserve sentiment, though I
didn't know I was capable of recognizing them."

It was a simple admission, yet from her, it revealed
far more than she perhaps intended, implying an emptiness to her life that even he had not experienced. When
Luc offered the ring, Henry had felt rage that his brother
could so blaspheme their mother's memory. The ring
had meant a great deal to her, as had the choker given
to her by their father as a betrothal gift. She had loved
the man beyond reason, and sacrificed her sanity to preserve the memories of that love. She had lived with her
illusions and taken her dreams to the grave with a
twisted smile on her face. The ring was, for Henry, a
valuable reminder of both the good and evil of his childhood.

Still, he felt Rachel's gaze, the probing intensity of it,
as if she searched for answers in his countenance that
he would not voice. "Unique," Luc had said of her, and
Henry realized the truth of it. "Comely," Luc had said,
and Henry recognized Luc's talent for understatement.
The stirring in his groin spoke of lust—a condition he
could deal with one way or another. But the stirring of
his curiosity unsettled him. There was only one way to

satisfy that. Again, the sound of his voice caught him unawares, echoing in his mind as if it came from somewhere outside the barriers of his control.

"You stare at me. What do you, see, madam?"

Her reply was long in coming and her stare wavered, as if she were reluctant to answer, as if the truth might be too horrible to utter. "I see nothing."

Nothing. In her expression he saw recognition, acceptance, and oddly, he saw understanding. The concept chilled him, and he wondered if he had hidden his soul so well that he was lost even to himself.

"*Nothing* is exactly what you have, Mrs. Ashford," he said with forced amusement. "You sell yourself cheaply."

She inhaled sharply, yet her hands remained folded in her lap. "I have neither bought you nor sold myself, sir. We have a bargain only—five years to ensure a future for each of us."

"Then we will both have nothing. There is only the present, which is often a continuation of the past." His eyes narrowed on her as color drained from her face and she clenched her hands. Tiny flakes of gold drifted onto her skirt from the scrape of her fingernails on the ring. "Tell me: What will you do in five years time when you become a woman with a past? Surely desertion and divorce by one's husband is not socially acceptable even here."

"Good God, Henry, speaking of divorce before we have toasted the marriage?" Luc said as he walked into the sitting room, a bottle of wine in his hand. His tone was light as silk, but Henry recognized the steel beneath. "I am famished. Do you suppose we could dine *en famille* without throwing our food at one another?"

"Do people do that?" Rachel asked as she accepted Luc's hand and rose from the settee.

"It has merit," Luc said in all seriousness, "and causes less damage than words." He led Rachel to the table and sat her with a flourish. "Shall we dine, Henry?"

"By all means," Henry said as he strolled to the table. "Feed your prize bull, so that he can perform properly." He took the only chair left—across from Rachel, where he could view and be viewed without hindrance.

It reminded him of home and times past when he had suffered through a meal served with liberal doses of condemnation and rejection. He'd learned early to carry on, to concentrate on the different flavors crossing his palate rather than the poison served up by his parents.

He glanced down at his plate and back up again at Rachel. She stared down at the damask cloth without moving. He and Luc waited while aromas of expertly prepared blue-wing duck rose on diminishing puffs of steam.

Henry shifted in his chair, cleared his throat, inhaled deeply to capture something of the meal that would soon be inedible.

"The gown becomes you, Rachel," Luc said in an oddly hearty manner as he annoyingly drummed his fingers on a fork.

Rachel's head jerked up and her hand raised to her throat. "Thank you."

The tapping became louder.

Wondering when Luc had developed such an irritating habit, Henry again cleared his throat. "Shall we begin?"

"Yes, we await your pleasure, Rachel," Luc said softly as he rudely picked up his fork.

Her gaze followed his movement, then lowered to her own cutlery. Her hand hovered over the selection of forks and chose one.

Henry sighed in relief.

Twice more Rachel watched Luc before picking up a utensil or goblet. She ate carefully, taking bites so small she would starve to death before dessert. For some reason, Luc matched her pace.

Good lord. She didn't know which utensil to use for each dish, and Luc was silently and obviously coaching her.

Shouts erupted in the street below, then died to a deafening, expectant silence. Henry stopped eating and cocked his head. Rachel and Luc seemed oblivious to the palpable atmosphere of danger as they continued their painfully slow progress through a meal grown cold.

Gunfire cracked through the air—one shot, two, then more shouts, a few cheers, and the bleat of a stray pig wandering through the town.

Henry laid down his knife and sighed. "I've had quite enough of this." He pushed up from his chair and closed the distance between them in two impatient strides. He leaned over her, taking her hands, guiding them none too gently from one utensil to another. "This is for soup, and this is for the main course. You use the knife for cutting and to coax food onto the fork . . . like this." He felt the chill in her hands, the sudden tremble beneath his fingers, as a strand of her hair brushed his jaw. He released her hands and straightened. "Forget the rest of the cutlery. I have no wish to still be eating this duck at breakfast."

"Your rudeness is unwarranted, Henry."

"It's kinder than starvation," Henry shot back as he sat down and cut into his meat.

Rachel's fork clattered onto the table. She looked up to meet Henry's gaze. "Thank you for pointing out the differences between pretension and good manners."

A small smile on his face, Luc sat back in his chair and twirled the stem of his glass in his hand.

Henry raised his drink and saluted his brother. "I congratulate you, Luc. You chose me a wife whose quick wit exceeds yours and mine put together." Without volition, his gaze skimmed over her form, her face, the dignity of her. Her mouth was exquisite. Her body was exquisite. It tickled his fancy to think that the woman might match her various parts.

Curiosity had gotten him into trouble before.

"Why, exactly, *did* you choose me?" Rachel asked, her hands clenched into fists on either side of her plate.

"Because your quick wit exceeds Henry's and mine put together," Luc said blandly. "I even believe that, if you had not met Henry last night, you would still have caught on to the deception very quickly." He looked up from his study of his glass then. "There are few who see the differences between us."

Rachel nodded. "You look the same, yet not."

"I'm fascinated," Henry said with sarcasm. "Do go on. There has not been a day in our thirty-two years that we've been so easily distinguished from one another."

"Until we open our mouths," Luc muttered.

"Yes, among other things." Rachel met Henry's gaze head on, held it, then did the same to Luc. "The earl's smile is a gift, while yours is a weapon. And his hair is a bit unruly, growing its own way. Yours is smooth, as if it has been ruthlessly tamed."

Henry stiffened.

The faint lines that radiated from the outer corners of Luc's eyes deepened with amusement. "I believe that sums it up. And in spite of Henry's pretensions and affectations, you are still willing to keep him?"

"I will keep him," she said gravely. "I haven't the time nor the will to resubmit my advertisement."

"Heaven forbid," Luc said. "God knows whom or what you might end up with. Henry at least is a known quantity."

"I don't know him. I know *you*," she pointed out reasonably.

"I would gracefully retire to my room while you discuss my virtues, but alas, I have no room," Henry said, his voice tipped with acid.

"You have already displayed a great many airs, Henry. Do tell your bride of the graces you possess."

"I am a man, clean and free of disease. Did you require more?"

"Do you have skills?" she asked.

"Madam, I am not applying for a position either as husband or hireling. I don't give a bloody rip whether or not I meet your standards." He leaned back, tipping his chair on two legs. "On the other hand, if you insist on *'keeping me,'* then keep me you shall. I have no money, no home, and no prospects for the future. As for skills, I can paint the broad side of a barn, and I can copulate. If you desire more than that, I will prove quite useless."

Rachel flushed as her gaze skittered away. "And the agreement?"

Luc's sudden preoccupation with checking the contents of the wine bottles alerted Henry. "Which one?" he asked suspiciously.

"You saw the papers, Henry."

"Which one, Luc?"

"The property agreement," Rachel said.

"The *what*?"

"It's quite ingenious, Henry. And fair under the circumstances," Luc said. "I read it thoroughly."

"Fair to whom? Just what part of my soul did *you* sign over to *my* wife?"

"Nothing, Henry. You retain your property and Rachel remains in control of hers. If you should part, neither of you can make a claim against the other."

"And what of joint property?" Henry's voice was as low and dangerous as he felt. These two people had discussed and portioned out what there was of his life and decided his future with impunity.

"It is Rachel's belief that should you extricate yourself from the arrangement, it will be within a short period of time. In that case, your contribution to her plans will still be negligible. I agreed. In any case, her life is here and she will be the one to remain, assuming all the responsibilities."

"Negligible. I see. Thank you, Luc, for seeing to my interests."

"I acted in good faith, Henry."

"Yes, well then, I suppose I can do no less than accept in good faith, especially since I have nothing better to do for the next five years." Henry pinned Rachel with a bitter stare. "Tell me, madam, will you place another advertisement in the newspapers if I should take my leave before the term has expired?"

"No. I will have what I want by then."

"Which is . . . ?"

"The res . . . the protection of a man's name." She smiled, the first he'd seen from her, and it was stiff, as if she had little use—or reason—for such an expression. "And if you should leave before our contract is completed, I won't have to suffer the social disgrace of being a divorced woman."

"You really should have read the documents before you signed them, Henry," Luc said with an aggrieved sigh. "If you leave Rachel precipitously, then you must leave the continent. It will be assumed that you died under any number of circumstances common to this country, and Rachel will be a very respectable widow with an equally respectable inheritance."

"I see." Pushing away from the table, Henry stood and looked down on Luc and Rachel. "Since you, *Mrs.*

Ashford, are interested only in my name, I take it that the man himself is free to find diversion at the Cheyenne Club?'' He strode across the parlor and picked up his cane and hat. At the door, he paused, then spoke over his shoulder. ''Luc, it would be wise of you to be gone by the time I return.''

''When will that be, Henry?''

''When I have imbibed enough Red Dog to fool myself into believing I am more of a man and less of a bull.''

''Henry, you're being a boor.''

''What else would I be, Luc?'' Touching the head of his cane to the brim of his hat, Henry saluted Rachel. ''I trust you and my name will find a way to pass the time.''

''I handled that very badly,'' Luc said as the door closed softly behind Henry. ''I have never had a taste for directing the lives of others.''

''Then why have you done so now?'' Rachel asked, knowing that she was just as guilty as the earl.

Luc sighed. ''Because he can't outrun himself anymore, Rachel. It is time for him to stop and rest. Unfortunately, he is determined to run for a while longer.''

''Why does he run?'' she asked.

''Why do you hide, Rachel?''

''I . . . my past—''

''His past has not been a kind one either,'' Luc said gently. ''I had hoped that small bit of common ground might be enough with which to go on.''

''I don't care about his past.'' She stared at nothing. ''Will he care about mine?''

''He doesn't have to know. It has nothing to do with you now or in the future.''

She wanted to believe him, wanted to dismiss her fears as easily as Lucien dismissed the truth. What did it matter, anyway? She had become a willing accomplice in the earl's scheme, knowing that Henry would hate her for it. She'd been relieved to learn that Henry was her husband and not Luc. Henry was not a man for closeness and tender feelings. He was a man whom it would be impossible to love. A man to whom it would be easy enough to say good-bye.

"He said he would return," she said.

"Yes, and that gives me hope for him. On the other hand, I know that being in Cheyenne is not comfortable for you. If you choose to wait for him in your own surroundings, I will be happy to escort you home."

Rachel swallowed. "No, thank you. I will stay here."

Leaning over, Luc kissed her brow. "You know a great deal more about patience than Henry, Rachel."

Her breath shuddered as she looked up at Luc. "No. All I know about is buying and selling flesh. It seems that I am no better than the men who frequent my mother's house."

7

➤➤●◖◗●◄◄

Patience. Rachel had always had it in abundance: as she spent evenings and nights locked in her attic room, listening to the comings and goings of the best and worst of society, as she fetched and ran for the women under her mother's roof and fought down the nausea caused by what she saw and heard. And as she grew older, she forced herself to be calm, to tuck her mind deeply within herself to escape the sounds of drunken men pounding on her locked door and her mother or one of the other girls offering themselves in her place.

Until now, she would have said that she knew a great deal about patience as well as hiding behind locked doors. But after waiting for three days and failing to elude her own thoughts, she was ready to brave anything, including a stroll down the main street of Cheyenne.

Including her husband.

The earl had been more than kind to her since Henry had walked out. So kind that she had begun to feel uncomfortable in his presence and urged him to resume his own life. No one had taught her how to deal with kindness, and she couldn't imagine that the earl's behavior might be inspired by anything but pity. She'd had enough of that from the decent ladies who had offered her their daughters' outgrown clothing, while taking the utmost care not to touch her.

As she paced the parlor floor, her robe fell open to reveal a simple muslin nightdress, yellowed with age and thin from many washings. A single lamp burned on the table behind her, casting a glow over the luxuriously furnished room. She cursed the life that had made her into a night creature, and she cursed Henry Ashford for being able to walk freely among others without censure, seeking his pleasure while she awaited his. A shiver halted her progress, held her rooted to the floor.

His pleasure.

She'd thought she was ready for this, ready to meet a husband's needs. It wasn't as if she didn't know the mechanics of it. It wasn't as if she feared it. She knew that pleasure could be found in the act. She knew that even if pleasure did not come, the worst that a man who had any sensibility at all would give her was indifference.

She was very good at cultivating indifference. It was the safest way to be.

Footsteps shuffled down the hall. A deep voice cursed as metallic scraping sounded outside her door. Instinctively she ran to the desk, opened the drawer, and pulled out the gun she kept there. She didn't have time to panic before the door swung wide and a man's tall form filled the doorway.

She lifted the gun, held it steady with both hands, pointed it at the intruder.

He lifted his cane and used it to push his hat back on his head. With slow, stalking steps, he entered the room and kicked the door shut behind him. "I see that you are angry beyond words, Mrs. Ashford," he said, his tone insolent, the words slurred. "I suspect that all young girls are taught the fine art of accusing silence at their mothers' knees."

Releasing her breath, she lowered the gun.

"Very wise, darling. In view of our agreement, you stand to gain a great deal more from me if I remain alive."

"Neither one of us will gain anything at all if things continue as they are," she whispered.

"A veritable fountain of wisdom. No doubt my brother has hopes that some of it will be absorbed by my thick skin."

Rachel returned the gun to the drawer and stood with her back to him, saying nothing, not knowing what to say.

He took another step into the room. "What? No words of recrimination for my debauched ways? Didn't your mother teach you how to nag along with her lessons on accusing silences?"

She heard his footsteps and braced herself for the odor of whiskey, the drunken gropings. Moments passed . . . a minute. She turned slowly saw that he had sprawled on the settee. In the dim light, she saw his gaze narrowed on her in speculation. Belatedly, she realized that she had bunched a handful of fabric in her hand. As she relaxed her fingers, the muslin fell back into place, wrinkled and damp from her anxiety.

"Do I frighten you, Rachel?" he asked.

"No," she lied. Here and now, without the presence of an injured child to divert him or his brother to temper him, he did frighten her.

"Well, that certainly makes it easier. Fear would be an unwelcome third in a marriage bed."

Her body jerked and her hand found another clump of muslin to mangle.

"Rachel," he said with forced patience. "You are, according to the marriage papers, twenty-four. Surely you know something about a husband's expectations."

"Yes."

"Ah. She knows how to say 'yes.' There is hope."

Rachel gathered her courage as she mentally reviewed the speech she had rehearsed. "I am aware of a husband's expectations, and a wife's duty to meet them. The agreement states that I will do so without protest, whenever you wish. I do not expect something for nothing, Mr. Ashford."

"Really? How strange. Most women expect exactly that."

"I am not most women. I will not nag or deny you. I will cook for you, make a home for you, give you children—"

"God!" Henry rubbed his hands over his face and shook his head. "Such perfection. Surely I am in heaven and in the company of a saint."

"Don't mock me," she said in a low, steady voice.

"I beg your pardon?"

"I said: Don't mock me!" she shouted. "You have no right. I've done nothing to you."

"You bought me, madam!"

Rachel reached behind her and groped on the desk, finding a small brass candle holder. Wrapping her fingers around it, she picked it up. "Don't call me that."

Henry leaned to one side, avoiding the missile, and slowly straightened. "Throw words at me . . . Rachel, but never ever try to strike me."

Her chest heaved with the effort to breathe. She

pressed her hands more firmly against her mouth to contain the whimper threatening to escape. His stare burned into her, making her feel naked and exposed, reducing her nightclothes to nothing. "I'm sorry," she whispered. "I don't know why . . . how . . ."

"I do."

The bitterness in his voice startled her into silence.

"We have just indulged in our first marital spat," he announced. "Such things are inevitable."

How could he go from biting sarcasm to barely leashed anger to resignation within the space of minutes? she wondered as she edged her way around the room to reach her door.

"Rachel."

She stopped.

"Since our agreement, which I was too lazy to read, gives me so many privileges, I assume that you also are accorded some concessions."

"Yes."

"Tell me now, Rachel. I don't like surprises."

She answered, hoping he wouldn't notice that she was inching her way closer to her room. "You will not beat me. You will be a good father if we should have children. You will not engage the services of pro . . . soiled doves."

"What a charitable way to describe them."

The way he'd said "them" was so full of hatred and venom that her stomach knotted. Her hand closed around the doorknob.

"Rachel . . . come here."

"I'm going to bed now."

"Is 'obey' no longer in the marriage vows, Rachel?"

Reluctantly she retraced her steps.

"If you are going to meet my expectations whenever I wish, why would I pay good money for a prostitute?"

"Men do."

"I won't," he said in a husky whisper. "Life offers many alternatives, Rachel, but suicide isn't one of them."

"Thank you. If that is all, I'll—"

"I wish, Rachel."

"You must be tired."

"Right now."

Her mouth dried and her lips felt as if they had grown together.

He pointed to a spot directly in front of him. "Right here."

"The bed."

"No."

"The lamp."

"Leave it." His gaze met hers, held it, drew her with their feverish light.

She walked toward him, stopped on the exact spot he'd indicated. He didn't move, didn't rise or reach out for her as he watched her with a cold purpose that she identified as revenge. "Unbind your hair."

And he watched her as she removed the net and combed her fingers through her hair.

The single lamp cast a dim glow over half his face, accenting the mystery of him, the darkness in him. His eyes were hooded, yet missed nothing.

A tremble began in the pit of her belly, and her body shook with the force of humiliation. Her hair felt heavy on her shoulders, threatening to drag her head back . . .

"Take off your robe," he ordered softly.

The plaid wool slipped from her shoulders. She shivered, then felt heat streak through her.

"The gown, Rachel."

Pain tightened her chest, and her throat swelled. She looked down and saw that the light revealed half of her body through the thin gown. Her breasts were swollen, the nipples hard and puckered. Yet still, the pain increased.

"Remove it."

She was smothering, dying. Her legs wanted to fold while pride held her upright. With one hand, she swept her hair away from her face as she squarely met his gaze. "I am not a whore. Don't expect me to act like one."

"What do you know of whores, Rachel? Or wives for that matter?"

As Rachel stood before him, barely clothed, open to his cold, assessing gaze, she wondered if there really was a difference.

"Shall I help you, Rachel?" He reached out, fingered the fabric of her gown. "Is that what you want—seduction?"

"No."

He opened his fingers, releasing his hold on her gown. "Then remove the gown. I would see my share of our bargain."

Her hair fell forward, a curtain shielding her face and her body as she bent to catch the hem of her nightdress. She was beyond emotion as she slowly raised the gown over her body, beyond hearing any sound but the slow, measured cadence of his breathing as she pulled the gown over her head and lowered her arms, beyond seeing anything but his reaction rising beneath the front of his trousers as she stood naked before him.

"Your hair obstructs my view, Rachel. Bind it in the net."

She leaned forward, picking up the discarded net. She raised her arms to gather her hair, feeling her breasts lift, her stomach tighten, as she confined the long strands and tied the ribbon that held the heavy mesh in place. Never had she been so aware of her body, its movement, the changes wrought by the brush of air, the gaze of a man . . . this man. And with her hair bound, she felt even more naked and utterly defenseless.

Again she glanced at the bulge beneath his trousers, fully grown now, straining against the fabric. Suddenly Henry seemed to be the one without defense against her or against himself. He could have revenge only if she allowed it.

"Come here," he said softly.

She went to him.

He reached up to caress her breasts, first one, then the other, a practiced ritual brush of fingers, as if he were testing the temperature of water in a tub. Her body responded. Her mind analyzed the sudden tremble of his hand, the slight quickening of his breath, the way his hands lingered as they moved over her ribs, her waist, the curls beneath her belly . . . between her thighs, down, then upward. She bit her lip to stifle a cry as shock after shock lanced through her at the touch of his finger on her, inside her. His other hand teased her breasts, sending a flood of heat downward . . . heat that melted something inside her, creating moisture that encouraged and enhanced the caress of his finger, inviting more.

She felt the liquid warmth of desire, the restless anticipation of ecstasy, the abandonment to pleasure. Yet still her mind worked, beyond sensation, independent of physical need. She still belonged to herself.

As if he felt her unblinking stare, Henry raised his head, met her gaze. His hands stilled on her. His eyes narrowed and his mouth slanted in familiar mockery. "You are ready for me, Mrs. Ashford."

"Yes."

"Accommodating, but not submissive."

"No."

He stood abruptly and gestured at the buttons at the front of his pants, his meaning obvious. "Accommodate me, then."

Without lowering her gaze, she found the buttons and slid them free, one by one. Anticipating his next order, she slipped her hand inside his underwear, finding him, easing him free of the soft linen. Her breath caught at the size and heat of him, the softness sheathing strength. She wanted to fear him, hate him. But she'd seen too much, had discovered too much about herself in the indulgence of youthful curiosity to fear the promise of her own response. She wanted to think him ugly . . .

She wanted to look, to explore. She wanted the completion she had dared not pursue in the solitude of her own bed.

His hands grasped her shoulders, as if he were in pain, and she realized that she still held him in her hands. All of him—heavy fullness and rigid length. He shuddered and his fingers tightened on her shoulders, pushing her down onto the settee, covering her body with his. He glared down at her, a look of fury and frustration, and she glared back, waging a battle with herself as well as with him.

He plunged into her, and her body resisted even as it bathed him in welcome. Her mind acknowledged the pain as he pierced her virginity, and that, too, was welcome. This was her choice—the man and the act itself.

She arched up to meet his thrust and heard him groan. He paused, holding himself on his elbows, watching her.

"Damn you, Rachel." His whisper was harsh, forced out of him as his hips moved on her, and his heart pounded against her chest. She countered his every movement, drawing him into her, deeper . . . deeper . . . His mouth ground down on hers, his tongue forcing her lips apart, engaging her in a carnal war as he slowed his movements, groaning again as she followed him, refusing to release him. He sank into her and shuddered over and over again, his body rigid, his breathing arrested as his life seemed to flow into hers.

It was pleasure without completion, need without fulfillment. Rachel closed her eyes, surrendering—too
late—to sensation. Henry rolled to the side, his body still
pressed to the length of hers in the confined space, yet
she felt as if she were alone, forsaken. She felt his breath
on her cheek and even that felt cold.

"Damn you, Rachel."

She knew then that she was not powerless unless she
chose to be. She had denied him his revenge. Yet she
felt no satisfaction, no sense of victory.

She felt empty.

8

The sounds were so familiar to Rachel—beds creaking in the rooms adjoining her suite, coughs and murmurs behind the walls, laughter and shouting from the streets, shuffling footsteps down the halls and discreet knocks on the doors. How far she had come in seven years. How hard she had worked only to find herself lying naked beneath a man, behind one locked door among many, feeling shame, disgust, frustrated need.

It had been such a grand scheme. Such a simple scheme to acquire a home, a husband, respectability—treasures that few valued as more than conveniences, like furniture and indoor plumbing.

A good man had responded to her advertisement. A good man had married her in spite of her origins. A good man had told her that she was worthy.

In place of another, less forgiving man.

Henry had said nothing beyond damning her, con-signing her to a hell with which he seemed all too intimate. Rachel remained still beneath him on the settee, held by his fury and her own sense of failure, needing to find a way to change what had happened, what they had done to one another. She turned her head to look at him. His head had fallen back at an odd angle and his soft snore broke the silence. The drink had finally claimed him.

With careful movements, she eased out from under him and left the settee, picking up her robe and gown on the way to her bedroom. She heard him mumble in his sleep, and Rachel paused, shivering as she stood in the middle of the room, aware for the first time of the dying fire and the night chill in the air. She closed her eyes for a moment, waiting, afraid that the slightest movement might wake him. She couldn't face him right now, not until she had a chance to think, to understand.

He mumbled again and she heard his teeth chatter. She retraced her steps and added wood to the fire, keeping one eye on Henry and one eye on the flames. He lay half on and half off the settee, his head wedged in the corner.

She stared at him, at the way his brow creased and his jaw worked, as if he were fighting something, as if, even in sleep, he found no peace.

Sighing, she lifted his legs onto the cushions, pillowed her nightdress beneath his head, and spread her robe over him before running to her own bed.

Henry was gone when she awakened, and had not returned for two days.

At first she had been glad to have him gone. With every thought of him, she experienced the humiliation of standing naked before him while he remained fully clothed, the utter degradation of his cold possession, the shame of knowing that she had rejected what tenderness he had offered. Over and over she fought the memories of Henry's contempt and then his frustration, her shame and then the pleasure she felt yet refused to show. She'd been afraid to feel pleasure, afraid of needing, afraid of becoming lost to it . . . to Henry.

·She'd been fighting that fear for far longer than she'd known Henry Ashford, pretending it didn't exist beyond a vague niggling of doubt, a fleeting uneasiness. Two nights ago, she had become intimate with her fear and its name was Rachel Ashford, her craving for intimacy . . . and for passion. Her need to belong to more than her own loneliness.

Rachel stopped at her familiar place by the window to watch the frenzy that was life in Cheyenne, and felt as if she were in another place and forever separated from a normal existence. She crossed her arms and rubbed them with her hands, though the day was warm and the air close in her suite. How far she had come, only to meet herself at the beginning of her quest, alone and frightened and shut away from the very world she sought to join. Outside, friends gathered and laughed, enemies met one another face to face, families shared the warmth and companionship of love and belonging.

Inside, she did as she had always done—watched and yearned to step beyond her prison and wondered why she could not be a part of it all. But of course she knew why. She was Madam's daughter, a pariah before she'd ever been born.

Did Henry know? she wondered. Several times over the last two days, she had seen him walking down the street, stopping to talk with one man or another, and touching the head of his cane to the brim of his hat when he passed a lady. Not once had she seen him glance up at her window. Not once had she seen him enter a brothel or return the ribald comments tossed at him from ladies of the evening.

How strange it was that she should be waiting for her husband to call on her. Stranger still was the spark of hope that he would appear, when all he had done was curse her for . . . what? For forcing him to honor an unspoken vow? For defying him with her body and her mind?

Had her marriage ended in less time than it took a customer to relieve himself with one of her mother's girls during his lunch hour?

A gunshot echoed from a saloon down the street, and Rachel shivered at the finality of it. Pushing away from the window, she closed the drapes and stepped back as she unconsciously rubbed her thumb over the dents in her tin wedding band.

She had to get out of this place.

Her gaze sought out the packed carpetbag sitting by the door. Today she would brave the society of Cheyenne long enough to buy supplies. This was the quietest part of the day, when women had left the shops in favor of their kitchens and children had gone home to their chores. The activity of a half hour before had muted to near silence.

Tomorrow she'd return to the Big Horn Basin and her home . . . with or without Henry Ashford. The thought of making the journey without escort created its own anxiety, but she'd done worse things in the past seven years, and she'd done most of them alone.

With or without him, her future still belonged to her.

Rachel snatched up her bonnet and fastened her reticule to her wrist. In spite of the spring warmth, she donned a concealing cloak and left her elegant prison for the dirt and gossip of the street.

Henry stared into a shop window and saw what he had always seen—a reflection of himself distorted by layers of grime. As if his father stood beside him, Henry heard the echo of his voice, words spoken a hundred—a thousand—times before.

"Be a man, Henry. Make your father proud." The memory of his fourteenth birthday had no images anymore, just odors of a whore's musk and the scent of those who had preceded him—how many, one? ten?—drying between her thighs as his father stood at the foot of his bed, watching as she forced Henry's virgin body to respond to her ministrations, forced him to humiliating acts in the name of "education." And as he vomited all over her, his father had sneered at him.

"So I was right. You're nothing but a limp-stemmed pansy."

The memory faded as a woman's face flashed briefly in the glass—a reflection that seemed clearer than his own—then a sunbonnet and cloak of soft gray, both so concealing that they seemed to move independently with no substance beneath. And though she was shrouded from head to foot, he felt the same quickening in his gut, the sharpened awareness of her presence. If he were closer to her, he knew he would catch the scent of lavender.

She moved with slow grace and dignity, though her body seemed to fold into itself a little more with every step she took away from the hotel. Beside him, Luc, too, watched her progress. "She will leave soon, Henry, with or without you."

Extracting a cheroot from the inside of his coat, Henry clamped it between his lips and struck a match. "Yes? She told you so?" He inhaled the smoke deeply.

"No."

"It is gratifying to know that one of us has such intimate knowledge of the workings of her mind," Henry said with sarcasm as his gaze followed her every move.

"How long would *you* wait, Henry?"

"I would not wait at all," he said as he saw her hesitate at a milliner's window and gaze at the display, keeping at a small distance, as if she denied herself the luxury of wanting anything too much.

She'd been like that two nights ago, refusing to give in to desire though he knew she'd felt it. He'd wanted her to feel, to lose control as he had. Instead, she'd been remote, a body separate from the mind, a heart spurning discourse with the soul. He'd wanted her as vulnerable as she'd rendered him with her damned contracts and agreements. Instead, she'd rendered him as helpless as a boy who'd just discovered more than one use for his cock. "It looks as if your bride has a fancy to indulge herself with feminine frippery," Luc said from beside him.

Henry focused on the sight of Rachel. She stood close to the display now, unmoving but for her hand on the window, her finger tracing the outline of what she saw behind the glass. His breath shuddered and caught at that slight movement, and he imagined it to be a caress, full of longing.

He tossed the cheroot onto the boardwalk and ground it with his heel. "My *bride* knows nothing of frivolous indulgence." His mouth tightened as he watched her hand slide down the glass and retreat into the folds of her cloak. She lingered a moment longer, then lifted her skirts and continued on toward the general store.

"Perhaps, Henry, that is because she has never been frivolously indulged."

"She wears the smallclothes of a servant and the shoes of an Indian, yet you and she both claim that she is a landed heiress. Tell me, was she chosen to inherit her estate at random by some dotty old woman?"

"The land came to her by her maternal grandfather. It was held in trust for her until her majority . . . you needn't worry, Henry, her dowry is quite respectable."

"God save me from so much *respectability*, Luc."

"You are not curious about the size of her estate?"

"It is *my* estate I am concerned with."

"Then I suggest you make ready to depart, Henry. If I am not mistaken, she is going to purchase supplies for the journey home." Luc said as he stared across the street at the millinery that had so fascinated Rachel. "And if I know Rachel, she will go with or without you."

Henry's mouth slanted in a derisive smile. *With or without him.* Why not? Rachel was obviously capable of acting independently in bed or out of it. With a snort, he strolled toward the shop, uncaring whether Luc followed him or not.

He paused in front of the window that had enthralled Rachel. A single hat was displayed simply, without background or props. It was an elegant affair, quite fashionable without the overdone gaudiness of current style. The color and texture of it caught his fancy, and the graceful sweep of wide brim and shaped crown were continuations of one another, curving and flowing into a whole that pleased the eye and challenged his artistic instincts.

A handsome woman of about thirty years moved into view as she unnecessarily fussed with the position of her display, her fingers lingering on it as Rachel's had through the glass. The feathers swayed at the touch, caressing the back of her hand as if they were drawn to the warmth and life of a human touch.

"Did I forget to tell you, Henry," Luc said from just behind him, "that I have reopened my accounts and given authorization for you to purchase whatever you need for the journey?"

Henry ignored him.

"The door is just to your left." Luc pushed Henry from behind, giving him no choice but to open the door or smash his nose into the glass panes decorating the top half.

"Good afternoon, gentlemen," the milliner said.

Gallantly, Luc doffed his hat and bowed from the waist. "Good morning, madam." He nodded at Henry as he straightened. "You're quite right, Henry. The creation in the window will suit your wife nicely."

"It's expensive," the shopkeeper said. "Is your wife worth it?" she asked teasingly.

Luc and Henry stiffened at the same time.

"Actually," Henry said as he brushed past her to inspect the hat more closely, "it's not good enough for her. Perhaps one of the women from the brothel will find it pleasing." Touching the tips of his fingers to the brim of his own hat, Henry strode to the door. "Good day, madam."

He was half a block away before he noticed Luc's presence at his side.

"A bit harsh weren't you, Henry? It was a lovely hat."

Henry said nothing.

"On the other hand, your defense of Rachel was quite gallant."

"She is using the Ashford name," Henry mumbled.

"Ah, so you do possess some family pride."

"Pride is the only legacy allowed to second sons, Luc." Henry stopped at the corner to light another cheroot.

"A legacy or a curse, Henry. Remember that, and spend your portion wisely in the years to come," Luc said, an odd note in his voice and a grim cast to his expression, as if he were foretelling either a disaster or a miracle.

"I have no doubt that you and my wife have already put the disbursal of my pride into writing, Luc."

Shaking his head, Luc stepped off the boardwalk. "Be careful in your condemnations, Henry, lest you lose the opportunity to live beyond the past.'' With that, Luc turned and walked back the way they had come.

Opportunity. The word sounded different coming from Luc, like hope rather than an empty promise. He had been bashing in doors all his life in search of that elusive commodity.

Henry's mouth slanted in a derisive smile as Luc rounded a corner and disappeared from view. Luc was a demented fool if he thought that a woman's touch would make purgatory more habitable.

With a snort, Henry strolled in the opposite direction, his gaze searching both sides of the street for the stiff brim of a sunbonnet, the twitch of a light woolen cloak.

Let her go, his mind counseled while something in the black pit of his emotions struggled against reason. Something like fascination for a woman who seemed more phantasm than reality. A woman who rejected rather than possessed with her body.

Why had she waited? he wondered. He had kept his distance and watched, hoping that she would abandon him and their marriage, but she had remained sequestered in their suite, giving him no evidence of her existence beyond his thoughts. The sight of her on the street had jolted him, physical proof that she would not dishonor her vows so easily.

As he had tried to dishonor her.

Until this moment, he had duped himself into believing that their last encounter had been seduction rather than a drunken attempt at revenge. She had set her terms. Pride and resentment demanded that he set his. Instead, she had disarmed him, turned his own body against him, denied him pleasure even as she gave him satisfaction . . . made him want more of her and less of revenge. He'd damned her aloud as she'd begun to shudder and arch beneath him—too late—and then silently as he'd

awakened to find cold comfort in the nightdress bunched
under his head and her robe shielding his body from the
cold.

"Don't mock me."

He'd heard her dim cry that night through a fog of
spirits. But with each day, he heard it repeated louder
and louder in his head, and with each day, he was less
sure whether the cry was Rachel's or his own.

His father would be proud to see how lust had rendered his second son insensible . . . another tradition upheld by the Ashford men.

His mind cleared of the shade that always seemed to
hover within a thought's breadth as he sought the reality
of Rachel, to discern the dimension of her, as vivid and
clear as his remembrance of rounded flesh, puckering in
the chill and growing more pale with each of his demands.

Let her go.

Henry's feet seemed to move of their own volition,
taking him off the boardwalk and into the street. Something squished under his shoe and a ripe odor wafted
upward to offend his nostrils. "Hell," he muttered under
his breath as he raised his foot to scrape the sole of his
shoe on the wheel of an elegant and obviously new carriage parked in front of a dance hall.

He was still alternately cursing vagrant livestock and
Rachel when he found her in a dry goods store a block
away. Blinking several times to adjust to the change in
light, he walked up behind her in time to hear the clerk
speak to her.

"It'll take cash, unless you want to make other ar-
rangements to pay."

On the surface, it sounded like a simple statement of
business practice, but something in the man's voice irritated Henry. "That won't be necessary. I believe the

Earl of Fairleigh has an account with you. My wife is free to use it.''

The two women tittering in a corner of the store hushed suddenly and turned to stare with avid anticipation. The shopkeeper gaped at him. Rachel spun around and collided with him, the folds of her cloak wrapping around his legs. He grasped her elbows to steady himself.

"You have led me a merry chase from shop to shop, darling. What is it you fancy—a ribbon or trinket?'' he said as if they had shared an intimate breakfast together. Was it relief he saw cross her features before all expression fled?

"Supplies.'' She stared at him as if *he* were a shade haunting her.

"Have you a list?''

Her face seemed to redden and her hands disappeared inside the folds of her cloak. "No . . . it's easy enough to remember.''

Silence still enfolded the store, as if the occupants were hanging on every word, every gesture. The devil in Henry drove him to mischief, and something else. With everything he knew of tenderness he reached inside the walls of her bonnet and cupped her face in his hand, lifted it to his as he lowered his mouth over hers.

Rachel began to step back, but he wrapped his other arm around her waist, gathering her close, and felt her tremble. His lips touched hers, brushing, once, twice, and again, soft strokes meant to leave a gentle impression.

Her hands appeared from their hiding place and clutched at his elbows. She pushed at him and arched away. A corner of her bonnet brim stabbed him in the eye. Reluctantly he withdrew from her, his eye closed against the sting of invasion.

The women began to titter again. The clerk watched from behind the counter as Henry glared at him.

Rachel remained still, her face pale rather than flushed.

He meant to continue the gentleness he'd begun, but his voice came out jagged as broken glass. "Forgive me, Rachel, for an eager groom's indiscretion."

The clerk snorted rudely.

Rachel closed her eyes and seemed to shrink within her cloak.

Let her go, the voice inside his head counseled.

But Henry knew he could not. Not yet.

Rachel tore off her bonnet as soon as she reached the safety and anonymity of her rooms. The shops were closed. The population had long since found pleasures inside the houses of their choosing. She had braved the human elements of the town and returned relatively unscathed . . .

Alone.

Henry had sought his own pleasure elsewhere after escorting her to the next establishment she needed to visit. As she had watched him walk away, she had said good-bye, silently, finally, knowing that tomorrow she would leave all that Cheyenne offered behind.

Maybe a name and a tin ring would be enough.

Suddenly she felt weary, drained. Her steps dragging, she walked into her bedroom and dropped her cloak on the floor, for once not caring of the abuse of fine cloth or the clutter it caused. With quick, tearing motions, she pulled out the pins securing her hair and sighed at the freedom of having it fall loose down her back.

A flash of color on the bed caught her eye in the mirror and she whirled around. Delicate flowers danced on a cloth-covered round box. A bit of tissue paper peeked from beneath the lid, secured by a velvet ribbon.

Slowly she groped for the end of the bow, tugged, and let it fall to either side of the box. Her hand shook as she lifted the lid. Her eyes widened in disbelief as she reached out to touch roses of peach satin and strips of peach and ivory lining the underside of a sweeping brim, a band of finely gathered silk chiffon adorning a scalloped crown of ivory felt.

It was the hat she had seen and touched through the cold glass of a milliner's window.

Henry had cursed the starched flaps of her sunbonnet as he rubbed his eye.

She thought of the kiss, the gentleness, the stiffness beneath his trousers as their bodies had brushed. He had been impatient in the mercantile and appalled at the quantity of her purchases. He had been even more horrified when she'd pulled a roll of currency from her bag to pay the clerk. The women in the shop had hidden their smirks behind their hands.

And then he had left her to finish her shopping alone. He'd neither asked about her plans nor questioned them. She thought he didn't care, and the knowledge cut more deeply than it should have.

Her finger traced the broad brim of the hat, the cool silk and scalloped crown. Hues of peach and white blurred together as her knees buckled and she crumpled to the floor, her arms crossed on the bed, her gaze held by the hat in morbid fascination. It wasn't money left on the nightstand, or a tawdry bit of fluff in exchange for a satisfying performance. Henry was too refined for such vulgar tokens of farewell.

But then, she supposed that a wife merited a more tasteful show of gratitude for a few moments of her time.

Cradling her head in her arms, she cried for the first time since she had left her attic room behind.

9

It was over. Rachel quickly completed her packing, quickly, because endings were easier when sharp and clean. Lingering cuts brought too much suffering, too much time to think.

She glanced out of the window for one final glimpse, one final search for the sight of Henry. Early-morning dew gave the town a softness and gentility that would disappear as soon as the inhabitants fully awakened and rubbed the stardust from their eyes. When she drove beyond the city limits, the time for dreams would be over, and she would bind them well in chains and keep them from her thoughts.

Below, she saw that her wagon had been loaded and awaited her in front of the hotel—a brutal reminder of the small privileges and courtesies that were hers at the mention of Henry's name. Perhaps it was enough.

Without a backward glance, Rachel donned her cloak and bonnet, picked up her carpetbag, and walked out of the luxurious suite.

Her step faltered as she approached the wagon, a final acknowledgment of trepidation in taking such a journey alone, and in a wagon rather than with pack mules. But a wagon would be easier to manage and she could change to mules closer to home. Indians were no longer much of a problem, and they thought her to be mad—a protection of sorts—but outlaws ran rampant, and those who knew who she was would not hesitate to take for free what she would have been well paid for under her mother's roof.

She set the carpetbag on the ground and bent to retrieve her pistol and the bandolero she found useful in keeping bullets close at hand. After stowing her bag under the plank seat of the wagon, she opened a carton in the back and pulled out a two boxes of ammunition and a new shotgun to keep beside her.

"I see I'll be well protected," a lazy voice said from behind her.

Holding the shotgun in front of her, she straightened and turned. Never could she mistake that sardonic voice. She ignored the heavy throb in her chest, the panic his presence always created.

Henry strolled toward her, carrying a flat leather case and leading a horse of fine proportions that was outfitted with the finest Sheridan saddle and tack. His deep-blue Levi's were a little too loose on his narrow waist and hips, and they were stiff with dye and newness. Suspenders held them up in place of a belt—fine suspenders better suited to more formal wear—and contrasted with the tailored perfection of a crisp white shirt. His boots had the creak of unworn leather. On his head was the same hat he wore with his English suits. Over his shoulder he carried the latest in rifles, belying his stated need for protection. She stared at him without blinking.

He looked utterly ridiculous.

The earl stood behind him, a twinkle in his eye and a large box under each arm. "Good morning, Rachel."

"Good morning," she said, unable to separate her gaze from Henry's.

Henry tied his horse to the back of the wagon and removed the saddle to place it in the wagon bed.

The desk clerk called out from the door of the hotel as he held up a gaily patterned hatbox. "You forgot this."

Glancing up, Henry scowled, then dropped the saddle with a thump and strode toward the clerk.

Rachel lowered her head as she pulled the bandolero over her head and across her shoulder, then wrapped her cloak about her.

"Have you room for these, Rachel?" the earl asked.

"Yes." She waved her hand toward a bare corner in the wagon bed.

"These are for Henry . . . a wedding gift," he said as he hoisted one box, then the other into the wagon. "Will you give them to him when you arrive home?"

She could only nod before Henry returned carrying the box containing the hat she had hoped never to see again. He held it out to her, his expression cool, forbidding, belying the light note in his voice. "Any other woman would leave behind a handkerchief or small trinket in hopes of having it returned by the man of her dreams."

She lifted her head, meeting his gaze squarely. "Why are you here?"

Carelessly he tossed the box into the wagon, then shrugged. "We English are obsessed with appearances. It wouldn't do to have an Ashford bride leave town unescorted." With all the aplomb of a courtier, he lifted her onto the seat, then ruined the effect by banging his shin on the wheel as he turned to his brother, his cursing as colorful as that of the drovers and teamsters.

Caught between relief that he was merely seeing her out of town and disappointment that she would actually have to say good-bye to him farther down the road, she groped for words and found none. What could she say? That she was grateful he was concerned with appearances? That if he was concerned with such things, then she was the last person he should be "appearing" with?

From the corner of her eye, she watched him face the earl, his silence speaking of pride and anger, his stiff posture speaking of reluctance to turn away from a life-long bond.

"Take care of her, Henry," the earl said, his expression seeming both guarded and hopeful.

"As you can see by her armaments, Rachel is quite capable of taking care of herself."

The earl nodded. "Then I hope that you will take care of each other." He extended his hand toward his brother.

Henry's hands clenched as he faltered on a backward step. He stood motionless, as if he were caught between two sides of himself. His shoulders heaved as the earl closed the distance between them, and unheeding of the curious stares of passersby, the brothers embraced with an ease few men displayed when confronted with emotion.

Rachel turned away, fixing her attention on the road that led out of town. Her gaze blurred. She could almost feel it—the love between Henry and the earl, the loyalty that seemed to bind them together in spite of their grievances.

The wagon rocked on its springs as Henry mounted the seat beside her. The cloth of his Levi's squeaked as his legs rubbed together. The waistband gaped at the back as he leaned forward to grasp the reins. Rachel stifled a reluctant smile. In a few hours his legs would be chafed and sore, his pristine white shirt would be dun colored, his feet would be raw with blisters.

Some devil inside her kept her from warning him of his impending misery.

Buildings slid slowly past as Henry drove the team, tipping his small-brimmed hat to pedestrians and whistling under his breath as if he were on his way to a picnic.

Rachel stared straight ahead, remembering other times when she and her mother had been escorted out of town by a sheriff or pastor—

Abruptly Henry pulled the wagon to a stop as a woman ran out of a shop and called out to him.

"Mr. Ashford, good morning."

Henry nodded curtly.

"Does your wife like the hat?" the woman asked, her neck craning as she tried to see Rachel's face.

"*Does* my wife like the hat?"

His whisper was so soft, it took Rachel a moment to realize he had spoken at all. She turned her head and recognized the milliner's shop, the window that held a new display. "It's lovely," she said flatly as she met the woman's gaze.

The milliner's eyes widened as she saw Rachel's face beneath the sunbonnet. *"This is your wife?"* Without waiting for Henry to answer, she met Rachel's gaze with a smile of bitter irony. "I was flattered when he decided the hat was good enough for you," she said.

Fear opened its wings in Rachel's chest, beating frantically as she neither moved nor spoke.

"On the contrary," Henry said, giving the woman a look that would turn water to stone. "But she is worthy of having her whims indulged no matter how modest they might be."

Her mouth hanging open, the milliner stepped back and stumbled on the edge of the boardwalk.

A flush heated Rachel's cheeks and her fear became a soft curl of pleasure inside her. Henry's defense of her

was her first dose of respectability, and she found it to
be heady stuff indeed.

"Why did you send me the hat, Mr. Ashford?" she
asked as sudden doubt surfaced at his contradictory behavior.

"Because your damned sunbonnet keeps poking me
in the eye," he snapped.

She studied his expression, searching for the truth,
finding nothing. She wasn't surprised. From what she'd
seen, men rarely bestowed gifts unless it served their
own purposes. So many times she'd seen a customer
come to Roz's house with some tawdry bauble for his
favorite "girl" in hopes that in her gratitude, she would
increase her efforts to give him pleasure, then return to
his wife with a fine hat or string of pearls to ensure her
tolerance of his transgressions.

Was an exchange of goods for favors all that existed
between men and women, even in marriage? Wasn't it
possible to share companionship and respect, along with
home-cooked meals and children? Funny, but she'd
never considered that possibility until she'd met Henry
Ashford.

Henry returned her regard with a mocking smile, then
slapped the reins and drove the wagon through the
gauntlet of polite society without a by-your-leave.

Men shouted and winked. Catcalls and sneers came
from doorways. But because Henry had declared her
worthiness to the milliner, Rachel displayed it to the
world as she held her head a little higher, straightened
her back a little more, and hid her pain within the broad
wings of her sunbonnet.

"Do you know these people?" Henry asked.

"Some . . . are familiar," she replied carefully.

"Then I suppose we should be grateful that we
haven't been treated to a shivaree," Henry said with

grim amusement. "I observed one the other night, and the prospect of being the butt of such mischief is frightening to say the least."

She couldn't help it. All the emotion of the past week bubbled up into her throat, an intoxicating feeling of absurdity at Henry's assumption, a wild sense of reprieve that they were passing the tattered fringes of Cheyenne and the prairie lay ahead like a clean slate. It began with a short burst and lengthened into full-bodied laughter. She raised her hand to her mouth, but couldn't contain it. Her other hand held her stomach and she kept on laughing.

And then she jammed her fist against her mouth to stifle a sob. A shivaree. He thought that the catcalls and hoots and smirks were simply an obscene way to wish the newlyweds well.

Henry frowned at her and urged the team to faster pace as he muttered about primitive society and its equally primitive amusements. His assessment of life in the territories sobered her, and she tried to see it all as he must—the opera house and gambling dens, the roller-skating rink and saloons, the broad collection of shops and churches and the brothels—and she thought of a child playing dress-up with old clothes from the attic. If Henry thought this was primitive, only God knew what his opinion of her home would be.

It was just as well that he wouldn't be accompanying her to the Big Horns.

They drove on, away from Cheyenne until it was a smoke- and dust-wreathed smudge on the horizon behind them. The wagon bumped and rocked and Henry cursed the team of horses with precise regularity. She waited and watched and wondered when it would happen, when he would have enough. But still they drove on. It could have been dread or hope—she didn't know which—that tightened her throat against the words she wanted to say, words that would release him from further obligation to her.

Another mile and another and the smudge behind them disappeared. She swallowed and gripped the edge of her seat on either side of her. She couldn't stand the waiting anymore, couldn't breathe for the strange fluttering in her chest.

"I'm pleased that you finally came to your senses," Henry said conversationally.

"I'm always in full possession of my senses," she replied stiffly.

"Ah. Is that why you remained in town waiting for a ne'er-do-well husband who might never have returned?"

"Everyone deserves a chance," she said, still not looking his way.

His mouth slanted in a cynical smile. "How tolerant you are."

"You can stop now," she said on a rush of air. "We've come far enough."

Silence.

Her gaze focused on the distant mountains as she waited for . . . something. "I can go on from here. Thank you for—"

He turned his head sharply toward her, his eyes narrowed. "Is this a dismissal?"

"No," she replied, puzzled by the intensity of his regard, the softness of his voice, as if he were waiting and taking great care not to startle her, as if he were the hunter and she the prey.

"No," he repeated. "Then what are you about?"

"You've seen me out of town. No one will know if you take another direction."

"Ah, I see. You are intelligent enough to know you've made a bad bargain, and careful enough to leave the decision to quit our arrangement to me," he said in the same tone he'd been using on the horses, grating, impatient. His eyes had a faraway look, fixed on nothing that she could see. He brushed at the dust collecting in the creases of his shirt, as if he could wipe away more than surface grime.

"No," she said again, not knowing what else to say, afraid to say anything at all.

"First you are mouthing farewells and trying to send me on my way, then you deny my inferences. My ability to read minds is limited, Rachel," he said bitterly. "Pray enlighten me as to your wishes."

She ran her tongue over her lips, listened to her reply as if it came from someone else. "The journey is difficult alone."

"That depends on where you want to go, Rachel," he said enigmatically as he turned his head to look at her.

"I want to go home, Mr. Ashford—a home that is meant for a family."

He cursed again and she wondered if it was directed at the team or herself.

"You'd be better off if I did stop," he said, his voice even yet forced.

"Why?"

"Damn it, I *am* a ne'er-do-well," he shouted. "Are you listening? *I'm no bloody, frigging good!*"

"By whose standards, Mr. Ashford?" she asked softly.

"Ask anyone who knows me."

"I'm asking *you*."

"I am what I have become, Rachel," he said wearily. Still he drove on.

If he had stopped, she thought she might want to let him go. If she had the courage, maybe she'd tell him the truth about her mother and watch the grim, straight line of his mouth curl into a sneer. If he hadn't started talking again, softly, deliberately, as if he were trying to diminish the humiliation and anguish she sensed in him, maybe she wouldn't care.

Hadn't caring too much always been her problem?

"It's not every day I admit to being less than perfect or right, you know. Only God knows that I'm a fraud. Everyone else who knows me simply thinks I'm an arrogant bastard who's earned the right by birth and privilege."

"Are you?" she asked seriously.

"Arrogant, definitely. A bastard, no . . . not in the literal sense at any rate." He shrugged. "The rest of it is a matter of universal speculation." The horses grunted as he reined them in suddenly. He struggled with the brake until she leaned over him and set it herself. "See there. I'm a total incompetent." His mouth twisted briefly, then smoothed out, all expression gone from his face. Again he looked hard, uncompromising, a storm waiting to happen.

Rachel glanced down at her lap, at how her hands seemed to have relaxed without her realizing it. He had given her reassurance with his self-condemnation. Reassurance that perhaps they had something in common after all, and maybe, just maybe, they both had good reason to build something new from the past. She couldn't help but be curious about him, about his past, but it was something she could live with. Not all secrets had to be told.

She hoped.

"None of us is perfect, Mr. Ashford," she said.

His gaze snapped around to hers, his expression wiped clean. "You ask a great deal of yourself, Rachel."

A sigh shuddered in her breast as she met his probing stare, unblinking. "Yes," she answered, and looked ahead to the mountains and home. "Don't you?"

"I've made it my life's work to avoid it," he said, and slapped the reins against the horses' rumps. "But who knows? Perhaps five years might be long enough to convince me otherwise.''

"Five years," Rachel said musingly, unaware that she was actually voicing a thought. "Long enough to either build a new life or resign ourselves to hell.''

"It's always that way, Rachel. There is nothing else.'' He said it with such utter conviction that Rachel wanted to cry out against him. "Do we go on?''

She wanted to say no, wanted to separate herself from the turmoil he had brought her, the questions and the doubts. But she couldn't stop looking at him. She couldn't tear herself away from the dreams that bound her. "Yes," she said with more certainty than she felt. "I don't think we have anywhere else to go.''

Yes, she had said.

The force of that simple word had knocked Henry off balance. Pressure built in his chest, as if his heart expanded and twice as much blood flowed in his veins. He hurt everywhere, deep inside, as if his soul were coming back to life. But no, that part of him had died long ago by his own hand.

Safely dead. Peacefully buried.

Unlamented.

He drove on as hours passed and doubts multiplied with the dust on his clothes. What was he doing here? Why had he given in to Luc's plans for him without a single convincing argument? Had he sunk so deeply into apathy that his only remaining concern was to drift through the days without touching . . . or being touched? What in God's name was he going to do in this wilderness with a woman he didn't want? A woman who had taken him out of desperation?

But he knew her.

The realization had come frequently since she'd turned so sharply away from him to stare ahead, her face and her feelings concealed within the shadows of her ridiculous bonnet. Oh yes, he knew her well.

The recognition had been subtle at first—brief glimpses and fleeting insights. Then it had come at him like a wave when she'd spoken of life and hell as if she weren't sure whether they were opposite ends of existence or one long and twisting path that never offered a change of scenery. He preferred it that way, always knowing what to expect, never being tempted to look for more. How long had it been? he wondered. How long since he had been like Rachel, with her shreds of hope? How long before she, too, saw nothing ahead but an endless expanse of drab, dirty prairie?

Yes, she was familiar to him. Too familiar. In her, he saw his past. In her, he saw the disappointments, and a moment ago, he'd imagined that he heard the desperate cries of a dying soul.

He didn't want her to share his fate, to be constantly tossed around by the storm and wonder when it would overwhelm her, drag her down into the eternity of dark and cold. Contrary to his nature, he found himself worrying about her, wanting more for her, wanting her to find the beauty he could no longer see. He wanted . . .

Her.

Against his will, he glanced at her and felt it again— a surge of life at the wistfulness he'd seen in her eyes more than once, a rush of passion for her innocence of youth and faith in the ideals that had driven her to seek a future however she could. And he felt a lift of weight from his heart because she didn't seem to be afraid of storms.

She met his gaze, the wistfulness a mere drift across her features as her mouth curved upward in a hesitant smile. It was still there, the touch of summer in her eyes and the sunlight melting golden over a strand of hair curling against her cheek. And he seemed to fly, just for a moment, as if the world had dropped away from beneath him and there were a thousand more inviting him to find solid ground again.

"Thank you for staying," she said in that firm, direct way of hers.

Damn her.

"As you said: There is no place else to go." He gave her a stiff, cynical smile and forced the old practiced mockery into his voice. "And for the next five years, I am your husband . . . for richer or poorer, in hopelessness and hell."

10

The sunbonnet didn't seem so ridiculous now.

Heat congealed beneath Henry's suspenders, between his legs, under the crown of his hat. Every time he moved his feet, stiff leather scraped against the bare bones of his heels, irritated by the drying blood where flesh used to be. He thought of taking a cool bath and sprawling beneath the shade of an ancient tree . . . if there were any trees.

He had seen emptiness before, but not like this. The land stretched before him in shades of stone and dirt, in textures of forbidding mountains capped by snow and oddly sculpted pinnacles rising from the ground like gnarled fingers reaching toward heaven while their foundations were firmly rooted in hell. Dust whirled and danced in pagan delight, smudging a sky so blue and clear it seemed transparent, stirring grit into air so fresh it almost hurt lungs more accustomed to the odors and chemicals of the city. And through it all the wind

whipped and battered and cried out plaintively as if a
thousand souls were begging for release.

This, too, seemed a familiar place to Henry. A place
of nightmare landscapes and tormenting silence.

Rachel seemed at ease here, comforted by the emptiness, as she sat quietly beside him, her hands folded in
her lap, her back straight, her head moving constantly
from side to side, as if she were searching . . .

"What do you seek?" he asked, needing to hear
something besides the creak of the wagon wheels.

"Trouble."

His mouth tightened at her answer. "Would you be
so kind as to elaborate?"

She glanced at him briefly. "Even where there is
beauty, there is danger."

"Beauty? Here?" He searched the horizon, the land,
the sky.

Her head tilted affording him a glimpse of the lower
half of her face in the shade of her bonnet. "Don't you
see it?"

"I see a void."

"Luc . . . the earl told me that you have traveled. I've
wondered where you have been, what you have seen."

"Nothing that is beautiful." He felt her stare, but did
not look at her. "What dangers do you imagine in this
wasteland?"

She drew in her breath sharply and turned her gaze
back to the land in front of her. "The weather. Wild
animals. Men."

It caught his attention, the way she spoke of the
weather and animals in a more casual manner, yet her
voice flattened when she spoke of men. It was as if she
afforded respect to the first two dangers, but was resigned to the third. "And which are the most menacing?"

"Animals can be avoided," she said, "and they seldom attack without provocation. We can take shelter from the weather. With men you must either run faster or shoot straighter than they do."

"I see," he said. "Is there no other way?"

She glanced over at him, her expression thoughtful, a little perplexed, as if she were surprised that he would ask such a question. "Yes. You must be smarter than they are."

"Ah. So have you shot many men, Rachel, or have you outwitted them?"

"I have only shot at one, to frighten him."

"What do you do then, when confronted with a two-legged enemy?"

She smiled, but with a slightly bitter twist rather than with pleasure or fond memory, as she returned her gaze to the land. "I convince them that I am crazy."

His bark of laughter resounded over the creak of wagon wheels and was swallowed up by the emptiness surrounding them. He knew well how a hint of madness instilled fear in the most enlightened mind, as if it were contagious. It was a defense he had perfected at an early age. Even his demons tormented him from a safe distance, as if they feared his madness was deeper than theirs.

He turned his head toward Rachel, studied the way she sat so straight and still, the way she watched without seeming to watch at all. Behind the concealing brim of her bonnet, he imagined her profile, the straight, clean lines of her nose, forehead, and jaw, the curve and shadow of her high cheekbones and full mouth, the depth of eyes that saw too much. Wariness was such a part of her that he hadn't realized it until now. The irony of it amused and intrigued him. A husband and wife who searched for demons behind every shadow.

Except that Rachel appeared to see dreams instead.

The wagon jolted over a scar in the land and he turned his attention to what lay ahead.

Perhaps she *was* mad.

Who would live in such a place but a madwoman? Why would anyone choose to travel under such primitive conditions for so long unless the only alternative was Bedlam? How could anyone with a shred of sanity choose to live in such a nightmare?

He had asked how long they would travel and the answer had appalled him. Three weeks? He could cross England in less time and certainly in more comfort. Everything was an extreme: the land, which was either vertical or horizontal; the climate, which was hot and windy during the day or cold and windy after the sun dropped beneath the horizon; the emptiness, which seemed so full of sound and unseen presences.

His bones ached and felt fractured in a dozen places from the constant jolt of the poorly sprung wagon. The flesh beneath his clothes felt as if it had been peeled back and scraped away. The skin on his face and lips was so dry he was amazed that it had not turned to dust long ago.

"There is a good place to stop for the night up ahead," she said, her voice a rich alto counterpoint to the high metallic soprano of turning wheels.

"Ah. A bath, a hot meal, and a bed. I was beginning to wonder if you meant to travel throughout the night."

She gave him an odd look, her mouth open as if she had wanted to say something and changed her mind. The corners of her mouth tipped up slightly. "If you want a bath we will have go about two more miles down the trail."

"For a bath I would go ten miles." He thought of immersing himself in a tub of cool, soothing water. He imagined a hot, satisfying meal followed by a trifle of some sort. He couldn't wait to fall asleep between cool linen sheets on a comfortable bed. Slapping the reins on the rumps of the horses, he urged them to a faster pace.

Rachel pointed to a stream of water bordered by a stand of trees and announced that they would make camp within the almost circular shelter bordered by an outcropping of rocks that abruptly gave way to stunted trees and brush. She selected a few articles from the wagon and carried them to a sheltered spot backed by the boulders that were like the petrified eggs of some giant mythical beast. There was no inn, no feather mattress, no pillows, only dirt interspersed with coarse clumps of long grass.

And now Rachel was checking her rifle as if she intended to use it.

He refused to ask.

She checked the shotgun next, then the two pistols, handing one over to him as if she expected him to know why. They had seen neither beast nor man all day. "Am I to shoot the wind?" he asked as he tested the balance and grip of the weapon.

"Anything bigger than a squirrel or longer than a worm," she said casually.

Bloody hell.

Sighing, Henry pulled his own rifle from its scabbard and checked the load, then set it beside the other weapons. His horse snorted and pawed the ground, impatient at being tied to the back of the wagon. At a loss, Henry did the most logical thing he could think of: he unhitched the team and led them with his mount to the stream, then after they drank their fill, he tethered them to the rope Rachel had strung between two trees.

With swift, economical movements, she gathered small pieces of wood and brush, then retrieved an ax from the wagon, placing them near the pitiful collection of items on the ground. He looked from the pile to her and back again.

"Where is our tent?"

She pointed toward the shelter of the rocky overhang on her way to the wagon where she ripped several sheets from a box of old newspapers. With pistol in one hand and paper in the other, she disappeared into a stand of dense bushes.

He'd wondered what the paper was for.

Wonderful. They had a wagonload of weapons and fabric, spices, foodstuffs, her supply of candy and one elegant hat, but nothing so luxurious as a chamber pot or tissue paper.

Leaves rustled and she appeared again, pausing to study the area, her gaze focused on the supplies still scattered on the ground where she had left them. "You don't know how to make camp," she stated.

"We have inns and posting houses in England."

"The earl told me that you were in the army, that you were in the field," she said as she covered the space between them in brisk strides.

"I was an officer," he explained patiently, annoyed that he had to explain anything. "I had a batman to do the housekeeping."

She stared at him, her face tilted in a considering manner. The corners of her mouth curved up in that odd little half smile of hers as she pointed to one article, then another, and spoke to him in exactly the same tone he had used on her while pointing out eating utensils and glasses. "That is an ax to cut wood for the fire. This is kindling to start the fire." With the same brisk movements, she bent to pick a rolled object. "This is a bedroll to sleep on. Extra blankets are in the wagon." She straightened, her hand finding the small of her back and massaging, as if it pained her. She waved her other hand toward the stream. "There is your bath."

He narrowed his eyes at her and clenched his fists, breathing deeply to tame the savage mood that descended upon him at her patronizing manner. But then the moon shot mellow rays of light through the trees and he saw a hint of mischief gleam in her eyes. Just a hint but enough to remind him of their first meeting and how he had lost patience with her fumbles over the silver and crystal.

Lowering her hand from her back, she waited, her gaze steady on him, watchful, as if she expected anger because she had thrown his own behavior back at him.

He cocked his hat and nodded mockingly at her. "I believe we are even, Mrs. Ashford."

Her eyes widened, and she breathed deeply. "You remember?"

Remember? He favored her with a wicked smile as visions of Rachel standing in the firelight, removing her clothes for his amusement were superimposed over the vision of Rachel standing in the moonlight, here and now—

He cut off the memory, denied the temptation, and picked up the ax, resting it negligently on his shoulder. "Oh yes, I remember . . . everything."

Her gaze faltered and fell before his deliberately suggestive regard of her body, from ridiculous bonnet to breast and waist and hip. She shook out a bedroll and spread it in the shelter of the cliff. "You should have time to bathe while the food is heating."

Heating? He'd been in the territory long enough to know what that meant. A warmed-up can of beans and bacon and cold bread, most likely stale. His stomach turned over and curled upon itself at the prospect.

Rachel sighed: "It's too late to cook fresh meat tonight."

Nodding, he picked up the ax and searched for a likely tree.

''The one behind you has some dead branches,'' she said as she unsheathed a wicked-looking knife and efficiently opened the first of two cans of beans and one of peaches.

With a crooked smile, he saluted her and began hacking off leafless branches that he presumed to be dead. At least he knew how to build a fire. It couldn't be any different from laying one in a grate, and he had idly watched his batman perform the task a time or two.

He angled his head to watch Rachel set up the camp, absorbing the mechanics of each task. It was one thing to allow an employee to serve him, but quite another to be dependent on a woman. Particularly a wife who already held too much of his life in her hands.

Rachel heard Henry curse as he stepped into the stream. From the corner of her eye, she watched him, a tall figure blurred and dappled by moonlight. He had waded in without testing the water and was fully immersed before his senses reacted to the cold. And then she heard him groan, an abrupt, undisciplined sound, as if he were in pain.

In one way he was like every man she had ever known—so full of cockiness and stubborn pride. All day he had shifted in his seat and plucked his clothing away from his body when he thought she wasn't looking. And she'd seen how he hesitated in every step, setting his weight gently on his feet, preventing the leather of his new boots from rubbing too harshly against his heels.

Water splashed and she knew that he had left the stream. She shifted to better see his dim outline through the trees as he gingerly dried himself with a length of linen and stifled another groan.

Hoping that he had something soft and worn to put on, she poured two tin mugs of coffee and sat down near the fire.

She nearly choked on a swallow of coffee as he emerged from the trees. His legs were bare except for soft carpet slippers on his feet, and he wore nothing but a fine, brocaded dressing gown.

With a sigh, he sat down on a rock next to her and cocked a brow as he accepted the mug of coffee she held out to him.

Well, she had hoped he had something soft to wear.

"I don't suppose we have cream or sugar?" he asked after tasting his coffee.

"I could open a can of condensed milk."

"Anything."

"What you don't use will go to waste."

"God forbid."

Taking pity on him, she reached for a tin and dipped into it as she leaned over.

"What is this?"

"Sugar." She held her hand over his mug and dumped in a palmful of grains.

"Are you sure you can spare it?" He shifted and winced. The robe fell open, revealing the chafed skin on his calves.

Unable to look at him without laughing, she bent over the pot simmering on the fire. "Would you like some beans?"

He shuddered and sighed and nodded, and took the tin plate of beans. He took each bite as if it were going to rise up and bite him back.

"I added some carrots and baking soda so the beans wouldn't . . ." She stared down at her lap. It had been so easy to speak of such things with her mother's girls, and even the men who had come to the house had no qualms about joking about bodily functions. But Liddie had told her that it wasn't done in polite society, and such things were to be treated with the utmost delicacy.

With this in mind, Rachel searched for a delicate word to complete her sentence.

"Create wind?" Henry said as he set down his plate. "I'm relieved to hear it."

She smiled then. She couldn't help it. What would Liddie say if she could see Henry sitting before a campfire in a silk dressing gown and carpet slippers, speaking of gastric disturbances while Rachel searched for a way to avoid it?

Henry's hand stilled halfway as he raised the mug to drink. He stared at her mouth, then her eyes, locking her gaze with his, holding her captive as the moon silvered his eyes and the fire cast unearthly shadows in the hollows of his face.

The smile slipped from her face, and she moistened her lips with her tongue. He'd looked at her like this before, only then it had been her body that held his attention as she stood before him in a thin muslin gown with her hair unbound and falling over her breasts, shielding her. Then he'd seen only what others saw. Now she felt as if he were searching for more.

She shivered and jerked her gaze away from him as she picked up the plates and carried them to the stream, lingering over their cleaning. Sounds reached her from the campsite—of Henry moving about, checking the horses, then sighing as he settled once more.

It was only a look, she told herself. Nothing more.

He was standing by the fire when she returned, his legs braced apart beneath the robe, his chest a wedge of hair-dusted flesh where the front parted. "Is it time to retire, or is there some other chore to perform?" he asked, not looking up.

Grimacing as she bent to pick up a pail and a small pot, she spoke with the quiet authority she'd learned to use on the men who worked for her. "Remove your robe and lie down on your stomach."

His head lifted with a jerk and his expression was instantly wary. She waited, facing him with the pail in one hand and the small pot in the other, saying nothing.

His features relaxed and his mouth took on a mocking slant. "On my stomach? I doubt either one of us will find satisfaction in such a position unless you plan to be my mattress."

"I am trying to help you," she said evenly, refusing to rise to his bait and suppressing the urge to fling the contents of the pail in his face.

"No doubt," he said dryly. "And I appreciate your gesture, but it has been a long day. Perhaps you will bestow your generosity another time?"

"This," Rachel said as she strode toward their bedrolls, "is the last time I will offer to help you in any way. Do you want relief or not?" Again she grimaced as she set her burden down.

He sauntered toward her, his hands in the pockets of his robe, his face arranged in an attitude of mock resignation. "If you insist." His hands appeared and found the sash knotted at his waist, lingering as he arched his brow in a way she was finding annoyingly familiar. "But I assure you it is not necessary."

"It's necessary," she said, "or we will be stuck here for at least another day."

His brow climbed a little higher.

"Take off the robe or it will be ruined."

The knot gave and the robe parted as he watched her with a challenging smirk. "Be gentle with me," he whispered suggestively as he shrugged the dressing gown off his shoulders and tossed it aside.

Her gaze raked him from head to carpet-shod feet, missing nothing—not his broad shoulders and chest, nor the arrow of fine hair that pointed downward to a full erection.

It didn't last. His shaft began to sag the moment she tossed the contents of the bucket all over him. Now she had his attention.

He sucked in his breath and expelled it, then took a step toward her, his eyes glittering with fury.

She stood her ground, knowing somehow that he wouldn't hurt her, knowing, too, that if she backed away, she would be inviting more of his taunts and disrespect. And suddenly his respect was important to her.

She dropped the pail and studied the results of his dousing, watching as liquid streamed from his chest to his groin and down his legs. "Cooled chamomile tea," she said, imitating his mockery. "It is efficacious in soothing skin rashes." Her gaze swept him once more and she nodded as his erection dropped between his legs. "If that doesn't relieve you, I'll apply some balm once you've dried."

Henry felt it—the soothing coolness on his abraded skin—and he heard Rachel's mimicry of him, her defiance and lack of fear, as if she knew that he would turn no more than words against a woman, against her. It had always been adequate before—to keep people from getting too close, from getting under his skin as she had done without him being aware of it. She defied all the lessons he'd learned about women, all the opinions he held about humanity in general.

Clenching his hands, he stopped midstride and closed his eyes, willing his body to relax an inch at a time. Tea, for God's sake. She'd drenched him in tea, when he had anticipated being drenched in her hair, the scent of lavender, the heat of her passion.

He opened his eyes and found her standing exactly in the same spot, her stare unflinching, the pot of balm in her hand. A curl had escaped the long braid coiled at the back of her head, a hint of softness in her otherwise stern countenance. He groped for something to say, disturbed that nothing came readily to mind. It unsettled him. Words had always been his greatest weapon, and his greatest defense. But then it was a dicey business, defending oneself while standing naked in the middle of a wilderness. He'd learned that when he'd fallen victim to a whore at fourteen, and he'd known it when he'd insisted Rachel disrobe before him that night in the hotel. In light of such a travesty, he supposed she was entitled to retaliate, and in this case, he was more amused than angry that she should turn his own actions on him.

The line of least resistance seemed appropriate. "Do your worst, Rachel." With a gallant bow that he'd last practiced before a duchess of formidable stature, he lowered himself to the bedroll and reclined on his stomach.

Something cold and slimy plopped onto his buttocks, and he groaned, not realizing until then that even that part of him was chafed. More of the stuff was slapped between his thighs. He gritted his teeth and forced himself to lie still, his discomfort for once dictating prudence. After all, the tea had eased the burning in his flesh, and only God knew what she might do to him if he balked.

"It's salve made with aloe," she said, her voice as feather light as her touch between his legs, not at all the roughness he expected. Her fingers circled gently, rubbing the slime into him until it was comfortably warm from her touch. His skin tingled as it absorbed the concoction, and her fingers increased their pressure, kneading away the tightness in his muscles as they massaged his thighs, around to his buttocks, and back again, the sides of her palms brushing his sac, yet not teasingly, not suggestively.

She was seducing him with something he was not accustomed to—with tenderness, and a simple caring for his comfort.

More cold slime plopped onto his upper back. He groaned in sheer bliss as her hands began to work their magic over his shoulders, down his spine, harder there, more insistent that his muscles surrender to her ministrations. Her fingers seemed more like twenty than ten as they kneaded and coaxed and seemed to caress him all the way to his bones. She rolled the cords in his neck and over his shoulder blades, then down again in long sweeps, up again with the heels of her hands. Even his face was not exempt from her care as she worked over his jaw until it, too, relaxed. And then her hands stroked his arms, gently, then with more strength as they rubbed in a circular motion down to his hands, still moving in circles over and over again.

She took his fingers one at a time, running her own between them and wrapping her hand around each one to stroke up and down on first one hand, then the other. He felt boneless, formless, mindless as she instructed him to turn over and he obeyed, willing in that moment to let her gut him if it would feel half as good as her hands on his chest, his stomach, and down to the chafing between his thighs.

He watched her as she leaned over him, her body swaying back and forth, up and down in rhythm with her hands, the stray lock of her hair brushing her cheek and gleaming with a silver-gold patina over rich, dark brown. Her eyes were distant, as if she were elsewhere, perhaps dreaming, perhaps thinking of nothing at all. He saw no calculation in her expression, felt no deception in her touch. An intimate touch that left not an inch untended, yet he remained unaroused, feeling only the simple, undemanding generosity of her actions light a spark in his dormant soul.

She removed his slippers and massaged his feet as she had his hands, and again he groaned as her fingers rubbed balm into his raw flesh, up and down, over and between.

It would not last. It could not, because nothing ever did. But for now, he would accept it—the comfort and the caring that were surely temporary. Seldom had he allowed himself to be so vulnerable. Only rarely had he been allowed to need, and then he'd had to pay a high price for his weakness. He closed his eyes, accepting the thoughts that grazed his mind, too light to leave an impression, knowing that tomorrow the sun would beat down on stone and dirt and the wind would blow away any illusions that lingered in the shadows.

This would not last.

Nothing ever did.

11

Henry slept without moving as if he were afraid of disturbing his own peace.

Rachel sat motionless as she watched him, careful to blend with the night as she held the shotgun across her lap, her back to a large rock and the fire off to the side where it would not blind her to the shadows. Confusion kept her awake long after the moon fell beyond the rim of the world and the howls and titterings of nocturnal beasts grew silent.

Henry had fallen asleep while she was still applying ointment to his abraded skin. She'd known the exact moment when he had relaxed, accepting the relief she offered for what it was—a simple act of kindness. That display of trust surprised her. Until tonight, she had seen only his anger, his strength and power, the darkness that seemed to hang over his thoughts. She hadn't expected to learn—to recognize—that his strength might be like

hers, a disguise for his vulnerabilities, that his anger was
his defense, the darkness his sanctuary.

She'd recognized the darkness that swallowed light
and devoured hope. She'd lived with it for so many
years, huddled in her attic room, dreaming of a life that
could never be hers, accepting it, mourning the loss of
something she had only imagined. But Liddie had taught
her how to dream in the darkness, to see the light of
hope within herself. From what she had seen, Henry had
forgotten how to dream, and he had lost faith in hope
altogether. It disturbed her to know that he saw only a
void where beauty existed, that his emptiness was more
complete and binding than hers had ever been. It mattered because her touch had penetrated that darkness so
easily, mattered because she'd never imagined that she
would ever touch or be touched by any man in such a
profound way.

A sense of sadness crept into her thoughts, aching and
bittersweet. Until tonight she hadn't thought in terms of
personal involvement with anyone. Especially Henry
Ashford, a man who treated her as if she were some sort
of penance. He'd made it obvious that he didn't want to
be there with her, that he was resigned to the fate his
brother had set for him.

Resigned, as the girls at Madam Roz's were resigned.

A renegade coyote howled in the distance. Rachel tore
her gaze away from Henry to survey her surroundings and
check the fire that she'd kept burning hotter than she normally would have done—for Henry's comfort. Again her
gaze was drawn to him, her thoughts not far behind.

He lay exactly as she had left him, on his stomach,
the contours of his body limned in silver light from the
waning moon—the broad spread of shoulders and back,
the sleek wedge of waist and hips, the masculine rise of
firm buttocks that swept down to a long stretch of strong
legs.

She'd actually enjoyed touching him, savored the resilience of flesh and sinew as it responded to her hands, found pleasure in his body. That, too, had surprised her. She'd seen men before, strong men who were pleasing to the eye, but never had her reaction gone beyond a simple aesthetic appreciation.

She glanced at his pile of clothing, so carelessly tossed aside as if he expected a valet to magically appear and set the campsite to rights. And there on the ground where he had dropped it was the silk brocade dressing gown. She shook her head. He was so green he could lie down in the grass and get lost. At least he hadn't strapped a pair of pearl-handled Colt revolvers low upon his hips.

Sunrise glowed in the distance, a thin ribbon of pastel light across the eastern horizon. Sighing, she fed more wood to the fire, making as much noise as she could, then added coffee to the pot she'd filled earlier, letting the lid clatter back into place and setting the pot onto the grate next to a frying pan. She unwrapped a packet of bacon and cut it into thick slices before slapping them into the pan. Fat sizzled and spit and the mingled odors of breakfast wafted through the early-morning air.

She sensed eyes watching her, following her movements as she opened a paper bag of biscuits she'd ordered from the hotel cook. Tensing, she picked up the shotgun as she scanned the area, then set it down again and turned to meet Henry's ice-blue gaze.

He lay with his head on his folded arms, his stare intent and drowsy at the same time. And he was still, so very still, as he watched her, missing nothing. She recognized that, too, the watchfulness, the readiness to defend at the slightest threat. Out here, where the land was raw and needs were at their most primitive, it was easy to see what she had only guessed at before.

Her husband was a dangerous man.

"It is not yet light," he said.

"No," she said as she turned the bacon.

His gaze slid over her. "You slept in your clothes?"

"No." Lifting the pan from the grate, she removed the bacon and divided up the slices between two tin plates.

"You didn't sleep at all. Why?"

Rachel drained the mug of coffee she'd poured and stooped to pick up his robe as she carried the shotgun over to Henry. "You'll need to keep watch while I clean up and change." She didn't look at him. She couldn't. Henry asleep and naked was not the same as Henry awake and naked with his muscles tensed and more sharply defined, in his back, his arms, the tightness of his buttocks and legs. Her own body responded all too readily to the sight. She knew the signs, the sensations. Her mother's girls had been free with their conversations at the breakfast table.

She didn't want to be like them.

Abruptly she dropped the silk brocade onto his back, picked up her saddlebags, and turned toward the stream.

She inhaled deeply the scent of the French-milled lavender soap—an indulgence she refused to sacrifice in the cause of thrift. That and a few gowns of high quality were the only luxuries she allowed herself, both reminders of the respectable wives and daughters she had so longingly observed from the attic window of a brothel, while their men cavorted with whores.

She didn't want to be like them either, so accepting of their places in life that even the infidelity of their husbands was expected and tolerated. Since meeting Henry, she wasn't sure of what she wanted beyond . . . Henry.

She slipped off her shirtwaist, unfastened her skirt, and stripped down to pantalettes and camisole. The lather of fine soap soothed her and the water cooled her flesh as she used a linen cloth to wash her face, her neck, her arms and chest. It wasn't enough. She needed to wash away all memory of the night, cleanse away the moisture that had gathered between her legs every time she had looked at Henry, thought of him. Sighing, she shed the rest of her clothing and walked into the water, liberally using the soap on every bit of flesh she could reach.

"You kept watch all night?" The voice was low, controlled, and far too close.

She kept her back to Henry and told herself that he had seen her body before, that he had as much right to see it as she had to see his. "Yes," she admitted. Henry might be green but he was not stupid. But then she had known that. He watched carefully and learned with ease.

"I do not require you to guard me."

"You were tired and I was not." She shrugged. "You wouldn't know what to watch for or—"

"What to do?" he said with a touch of roughness in his silky voice. "I assure you that I can and will shoot anything larger than a squirrel or longer than a worm. My batman did not fight my battles for me, and neither will you."

"All right," she said. "But neither one of us can stay up all night. We'll have to sleep in shifts." She forced herself to continue rinsing off the soap, as if he weren't standing a few feet away.

"Ah, an interesting concept—to conduct a honeymoon in shifts," he murmured with evident sarcasm.

There was a rustle behind her and then silence.

She turned and laid the soap on the bank . . . next to a pair of new leather boots. Her gaze traveled upward, over long legs encased in fine, soft fabric, a narrow waist and white-shirted chest. The embroidered suspenders were there, attached to his trousers and emphasizing his shoulders. His head was bare, his hair tousled above arched eyebrows and a mocking stare. The clothes were much too elegant, but would certainly be more kind to his chafed skin. His gaze was much too knowing as it slid over her, pausing at her chest, which she knew was rising and falling too quickly, her breasts, which were puckered and erect with the chill . . . with his perusal. "Are you quite finished with your ablutions?" he asked in an amiable tone.

"No."

"Good." With another cock of his brow, he stepped back and lowered himself to the ground, languidly reclining on his side, his weight supported on one elbow, his gaze never leaving her.

"Is this how you keep watch?" she asked as she sank into the water up to her neck.

"I am merely following your example, and 'keeping watch' as you were doing when I awakened." He crossed his ankles adding to the illusion of natural indolence. "So, I am assuming that this is how one stands watch in this country."

There was something in his expression and his voice that told her he hadn't liked being observed while he slept, that he considered it a threat, and she might see beneath his nakedness.

She knew exactly how he must have felt. It was unsettling to bathe while he reclined on the ground, fully clothed, watching her every move. How long had he been standing behind her watching her rinse out her hair, brush her teeth, and wash her most private parts? From the look in his eye, long enough. The embarrassment of it surprised her. She had thought that condition shocked out of her long ago.

But then none of the men she had seen roaming the halls in various states of undress had been her husband, and she had never been alone with any of the "customers."

"Come out of the water, Rachel. You'll take cold."

She stared at her towel halfway up the bank, out of reach, then over at Henry, seeing a corner of his mouth slant upward in a way that she'd seen once before as she'd unbound her hair and shed her clothing for him. "I will not perform for your amusement."

With an aggrieved sigh, he pushed to his feet and strolled over to the towel, bending to pick it up, shaking it out as he closed the distance to the bank. He stopped in front of her and sketched a courtly bow. "You misunderstand me. It is not entertainment I wish, but to share breakfast with my wife."

"I will be there in a moment."

He smiled slightly, barely a smile at all as he looked down at her in the water, his feet planted apart, his arms outstretched to hold the large rectangle of linen open in front of him. "Come, Rachel. My appetite will be quite spoiled if I must look at a prune-skinned woman on the verge of consumption."

He gave another exaggerated sigh and turned his head away from her, presenting his profile to her and staring up at the boughs of a tree, as if he would stay there forever, admiring the pattern of blue sky peeking through the leaves.

Gritting her teeth even harder, she mentally recited every curse she had ever heard as she straightened and stepped onto the grassy bank. Immediately his arms closed in, wrapping the towel around her, overlapping the ends across her back. His body was close, so close and warm. His gaze didn't waver, focused only on her eyes, yet she felt as if he were staring at all of her.

She leaned back, trying to separate herself from him, but he shook his head and strengthened his hold.

"Be still, Rachel," he ordered in a tone she'd heard before, low and grave, creating fear, making promises. On that night in the hotel, she'd thought she was afraid of him, of what he would do before she was ready. But now she knew that she was afraid of herself, of what she wanted. Fear of what she might feel . . . what she *did* feel. . . .

Like the moist trails the water left on her back and each coarse blade of wild grass beneath her feet. Every waft of air that touched her seemed as if it were Henry's breath whispering of sensations she'd only imagined through the night. And she became aware of his hands rubbing the towel over her back, tentatively, a little awkwardly, applying pressure, then drawing away, as if his hands were acting against his will, and they had no experience in tenderness.

Still, he held her gaze, only that, and she could not look away from those ice-blue eyes that seemed to hold his emotions frozen within him.

She stood rooted to the edge of the bank, wanting to duck beneath his arms, to escape, yet knowing that it would be foolish to try. Showing fear to any animal was often a mortal mistake, and man was the most dangerous animal of all.

His hands widened the circles they were making on her back, working their way downward, to her waist, and farther still to the base of her spine, to her bottom. His arms tightened, pulling her closer, warming her with the heat of his body.

Was this the moment he would again claim what she had promised him? Now, while the sun burned a gentle dawn blaze across the sky? Was this to be the place where she would surrender to herself and claim the promise his body had made to her two nights ago? Not a bed, not a room enclosed by four walls and a door, but the earth, grass moist with morning dew, and a horizon that stopped short of home.

Anticipation and dread trembled in her legs. Her body was rigid as she fought the seduction of his touch, showing nothing of what she felt, what she wanted.

His hands skimmed upward, the fabric of the towel creating friction as his fingers followed the valley of her spine up to the base of her neck. Her head bent forward, and her gaze lowered as he swept her wet hair over her shoulder and kneaded the tightness in her shoulders and her neck with that faltering rhythm that held no hint of experience with such gentleness. But then she had never thought him to be a gentle man.

The top of her head touched his chest, rested against it as she stared downward, saw the bulge beneath his trousers grow, straining the cloth, fighting confinement. She wanted to touch it, hold it in her hands, caress it.

He breathed harshly, just once, as his hands paused and clenched on her back, bunching the towel between his fingers. He exhaled slowly, as if he were fighting pain, trying to control it, and she wanted to cry out at him, to beg him to stop fighting.

His hands relaxed on her back and one end of the towel slipped from his grasp, falling away from her, leaving nothing between them.

Her eyes blurred, seeing nothing now as her desire grew stronger, overwhelming her. She arched her neck and closed her eyes against the helplessness she felt— against Henry, and herself. She waited, anticipating the return of his hands on her, wanting more than the brush of his shirt against her breasts as she parted her lips, inviting his kiss.

It happened between one sensation and the next—his mouth descending on hers, his tongue penetrating and exploring hers as his hold tightened, crushing her against him with urgent strength. She could only grasp his waist, crumpling his shirt in her hands, hanging on to him with her own desperation.

He tore his mouth from hers and wrapped his arms around her waist, lifting her, taking her breasts into his mouth, one and then the other, drawing on her as bolts of pleasure chased through her body and pooled in the pit of her belly. She wrapped her legs around him and cried out at the friction of cloth against her most tender spot as he moved his hips, thrusting upward.

Again he tore his mouth away from her and she looked down at herself, at her swollen nipples, at the way they seemed joined together, one being rather than two. She sobbed in passion and need.

His touch was slight, a mere breath of feeling on her waist, skimming upward to the side of her breast as he began to slowly release her. Her legs fell away from him and she swallowed a shudder of anticipation. Now he would lower her to the ground, cover her body with his. Now he would take her—

She swallowed a shudder at the sensation that suggested pleasure. Her heart paused a beat and jumped as she heard a rustle of movement, felt damp linen being wrapped around her once more, one end tucked into the other over her chest. His hand lingered, his thumb inside the towel, finding the erect center of her breast, circling once, twice, three times. The pleasure was real now, piercing her, invading her. And then she felt nothing but phantom sensation and the sudden absence of the warmth of his body as his hand slid away from her.

She raised her head and opened her eyes, seeing the intensity with which he gazed at her, and it seemed as if a battle raged on his face between mockery and desire and something she could not name.

The swelling beneath his trousers was more pronounced, harder. His breath was slow and even, despite the way he seemed to force it in and out. The knuckles on his hands were white from the strength with which he clenched them at his sides. She stepped back at the same moment as he did, and felt the lap of water on her heels.

"No." She heard his voice, a strained monotone, and it didn't seem like his voice at all.

He hooked his arm around her waist, jerked her back against him, then grasped her chin in his hand, tilting her face up to his. "No," he said again, and she wondered what he meant, what he was denying as he opened his mouth over hers and thrust his tongue between her parted lips.

There was no gentle awkwardness, just hard demand. No tentative stroking, only bold possession. A heavy beat pounded in her ears, seemed to fill her with its rhythm. Urgent. Frantic. She wanted. She needed. She desired Henry.

The birds were singing. Leaves rustled. Water flowed lazily over rocks in the streambed. Yet all she was aware of was the throbbing inside herself, the invasion of his tongue, thrusting and dueling with hers, and the sound of Henry's breathing, harsh and controlled at the same time as he held her chin with one hand, held her body away from his with the other.

Controlled. She blinked, wanted to cringe away from him. More than anything that had gone before, his control made her feel as if her nakedness beneath the towel went deeper than flesh because he could govern his urges when she could not govern hers.

Sensation diminished to a tingling memory as he separated himself from her. She felt only air where his hands had been, saw his back as he abruptly turned away from her, his hands flexing at his sides as if he were trying to keep them from digging into his palms.

In that moment she didn't care about his struggle, or his whims, of which she was obviously one. She was frustrated and humiliated by his rejection, whatever the reason. She spoke carefully, releasing each word when she was sure it wouldn't tremble as she was trembling, with desire and anger. "I won't play games with you, *Mr.* Ashford. If that is what you want then Cheyenne is full of poker games and horse races."

He bent over, then straightened before turning back to her. Against her will, her gaze jerked up to his. Suddenly she felt the chill of the morning as he stared down at her, his expression remote, his stance relaxed, as he held her clothes hooked on his finger.

"Haven't you heard, *Mrs.* Ashford?" His voice was calm and wry, with the familiar edge of sarcasm. "I come from a long line of dilettantes. Our sole purpose in life is to pursue diversion without having to work for it." His gaze raked her body. "And you are quite diverting."

She wanted to grab the clothes and run behind the nearest tree. But she stood firm, taking the garments from him with movements as controlled as his. "I'm happy to have entertained you. Remember it well because it will not be so easy for you again. Next time you *will* have to work for it." She brushed past him then, walking sedately toward the campsite in her damp linen toga to dress by the warmth of the fire. Never had she felt quite so cold and alone and empty. And as she jerked on her clothes, she muttered under breath, cursing the man who had the power to fill her with pleasure even as he stripped her of pride.

Henry dipped his face into the stream over and over again, needing the sharp chill of the water to cool his anger. What was it about Rachel that chopped at his emotions until they were nothing but splinters and jagged edges? Why could he not view her with the same detachment with which he viewed other women? How could he want her when she had done nothing but hack away at his pride and his control with her competence and composure, her dignity and serenity?

When had he become so weak that he responded to every nuance of a woman's presence? He'd trusted her last night as he hadn't trusted anyone in many years. Except Luc. Luc, who had trapped him a right tangled coil this time.

Drops of water flew around him as he raised his head and shook it. He sat back on the bank and shifted as something hard jabbed him. Raising up on one side, he reached beneath himself and grasped the object. He opened his hand and the scent of lavender wafted through the air. It was soap. Finely milled, imported soap that brought back memories of lavender in his dreams before he'd ever met Rachel. Rachel, who stirred his emotions and his body as no woman had before. Was Luc feeling it, too? Henry smiled grimly. He hoped so— hoped that his twin was suffering as he was, with frustration and desire and the impotence of being trapped by vows and duty and an anger he'd forgotten how to release.

Until Rachel.

Luc had neglected to warn him that Rachel, in her own quiet way, was a dangerous woman.

He'd hurt her, yet that had never been his intention. He'd wanted her, yet he didn't want the same emptiness he'd experienced when she'd lain beneath him enclosed within herself, taking all and giving nothing. He'd wanted revenge, but when she'd leaned against him so pliantly, responding to him, wanting him, he had realized that her response could be far more threatening to him than her indifference. He told himself that his behavior toward her was spawned by his aversion to being beholden to anyone for anything, even gestures of kindness and compassion. Especially gestures of kindness and compassion.

His father had been good at dispensing such tokens of goodwill and love only to use them as weapons later, reminding him and Luc of his *benevolence* whenever they began to feel secure enough to behave like normal children. Henry snorted as he swiped at the dampness on his face with his sleeve. *Normal.* Their family had been anything but normal. Yet still, they'd hoped, as their mother had hoped, that the ugliness that ruled their lives would reverse itself, until their mother had died whispering the name of the demon who had destroyed her.

Henry had vowed never to fall into the same trap, never to fall prey to emotion and need, never to become a victim to his own weaknesses as his parents had done.

Luc still believed in the basic good of man . . . and woman. But then Luc was the first son, the heir, and treated with far more care and respect than Henry, who was a mere inconvenience and thorn in the old man's side since he'd appeared in the world five minutes after Luc. It was easy for Luc to live within his illusions. Henry could not. His demons were too close, writhing in his memories, howling at him whenever his guard was down. He'd learned early to avoid them by masking his thoughts with activity until his weariness drowned him in thick, shielding darkness.

Like last night. Rachel had given him peace, as if she had, through her hands, magically infused him with her own serenity. It had angered him, waking up to discover that she'd had such power over him, that she'd watched him all night as he slept naked a few feet away . . . that she'd taken care of him, and he had been such a willing charge. And so he'd acted in kind, rendering her as vulnerable as he'd been the night before, molding her responses as she'd molded his, reducing her to naked vulnerability in revenge.

But his revenge had been double-edged and caught him on the backswing, as she stood before him, speaking calmly, walking away from him with a straight-backed dignity he could only admire. He'd seen the flash of shame in her eyes just before she'd turned away from him and known what that dignity must have cost her. Hadn't he done the same thing time and time again? Too late he realized that she was as driven by demons as he was.

Only Rachel still believed that she could defeat them. Hell's bells, she believed that she could trust a complete stranger to be her husband and share in her dreams.

Work for it, she'd said. What a cruel jest that was. At least she didn't know just how bloody hard he was working against her and against himself.

12

He shouldn't give a bloody damn about Rachel's silence, Henry told himself for the third or fourth time, as he ate a cold breakfast of bacon, biscuits, and coffee and tried to ignore Rachel's equally cold companionship. How odd that her silence felt like loss when he hadn't cared a bloody rip before. Now he found it necessary to focus on anything that would keep him from his own thoughts ... like the sight of her hips clothed in Levi's, or her breasts straining against a shirt that had not been made to accommodate such an attribute, or the length of her legs accentuated by knee-high boots that were likely as old as she was. Even struggling against his desire was a welcome escape from his own company.

He tossed the remains of his coffee on the fire. "Do all women here dress this way?"

Rachel kicked dirt on to the fire, extinguishing the last of the flames. "Why?"

"It's inappropriate for a woman to show herself—"

She rounded on him, stared down at him with challenge in her eyes. "Is it? I'll have to remember that . . . and so will you."

"I am your husband." Deliberately he cocked a brow. "You dress or undress to please me."

She walked away from him to hitch the team. "Haven't you heard, Mr. Ashford, that this is a new world? Dresses and sweeping hats are for gentle places and gentle pastimes. So are silk dressing gowns and embroidered suspenders." She hoisted the saddle onto his horse and adjusted the stirrups. "And in this new world," she said conversationally, as if she were simply passing the time, "women dress and undress to survive." With that, she mounted the horse and walked it through the campsite. "The wagon is ready. All you have to do is follow my dust." Before he could reply, she rode away.

Henry watched the plume of dust rise behind her as she kicked the horse to a gallop once she cleared their campsite.

"Damn," he muttered as he gathered up the tin plates and mugs from their meal and dumped them into the wagon, food and all. After vaulting into the seat, he pointed the team in the direction Rachel had taken and urged them ahead. His teeth jammed together as the wagon lurched and jolted over the uneven ground. The landscape jumped in and out of focus, and he squinted to keep sight of Rachel. Her words hadn't been idle. There was no evidence of her presence except for a plume of dust on the horizon.

How she could scout anything while riding as if the demons of hell were nipping at her heels, he didn't know. He glanced up at the sky, noting that the clouds had become darker and lightning flashed in the distance. The air had cooled drastically, giving the wind sharp teeth that bit through his shirt, chilled him with apprehension. A storm was coming from the direction in which Rachel had ridden. Why hadn't she returned?

Of course he knew why. She hadn't wanted to scout anything. She'd wanted to escape him. He'd seen it in her rapid, jerky movements as she'd saddled the horse. She'd been angry, yet she'd controlled it, and taken it with her. He wouldn't be surprised to hear her screams of fury echoing in the wilderness. He wished she would scream. It would make her seem more like the other women he had known, less like a bloody paragon stoically suffering the callousness of her husband . . . as his mother had done.

Luc had been right. Rachel was an extraordinary woman. A woman whose honesty seemed as tangible as her sensuality. A woman who was unlike any he had ever known. He wondered how she had developed honesty in a world so full of deception and so much pride in a world that had no respect for such things.

She appeared in the distance, riding hard, her single long braid flying out behind her, her Stetson whipped off her head by the wind and held only by the cord around her neck. She slowed the horse as she drew closer, and her lips were moving as if she might be comforting the animal, soothing it.

He pulled back on the traces and set the brake on the wagon, waiting for her.

Her cheeks were red from windburn and exertion, and her expression was grim as she vaulted off his horse. Her hands held the gelding gently, caressing his neck as she spoke in a low, breathless voice. "There is shelter up ahead." She pointed toward a group of monoliths rising from the ground like broken bones that had torn through the flesh of the earth. Tying the horse to the back of the wagon, she murmured reassurances to the animal and promised that she would care for him later . . . after . . .

"After what?" Henry asked.

"Twisters. I saw one about five miles east of here."
She pointed to the clouds, towering ever higher, becoming blacker. Rachel climbed up onto the seat beside him.
"We'll have to hurry."

Henry felt it then—the absence of currents in the air,
the unnatural stillness of wind and the animal life he
hadn't noticed until they had silenced. Urgency crackled
in the atmosphere, and he'd never seen anything like the
dull golden glow of sky and land alike despite the dark
clouds that seemed like a wall separating heaven from
hell on earth. Twisters. An ominous implication. He
didn't ask for an explanation. He didn't want to know.

Bloody hell.

He released the brake and urged the team to greater
speed, turning the wagon toward the rocks as soon as
Rachel vaulted onto the seat.

Shelter was within reach when it began, a dull rumble
in the distance and the wind battering them from one
direction, then another. Rachel leapt from the wagon and
led the team into a wide crevice between the rocks as
she shouted at Henry. "We have to cover their eyes."

Without question, he copied her movements—pulling
kerchiefs from a box and blindfolding the animals, talking to them as they frantically danced in place, tying his
own black silk kerchief over his mouth and wedging
himself deeper inside the natural shelter, toe to toe and
face to face with Rachel.

The rumbling became louder, like a thousand trains
bearing down on them. He glanced through the opening
in the rocks that loomed overhead. The air was the color
of dust, as it collected in whorls, concentrating power
within each grain until it stung even through their shelter
and clothes. And from the dark clouds that seemed to
tower into infinity, an appendage grew downward like

the black tail of Satan himself, wide at the top and narrowing to a blunt point as it snaked toward the ground.

And as the funnel grew, it seemed to suck the air itself dry of oxygen, creating a vacuum that paralyzed all life in its path, imprisoning it in horror and fascination. Dirt and rocks spumed upward as the point of the tail struck with a deafening roar and plowed ahead at alarming speed, its path serpentine, ruling the wind itself, gathering its force and hurling it out again, using whatever was caught in its path as another weapon to bludgeon life from the land. A prairie squirrel flew past, caught in the grip of the wind, helpless and tossed about by the fury of nature.

The fury grew and Henry stared at it, mesmerized by the power contained within symmetrical boundaries. It was hell without fire, smoke without flame, roiling in an ever-widening circle as it rumbled past their shelter, then changed course and lifted up from the ground, the column spreading out and fraying like the wings of a dark angel unfurling to ride the wind.

The squirrel circled in the air, still in the grip of the fading storm, and landed with a soft plop within the crevice, as if it had been cast aside in disgust, too small and insignificant for hell to bother with. The creature lay on its back, stunned or dying, its feet twitching in the air.

Drawn by the squirrel's struggle, Henry tried to ease away, but Rachel's arms were around his waist, holding him tightly. He'd forgotten how close they were, had forgotten even her presence in his fascination with the storm.

"No," she shouted above the wind. "Not yet. It's not over yet."

He followed her gaze beyond the rocks and saw that another tail was snaking down from the clouds—Satan

still in search of souls to sweep into his domain. He
realized that Rachel was trembling against him as her
hands dug into his waist. He looked down at her, saw
her eyes wide and unblinking above the silk kerchief
protecting her mouth, heard the rapid breaths that pushed
the cloth out and drew it in again.

She was afraid and clinging to him. He didn't think
beyond that, but cupped the back of her head with his
hand, urged it against his chest as he stroked her hair.
He felt awkward, his fingers tangling in the long strands
that escaped her braid, unable to find a soothing rhythm,
yet still he stroked . . . because she sighed as her body
relaxed against him and her hands spread out on his
back, because her trembles eased, and she released a
single sob. Because no one had clung to him in such a
long time.

The tail forming in the sky shattered on a gust of wind
and dissolved. Henry watched for more, but none came
as the clouds began to flatten and race and rain fell in
slanted sheets, washing away the flying grit that coated
them from head to foot. He reached down Rachel's back
and caught her hat, setting it on her head. Water ran
down the brim and doused his chest, but he didn't care.
Rachel was all that was soft and warm in a place where
only hard stone seemed able to survive.

The rain moved on with the clouds, leaving blue
patches in the troubled sky. He turned his head and saw
the squirrel sit upright, its head cocked toward them,
watching them. Such a small creature to ride the storm
and survive the lash of Satan's tail.

What was it like, my friend? Henry asked silently, and
wondered if a man could fare as well.

Rachel's hands fell from his back and she drew away
from him as she raised her head to inspect the destruction outside their haven. A wide swath of rocks and
brush lay broken and mangled within the path the storm

had followed, as if that strip of earth had been turned upside down and shaken out, leaving everything outside its boundaries undisturbed. A rabbit lay beside a bush torn up by its roots, its sides heaving and a hind leg twisted at an odd angle. The ground squirrel scurried away.

"It's over now," Rachel said as she eased past him, calm once more. She left the shelter of the rocks and bent over the rabbit. A moment later, she returned, the animal hanging lifeless from her hand. "We'd might as well camp here. It will take awhile to cook this."

"Cook?" he asked, staring at the rabbit, wondering why the only sign of life he'd seen during their journey was a squirrel too mangy even for death and a harmless rabbit left to expire in helpless agony. It angered him to know that life was the same for man and beast alike.

He clenched his fists against the rock and spoke without looking at Rachel. "There was a squirrel here a moment ago. Shall I hunt him down for you to add to the pot?"

She set the rabbit down and walked over to him. "He was dying, Henry," she said quietly. "We would have had to hunt for meat soon, anyway."

Henry's jaw clenched and locked as he stared at the creature. His hand reached out and he stroked one long ear with his finger—only once—then abruptly jerked away.

Rachel tilted her head. "Have you ever eaten rabbit?"

He turned away from her. "I have eaten meat that was called rabbit," he said without inflection. "But it was in parts and had no eyes, nor ears nor fur." Striding to the entrance of their shelter, he called over his shoulder. "I will gather wood for the fire. At least the storm has chopped it and laid it at our door." He gathered the pieces of brush and wood strewn over the ground and dumped it at Rachel's feet, then retrieved a silver flask from his carpetbag in the wagon and disappeared into the gathering dusk.

He stood at the entrance to the crevice, backlit by the full moon as he gazed down at the small mound of newly turned earth. His hair was tousled by the wind, a lock falling over his forehead, and the day's growth of beard shaded the planes and hollows of his face.

Rachel chewed on pemmican and dried fruit and sipped coffee as she watched him, his head bent over his leather folder, his pencil flying over the paper—sheet after sheet of it, rendering images of what? The small grave of a wild animal? The looming walls of their shelter? Or was he drawing something only he could see? She'd never had a desire to pry into the affairs of others before. It had been hard enough to see what was obvious without searching for more. But Henry stirred her curiosity and her imagination. It seemed important to know what drove him . . . what would touch him.

With slow, heavy movements, he closed the folder and approached her, accepting the mug of coffee she held out to him.

"There are biscuits left from this morning." She picked up a jar and opened the lid, then scooped precious jam onto the split biscuits with her finger.

Silently he lowered himself to the ground and took her offering, holding the bread stacked in one hand, staring at it.

"May I have some brandy, please?" she asked.

He slipped the flask free of his waistband and handed it to her, saying nothing, showing nothing of his thoughts in his expression. She poured brandy into her coffee, then added a like measure to his. There was so much silence in him, Rachel thought, and wondered that he hadn't drowned in the darkness within himself. A darkness that reached out to her and filled her with a melancholy she could not name.

The brandy-laced coffee warmed her, soothed the restlessness that had been a part of her since she had left Henry sleeping on the settee. Draining her mug, she set it down and rose. "I collected rainwater from the rocks"—she pointed to a pot—"if you want to wash. You can take the first watch and wake me in four hours." Without waiting for him to answer, she lay down on her bedroll and closed her eyes, immediately caught up in the rush of weariness sweeping through her mind, obscuring everything but dreams.

In sleep, she saw Liddie and Grace imprisoned in the writhing clouds of a twister, and she saw Phoenix standing in the midst of it, unscathed by the wrath of nature. And she saw Henry standing too close to the storm, watching, waiting, daring it to take him, daring it to keep him once it had.

Her eyes snapped open and she inhaled, feeling as if it were the first breath she had taken in a long time. Storms had never frightened her before, but this time it had been too close, too threatening in its kinship with Henry. His fascination had been as palpable as the grit-laden air. She'd held him as tightly as she could, afraid that the savage beauty of the storm would lure him into its macabre dance . . .

She'd known then that she would not surrender him so easily.

Unblinking, she lay still, remembering where she was, who she was, and where she was going. She remembered that Henry had held her just as tightly as she'd held him, as if she might save him from himself.

He was there, sitting in front of the mound of dirt, his elbows resting on his outspread knees, his head bent. "Why?" he said without moving, his voice low and raw as if the word had been wrenched from him. "Why didn't you cook the rabbit?"

She shifted onto her side and sighed. Why? A simple enough question for a simple enough act, yet the answer was difficult to give, like tearing off a piece of herself and handing it into his care. Yet she knew she would answer. As she'd held the rabbit, she had seen emotion cross his features, briefly, but enough to touch her. Since that moment, she had wanted to touch him, too. "When I first went home—to the Big Horns—I had to learn how to live without city ways," she said softly. "We had chickens, and they were noisy and dirty and always pecking at me when I'd gather their eggs or feed them. Someone else always killed them and dressed them out for food, and I always ate them. They weren't the same—the meat on the table and the smelly things out in the henhouse." She lifted her head and propped it up on one hand. "One day when the hands were all busy, I had to pick out a hen for dinner. I thought it would be easy, but when I'd caught the meanest one and wrung her neck, I got sick. I didn't eat that night. It was a year before I could eat chicken again."

"But you still hunt meat and eat it."

"It's better than starving."

"Ah, yes, a human failing—to blind ourselves to our own sensibilities in order to survive." He smiled then, a small, whimsical lift of his mouth. "The jam—I take it that it is a luxury out here."

"Yes."

"The rabbit would have made a good, hot meal."

"Yes."

The smile disappeared. "Then why in bloody hell did you bury it?"

"Because you wouldn't have eaten the stew and it would have gone to waste."

He poked a finger in the dirt and seemed to be drawing pictures on the mound, his brows drawn together as he squinted down at his handiwork, his head angling one way then another while he worked. "No, I wouldn't have eaten it," he said, the familiar mockery back in his voice.

"Why?"

His mouth slanted up at one corner, a grimace more than anything else, as he turned his head to look at her. "Because there was no hunt, no chase. The animal was a victim of a force too great to elude. He didn't have a chance. Because he suffered and didn't die cleanly." Abruptly he shook the dirt from his hands and rose to feed more wood to the fire, his movements stiff and awkward. "Go back to sleep, Rachel. It is two hours before your shift."

Rachel laid her head down and closed her eyes. It was over—that brief moment of sharing small pieces of themselves, pieces that seemed to match so perfectly that it frightened her. She felt a part of him in some indefinable way. She cared though she knew that she shouldn't, that it would make no difference when he was gone from her life. And she knew that he would go once the term of their agreement had expired. He showed no interest in his new life, or her part in it. He'd asked no questions, as if even the answers were more than he was willing to accept from her.

"Henry?" she murmured as she heard him settle against his saddle on the ground.

"Go to sleep, Rachel," he said gruffly.

It gave her the courage to go on—that gruffiness. "Henry, kindness, too, is a luxury out here, and not to be wasted."

"Kindness," he said, "is a luxury anywhere, and one that we can seldom afford."

Her breath shuddered at the bitterness in his voice. She knew how very much bitterness hurt, inside where no one could soothe it but oneself. "Mine will cost you nothing, Henry," she whispered. "There is no need for you to throw it back in my face."

As she drifted off to sleep once more, she wondered how many times Henry had been a victim of forces more powerful than he, how many times he had been left to suffer alone, without the luxury of human caring.

"I will try to remember that, Rachel," she thought she heard him say, a soft whisper on the edge of her dreams.

13

Rachel had been wrong. Henry didn't know how to play games, but took everything seriously—too seriously. Everything he did was a crusade in the name of pride. To Henry, travel was carriages and coaches, sleek ships and fast trains. It was a fine, expensive horse and posting inns with hot fires and warm food and soft mattresses. Yet over the past two weeks he'd learned surprisingly fast, and with predictable silence. The second night out, after the storm, he hadn't awakened her, but kept watch all night, paying her back for her vigil the night before. She had finally gone hunting for meat—a rabbit—which he'd eaten with an aversion he couldn't quite hide. When that was gone, he'd shot a deer that had wandered down from the foothills that loomed closer every day. He'd stared at it with a frown creasing his forehead, and she realized that he had no idea of how to dress out his kill. She'd taken over, working slowly as he watched, giving him a good view of her movements.

She didn't have the heart to tell him that there was too much meat, too much waste in such a large animal. Instead, she'd suggested a day of rest and used the time to salt down and cook the remains and pack it as best she could. "I can use the hide," she'd explained, peering at him from beneath her lashes and seeing that he'd clamped his mouth shut on another question he would not ask. "We can trade the meat at Finnigan's horse ranch for some vegetables and maybe some fresh bread."

She glanced over at Henry and saw that he was once again making pictures in the dirt, this time with a sharp pointed rock. The image was large, easy to see from where she knelt beside the deer. An image of the shape of the hide she'd cut from the animal, and other shapes, of the various parts of meat she set aside as she butchered the carcass. Henry drew everything he saw and everything she did, as if it were second nature to him to translate what he saw in the land around him into patterns in the dust, and he was engraving it in his memory for future use. And always when he caught her studying his handiwork, he brushed it away as if his vision of the world was his alone and not to be shared.

He caught her now, looking up at her just as her gaze swept over the last image. Abruptly rising from his crouch, he kicked it all away and watched it scatter to the wind.

She had the absurd urge to apologize to him for eavesdropping on his thoughts, for that is what his pictures seemed like to her—his thoughts.

Finished with the cutting, she sat back on her heels and grimaced at the mess on her clothes and hands. At least they were camped near a creek where she could bathe. "We should smoke the meat or jerk it," she said idly as she began to salt each chunk and wrap it in burlap. "But since we will arrive at the Finnigan's within a day or so, it will keep this way."

Henry helped her, mimicking her movements. For such a dandy, he was surprisingly willing to work, though more often than not, his distaste for whatever chore he performed was evident.

"After two weeks of seeing nothing but an occasional creature, I find it difficult to credit that anyone lives out here," he said conversationally. "Let alone anyone so civilized as horse breeders."

"There are homesteads and farms and ranches scattered throughout the territory," she said.

"Then why have we been sleeping on the ground and slaughtering our food?"

Rachel rearranged the contents of the wagon, emptying a sturdy wooden box to store the salted meat in until they reached the Finnigan's. "We haven't time to stop and visit," she lied. "I've been away from home too long already." That was true enough, as far as it went. She wouldn't tell him that she wasn't welcome in most of the homes in Wyoming, and most likely Colorado. She couldn't tell him that her mother had serviced men from the lowest and the highest planes of society from Denver to Montana. While he made disapproving comments on some of her activities and her mode of dress on the trail, he still treated her like a lady, refusing to allow her to carry heavy objects and helping her down from the seat of the wagon, as if it were the finest carriage and she were dressed in silks and satins. They were little things, but courtesy and respect in any form was a novelty she wasn't anxious to lose.

"Is 'home' a pile of wood and mud dropped in the middle of this wasteland?" he asked, as if he were simply making small talk.

She looked up, toward the mountains barely visible in the distance. "No. It's mountains. High mountains surrounding a basin of green grasses and bright flowers and tall trees that are green all year round. We have aspens, too, that turn gold and red and orange in the fall." She smiled then, thinking of the beauty and richness, the protection and isolation from a world that did not want her. "It's like living in a world separate from this one."

"And is there a dwelling or am I doomed to live like a primitive for the next five years?"

Her gaze jerked to his, and she tilted her head as she wondered why he was asking questions now when he had shown no interest before. It pleased her—that small curiosity. It surprised her to feel a flutter in the pit of her belly and realize that it was pleasure. Pleasure in sharing her own visions of life with Henry. "There are houses, and we are building more."

"We? You mean that you and I will not be Adam and Eve in the Garden of Eden? There is actually a civilization at the end of the earth?"

His sarcasm failed to dampen her enjoyment of speaking about home. Describing the Big Horn Basin and her small corner of it made it seem closer, more real than it had been since Luc had persuaded her to venture into the world that she had left behind seven years ago. "Yes. Aside from the men that work for me and their wives, there are a few others. Across the basin there are ranches owned by some of your countrymen." As she spoke, she spitted a piece of venison and placed it between two forked sticks on either side of the fire.

"Ah . . . buildings and people. Dare I hope that there is a town as well?"

"Not yet," she said as she opened a can of beans. "But we have a good start on one. I have a trading post and saloon, and a bunkhouse that I've made into a hotel of sorts."

We? I? Henry didn't like the sound of that. "Are you implying personal involvement in building a town?"

She scooped beans onto two tin plates and shrugged. "Of course. It's my land, and my money. Who else would do it?"

"Who else indeed. Next you'll be telling me that you will be the mayor or sheriff of this town you're building."

"Why not? Women have the vote in Wyoming. We can own our own property, serve on juries, and two women have served as justices of the peace."

"Good God. No wonder all the men wear guns," he said, then took a bite of beans. A town. Rachel was building a town. He couldn't credit it—a woman building anything but a wardrobe and a list of suitors on her dance card. But then, Rachel was no ordinary woman.

He wished to hell that she was ordinary.

A town. Bloody damn.

"Of course," he mimicked. "My wife, a landed heiress, is a merchant. That explains Luc's fondness for you."

"Everyone is a merchant here. We buy, sell, and barter, even the rich men."

"I understand that you are rich."

"I suppose I am . . . but only because I have bought, sold, and bartered. When I took over my grandfather's land, there was nothing but an old soddy and a few crops gone to seed."

"Tell me, am I the only man you have bartered for?"

She inhaled sharply, but otherwise showed no reaction to his dig. He'd made others over the last two weeks, yet still she wasn't accustomed to the knowledge that her dream was his nightmare. That she, too, was his nightmare.

He hadn't touched her since the storm. She was beginning to think that he would never touch her again.

All of his passion seemed concentrated on the images he rendered on paper, then tucked away in his folder, hidden from the light of day.

With a sudden coldness that seemed to penetrate even her spirit, she met his gaze. "You know there have been no other men."

"I know only that no other man has had you. I doubt most men would dare for fear of freezing to death."

"You had no such fear."

"I, madam, have nothing to lose. You have my name, my fortune, and my future in your hands."

She stared down at her hands as if the things he spoke of were tangible and she could see them, feel their weight, then she spread her fingers wide and lowered her hands to her sides and met his gaze once more. "Except for your name and a child, I want nothing from you, Mr. Ashford."

"Nothing?" he said as he took a step toward her. "Are you quite sure?"

She saw the controlled anger in him, the deliberate way he moved toward her, the icy stare, the tightness of his jaw. And though he reached for her in a languid manner, his grip on her arms was tight and firm, brooking no resistance as he drew her fully against him, forcing her to lean her head back to look up at him.

She did not want to resist. There had been a tightness in the pit of her belly ever since that night in the hotel, a tightness that came with hunger. A hunger that would not leave her since the morning they'd both lost control for a few, desperate moments.

"Is it only a child you want, Rachel, or is there more?" He traced the line of her throat with his finger, circled the hollow at her collarbone over and over again. "Tell me, Rachel."

"I want more," she whispered, without thought of lying. They had both been cheated enough.

He lowered his mouth to hers slowly, tauntingly, his lips brushing hers, back and forth, over and over again. She could not raise her arms to draw his head closer, his grasp was so tight, and so she raised up on tiptoes, straining toward him, reaching for him, reaching for more than a deeper kiss.

"Say it again, Rachel." His tongue skimmed over her lips and barely dipped inside.

"I want more, Henry. I want to—"

Her arms were suddenly free, and she lifted them to encircle his neck, but she found nothing but air as he backed away, that familiar mockery slanting the mouth that never really smiled.

"Then, madam, you must work for it."

At the end of the second week they'd arrived at the horse ranch where Finnigan and his wife had taken the meat in exchange for a Morgan gelding they'd raised and trained for Rachel. She didn't have the heart to tell Henry that she had long since paid for the horse, and she'd given Eamon a warning shake of her head when he had tried to refuse the meat. Instead, their host had insisted that they accept a night's lodging in their barn and a meal of venison stew and hot, fresh bread.

"Good God," Henry said as he surveyed their quarters for the night. Everything in the barn was spotless, from the loft to the stalls housing Eamon's breeding stock. Below was a shiny new pump to bring water from the well to the stabled mares. "Leave it to an Irishman to live in a hovel while his animals enjoy all the comforts of home."

Eamon and Maeve Finnigan had put all the money he had earned laying track for the railroad into their Morgan breeding stock rather than their dwelling. They lived in a soddy while their Thoroughbreds enjoyed the comfort of the finest barn in the territory. She didn't point out that the condition of stock meant the difference between life and death in the territories. Henry didn't appreciate her pointing out practicalities. Instead, she asked, "Don't you like the Irish?"

He'd mumbled something about "bloody troublemakers" and then sought out their host to discuss the Morgan breed. She'd smiled at that. From Luc she had learned that Henry's regiment had been posted in Ireland "to keep the peace" and Henry had irritated his superiors by sympathizing with the natives' plight. She'd learned enough about Henry during their journey to know that he embraced any cause as long as it was the losing one, consistently sympathizing with anyone that he judged to be a victim of superior forces.

"Does he know?" Maeve asked after Henry had followed Eamon out to the paddock to look over a new stallion.

Rachel paused in kneading dough. Few people along the trail would extend hospitality to "Rachel's kind," but Maeve *was* Rachel's kind—one of the rare lucky ones who had escaped the brothels with a man who saw beyond her past to the reason for it. In fact, Maeve and Eamon had met at Madam Roz's while Rachel was still a child, and she remembered her mother telling the burly Irishman that he spent so much time and money in Maeve's room that he ought to marry her and be done with it. To everyone's surprise, he had done just that.

"Rachel?"

She forced a smile and began kneading furiously. "No, he doesn't. He thinks I'm an heiress."

"True enough in these parts, I suppose," Maeve said as she tipped chopped vegetables from a cutting board into the cast-iron pot of meat simmering in a thick, seasoned gravy. "I saw the advertisement and knew it was you. There'd been some talk, but I didn't believe it until I saw it with my own eyes." She turned and leaned a hip against the crude wooden counter built around an old, chipped sink. "You got yourself some trouble in that man."

"Yes, I know." Rachel sighed. Henry was trouble—like a dark, turbulent night out in the open, with no shelter, no protection, no mercy.

"I'll bet it's been a real barrel of fun traveling with a dude like him."

Rachel looked up at Maeve. "He's the only man I know who can turn the wilderness into a drawing room."

With a gleam in her eye, Maeve wiped her hands on her apron and sat down across from Rachel. "This I gotta hear."

Rachel told her, about how Henry bathed every time they camped by a stream or creek and donned his silk dressing gown and carpet slippers, how he would lean back indolently against a rock or his saddle or a tree and light a fine pipe and pour himself a tin cup of brandy, wrapping his hands around the cup to warm the liquid and inhaling it before sipping it as if that cup were the finest crystal goblet. She didn't tell Maeve about the rabbit or the storm or Henry's grim insistence that whatever service she might perform for him—no matter how small—he would repay in kind. Those bits of information were private, belonging to her, moments and memories that, oddly enough, made her feel in some small way that Henry belonged to her.

In a large, overwhelming way that she didn't understand, she wanted him to belong to her. She wanted to belong to him, and as she always did when confronted with something she could not change, she accepted it.

A deep belly laugh interrupted her thoughts, brought her attention back to Maeve. "You're pulling my leg," Maeve said between gusts of laughter.

"No." Rachel smiled. "As you said—he's a dude, right down to his tailored Levi's and silk underwear."

"Silk? *Silk?*" Maeve wiped her eyes and laughed some more.

Rachel joined her, seeing the humor in it, when only a few days ago when she'd washed their clothes in a creek, she'd shaken her head at the extravagance of it. "Silk," she confirmed between chuckles. "With his initials embroidered on one leg."

"Oh, my." Maeve gasped. "I always wondered what those dandies wore under their fine clothes. I'll never keep a straight face when Morton Frewen and his cronies come through." She peered at Rachel through watery eyes. "Do you suppose men like that fart?"

"According to Henry, they 'create wind.' "

"Oh, lordy me." Maeve wiped her eyes again. "Well, your Henry might be useless as a stiff pecker on a dead man, but he sure as hell will be entertaining."

"Who's entertaining?" Eamon asked as he entered the soddy. "The Medicine Show comin' through?"

Rachel's gaze jerked to the doorway. Henry stood in the doorway, watching Eamon wipe his feet on the old rag rug just inside the door, as if he couldn't understand why a man would clean his shoes to walk on a packed-dirt floor. His gaze met Rachel's, and the bemused frown slipped from his face as he stared at her with concentrated intensity. She heard Maeve answer Eamon's question, heard him mumble something in reply, but it was so much babble as she stared back at Henry. He seemed to be focused on her mouth and she realized that she was still smiling broadly, that tears of mirth were still trickling from her eyes.

And when he stepped inside and wiped his boots on the rug, she couldn't stop herself from chuckling again. She couldn't imagine Henry performing such a simple courtesy in his fine mansion in England.

Still, he stared at her as he walked deeper into the one-room dwelling, slowly, as if he were being drawn closer to her against his will. Her smile smoothed into something else as her lips parted and her breath lodged in her throat. He reached out a hand and touched her cheek, chasing a tear down to her jaw, then wiping it away with his finger. Her hands were still in the bowl and she clenched her fingers, feeling the dough squeeze through her fingers, smelling the yeasty fragrance . . .

Henry lifted his finger to his mouth, licked off the drop of moisture he'd taken from her, and closed his eyes, as if it were sweet rather than salty, as if laughter were a flavor he'd never tasted before.

Rachel dropped her gaze to the bowl and her hands buried to the wrists in dough. She didn't want to see such things in Henry, didn't want to speculate about him. It always hurt to have those glimpses of him as he really was, to believe that he was as hungry as she was for sensations and experiences, for such simple pleasures of the mind and heart. It was one thing to accept the presence of trouble and quite another to invite its consequences.

"Out!" Maeve flapped her hands at the men, shooing them back into the yard. "We're working in here so you can eat, and you haven't done more all day than shoot the breeze. Go find me a nice fat chicken that I can fry up for Rachel and Henry to take with them tomorrow." She tossed her husband a bottle of whiskey, which he neatly caught one-handed. "And don't come back until you're called." The door slammed shut on Eamon's shouted reply.

Maeve pulled Rachel's hands from the dough and slid the bowl across the table to form the loaves. "You got real trouble, Rachel," she said.

"I know." Rachel winced at the tremor in her voice as she bent her head to focus on wiping the dough off her fingers with precise care.

"He's fighting you too hard, and he'll either have to give in to it or put more distance between you."

"He'll fight harder and then he'll leave," Rachel said and twisted her hands in her apron.

"Uh-huh. What'll you do?"

Forcing her hands relax their grip, Rachel stretched her fingers flat on the table. "I'll go on. I'll build my town and build my future with or without him."

"Just like that?"

"No," Rachel said, her strained smile at odds with the sadness she felt. "It will be hard, and it will take the rest of my life."

"It'll be worse than hard. You could always go back to your ma."

Rachel inhaled sharply. "No. I'd rather work in the dirt than wallow in it."

Maeve slapped the loaf she had formed into a pan so hard that the rounded top sank. "Is that what you think I did—wallowed in the dirt?" She waved a hand, cutting off Rachel's reply. "Never mind. That's exactly what I did and I make no apologies. I survived and I got out first chance I had. I plowed a field for hay this year and I clean out the horse manure every day, and I don't get paid for spreading my legs for Eamon with anything but knowing that he'll be in that bed beside me come morning."

"Don't you like being that way with Eamon?" Rachel asked, needing to know if it truly was different between husbands and wives than between whores and customers. She needed to know if only whores were free to find pleasure in the act.

"Like it? It's a hell of a lot easier to like it when you're doing it for love instead of money." She smiled and winked at Rachel, a bawd's wink that told a story of its own. "I like it fine, Rachel. Just fine." Her voice softened as she regarded Rachel shrewdly. "You think it's different when you get that little piece of paper? You think it's shameful to shiver and shake beneath your man just because it's respectable?''

''I don't know, Maeve. So many of mother's customers had wives at home, yet they came to the house for their 'pleasure.' ''

Maeve shook her head. ''Men can do what they please, Rachel, you know that. Half those so-called respectable men married so they'd have all the comforts of home, and they'd rather pay money to a whore than pay real respect to their wives. The other half don't care about anyone's pleasure but their own. They think the only kind of woman who can holler and sweat in bed is our kind. The wives put up with it because they don't know how to be women, and the husbands go to Madam Roz to feel like men.'' Carrying the loaves of dough to the counter near the oven, she covered them with a light, damp cloth. ''In some ways, you're lucky, Rachel. You know more than those cultivated ladies who think that cooking and sewing and birthing babies is all there is to being a good wife. You know how to please a man and yourself at the same time, and there's nothing shameful about that.''

''But I've never—''

''I know that,'' Maeve snapped. ''But you know what every woman ought to know and doesn't, and you have instincts just like any other woman. I'm telling you to use them. I'm telling you that you have an education that most women don't have. I'm telling you that you can use it to show that man what he'd be doing without if he leaves.''

''Use my body to buy a husband,'' Rachel said flatly.

''No! Use your body to show your feelings.'' She planted her hands flat on the table and leaned over, meeting Rachel's gaze. ''*God* invented sex, Rachel, not some randy cowpoke looking for relief on a Saturday night.

You know what's so good about having your man stay
with you when it's done? It's the little touches and the
talk and having his feet tangling with yours to keep
warm or maybe just because he needs to know he's not
alone. It's knowing that he'll still be there in the morning
because he wants to be there. And it's knowing that he
wants to be there because you're sharing more than a
hard day's work, and I'm inclined to think that's exactly
what God had in mind.''

"It seems so different."

"Hmph. You either do it 'cause you want to or you
do it 'cause you have to. Plenty of women on both sides
of the tracks do it for one reason or the other—married
or not. The thing that makes the difference is *why* you
do it."

"Five years, Maeve. I have five years of his life because he was tricked into marrying me.'' She couldn't
say more, couldn't voice the fear that if she gave all she
had to him, and he left her anyway, that she would still
be like her mother, with nothing to show for it but value
received for services rendered. Wasn't that the nature of
her strange relationship with Henry—a mutual "using"
of one another, each paying the price that the other
needed to survive? "He'll have what he wants after that
and it won't matter whether he knows what he's missing
or not. He'll leave.''

"Then take what you want while the takin's good.''
Maeve checked the rising dough, her back to Rachel, her
head shaking at the one loaf that still had a flat top.
''And when he's gone, you go on without him, and do
the best you can, just as you've always done.''

   He hated her. The emotion had sprung to full malev-
olent life the moment he'd heard Rachel's laughter, the
husky richness of it, and seen the dimple that danced in
her cheek, the bright tears of mirth tumbling down her

face that gave her eyes a luminous glow. She had seemed a stranger then, a vivid creature of light and promise, even with her hands buried in mounds of dough, her body wrapped in a voluminous apron made of flour sacks.

He'd itched to paint her like that, to capture the shine in her hair, to re-create the high blush that had tinted her cheeks when he'd touched her. But he had only pencils and chalks in black and shades of gray, and even if he did have the paints he'd been forced to leave behind in England, he would not have painted such a portrait. He left bright colors and beauty to those who believed in such concepts.

He hated her for knowing how to survive in this wilderness and making him feel the fool as he tagged along behind her, copying her movements. He hated her for her remoteness, for the way her laughter had died when she'd seen him.

He hated her for making him want her.

For good measure, he hated her for tempting him with the notion of a real bath only to be presented with a common galvanized steel washtub. He sat in the hot water, his body pleated like a lady's half-opened fan, viewing the stool at arm's reach that held a glass of Eamon's homemade whiskey and a towel cut from the ever-present flour sacks.

A pipe—a homemade affair called a "corn cob," courtesy of Eamon—hanging from his mouth, Henry leaned back and winced as the edge of the tub cut into the back of his neck. He reached for the towel, rolling it into a pillow and stuffing it behind his head. With a grunt, he eased his legs, one at a time, up and out to dangle outside the tub. Raising the glass, he toasted the shadows in the barn, downed the whiskey in one swallow, and closed his eyes.

It seemed a lifetime ago that he had languished in warm water and expensive bath salts in a marble facility so large that it could better be called a pool than a tub.

It *had* been a lifetime ago, when he'd been wealthy and privileged and free to raise hell on a whim. From what the Irishman had told him about the Big Horn Basin and Rachel's place there, and from what he'd already seen, the grim reality of his position had become painfully clear. It hadn't occurred to him that in this country a landed heiress cared for her own acres without benefit of tenant farmers, gardeners, and stable hands. It hadn't occurred to him that out here, "heiress" was a relative term—relative to whether one owned a pot to piss in or had to borrow a bush from Mother Nature.

And he was, God forbid, adjusting and taking a grateful pleasure in the makeshift luxuries of her existence.

A short burst of chilled night air hit him as the huge door opened a crack and Rachel slipped in, hastily shutting it behind her. It annoyed him—Rachel's habit of performing small acts of consideration, as if they had more between them than business contracts and a tin ring, as if she actually gave a damn.

He noted the slight twitch of her mouth as she glanced at him, but the amusement didn't reach her eyes.

"Have you come to wash my back?" he asked idly.

"No." She set down the blankets she carried and arched her back.

"If you wish to use the bath, I fear you will have a long wait. After disjointing myself to climb in, I am reluctant to risk further injury until the water is cold."

"I washed in the house."

"Of course. And I am relegated to the barn like the servant I am."

She lowered her hands to her sides and straightened. "I'm tired. Please turn down the wick on the lantern when you come up."

"You're tired? Impossible. We both know that you are a better man than I."

She lowered her head and rubbed the bridge of her nose. Just then she looked tired, her skin pale in the lantern light and her hands trembling just enough to notice. "Yes, I'm tired," she said slowly, carefully, as if she were trying to teach a new language to a halfwit. "I'm tired of your arrogance and your sarcasm. I'm tired of your pride and your cruel remarks." She met his gaze, a bright flush of color on her cheeks. "I'm tired of your anger, and I'm tired of caring about you, and I'm *damned* tired of feeling sorry for you."

He forgot everything as he folded his legs back into the water and gripped the sides of the tub. Everything but her words that froze and heated him all at once. The water cascaded down his body as he levered himself up and out of his bath, uncaring that he was naked and the air carried a chill. "Pity?" he said, almost whispering as he stepped into his slippers and wrapped a towel around his hips. He strode toward her. "You pity me?"

She didn't move, didn't flinch. "Yes. I pity you because your vision is limited only to what you see. I pity you because you can care only about animals and children you will never see again, like Benny and the rabbit."

"You waste your time with pity, madam."

"Yes, I know. It's easier not to care, isn't it? You don't have to get involved."

"You begin to understand."

"Yes . . . unfortunately." She reached for the ladder that led up to the loft. "I'm going to bed."

He hated the disgust in her voice, the resignation. Again he told himself that he hated her. "Let me help you, Rachel, since you are so very *tired*." He scooped her up in his arms. "There is one thing, however, that you have not yet grown weary of." He glanced at the ladder and felt her weight in his arms. Weight that seemed doubled for her lack of resistance.

"Not tonight, Henry." Rather than pleading or desperation in her voice, he heard only flat resignation. Instead of fear or anger in her expression, he saw nothing at all. He felt it again—that recognition of one soul meeting another in the void.

A soul that pitied him.

He swung Rachel over his shoulder and grasped the ladder, placing his foot on the bottom rung. "Yes, tonight. In our marriage of convenience, Rachel, there must be at least one thing that is convenient to me." She clutched at him to keep from falling as he struggled to climb up the rungs.

He levered himself up from the top of the ladder onto the floor of the loft and carried her to the mattress set against the wall. Bending, he released his hold on her and allowed her to slide down his body. She landed on the mattress as if she were boneless, her arms and legs splayed. She whimpered, a tiny animal sound of distress immediately stifled as she pressed her lips together. She gazed up at him and he returned her blank stare. She *was* pale, washed out as if she were a painting that had faded in the light. And then she rolled to her side and drew her knees up to her chest.

Animals and children. She looked like either . . . or both, lying on their crude bed as if she were trying to curl into herself to deflect a blow—or perhaps to deflect him. He clenched his jaw and breathed deeply, struggling for control.

Memories swept through his mind, overwhelming him—of himself at fourteen trying to curl up in just that way and his father grasping his legs, holding him still for the ministrations of a whore. He remembered the humiliation, and the utter helplessness he'd felt as she'd used her mouth and hands to force his response, as she'd climbed on top of him and rode him as if he were an animal. He'd been little more than a child. He'd felt like an animal.

With a muttered curse, he climbed back down the ladder and stepped back into the tub.

Bits of straw drifted down from the loft as Henry completed his bath, standing this time rather than wedging himself back into the washtub. It struck him as odd that the water was still warm, that so little time had passed between his moments of relative contentment and his trial by Rachel.

She thought he was too lazy to care for anyone who might care back. Good. And she thought he was arrogant and cruel. Even better. Perhaps one day she would realize that those very qualities were the foundation of his pride.

He grabbed the towel from a sawhorse where he'd laid out fresh underwear and his dressing gown—a comfort he refused to give up regardless of Rachel's opinion. And, he admitted to himself, it had become an affectation because of Rachel's comments. Ridicule was easily deflected by flaunting the object of mockery . . . with arrogance, of course.

Dry and feeling truly clean for the first time in over two weeks, he stared at the ladder. Was there a law against building proper stairs in a barn? *He* would build stairs in a barn, if he was to build anything, which he wasn't.

Again he heard the rustle of hay and then a soft, weary sigh. It was gratifying to know that Rachel was not as tireless as she seemed. He was exhausted from trying to keep up with her, unwilling to cry quits before she did each night. And each night they retreated to their separate bedrolls, falling asleep without a word between them.

The silence, too, was exhausting.

The night shadows slanted across the floor of the barn as the side door opened and Maeve walked in carrying a basket. She smiled broadly as her gaze swept over him, taking in the dressing gown and slippers. "Oh, lordy me. You are a dandy."

A dandy what? Henry wondered. "May I help you?" he asked, feeling as if he would draw less attention if he were dressed in tar and feathers.

Maeve bustled to the ladder and set down the basket. "You can give this to Rachel. Might ease her some."

"Ease her from what?"

"The misery. Came on her after dinner. Hits her hard every time."

"And what misery might that be?" Henry stared down at the contents of the basket, wondering what Maeve was talking about. He had noticed no distress in Rachel as he'd watched her help clean up after dinner. She'd been as efficient as ever, as quiet as ever, as remote as ever. The exhaustion she'd complained of had explained her paleness to his satisfaction.

"The monthly one." Again Maeve gave him the once-over. "What she needs is a baby. That fixes it for some women."

Henry scowled. He was getting damn sick of hearing about babies.

"You just tuck that hot brick up against her belly and stick a pillow over it to keep the heat in longer . . . and don't tip the basket going up. I stuck in a jar with my special toddy in case she can't sleep. Tastes better than Killmer's Female Remedy and does the same thing . . . and keep your distance for a day or two. She gets a mite cranky. . . ." Maeve's voice faded as she walked out of the barn. For all Henry knew, she was still dispensing advice and information as she walked back to the soddy.

He saw the folded pads of muslin rags beside the jar and the brick wrapped in flannel, and belatedly realized the nature of Rachel's crankiness. Evidently, the husband was doomed to share in "the misery" in such a primitive society. It presented a convincing argument for separate bedchambers.

He picked up the basket and climbed to the loft. A lantern cast a soft circle of light that barely reached beyond the mattress. Rachel wasn't there. Swinging off the ladder, he stepped onto the floor and reached for the lantern, turning up the wick and squinting into the shadows.

She was huddled in a corner, another quilt draped around her shoulders, her legs drawn up to her chest and her head resting on her knees. Her hair was unrestrained, free from its usual braid. He raised the lantern and saw that she was asleep, her skin pale, her features drawn. She looked small and frail and helpless.

She had chosen to keep sitting up rather than share a bed with him.

Something stirred in him, pounding like the beat of rain in a storm, flowing through his mind like a river of mud dragging at him. It hurt like sadness hurt. It smothered like loneliness smothered . . .

He set down the basket and walked to her corner, his steps slow, hesitant. For the second time that night, Henry picked her up—this time gently, clumsily—and cradled her against him as he carried her back to the mattress, laying her down, turning her onto her side. He placed the flannel-wrapped brick against her belly with a pillow against it to hold in the warmth, and she curled around it, her arms around the pillow, embracing the small comfort. He leaned over her, covering her with the quilt, lingering as he smoothed out the wrinkles and tucked the edges around her.

Her eyes opened. "Not tonight, Mr. Ashford."

He shuddered and his sigh was a harsh snag in the silence. "No, not tonight, Rachel," he said.

She blinked. "Because Maeve told you that I am . . . ill?"

Ignoring the question, he stepped around her to sit on his half of the mattress and remove the jar from the basket. "She brought you a toddy. Perhaps it will make you feel better."

Rolling to her back, she scooted up until she was propped against the wall behind them and accepted the jar from him. "By the time I drink this, I doubt I'll care how I feel," she said as she took a long draught, then gave him the barest hint of a smile.

He jerked his gaze away from her, away from the curve of her lips and the tip of her tongue as she caught a stray drop of liquid at the side of her mouth. He examined the arrangement of hay on the floor.

"Mr. Ashford?"

"My name is Henry," he said, annoyed by her formal address.

"Henry?"

"What is it?"

"This is a very large jar. Maybe it would help if you didn't care how you feel either." She took another quick swallow, then held out the jar to him.

"I have it on good authority that I have no feelings at all. In fact, I am arrogant and cruel, not to mention too lazy to care in any significant way. You said so yourself."

"I lied."

"You? The paragon of virtue and strength?" He took the jar and drank before handing it back to her. "Not likely."

She held the drink between her hands, turning the jar around and around. "If I am a paragon and you are a— how did you put it?—a ne'er-do-well, then the next five years should be quite interesting."

"How so?"

"Because maybe I will redeem you and you will corrupt me, and we will meet somewhere in the middle, neither paragon nor wretch."

"Are you suggesting that we become *ordinary*?"

Frowning thoughtfully, she plucked at the quilt. "If we don't, I think we might drive each other mad."

"Too late. We are already mad as hatters, Rachel."

She smoothed out the little peaks she had formed in the quilt. "Yes, I suppose we are," she said softly. "If you are not going to corrupt me, then I won't try to redeem you, Henry. Maybe that is all we need to find some sort of peace with one another."

With those few words, she had accepted him as he was. Yet there was a quality of sadness and resignation in her voice that bothered Henry. He told himself that he didn't care, and knew himself to be a liar. *She* cared—enough to attempt a truce between them . . . enough to believe he was worth redemption.

He finished off the toddy and set the jar down. His throat felt tight, resisting, as he tried to speak. He swallowed and called her name with a strained hoarseness.

She did not answer, but simply lay there, her arms flat at her sides. He cleared his throat and whispered so she would not hear the thickness in his voice. "The next five years would become bloody tedious if you were to become ordinary, Rachel."

And with those few words, he accepted that he did not—could not—hate her.

14

The rest of the journey was endless as death, and Henry began to wonder if they would ever arrive at Rachel's home. They traveled through mountains, over rocky plains and a dirty white desolation that Rachel had called Alkali Flats. And always, she pointed to the distance, as if she actually believed the end was in sight.

He humored her, knowing that it reinforced the truce that had begun with such fragile expectations and had, over the last week, become hope. *Hope.* He'd denied it for so long that he'd forgotten how it felt—the lift and promise of it, the sense of being nurtured by it.

He wasn't sure he could forgive her for reminding him.

Henry stared ahead at the ragged shadow on the horizon that was supposedly the rim of the Big Horn Basin as he drove the wagon, allowing Rachel to keep watch, though he was convinced nothing more deadly than boredom existed here.

The shadow rapidly grew in height and gained substance as they drove on. More mountains, and on the other side was Rachel's town, Rachel's home, Rachel's future. If he was lucky, there would be a water closet. He hadn't had the fortitude to ask. There were some disappointments in life that didn't bear thinking about . . . and he had never been particularly lucky.

She pointed ahead to the curve of a river. ''We'll follow that into the basin.''

She didn't look at him, didn't move at all, and her damned sunbonnet was firmly in place, hiding her face from view. He'd learned to appreciate the Stetson hat she'd worn with her trousers and cotton shirt during the journey. They had revealed her face for his appreciation and the telltale language of her body for his enlightenment as to her moods. But today she wore a dress for her homecoming, evidently preserving the image of ''town mother,'' so to speak. ''I'd ask how much farther, but I'm not sure I want to know,'' he said, preferring mindless conversation to the image of himself as ''town father.'' It was too literal for his taste.

''Why?'' she asked. ''Because you are weary of traveling or because you don't want to arrive?''

Ah, she had added defensiveness to her repertoire. Interesting. And ominous. ''Should I dread it, Rachel?''

''It depends on what you are expecting.'' Now her voice held a challenge.

He felt more comfortable with that. Rachel was, above all else, challenging. ''I expect a bunk house, saloon, trading post, and a dwelling or two. Hopefully they are more than hollowed-out mounds of dirt.''

''They are not castles.''

''Thank God for that. Damned dank and drafty—castles.''

She did turn to him then, her gaze direct and blank. "There is only one soddy—the original homestead. It's unoccupied."

Still, he had the feeling that she was daring him to cast aspersions on her way of life. He might be tempted to do just that if he knew more about it, and if he was anxious to end their armed truce. Oddly enough, he wasn't. He was bloody tired of being on guard, of fighting her. She had a disconcerting habit of disarming him with a few words, a look, a drift of lavender and smiles.

Since that night in the loft, he'd known that his real battle was with himself.

"I'm relieved to hear it," he said. "With windburn on one end of my body and chafing and calluses on the other, I shall be quite content in a log house with walls and a ceiling. I assume that I will find a real bed with blankets that don't reek of horse, and pillows that are softer than the average rock on the ground."

"I would have thought you'd be used to it by now."

"Rachel, I cannot believe that anyone becomes accustomed to such conditions. One simply is too weary to care."

"Do you care about anything?" she asked.

"I care about arriving at our destination within my lifetime."

"If we follow the river, we will be home in another two hours or so. By now one of the men has spotted us and has ridden to tell the others."

Henry noticed what he had overlooked during their conversation. They had indeed drawn up alongside the river and were now rolling through what seemed to be a wide groove cut through the mountains by the rush of water. As for the actuality of there being another human being in the vicinity, he saw no evidence of it. And then he realized what she'd said. "Two hours or so? It's that close?"

"Yes."

"Yes," he repeated flatly, irritated that they'd need-
lessly spent another night with only a campfire for
warmth and canned beans and jerky for nourishment.
Another night of four-hour shifts, and watching Rachel
sleep across the fire from him, wanting her, missing the
closeness they'd shared in the loft, the reassurance that
there was another person in the world who needed comfort in the dark. She had curled around him in her sleep,
and later he had curled around her. And when they had
awakened the next morning, they had lain unmoving on
their mattress spread over a cushion of hay, saying nothing, together in need, yet separate in loneliness. He'd
pulled away from her finally, but it had been too late.
She'd crippled him, disabled his anger, with the silent
promises of simple consideration and willing closeness,
with her earthy beauty and unaffected honesty.

"Then why didn't we continue on yesterday instead
of stopping midday?" he asked, trying even now to re-
capture his shield of anger, but all he felt was the vulnerability of false hope.

"Because we would have arrived after sunset. I didn't
want you to see home in a bad light." She turned away
from him, concealed once again within the shadows of
her clothing. "I wanted to make sure that you see everything as it really is."

They crossed over the pass from endless drabness and
hostile elements into a giant palette of vivid colors and
gentle winds. Trees grew everywhere and wildflowers
speckled the mountainsides and meadows like splatters
of paint. Mountains rose around them, great walls crumbled by time, and sprouting lush grass wherever soil had
collected. It looked both ancient and new, like part of
an unfinished canvas that was in the final stages of completion.

And as they rolled forward he saw another work in progress in the distance, rising from the floor of a smaller valley tucked between mountain slopes.

Buildings in every stage of construction were arranged along a crude street, some weathered and false-fronted, some so new he imagined he smelled sawdust. On a small rise, a house stood alone, freshly built judging by the brightness of whitewash that covered every inch of the exterior save the roof. Beyond that, he saw an old soddy with a goat grazing on its top of grassy earth.

"I count five buildings, three houses, and an oversized animal hutch that must be your soddy," he said with studied boredom. "Your *town,* I presume?"

"Yes." Her voice had a breathless quality to it, and she leaned forward as if she might close the distance a little faster.

The trail widened and flattened, which qualified it, he assumed, as a road. Just ahead was a whitewashed sign surrounded by flowers. As they drew alongside, he read the neatly painted letters:

PROMISE
population 30 36 32 39

Bloody hell.

They were close enough to see detail with some distinction now, signs on the buildings and a group of people gathering in front of the house on the hillock at the end of the road. One man emerged from a long building that reminded Henry of a barracks—no doubt Rachel's "hotel of sorts." A woman followed him out and remained standing in the middle of the street, shading her eyes with her hand as the man mounted a horse and rode toward them at a gallop.

Rachel inhaled sharply and reached for the reins. "Stop, Henry."

Reacting the curious note in her voice—not quite a catch, not quite panic—he pulled on the reins and reached for his rifle. It would be the height of irony to have traveled through no-man's land only to find danger barreling toward them from a pathetic little place called Promise.

Her hand covered his on the Winchester. "No, he's a . . . friend."

Her face had bleached of color, and her hand felt cold, her grip tight on his as her "friend" halted his horse directly in front of them.

"Rachel," the man said, touching the brim of his black hat.

He looked like something from the dime novels Henry had read on the train, his lean body shrouded in black from the coal hair growing over his collar, down to his plain, soot-colored boots. His face was sharp and strong, his eyes a gray so pale, they seemed clear, like pure light penetrating all that he saw.

Henry returned his stare and thought this must be what it felt like to be cut apart, studied, and put back together again.

"This isn't the same man," the stranger said to Rachel, a simple statement of fact.

Henry's skin prickled and his scalp seemed to crawl over his skull. The sensation increased as he held the stranger's gaze, feeling as if the secrets in his soul had been laid bare.

"He is Henry Ashford, my husband," Rachel said.

The man merely nodded, asking no more questions, as if he already knew the answers.

Rachel loosed her grip on Henry's hand. "Henry, this is Phoenix."

Phoenix again touched the brim of his hat, then leaned forward in his saddle and focused on Rachel. "New arrivals in town—Roz and two of her girls."

Rachel snatched her hand away from Henry's and clenched it in her lap. But not before he'd felt the chill in her fingers, the tremble that seemed to rock her body. "I saw her. Did she say why she came here?"

"Vigilantes. Seems the town got religion. Roz and the girls are in pretty bad shape."

Rachel dug her hands into the folds of her skirt and he had the impression that she was struggling against saying too much, or asking anything at all.

Impatient with being ignored and left ignorant in what was obviously a weighty matter, Henry leaned back in the seat, propped his foot on the front of the wagon, and slid his hat down over his eyes. "Will you be so kind, madam, as to awaken me when you decide to move on?"

Rachel heard Henry, recognized the irritation behind his flippancy. She knew he wouldn't seek information, but would take it when offered with less than a grain of interest in his attitude. But he would be interested if the truth came out. Interested enough and angry enough to leave her.

Fear held Rachel in a relentless grip as she stared at the woman standing outside the bunkhouse. She couldn't speak, couldn't move, couldn't think. She felt as if she were being strangled by her own past.

She couldn't see the woman's features, but she'd instantly recognized Roz from the way she held herself with stately grace and from the ivory clothing she always wore—a symbol of purity that had yellowed with experience and age—"like snow that a dog had pissed on," Roz had once told her.

Her chest constricted as if her heart were curling into a ball, protecting itself.

Phoenix spoke again. "She asked if they could stay . . . said they wouldn't interfere with anything. She knows this is a respectable place and that you're just married."

Rachel understood Phoenix's message. Roz wouldn't ply her trade in Promise. She wouldn't reveal her relationship to Rachel. The more she heard, the more she felt an unwilling fear for her mother. Something was terribly wrong for Roz to humble herself so. Roz never begged nor bargained. "Is she—are they—all right?" she asked, feeling as if the question ripped her to shreds as it forced its way into the open.

Phoenix paused before replying. "They tarred and feathered her, Rachel. Her skin—"

"*Damn them,*" she said, startled by the vehemence in her voice. Something cold and angry bled into her, stiffening her courage. It was too late for fear. The decision was already made. She turned to Henry, called his name in a tight whisper.

Without changing position, he shoved his hat back with his thumb and stared at her with polite tolerance. It fueled her anger, threatened to fan the embers. He cared about nothing. She didn't want to care either. Not now. Not about Roz.

Phoenix kneed his horse and rode a discreet few yards away. He knew what she had to do even as she resisted it. Swallowing down her misgivings, she formed her words carefully. "Henry, the people here—there's nothing for them in the outside world. They come to Promise for a new start."

He listened without so much as a raised brow or curl of his lip. "Now why doesn't that surprise me? If I remember my lessons correctly, this entire country was founded by peasants and miscreants."

She held on to her composure, forced herself to speak without inflection, without betraying herself. "That's exactly how this town is starting, too—with played-out criminals and misfits of society."

"Since I am one of your strays, I suppose I must applaud your nobility, Rachel."

Ignoring his remark, she continued with a speech she'd had no time to prepare. "They are human beings, Henry. We all are."

He tipped his hat farther back on his head and propped his arm along the backrest of the seat. "What are you trying to say, Rachel? That I am to behave myself? That in this haven of democracy I shouldn't reveal that I am little better than an indentured servant? That wouldn't endear you to the downtrodden masses, would it? Perhaps you are about to ask me to pretend that I am besotted with you to preserve their moral sensibilities?"

"I'm telling you that the past isn't important here. I am asking you to pretend that your moral sensibilities are well laced with compassion and tolerance."

"For whom, Rachel? Him?" He pointed toward Phoenix.

"No." She refused to say more about Phoenix. In any event, what could she say? She knew nothing about him except that he was her friend.

"I don't give a bloody damn who inhabits your town, Rachel. I am far more interested in the physical amenities than the population."

"I am glad to hear it," she said. "Because a madam and her girls have come to us for refuge."

"*Us?* Should I infer that I have a voice in this matter?"

"You have a voice," she said, the fear rising again, attacking her control. "There are over thirty voices in Promise. Each one is heard with equal attention and respect. Since the . . . women are still here, we can both *infer* that they have been welcomed and will stay as long as they wish."

"They are not women, Rachel, but animals." He sat up and gathered the reins, slapping the team into action. "Since my voice has been drowned out by my fellow

misfits, I can only suggest that you confine them to a
pen well away from mine.''

Phoenix fell in beside the wagon as they drove on,
and for once Rachel couldn't find comfort in his presence. She stared at the town—her town—blind to the
promise of safe haven after a lifelong journey. All she
could see was the woman standing at the end of the road
waiting to either be welcomed or shunned by her daughter.

Madam's daughter.

Henry wasn't going to stop. And as they drove toward
the bunkhouse, Rachel knew that she wouldn't ask him
to. Not with his aversion to prostitutes. Not when she
didn't know how she herself felt about Roz. Her opinions had been so clear when she'd left the house seven
years ago. She'd been so certain that she could go on
with her life, sever her connection to the past. Roz had
encouraged it by not saying good-bye when Rachel
had left, by not contacting her in all that time. Rachel
had kept track of her mother by listening to gossip, by
asking Maeve. The second year, Rachel had returned to
the brothel with a birthday gift for her mother. Roz had
been too busy to see her.

Business as usual.

Rachel repeated the words over and over in her mind
as she saw more clearly the woman standing by the
hitching rail. Roz had taught her that business was everything, that it was survival. Rachel had to remember that
her business was the town and her marriage and the children she wanted so desperately. From what Phoenix had
told her, she knew that Roz understood that. No doubt
Roz even approved.

It didn't matter. Her memories had lost their clarity
until all she remembered was Roz's tea and honey-
colored hair that had always been braided in a coronet—

a lady's style to go with her lady's gowns—and her tawny eyes that were too sharp to be fooled by the most cunning of men.

They were within a few yards of Roz now, close enough to see that her gown had been torn and mended, that she was wearing a pair of old boots beneath the taffeta and lace, no doubt contributed by Cletus or one of the other men. She looked as if she'd been scoured from head to foot with the coarsest pumice stone, leaving her skin red and raw, layers of flesh peeled away with drying tar.

Bile rose in Rachel's throat and her eyes burned. She could almost feel it—the pain her mother must be suffering from the touch of air, the burn of the sun on the exposed flesh of her arms and face, the scrape of clothing on her body. Rachel covered her mouth and swallowed down a sob.

Roz was bald.

She didn't want to look, yet she couldn't close her eyes against the sight of her mother standing tall and proud in the street, studying Henry as they rolled slowly past her. Roz nodded once and turned away to walk back into the bunkhouse.

"Again you waste your pity, Rachel," Henry said as he urged the horses around a slight curve in the road. "Just as the vigilantes wasted good tar and feathers on her. Depravity goes far deeper than strands of hair and a layer of flesh."

She inhaled sharply as his words bit into her like rats in the dark. She thought of Liddie and Grace, Maeve and Cletus, and all the other people in Promise. She thought of her mother as she untied her bonnet, feeling as if she were removing blinders. "You mistake depravity for desperation, Henry," she said softly. "You of all people should have recognized the difference."

His face seemed to blanch and his expression closed against her. She waited for a caustic reply, but instead there was only silence.

The citizens of Promise began to wave as they approached the house on the hill—her house. They were happy to see her, the woman whose dreams had spawned theirs. She had saved them, they'd said over and over again. They needed her, depended on her, trusted her to keep those dreams alive, to build on them and make them real. She knew that she was their strength.

She'd never had time before to realize how lonely it was to be needed without allowing herself to need in return. Yet this was the life she had chosen, the person she had chosen to be. She would have to do the best she could and go on.

She straightened her back and fixed a smile on her face. And feeling the burden of Promise on her shoulders, she wondered if she had enough strength left to save herself.

15

They were the rubble of humanity—Rachel's collection of the hopeless gathered in this isolated pit to rest before continuing their journey into hell. It was a pretty enough pit, Henry supposed, but it took more than a colorful setting to make a common rock into a gemstone. And this lot was as common as they came . . . aging felons and renegades who apparently had escaped society but failed to escape themselves. In each eroded face he saw subjects to paint—of the nightmares they had suffered, the demons they were fighting still.

He counted them: three women and thirty-five men . . . and not a single child.

There were no promises here.

And he realized that he had expected—hoped for—just that: promises. He wanted to laugh at the irony of it all, but something else twisted inside him, paralyzing him with the shock of it. When had he last wanted anything enough to feel disappointment at its absence?

Truth spread a stain of melancholy in his mind. This is
what Luc had consigned him to—a graveyard of
wretched, wasted lives, a repository for bodies that no
one would claim.

What better way to shock his brother into an awareness of his own fate? What better place for Henry to see
the difference between what he could be and what he
was becoming? Luc believed in pretty little sentiments
such as trust and faith and hope. Luc didn't know, as
Henry did, that "pretty" was simply a dying flower
rooted in dirt, a figure squeezed into a comely shape by
a corset, a veneer of paint disguising a blank canvas.

Yet Rachel wore neither corset nor paint. Rachel with
her youth and beauty, her hopes and dreams. Rachel,
who gave kindness merely because it was needed. Rachel, who hadn't yet learned the difference between
keeping promises and maintaining illusions.

She was the only misfit here.

He stepped down from the wagon and lifted her from
the seat as the citizens of Promise stared at him with
avid curiosity. One by one, men approached him with
congratulations and slaps on the back as Rachel made
very proper introductions, and a few offered threats
barely veiled by paternal attitudes as to his responsibility
toward Rachel's happiness and welfare. With a curious
detachment he noticed that they appeared as menacing
as they'd surely been at the height of criminal careers.
And through it all the man called Phoenix stood a distance away, betraying nothing, yet posing the most dangerous threat of all by his lack of expression . . . his
silence.

Henry lounged back against the wagon, observing
them all as they turned to Rachel, telling her of progress
made in the construction of her "town." He saw their
pride in her, as if *she* were their child, the heir to their
own broken-down dreams.

Rachel glanced up at him, a look in her eyes that spoke of weary fatalism, and for some morbid reason, he thought of the whore, her countenance stripped of all artifice, her flesh appearing as corroded as her soul. Her eyes had a hard glaze and her mouth a cynical twist, and for a brief moment she had looked at Rachel in just such a way before turning her back on them as they drove down the street.

The women emerged from the house where they had deposited their dishes of food and gathered around him, one greeting him shyly, another with a brusque "How do?" and the last, an Indian woman, gave him a cursory inspection and a grunt. The crowd hushed and drifted to the edges of the property, their gazes fixed on him with a mixture of suspicion and expectation.

He understood the rest of it then. The poor blind fools still held on to a last shred of sentiment. They might not believe in promises either, but they would quite gladly live with any delusion that came among them, particularly if it was a loving husband for Rachel.

He smiled at her and stepped forward. They watched as he wrapped his arm around her shoulders and bent over her with the pretense of affection to whisper in her ear. "Do they know the truth or do they think we are in love?"

"They are willing to believe what they see," she whispered back.

"Can you tell me what you wish them to see, or am I to guess?"

"What do you wish them to see, Henry?"

The question caught him off guard, though he should have expected it. Rachel had a disturbing habit of making him reach down inside himself to touch thoughts he'd rather ignore, while the workings of her mind remained inviolate.

He scooped her up in his arms and carried her up the steps to the porch, pausing in front of the open door to spread his smile around the spectators. "Ladies . . . gentlemen . . . if you will excuse us?" He bent his head over her, taking advantage of her open mouth by indulging in a blatantly carnal kiss. It gratified him to feel her body lose the starch that had held her rigid since they'd come within sight of Promise, and even more to feel her pull at the hair on his nape in an effort to stop the assault. He lifted his mouth the barest fraction so that their lips still brushed one another as he spoke. "Rachel, they wish to see illusions." He kissed the corners of her mouth. "Would you deny them?"

Her eyes widened in surprise, then narrowed as he cocked a brow at her. Before he could again claim her mouth, she turned her head aside and rested it in the crook of his neck, the very picture of a shy bride.

The men cheered and two of the women applauded. The Indian woman grunted and walked away.

Taking their collective response as approval of his actions, he stepped inside the house and kicked the door shut with his foot. He lowered her immediately, careful to keep her body from brushing his, and set her at arm's length. Her voice a soft whisper of breath in the stillness.

"Why, Henry? Why such concern over the illusions of my friends?"

"You mistake concern for self-preservation, Rachel. Since I counted over a dozen guns among your protectors, it seemed prudent to hide behind your skirts until we were safely behind locked doors."

She stepped back, increasing the distance between them—a distance that had been growing wider with every moment since they had ridden within sight of town. "I'm relieved to hear it. I wouldn't want you to think of my friends as rabbits dying in a storm."

This time *he* stepped back, trying to avoid the reminder of how much of himself he had revealed during the journey, of the power it gave Rachel over him. Leaning back, he propped his shoulder on the door. It was too late to change what she knew of him. All he could do now was treat it casually, as if it had no importance. "We're all rabbits dying in a storm, Rachel."

"Speak for yourself, Henry. Most of us are like the squirrel who survived to build another place for himself in the ruins of all that was familiar."

So she had witnessed that, too—his silent communion with the creature in the wake of the twister. A chill shot up his spine. Through some mysterious bond of birth, Luc could feel his soul. He damn well didn't need Rachel seeing through him as if he had no soul.

Rachel turned away then, to open a refurbished sea chest set against the slanted wall supporting the staircase.

He folded his arms across his chest and studied his surroundings—the odd mixture of Victorian opulence and Colonial makeshift resourcefulness. The windows were covered with plain muslin drapes over airy lace curtains, the walls with softly patterned wallpaper above whitewashed planked wainscotting. Traditional furniture of rich woods and fabrics of brocade, damask, and velvet was arranged on plank floors and rag rugs. Dried flowers in Mason jars occupied tables next to crystal-hung lamps. Instead of the usual ornate bric-a-brac and framed miniatures, there were only a few wooden carvings of animals scattered about. Through a doorway, he saw what must be the dining room furnished in the same way with table and chairs that surely must have been imported, a sideboard that surely had not, and a chandelier made of antlers. From what he could see, the rooms were large and filled with light, though he knew that heavy shutters hung outside the glass-paned windows to keep out the worst elements of nature.

The house suited Rachel in the same way that the combination of elegant gowns, threadbare smallclothes, and Indian moccasins suited her . . . as the sunbonnet she pulled up from where it hung down her back and tied the ribbons firmly beneath her chin—more shutters keeping her in while shutting him out. She belonged here in this land that obviously gave so bountifully and took so harshly.

He felt unmade suddenly. Everything around him was sharp and clear, yet he felt blurred, without detail. He belonged outside, with the others who had failed to find their proper niches in the world. He'd always known it, yet it had taken not his father's blatant cruelties, but the incongruities of this house and this woman to convince him it was really so. And at the same time, it was this woman and this house and the human clutter outside that made him wonder if there was indeed room in the world for a few more niches to be carved out.

"You did all this?" he asked, still propped against the door, too wary of his thoughts to step more completely into Rachel's home.

"We all did," she replied as if those three words were all the answer required.

"You sent away for the furniture?"

"I gathered some, bought some from settlers on their way to Oregon, and Phoenix built some."

"Gathered?" he asked. Somehow that struck him as being an important detail.

"The Oregon Trail is littered with things the settlers can no longer carry," she said as she sorted through the contents of the basket. "I picked up what I could use."

"You said you bought from the settlers."

"If they were still around, I offered money or trade goods. But by the time they get to Wyoming, they're anxious to move on quickly before winter catches them in the mountains.''

"So ..." He pushed away from the door and took a step—only one—into the entryway. "You gathered outcasts to create your own society and gathered castoffs to provide all the trappings of civilization."

She closed the lid on the basket and met his gaze. "Yes."

"Why? You have money, or so I've been led to believe. You have beauty and wit enough to set polite society on its collective ear."

She gave him a smile he'd seen before, a familiar smile that he'd seen on Luc and their father, on his own image in the mirror—a mocking slant of lips employed in place of blatant rudeness. "All I had seven years ago was the land and the soddy and a ... small inheritance. I am now rich because I had the wit to make leather goods, preserves, and jerky to sell to the soldiers. I repaired what furniture and clothing I didn't want and sold that to the settlers, miners, and ranchers." She adjusted her cape and settled the basket over her arm. "I am here because I have no taste for using my beauty to 'set polite society on its collective ear.' " Brushing past him, she opened the door. "I will be back shortly. The women brought food; it's in the kitchen. They also cleaned and put fresh linens on the beds. If you want a hot bath, you'll have to wait until I return to heat water."

Her manner, too, was familiar—defiant and defensive at the same time, another of the dares she was so adept at issuing. "Might I inquire as to where you are going?" he asked, suspecting that he would not like her answer.

"To take some medicines to Roz and her girls."

"I do not believe that Roz is the sort to require nurturing, Rachel."

"Everyone requires nurturing, Henry," she said softly.

"I forbid it."

She arched her brow in another parody of his own mannerisms. "Forbid your servants, Henry, but do not presume to do so with me."

"An Ashford wife does not minister to—"

"Animals?" she interrupted, her voice flat. "Out here, we save our animals if at all possible. You might appreciate that some day. Aside from that, you might remember that human animals, no better and no worse than Roz, built this house and prepared the food you will eat. We are a community dependent upon one another for all things. Infirmity in one weakens us all." She brushed past him and opened the door. "I will help you unload the wagon when I return."

"Where are the bloody servants?"

"We don't have servants here," she said as she crossed the porch and descended the steps, Henry stood where she'd left him, his mouth hanging open. He clamped his teeth together and very quietly, very gently, shut the door behind her as he told himself that he was angry—no, outraged—by her behavior. Decent women did not consort with whores. Philanthropy was an idle pastime for women of class, not a divine mission. Decent women of any class obeyed their husbands.

But then Rachel defied convention—a decent woman who took care of herself rather than expecting her husband to do it for her. A woman who had the decency to teach him how to take care of himself without deriding him for his ignorance.

He wandered into the kitchen, absorbing impressions of cabinetry with clean, simple lines, an indoor pump and massive cast-iron stove with as many doors as the house. A stove that was certainly a luxury. Rachel had built all this, acquired all this by *working,* of all things. By sewing and cooking and bartering. For all he knew she had put on the bloody roof herself.

She *was* a paragon—and, dammit, he knew that amid his bafflement and ire he also felt pride for her, in her, and wished that he could feel as much pride in himself.

Rachel saw defeat rather than pride as she peered into the window of the bunkhouse. Inside, Roz leaned heavily on the table, supporting herself with one hand, her head bowed, her breathing rough with pain. She had removed all her clothing but a loose chemise that bared her arms, upper chest, and legs below her thighs. Her body was as firm and trim as Rachel remembered but the grace was absent, replaced by stiff, awkward movements. What had it cost her earlier to dress and stand so tall before her daughter?

She stared blindly at the doorknob as she blinked the mist away from her eyes. It had never occurred to her that Roz would ever be anything but the grandest and certainly most handsome madam in the territory. Roz, who had educated herself enough to do sums so no one would cheat her, to read so no one could lie to her, and, as she had said, "to screw better than any woman in the West" so no one could retire her before she was ready. Roz had survived in her business longer than most and had raised her daughter to be as strong and indomitable as she.

Strangely enough, where Rachel had only felt shame and anger for what her mother was before, she now felt pride in the woman herself. She didn't know why. It was simply there—a fierce tightness in her throat, a burning pressure behind her eyes. She leaned her forehead against the door and breathed deeply, calming the emotions that had been prodding at her since she'd seen her mother standing in the middle of the street in a tattered ivory gown, her head high as if her baldness were the finest of hats.

A shadow streaked up the door beside her and she lifted her gaze to find Phoenix beside her. Without a word, he opened the door and held it for her, shutting it behind her when she stepped inside.

Roz straightened as she met Rachel's gaze. "Rachel," she said, and her voice was a dry rasp, as if it had been scraped away by screams.

Rachel couldn't imagine her mother screaming. "Do you need a doctor?"

With slow, painful movements, Roz lowered herself to sit on the bed. "There was a doctor in the mob that did this to me." Roz smiled. "Two hours before that, he was in my bed. I'm not in the mood to trust any of his kind. Guess he figured that the only way to stop himself from coming to me was to make me too ugly to be tempting."

"You have infection," Rachel said, nodding at an open sore on Roz's arm.

"I can take care of myself. All I need is a place to hang my garters for a spell."

"And then what, Roz?"

"You worried that I'll stay here?"

"No."

"Well, you ought to be. I never saw so much hate in a man as I did when your husband looked at me. I figure it's either because he knows who I am or because of what I am."

"He doesn't like—"

"Whores," Roz said. "Most men are afraid of us, others think we're livestock. I've only run into out-and-out hate once before."

"Do you know why?" Rachel asked as she laid the basket on the bed and slipped off her cloak to hide the depth of her interest. She didn't want her mother—or anyone—to know how much it mattered.

"People are taught to hate, Rachel, either through experience or by example." Roz sat on the edge of a chair. "Either way, that man of yours is packing a load of misery. What I can't understand is how you got him to marry you. He's not the type to let anyone get too close."

"He had nothing better to do for the next five years. . . . Lie down on the bed and I'll rub some salve into your skin."

"Just leave it here and the girls and I will take care of each other."

The dismissal was clear as it had been the day Roz had tossed the bag of blood money at her, then refused to see her again. Rachel wasn't surprised, yet she was reluctant to leave and she didn't know why. She removed the lid from the jar and faced her mother.

Roz shook her head. "How you got to be such a do-gooder I'll never know. Maybe it came from me. I'm an expert at soothing a man's troubles. I guess that qualifies as charity."

"You get paid. Charity is free."

Roz snorted. "Everything has a price, Rachel. If you didn't believe that you wouldn't have advertised for a husband. What did you buy him with—money or your body?"

Roz's stab barely missed the truth, yet it drew blood. Rachel couldn't move, couldn't speak for the pain of humiliation, the twist of guilt, the agony of knowing that she was truly her mother's daughter.

"You didn't see it, did you, Rachel? You were trying so hard to avoid selling yourself that you didn't realize you were doing the buying. And you sure as hell didn't know what you were getting, or you would have run the other way from your Englishman."

It hurt to breathe, to think. She didn't want to think beyond finding a way to convince Roz and herself that it wasn't true. She inhaled and the air burned in her throat, her chest. "The man I married didn't care about my past. He knew what he was getting into and wanted what I had to offer."

Roz snorted. "Then it's too bad that the man you rode into town with isn't the man you married."

Abruptly Rachel turned to set the jar on the night-stand. "Phoenix told you."

"He didn't have much choice. He'd told me when I got here that your husband knew all about me. It was either warn me or risk the truth coming out. Everyone in town has been warned in the last couple of hours. I for one wouldn't want to cross Phoenix, so you don't need to worry that I'll start playing the doting mother."

"That's the last thing I'd worry about." Rachel tossed her cape over her arm and picked up her basket. She had to get out of there. Seeing Roz, listening to her, brought back too many old memories: of watching other girls walk down the street holding their mothers' hands; of being denied even that modest affection from her mother; of needing so desperately to be a mother and prove to herself that whores did not necessarily beget whores. She had to escape the sudden discovery that nothing would have mattered—not even Roz's occupation—if she'd been allowed to run into her mother's arms instead of an empty attic room. But Henry waited at the end of the road, a man who touched her heart without allowing her to touch back, and she wasn't sure which was worse—an empty room or empty dreams.

The urge to talk to Roz was strong, holding her in the doorway, tempting her to try one more time to reach out for what she'd never had. But it was too late for that. If she'd had any doubts, they had disappeared with Roz's refusal to let her help her. "I'm not worried," Rachel said instead. "You see, I've finally learned not to ad-dress you as 'Mother.' It would be bad for business."

· · ·

There were no servants, Rachel had said; she would help him unload the wagon. Not bloody likely.

Henry cursed as he hoisted a large crate from the wagon and carried it into the house, adding it to the growing pile in the kitchen. The thing that irritated him the most was that she undoubtedly knew he wouldn't take kindly to her help. He'd made that clear enough on the trail. Let Rachel nurture the whore down the street. He had no need for anything but tangible goods that he could purchase with tangible coin—an even trade with no commitment beyond producing the right change.

He swiped at his brow with his sleeve and peered into the wagon, expecting the boxes to reproduce themselves as they had seemed to do for the last hour. But there were only two—different from the rest, with tags attached to them. He reached for one and saw that the tag was instead an envelope, with his name written on the front in a familiar hand. Luc's hand. Ripping one from the string securing it to the box, he slipped out a single sheet of note paper and read:

Henry—a wedding gift of sorts as I noticed that you only brought your tablet and chalks on your escape from England. I wired my steward and had him send your old paintings and what supplies he could find. The rest were purchased from your favorite merchant in London. They arrived less than a day ago, thankfully in time to send along with you and Rachel on your journey into a new life.

In that spirit, I hope you will put my offering of peace to good use and not leave the happier colors untouched. You might try your hand at animals first and perhaps a flower or two. I understand both are in abundance in your new home. I know that I am again presuming to direct your talent, but I cannot, it seems, refrain from trying to guide your life into more pleasant directions.

I remain Your Devoted Brother—Luc

Henry felt nothing but the tremble in his fingers as he pried open the crate with his bare hands, then reached for the second crate and opened it in the same way. The splinters that dug into him were nothing. The bloody scrape on his palm was nothing. The full set of paints, brushes, and necessary supplies was everything.

He examined each color and every tool, smoothed his hands over the canvas, and smelled the solvent to make sure it was real. And he stared at the array in amazement. Somehow Luc had acquired the finest of paints contained in the new collapsible tubes, the most refined solvents, the specially made brushes with handles sufficiently long to accommodate his large hands. Then, in the bottom of the second box on top of a stack of his old paintings, he saw a smaller package with another note attached.

Henry—Another gift. Actually not a gift at all as I have always felt that this rightfully belongs to you. I know it is what Mother would have wanted and somehow I feel that she also would wish for you to find the happiness she dreamed about in her sanity and in her madness. Cherish these well and, when the time is right, put them in their proper place. Remember that Father is dead and can no longer use what you hold dear against you. Do not give him such power over you.

I bid you farewell for a time. I am off to winter in the Sandwich Islands. No doubt the distance will offer us both respite from our thoughts and experiences.

Yours have been particularly tormenting lately. As you know I remain free from that cursed hacking. Luc

Henry lifted the smaller parcel but did not open it. He knew what it held and had no desire to look again upon the symbols of his mother's anguish. Of course Luc expected him to present them to Rachel. Of course Luc expected that he would become so besotted with his wife that he would believe himself happy and at peace. But he had tried and failed to achieve such a state except in the bottom of a bottle, and even that was always followed by retching illness and nightmare that howled through his mind.

He crumpled the note in his hand and shoved it into his pocket. If their respective parents' dementia had been caused by bad blood rather than disease, he could almost believe that Luc had inherited the affliction along with the title.

A throb in his hand reminded him of the crates and the treasures Luc had sent, treasures that had the power to bring him more peace than any mementos of foolish dreams and empty lives, or any misguided hope of his own that with Rachel, he might again believe in promises.

16

———=●=———

Maybe it was all a dream.

It seemed like a dream as Rachel entered her home to find the lamps unlit, the outlines of furniture limned by the light of an full moon. It seemed as if she had never left the basin and Henry had never existed as she walked through the unoccupied house searching for evidence that he was real and waiting to tempt and torment her.

She cracked her shin on a box sitting in the middle of the kitchen floor. She hadn't noticed the boxes stacked about nor had she noticed that the back door was open. Henry *was* here . . . somewhere.

But the rooms were all empty and his bags were still packed and piled in a corner of the master bedroom. Her bags occupied an opposite corner, and she wondered if that separation had been deliberate. But then her heart paused and she felt a quickening in her belly that was

both anticipation and panic as she stared at the high test-
ers of her bed—a grand bed chosen with great care and
grand expectations. A bed in which children might be
conceived and birthed. Henry's hat rested atop one tester
at the foot. Her Stetson rested atop the other. And on
the lacy counterpane that had been the last thing Grace
had made for her was the fabric-covered hatbox from
the milliner in Cheyenne.

She sagged back and found support in the wall beside
the door. Yes, Henry was real, and he had left her a
message of intent. No longer would they sleep at different times, apart from one another. Remembering the first
and last time they had joined in passion, and all the other
times they had used their bodies as weapons against one
another, she wondered whether the bed would be battle-
ground or common ground.

She wondered if they would continue to keep watch
through the night, anticipating danger from one another.

Refusing to think beyond that, she removed the hatbox
from the bed and put it inside the wardrobe. She lit an
oil lamp on the nightstand and washed at the basin, using
cold water rather than taking the time to draw a full bath.
Then, wearing only camisole and pantalettes, she lowered the wick until a dim yellow glow encircled the bed.

Still there was no sign of Henry.

Hairbrush in hand, she climbed up onto the bed, remaining on her knees as she untied the ribbon that had
secured her hair while she washed. Her fingers brushed
her flesh and it began then, suddenly, as it always did—
the tingle and the heat spreading from breasts to belly
to thighs, the hollow ache that had never quite left her
since Henry's first touch on her body. She arched her
neck and the brush of her hair falling down her back
brought sweet anticipation of a firmer caress. Her limbs
trembled and every breath was a flutter in her chest, a
shiver in her throat.

She dropped the brush and untied the ribbons of her camisole to touch her breasts, then lower, feeling the mist of desire through the opening of her pantalettes, hoping that this time would be different, that she would chase away the need for Henry with her own self-reliance. But the urgency of her own touch was not enough, and she stared blindly up at the moon through the window, seeing only a silver blur as the ache throbbed with steady insistence for relief, demanding more than she could give herself.

A ragged sound broke the silence, a sob wrenched from her desperation. She sagged back on her heels and bowed her head, her arms wrapped around her waist, her hair falling forward as she inhaled deeply, fighting the weakness of her body.

Experiencing a woman's need was not a mystery to her. The need to share the experience with another was terrifying.

She heard a sound, a sharp breath, a rustle of cloth. Lifting her gaze, she saw the shadow of a man standing in the threshold, his body still, his eyes a blue flame as he watched her. A flame that beckoned. A flame that reached out to her, touching her more provocatively than she had touched herself, searing and consuming her.

Henry was here, more specter than man in the darkness beyond the circle of light. Henry, not quite real as the fulfillment of an old dream, the essence of a new one.

She turned toward him, holding his gaze as she knelt facing him, and spread her hands over her belly, skimmed them up the sides of her rib cage, touched two fingers to the tip of one breast as her other hand trailed down the center of her body to the part in her thighs, continuing what she had begun alone, showing Henry that she needed him, because she could not find the voice to tell him.

He emerged from the darkness, his shirt open to the waist, the hair on his chest glistening in the moonlight. Banked desire flared to new life, and she was aware of her body as never before, sensation became sharper— the caress of air on bared flesh, the rough sound of his breathing like another kind of touch, the scent of him primitive and natural, as if he'd been working—

"What are you about, Rachel?" he asked, his voice a soft slide that moved through her as he halted at the foot of the bed. His eyes remained fixed on her, a look both enthralled and knowing. But his face was rigid with control, his jaw clenched, his mouth tight. She realized her mistake then. She was going through the motions of seduction—motions learned from the girls in a brothel, to entice and tantalize, to tease and invite. It was the only way she knew ... obviously the wrong way for a wife to attract the attentions of her husband.

Henry arched his brows as he waited for her reply. She thought to brazen it out, to play the innocent, but the proper words and actions eluded her. She was not innocent and had not the slightest idea of how to carry out such a pretense.

"I was trying to seduce you," she said as she picked up her hairbrush and gathered her hair over one shoulder. "Now I'm braiding my hair."

"Ah, seduction," he said, the familiar mockery slanting his mouth. "A most appealing way to remind me that it is time to earn my keep. Still, it was a wasted effort since I am the one who is required to perform. All you must do is indicate the time, place, and method."

The words were ugly, yet she was not repelled. Her need was too urgent—to be held, to somehow reinforce the tenuous bond between herself and her husband, to hold him in any way she could for as long as possible. She combed her fingers through the braid, freeing it, and fanned her hair across her breasts. "Now, Henry . . .

here . . . the way men do when it matters . . . when they care."

He reached toward her, his hand brushing a strand aside to reveal her nipple, and his thumb caressed her there, back and forth and then in a circle. "I am accomplished at a great many pretenses, Rachel, but caring is not one of them."

He was so close now, his legs pressing against the foot of the bed, his body slanting slightly toward her as he continued to stroke her. He still seemed like a specter, half in shadow, half in light, his eyes dark as the midnight that surrounded them. She leaned toward him, going to him, placing her hands on his chest, stroking upward as she raised her head, parted her lips. "Perhaps we can both learn to pretend."

The word almost stuck in her throat. Pretense was for the women who, for a price, gave pleasure regardless of their own. She wanted more than that. Yet she was shamefully willing to accept whatever he chose to give her . . . for now.

Suddenly his mouth ground down on hers, with hunger and fury. She recognized the fury. He needed her, too, and she thought he must hate himself for that weakness.

She knew how he felt.

She met the kiss with her own desperation, becoming a part of Henry's storm as his hands moved over her like the wind, as he stole her breath and gave her his, as his fingers found the opening in her pantalettes and slipped inside, moving with a fevered rhythm, one way, then another until she felt the warm rain inside herself. She heard the thunder of her own heart and the counterpoint of his until it was a roar in her ears.

He tore his mouth away from hers and found the lobe of her ear, the hollow of her throat, her breast, tasting her, closing around her, drawing on her, and still his

fingers stroked her until she felt as if she were flying.
Abruptly he drew back, his gaze lowering to his hand
buried in the curls between her thighs, following as he
raised it to brush one nipple then another with her own
moisture. He stepped back, withdrawing his touch, as he
shrugged out of his shirt, unbuttoned his trousers, and
stood silently before her, naked in his desire, his body
shadowed as if clouds surrounded him and he was the
eye of the storm.

They stared at each other in that sudden calm, his
hands on her hips, his thumbs caressing her belly as he
slowly pulled her closer until the only thing between
them was passion.

In that moment, it was enough. Perhaps with time and
patience, it would become more.

He urged her back, following her onto the bed, his
body covering hers, the tempest claiming her as he surrounded her, caught her up in the fury of it, plunging
into her over and over again, and she embraced him with
her arms and her legs, arching to meet him. She gasped
at the force of the whirlwind, sobbed as he held her
suspended, his hands under her hips, holding her as he
thrust harder and faster, cried out as he poured into her.
Her body tightened around him, holding the pleasure
inside her, unwilling to let it go as the frantic throb inside her slowed to pulses, as if there were a separate
heart where their bodies joined.

She didn't know where Henry ended and she began
as he stiffened above her, held her tightly, and thrust
into her with a force that banished everything but the
pleasure consuming her.

He moaned against her ear and raised up on his elbows, his head turned away from her as she felt the chill
night air come between them and the fullness inside her
become less and less, as if he were shrinking away from
her.

"Rachel, let me go," he said. Still she held him, her hands clenched over his shoulders, her legs tight around his waist. He took in air, his chest heaving. *"Let . . . me . . . go."* It was both threat and demand, both equally raw with desperation.

She relaxed her legs, holding him only with her hands as she stared up at the ceiling. "I can't," she whispered. "I want to, but I can't."

His breath slowed to a soft breeze in the night as he lay there, pressed to her from waist to toes, parted from her in heart and mind. "I won't give you more than this, Rachel."

Won't rather than can't. "I didn't ask," she said.

He pulled away from her and she felt her nails raking his shoulders, heard him inhale sharply as he jerked away and rolled to his back with only his hand on her hip to soothe her trembling. She remained silent as the distance grew between them and then even his hand withdrew from her.

Henry turned away from her and lowered his feet to the floor, then donned his pants and shirt and rummaged through his bags for his leather case and extra supply of pencils and chalks. "Am I dismissed?" he asked flatly.

To go where? she wanted to ask. *Why?* she needed to know. *Stay,* she wanted to plead. But she held her tongue, saying nothing for fear of betraying emotions she couldn't name.

"I have taken over the soddy as a studio," he said. "I will have adequate solitude there and it is within range of my hearing should you wish to ring a bell or shout or whatever."

She moved then, reaching for a nightdress that was folded beneath her pillow and sitting up to pull it on over her head. "As a member of this community you are expected to work. Aside from that, I won't call for you."

He paused in sorting through a handful of pencils. "No?"

"I want a husband, Henry, not a stud. You are neither required to perform nor are you subject to my whims. If you come to me it will be because you wish to do so, because I am as pleasing to you as you are to me." She looked down at her hands that were still clenched around the fabric of her nightgown. "I find that I cannot settle for pretense—not from you."

He smiled at her, more sneer than amusement. "You mistake pretense for lust, Rachel. One body responding to another. It is elemental and unavoidable. And it is, after all, what you bargained for, is it not?"

Her gaze snapped up to his. "No. I did not expect even that."

"Ah, so we are both hoisted upon our own petards, me through misadventure and you through only God knows what skewed reasoning." He tucked his folder beneath his arm and walked to the door, turning toward her as he stepped into the hall. "Lust is all I can give you. It should be adequate to accomplish your purpose."

She watched as he strode out the door without waiting for a response, without looking back. Had the pleasure she knew she had given him meant so little that he could leave her as easily as he'd leave the table after a satisfying meal? That in itself answered her question. He wanted nothing from her but temporary appeasement of a natural hunger for which he had paid with his name and an experience she couldn't have imagined in a thousand dreams.

And then he had left because he hated whores.

The hallway stretched out before Henry as he left Rachel's room, the walls seeming to tip toward him, closing in on him. He gained the stairs and they felt like a bog beneath his feet. Taking the last three steps in one bound, he strode out of the house, across the porch, down more stairs. The sky and the space around him should have eased his sense of confinement, but everything around him was distorted, curving around him, over him, as if he saw it all through the bottom of a glass, as if he were trapped inside the glass and the scene between him and Rachel revolved around him, forcing him to see it over and over again.

His pencils and sketch pad were all he'd wanted when he'd gone into the bedroom, caught up in thoughts of the release he would find by rendering the images in his mind to canvas. He'd been lost in it—setting up a studio, arranging his paints and brushes just so, stretching canvas on the frames he had assembled. During those hours of single-minded activity, he'd almost forgotten that in the last weeks, he had wanted something else.

But then he'd also wanted his father's approval so he would feel worthy, his mother's survival so he would feel loved, his brother's health so he would not forget entirely how to love. And when the demons danced in his dreams, he'd wanted to reclaim his own soul.

He'd learned to stop wanting a long time ago.

Until he'd met Rachel in the dirty alley beside the saloon, watched her care for a grubby boy without regard for the grime and blood and stench of a life that was so obviously beneath her. He'd wanted her as she'd taken his insults and turned them back on him with quiet grace and dignity, and as she'd met his gaze squarely and honestly while being a willing accomplice to his brother's blackmail. He'd wanted her serenity and calm acceptance, her ability to wait out the storm and view the destruction as new ground on which to build. He'd wanted to tame and possess her, to peel away the color he saw in her and prove that she was as gray as the rest of the world.

Until she had imprisoned him within her body, possessing him, pronouncing sentence on him as he had suffered the little death in her arms and still wanted more.

That had never happened to him before. He'd indulged in brief affairs of the body with one lonely widow or another, yet once he achieved relief, he had no desire to repeat the experience until the next time matter overruled mind. Wealthy widows were a perfect solution for a man who wanted neither wife nor whore, requiring neither commitment nor recompense beyond the same relief he sought. And when widows were not available, he'd provided his own ease.

Rachel hadn't asked for more than lust, and Henry felt cheated. He'd wanted her to ask, dammit. He'd needed something to bring him back to reality, to remind him of why he shouldn't—couldn't—want her. It would have helped to indulge in the cruelty of mocking her. But, unable to match the brutality of her reticence, all he could do was remain silent. She'd given him the perfect opportunity to separate himself from her. Yet it was her very attitude that fascinated him—in her refusal to quail under his sarcasm as most women would do. Even whores such as the one who had taken up residence in town followed certain rules. Rachel, clearly a lady, made her own rules and convinced others to follow them by her very lack of insistence.

He pleased her, she had said, and her honesty felled him, pinned him down. She'd told him that she could not settle for pretense, implying that the facade he had cultivated for so long was *not* pleasing to her. How long had it been since anyone had bothered to sort through the layers, much less voice a preference for the man beneath the armor, the name, and the wealth?

He'd thought himself beyond being moved, yet she had cracked him open and exposed his emotions to the light . . . to himself.

As he reached the soddy, he was numbed by the shock and futility of it. Rachel had ensnared him with more than legal documents and money or even her body. He'd been trapped before—by his mother's need and Luc's illness, forced to remain when he would have escaped the beatings and the torture of his mind. The bond he shared with Luc was another kind of enslavement. Now he was held by the greater force of his own need to become more than a shell, for Rachel, for promises he didn't want to believe in.

For himself.

He leaned back against the door, still imprisoned in glass, his demons staring at him as if he were a curiosity to be toyed with and tormented. His paintings surrounded him where he'd hung them on the walls—portraits of his nightmares, each a different face, yet in that moment all he saw in each was himself.

Mocking.

Threatening.

Destroying him.

His only weapon against the shades that haunted him was the blank canvas on an easel in the middle of the room. A canvas that soon would reveal Rachel to him as she really was before she blinded him to his own visions of life.

17

Henry plowed his hands through his hair and extinguished the dozen lanterns that filled the old soddy with uneven illumination and a miasma of smoke that stung his eyes and burned his nostrils. If he opened the door and shutters—the only covering on the windows—his teeth chattered with cold and his hands shook too much to be of any use. Painting under these conditions for any length of time would surely render him blind, if he didn't die of consumption first.

Again he stood at the door and stared at the house through a gun hole cut into the wood. Rachel's house, where the rooms were large and the windows welcomed the sun inside. He could simply move his paraphernalia to the house and take over a room. He doubted Rachel would object. She was generous to aging derelicts and pet husbands.

He slammed his fist into the door and turned away to pace the one-room shack. He'd been humbled enough by Rachel's bloody benevolence and the labors he'd performed to avoid obligation. His art was vital to his existence, his peace. That and Luc were the bonds that held him together, and kept the secrets of his soul. He would work for Rachel all night and move his easel to the open-sided lean-to behind the soddy during the day before he allowed himself to become indebted to her for all that had value in his life.

The night sky overhead graduated to dawn at the horizon. Smoke drifted up from the chimney of the house, and already he saw activity in the settlement below. Rachel stepped outside, a basket in one hand and a bucket in the other, and walked toward the chicken coop alongside the barn—no doubt to gather eggs and milk for their breakfast.

He jerked open the door and strode out of the soddy, meeting her before she reached the wire fence, taking the containers from her and walking ahead before she could protest. She didn't meet his gaze, didn't speak as she veered into another direction. He forced himself not to look at her.

The hens pecked, scratched, and squawked at him as he gingerly reached beneath them to collect their eggs. The rooster flapped his useless wings and strutted beside Henry to the gate. He rather liked the little bantam for maintaining a stalwart pride in spite of a harem that wanted nothing from him but impregnation. He favored him with a wink as he left the pen and secured the gate. "Just do your duty and get out of the way," he advised.

The odor of manure and the insistent bawl of cattle assaulted him as he sauntered into the barn. Pausing, he frowned at the bucket in his hand, glared at the row of bovine rumps and tails protruding from the line of stalls to his right, and cursed roundly. How in blazes did one milk a cow, let alone four?

A tail swished and one hind foot stomped the earthen floor and was quickly repeated by the others. Surely it couldn't be that difficult, since he knew that children performed the task every day on the tenant farms of Luc's estates. Resolutely he set the basket of eggs on the floor of the aisle and entered the first compartment. He'd rot in his own ineptitude before he asked Rachel.

But she was there, calmly sitting on one of two stools set alongside the cow, soothing the beast with soft shushes and a stroking hand. She glanced up at him and swept her skirt aside in silent invitation—or was it command?—for him to take the second stool. "Were the hens generous today?" she asked as if they had done this a hundred times after spending a routinely pleasant night together. If only it had been routinely pleasant rather than an experience so consuming that it seemed every emotion he'd ever felt had gathered and exploded into that one moment of mutual and complete submission to one another.

"The hens are vicious creatures with no respect for the hand that feeds them," he said as he struggled to maneuver his long body onto the low stool in such confined space. The cow immediately kicked out and caught him on the thigh.

Rachel's shoulder brushed his as she reached for the cow's udders and a thrilling frisson streaked from his arm to his groin in sudden, stunning awareness of her lavender scent and the heat of the barn. He sucked in his breath and heard her do the same. He glanced over at her and met her gaze, seeing that she was held as surely as he by the simple contact, and she was as unwilling as he to break it. Her lips parted and her eyelids lowered a bit as she stared at him with the same need he'd seen the night before. How easy it would be to lean toward her, to take her mouth and draw her sweetness into himself. How tempted he was to lay her down in a pile of fresh hay and surrender himself into her keeping.

The cow bawled and stamped a hoof. Rachel started and shifted away from him, withdrawing her touch to begin a rhythmic kneading of one bovine teat and then another. And though her hands trembled, milk squirted into the bucket in steady spurts. Spreading his knees, he clasped his hands between his thighs to conceal his stiffening member as he watched the way her hands moved so deftly, up and down, in and out, over and over again. His body responded more fully, feeling the memory of her hands on him, soothing away the aches of his first day on the trail, of the way she had held him inside her last night in just such a way, draining him. . . .

Bloody hell.

"I didn't hear the rooster. Did he try to keep you out?" Her voice was slightly forced, yet she seemed damnably calm and in control.

He resented her for it.

"The rooster and I developed an immediate regard for one another. Cocks of a feather and all that." He'd meant the comment to be offensive, and judging from her sudden release of the teats, he'd succeeded admirably.

"Yes, I can see that," she said as she rose from the stool and stepped around him. "Neither of you can see past your arrogance to the sensibilities of others."

Suddenly Henry felt as weary as she sounded. There was no longer any satisfaction in hurting her, no sense of justification in continually pecking at her pride. The stool balanced on two legs as he leaned back, his head connecting with the side of the stall, and closed his eyes. He reached out and caught her skirt in his hand, holding fast, yet not drawing her nearer as she tugged and tried to free herself. "I suppose I deserved that," he said flatly.

The silence lengthened and even the cows were still. He opened his eyes to find her staring down at him, her eyes wide and her lips parted in surprise. Now, that gave him satisfaction—to stun her into silence. And then, melancholy overcame gratification because she *was* surprised at his implied apology. Because he should rue words he had so deliberately spoken. Because he had hurt her and somehow hurt himself as well. "I *did* deserve that."

"Yes, you did," she replied softly. "I cannot live with your anger, Henry. If you can't rise above it, then I will release you from our agreement."

"Is that what you want, Rachel—for me to go?"

"No. But I can no longer ignore what you apparently want."

"Why not? Even my beloved brother has no such compunction."

"Because you make me see beyond myself." Her words reached him on a sigh—seeds carried by a breeze to find root in his mind, to multiply with questions only he could answer. Questions frozen in a winter heart until he had seen a touch of summer in a woman's eyes.

His hand fell away as she freed her skirt from his grasp, and he closed his eyes again. To see beyond oneself. Oh, God, but it was painful to feel such a thaw, to struggle against the flood of insight that followed. An image formed in the darkness of his mind: of Luc sitting back in a chair, toasting the air with a cup of coffee . . . Luc smiling . . . and Henry knew that the smile was for him. Why now, he wondered, when he had not "felt" or "seen" Luc since leaving Cheyenne?

"Damn you," he whispered to the presence that intruded into his soul.

"No more than I have damned myself, Henry," Rachel said in a thready voice that seemed to be another image in his thoughts. He heard the swish of cloth and knew that he had hurt her again and she was leaving the barn.

"Rachel," he called out to her, and looked up to see her pick up the basket of eggs. She did not turn as she straightened, but neither did she walk away. It was easier that way, not having to meet her gaze, to be spared seeing the regret he had heard in her voice.

He was so bloody tired of being a regret.

He spoke clearly, firmly, leaving no room for doubt that he accepted his own decision. "The agreement stands, Rachel."

"All right, Henry," she said, her shoulders jerking slightly before she walked down the aisle of the barn.

He watched her disappear out the door and stared at the wedge of sunlight falling over the floor. And he heard his voice reach out in desperation. "Ah, Rachel, what are you doing to me?"

"You will not turn me into a farmer, Rachel," Henry said later that morning as he glared at the furrows of newly turned earth.

Rachel ignored him and dug a small hole with her finger, then dropped in a seed and covered it with dirt. If he was truly adamant about maintaining his lofty station in life, he would not be sitting beside her on the ground, studying her every movement. "These grow into bushes, so you must allow space between them. I've marked the seed packets and put signs out to show you where to plant each vegetable."

"Surely there is someone in town whom we can hire to do this."

"Everyone already has work, between tending their own gardens, seeing to our cattle, and building houses before winter comes."

"So I have a choice of being a 'cowpoke,' a merchant, a tradesman, or"—he flicked a disgusted look at the ground—"a farmer."

"Not exactly," she said as she dusted off her hands and stood. "We all, by necessity, perform whatever task is required. Last summer I helped put on the roof of our house." Before he could ask her to elaborate, she left him sitting in the dirt with a mound of cloth seed packets by his side. By the time he finished planting she guessed he would be only too happy to vent his outrage with a hammer and nails. And when his fingers had taken on enough splinters and errant blows, she thought he might welcome a turn behind the counter of the mercantile.

"Rachel," he bellowed behind her. "An Ashford wife does not climb about on a roof."

"Then you will have to take my place," she called back, knowing he would do just that. His pride would demand it, just as his pride had demanded that he not appear for breakfast until he had milked all four cows, though it had taken him two hours to accomplish it. She'd had to go to the barn to see what was keeping him, and found him sitting on the floor of the last stall, his knees flexed beneath the cow, the stool abandoned. She could only assume that his height had made the stool too high for him to reach the teats without having to bend almost double. His charge had lowed contentedly as Henry's hands maintained a steady rhythm and milk squirted, more often than not, into the bucket.

He'd eaten more for breakfast than she'd seen him consume in an entire day on the trail.

It had pleased her to cook him a proper meal and have him enjoy it with such enthusiasm. While she washed and dried the dishes, she'd felt an unaccustomed warmth in her chest to see his head fall back as he sat at the table and hear his soft snores accompany the clink of china and silver.

She hadn't questioned why he had insisted that their agreement stand when she would have sworn he'd tear up the papers with relish. It was enough that he had made the decision to stay when she'd offered freedom. Enough that she had a chance to see her dream become a reality.

Her steps faltered as she glanced toward the end of town. A woman wearing a tattered ivory dress sat in a rocking chair on the porch of the mercantile, staring up at her, and beyond . . . to Henry. Roz—watching her, observing the new patterns of her daughter's life, threatening them with her presence.

And all Rachel could do was wonder if the girls had applied the ointment correctly to her mother's tortured skin.

18

I n the last month, Henry had learned that a paste
made of Saleratus and water was efficacious in
treating bee stings, that black silk kerchiefs were not
effective in filtering out the odor of fertilizer if one was
spreading the stuff, and that his favored Derby was best
replaced by a wide-brimmed Stetson. The dubious merits
of horse liniment on aching muscles didn't bear thinking
about.

Yet he couldn't think of anything else as he bent and
stretched and angled his body to put the finishing
touches on his latest project.

He felt as if he had been stretched on a rack, tortured
with thumbscrews, hung out on the clothesline alongside
Rachel's pantalettes and crinolines. The blisters he'd acquired from gardening had broken while he'd helped to
build an outhouse, of all things. He had vowed then and
there to buy an indoor convenience for every dwelling
in Promise before he would repeat the experience. He

didn't know which indignity was worse—digging holes in the ground to hold human waste or listening to the grunts of the Indian woman while showing her the new stock of female underpinnings. Actually, he thought that milking a wretchedly vinegarish goat was probably the worst—if he didn't count the sunburn he'd acquired while painting the broad side of Rachel's barn.

The sunburn was a small price to pay, he thought as he stood back, paintbrush in hand, to study his handi-work. Rachel wanted white and so she had it—a stark background for exaggerated images of a goat with the face of a crone, hens squatting on their nests like gar-goyles, cows shaped like slugs, and a strutting rooster in danger of being toppled by the weight of his coxcomb. He had begun the caricatures out of pique that he should be expected to paint something so mundane as a barn, but as the images took shape, he'd been caught up in a peculiar sense of excitement. In the back of his mind, he thought he might even be enjoying himself.

Though the citizens of Promise showed no particular interest in him, they seemed to find amusement in his handiwork, and that added to his determination to see it through. To give Rachel's vagabonds credit, he had to admit that they were willing enough to instruct him in the arts of rural living, and patient enough to wait for him to catch up to their superior speed and abilities.

Regardless of the trials he faced, there were times when he almost appreciated his provincial existence. He could not deny that there was peace here, even in the midst of frenzied activity. Nor could he ignore the colors that grew more brilliant as spring wore on, the variety of wildflowers, the changing hues of mountain shadows from one hour to the next, the richness of trees standing among the structures of Promise, the vivid blue of a sky that transformed into eerie patterns with the lightning flashes and dark thunderheads of a storm. At times, he compared the color outside with the ones in the tubes Luc had sent, yet he hadn't been tempted to paint what he saw . . . except for the storms. He'd lost the knack of capturing color and light unless it was the blood of a demon or the macabre glow of a tempest in the air.

He had repeatedly painted Rachel, yet none of the canvases were complete. He'd tried to portray her in the garden and in the kitchen, sitting before a mirror and lying in bed, her legs still parted after he left her body, her face flushed and drowsy from exercising the privileges of marriage. That she enjoyed such a privilege, he had no doubt. She received him readily, with an expression of relief in her eyes each time he appeared in the threshold of her room, as if she had feared that would be the night he would stop coming to her.

He could not stop going to her just as he could not complete any of his paintings of her. Both frustrations seemed to be linked somehow, but he shied away from exploring the reasons why.

He cast a calculating eye at the sun and judged that he had a few hours before the light failed. Prudently, he didn't question why his ''chores'' always seemed to end before those of the others, thus giving him time to paint at least a little every day. Being the consort of the town's founding mother, he supposed he was entitled to such consideration. He didn't give a bloody damn whose rank afforded him the privilege.

A form leaning against a tree caught his eye, and it was so still that for a moment he thought it a shadow, more ether than substance. An appropriate thought for a man who rarely spoke and seemed to interrupt space rather than occupy it. A man who always appeared to be watching him. A man, Henry thought acidly, who was altogether too proficient in the skills Henry struggled to master . . . a man who was altogether too chummy with Rachel.

Phoenix, dressed in shades of coal and ash, met his stare.

"So nice of you to call," Henry said his voice bland, though he felt anything but. Aside from the unsettling suspicion that Phoenix had been watching him for some time, he welcomed the company of no one when he painted. This was the only part of his life that belonged to him—the only part that had ever belonged to him. "In such primitive society, I suppose one must make allowances for shabby manners."

The cut didn't take, and Phoenix's gaze swept from one end of the barn to the other. "A shipment of good whiskey and new playing cards just arrived and Rachel paid wages today. The men are gathering at the saloon to celebrate."

"I will not tend bar."

"We serve ourselves tonight and leave payment in the cash box."

"If anyone remembers. A damn slipshod way to do business."

"They remember," Phoenix said. "If there is no money, then there will be no new shipments of whiskey."

"I should have known. My wife is adept at blackmail."

Phoenix's mouth tightened. "There is a place at the poker table for you."

A place for him? It startled him—that statement that seemed more supposition than invitation, as if it were taken for granted that he would join in, that perhaps he belonged. He was not accustomed to being sought out. In England, his presence was tolerated by virtue of his family name and connections. But here, a man's measure was taken by the amount of perspiration he shed in the course of a day's work rather than the color of his blood. In that, he supposed he was one of them. It was a dubious distinction at best, yet he felt a twinge of pleasure at the notion, a sense of pride for his efforts rather than for his ability to exploit his brother's title. Yet on the coattails of that thought rode wariness. He knew from experience that his money and position were far more desirable than his company.

"Why?" he asked flatly. In the last month he'd also learned that subtleties were lost on the citizens of Promise.

"The others wonder if you play poker as well as you work. They need a challenge." Phoenix's teeth flashed in a smile then. "And they're hoping your pockets will be easily lightened."

. . . *as well as you work.* Something snagged in Henry's throat at the implied respect and approval of Phoenix's statement. Something that grew until he was filled with it, held immobile by it as he struggled to understand why he should be so affected by the approbation of others . . . why he should suddenly feel lightness and pleasure at being included in the community of men. At the moment it seemed insignificant that the community in question was one he would have viewed with distaste not so long ago. The irony was not lost on him that his own class viewed him in the same way.

Phoenix remained silent as Henry washed his hands at the outdoor pump that fed the animal troughs and stowed the paint and brushes in the tack room as he mentally counted the remains of the funds Luc had given him in Cheyenne.

Phoenix began to stroll down the hill, leaving Henry to go or stay as he chose.

Jamming his hands in his pockets to hide his sudden eagerness to join him, Henry followed, catching up in three long strides. He felt idiotic, trailing behind Phoenix and wondering why he did so when the light was yet adequate for painting in the soddy. He'd observed Sat-

urday nights in Cheyenne when pockets were newly
lined with money and spirits ran freely both in human
and liquid form. At the time he'd had no desire to do
more than draw the odd ritual of men drinking together
one minute and shooting at one another in the next when
friendships ended with the draw of a card. The more
civilized proceedings at private clubs in England had
held no appeal for him, so why in blazes was he at the
heels of a man he barely knew and wasn't sure he liked
for the questionable pleasure of communing with ple-
beians in the back room of the mercantile?

As they entered the store and crossed through the
rooms full of merchandise, he supposed he would find
out, though he couldn't imagine what they would find
to talk about.

"Yep, his sweat stinks just like ours," Cletus said
with good nature as he conspicuously sniffed the air
above Henry's head.

"Mebbe it's those drawers he wears," another man
commented. "Saw 'em hanging on Rachel's clothesline
and thought nuthin' that fancy can be good for a body."

The more he drank, the less the banter concerning
everything from his clothing to his various bodily fluids
bothered Henry. He had enough to do concentrating on
his cards and keeping track of what his fellow gamblers
were losing. His stomach gurgled rather than growled in
protest at his liquid meal, and he ignored that, too. It
was long past time to concern himself with the folly of
drinking so much without eating more than a few pickled
eggs.

"What d'ya expect from a Montgomery Ward husband?" Cletus asked the room in general. "Ol' Hank
here is so green I'll bet he pisses pea soup."

"Don't call me Hank," Henry warned for the hun-
dredth time, and discarded three queens, breathing a sigh

of relief when Phoenix dealt him nothing he could use. By virtue of his ability to bluff, he was by far the best player in the group . . . aside from Phoenix. It was becoming more and more difficult to lose enough hands to keep from cleaning out the others.

A pot-bellied, retired bounty hunter belched, and each man in the back room reciprocated with some interesting variations on the theme. Comments accompanied each entry in what Henry thought must be a contest. Even Phoenix obliged.

"Sounds like you got barb wire in your throat, Cletus."

"Gawd, Horace, but you shore kin make it talk."

"Praise be that weren't a fart or we'd have to knock down the walls to clear the air."

Henry bet and raised on his losing hand and drew on his cigar, then performed a trick he had perfected as a boy in boarding school. A perfect smoke ring drifted from his mouth along with a long, steady eruption of sound. A hush descended as the belch ripped through the room and bounced off the walls with a stunning crescendo. He glanced around the room, feeling smug that he had finally rendered his companions speechless. Apparently some things were universal—such as men using rude noises to prove that they indeed reigned supreme in spite of the rules of gentility women tried to foist upon them.

"*Sheeyut*, Hank, you could get rich givin' lessons in that."

"Ain't never heard the like."

"That sound came right through the hole in his smoke."

"Nobody ain't never goin' to believe it happened," Horace said glumly. "They'll call it a cock-and-bull story fer sure."

Henry laid out his hand and leaned back in his seat, feeling inordinately pleased with himself. Evidently, he had been accepted into what he thought of as the Order of Benevolent Sots and Careless Gamblers. It appalled him to discover how eager these men were to bet and drink their meager earnings away in the space of a few hours. He'd spent more on the underwear they found so fascinating than they earned in a month.

"Either you jerked when God was pouring brains or you're cheatin', Hank," Horace said as he studied each hand.

The absurd camaraderie of the gathering dissipated as chairs scraped on the rough plank floor. Some of the men balled their fists, while others caressed their guns. Phoenix, too, had scooted his chair back and held his Colt aimed at the man nearest Henry. "Drop your guns behind the bar and keep it clean, boys."

Henry didn't like the sound of that, yet with over a dozen men glaring at him, he couldn't help but appreciate Phoenix's quick reflexes. Before he could fully comprehend the menace surrounding him, he was hauled out of his chair and held by two aging cowpokes with surprising strength. To his great relief, the men unbuckled their gunbelts and dropped them behind the bar.

"Might I inquire as to the nature of your complaint, gentlemen?" he asked, bluffing for all he was worth.

"You been cheatin', Hank."

"I would like to think," he replied, counting on reason to divert his doom, "that I would benefit from such an act. As you can see, I am barely breaking even."

"Ain't you slicker'n snot on a doorknob?" Horace said, and received a few grumbled assents. "Thing is that out here, a man likes to win or lose honest. Don't need no dude with embroidery on his balls to come in an' turn our poker game into a charity social. I been watchin' you, Hank. You're good but I was better in my day."

Henry realized his mistake in underestimating the pride of these men, yet he wasn't about to give a verdict on his own guilt. "Don't call me Hank."

The two men released him abruptly and stepped back into the circle the others formed, leaving him and Horace in the center. Before he drew another breath, a fist slammed into his jaw.

Rachel wanted Henry to fit in with the other men. She wanted them to like him, she told herself as she paced the floor of the parlor. Most of all, she wanted things to be as they were—the spirit of community that had thrived in Promise until recently, the sense of family she'd always had with the people here.

The settlers in town treated her with a deferential respect rather than the common friendliness of the past, as if her husband and his name had somehow elevated her in their eyes and she could no longer be approached as an equal. They avoided Henry altogether, yet she'd overheard their snickers and complaints for his lofty ways and remote demeanor. Because of him, she was suddenly too respectable for the society in Promise, while he was the town curiosity—too arrogant to be admired and too green to have earned a place among them. Promise had developed a class structure and the commoners ruled. How ironic that they viewed a whore's daughter as their leader, and her aristocratic husband ranked as fodder for ridicule and censure.

Only Rain, who hadn't spoken a word in the four years she'd been here, received Rachel as she always had—with a toothy grin and a grunt. Of course, Phoenix was the same, and it was she who felt restraint when he was near. The temptation was too great to seek him out,

to share conversation as they had in the past, to feel
closeness with at least one person in the world, but it
would not be the respectable thing to do.

She'd been pleased to hear that Henry had gone to
the saloon with Phoenix, yet now all she could do was
worry. All Henry knew of society was what was practiced in the drawing rooms of England's aristocracy. The
earl had told her enough about it for her to realize that
Henry could draw a bullet with one ill-advised word.
She should have stopped him, but by the time she knew
of the poker game, it had been too late. Besides, she had
seen how easily men who supposedly cared for their
wives left them night after night without regard for their
sensibilities, using their nagging to justify their actions.
Henry did not pretend to care anything about her beyond
the pleasures they shared in the bedroom.

There was no reason for her to wait up for Henry, no
reason to believe he would still come to her bed that
night. She should take advantage of the freedom from
the passion he spent so desperately in her body, the
peace of not having to anticipate his abrupt departure
when it was over. But she missed those shared moments
of wildness when their bodies spoke honestly to one another in the silent language of need. She missed him.

The grandfather clock chimed four, followed by the
voices of men raised in song. When they paused for
breath—or possibly a swallow of whiskey—she heard
the creak of wagon wheels rolling up the hill. At least
they sounded happy enough. It was all she could do not
to peer out the window.

The wagon stopped and there was grumbling and
laughter, then a loud thump on the porch.

"Rachel," a slurred voice called out. "We got a package fer ya."

Oh, Lord, Henry must be insensible. She tightened the
belt on her wrapper, picked up a lantern, ran to the door,

pulled it open, and stepped outside. An obstacle brought
her up short and she lowered her gaze.

Henry lay flat on his back, staring up at her from two
blackened and swollen eyes. His lip was cut and his nose
bent slightly to one side. His knuckles were skinned.

"What happened?"

Cletus stepped forward, hat in hand. "He cheated."

Her gaze flew to Phoenix. Cheated? She couldn't
imagine it—not with Henry's pride and arrogance. Phoenix nodded once, a small smile playing about his mouth.
She couldn't credit it—that smile and the sheepish ex-
pressions on the other faces watching her from the bed
of the wagon. "How much did each of you lose?" she
asked.

"It was the damnedest thing, Rachel," Cletus said.
"He cheated so we *wouldn't* lose."

She sank to her knees beside Henry, partly out of a
sudden weakness in her legs and partly to assess the
damage. It made sense—Henry not wishing to take
money from those he considered to be less fortunate than
he. Her heart seemed to tremble in her throat as she
lightly touched his face. He grinned up at her—proof
that he was as pickled as the eggs she had sent over to
the saloon, knowing he had a fondness for them. Obviously he was feeling no pain . . . for the moment.

One by one she studied the other men, cataloguing the
injuries that seemed to be evenly distributed among
them. "Who won?" she asked.

Cletus shrugged. "Don't rightly know who won, but
Hank here lost fer sure." There was an insistent tug at
the sleeve of her wrapper. She glanced down at Henry.

His grin had widened, but his voice was solemn as a
boy's when announcing a feat of great importance. "I
won the belching contest, Rachel. Mine was the loudest
and the longest."

"Hank?" Rachel blinked, unable to comprehend this new vision of Henry beyond the simplest impression. *"Hank?"* she repeated, and again felt his tug on her sleeve.

And as his eyes rolled back in his head, his brows drew together and his mouth twisted in a glower he couldn't quite form. "Don't call me Hank." Then he passed out at her feet, his expression fading to a contented smile.

19

June

The land was studded with color and growth, the air gilded by the sun as spring promise was fulfilled by summer prosperity. Crops and gardens flourished. Buildings were completed and new ones began. It was business as usual, yet everything had changed in seven weeks—including Henry's face.

After the men had driven away in the wagon, she and Phoenix had taken advantage of Henry's stupor to carry him into the house and attempt to straighten out his nose. They had succeeded in pushing it back into place, though it now sported a slightly hawkish crook just below the bridge. A cut above his eye had healed, but had left a scar that further roughened his features. He looked a proper rogue now with his tanned face and hardened muscles. He behaved like one, too, when playing—and winning—poker with the other men. Under Phoenix's tutelage, he'd learned to fight without using the Marquess of Queensbury Rules.

And still everyone called him Hank.

He grew firmer, broader, as he worked beside her or with the men during the day, learning quickly as he had on the trail, becoming proficient in most tasks, remaining awkward and grimly determined in others, yet he was remote and preoccupied. He appeared for meals as if he were a paying guest and ate mechanically as he concentrated on the pad and pencil that were always within his reach. She'd become accustomed to seeing him drop whatever he was doing to execute a quick sketch before returning to the job at hand.

When the work was done, or a meal finished, he disappeared into the soddy.

He spent his passion in her bed, taking her with a fierce ardor, giving her completion without giving of himself. He spent the rest of the night in the soddy with the light of every spare lantern he could find shining out of the four windows.

She wondered if he found more satisfaction in what he created on paper and canvas than in what he saw around him. She wondered how he saw her. And then she wondered why she cared when he seemed to prefer his own company or that of the men in town to hers.

Of course it pleased her to see the grudging respect between him and her friends, and it was gratifying to know that they were becoming his friends, as well. From the almost boyish way he prepared for their gatherings, she thought that perhaps he had little experience with friendship. From the way he had grinned happily as he lay drunk and bleeding on the porch, she guessed that he knew nothing about play—either as a child or an adult.

She was pleased, yet she also felt left out, insignificant. Henry was a stranger to her, less familiar than he had been when they'd first met. The desolation she'd often seen in his expression had been replaced by wry smiles and bemusement. Gone was the anger that had seemed so old and worn that he had conformed to its dimensions, becoming a part of it. He appeared more relaxed, yet she sensed his wariness, as if he thought their truce was too fragile to withstand a direct confrontation.

She wished that she could interpret Henry's behavior as an echo of her own guarded hope for the future, but she had the feeling that if he did have hope, he expected it to turn on him at any moment.

She knew how he felt.

Bleakness settled into her a little more deeply, a chill that wouldn't leave her, a fear that reckoning drew closer with each day that Roz remained in Promise.

Roz's girls had stayed long enough to care for her, then elected to seek employment near the lumber camps in the Northwest. One of the men had relinquished his cabin to Roz, and she had planted a garden in the back and flowers along the sides, leaving the front bare and uninviting. It appeared that Roz planned to remain in Promise, and Rachel hadn't found the courage to seek either confirmation or denial. In any case, her mother did not welcome discourse with anyone, as if her life as well as her garden was for her own pleasure and not to be shared with anyone who happened by.

It was odd to see Roz in solitude, walking the meadows and working silently in the garden behind her one-room dwelling. Oddly, she felt a certain comfort in knowing her mother was close . . . and safe. Seeing Roz was more reassuring than having to rely on gossip, and Rachel had made it a point to see her mother several days a week even though more often than not she was ignored or bluntly turned away.

But it was late June and preparations had to be made for the coming winter. Every person in the small community had to be considered. And today Rachel needed to find solace in the company of another woman, to feel connected to another human being. Today she had realized that she was pregnant.

Roz glanced up as Rachel walked around the side of the cabin. Her skin was almost healed, though several scars marred her arms and neck. The lines that Rachel remembered fanning out from Roz's eyes were gone, and the flesh of her face was smooth as a young girl's. A half inch of hair covered her scalp, straight rather than the curls Roz had been born with.

It was stark white.

Rachel averted her gaze and swallowed.

"You must be lonely as hell to keep coming to see me," Roz said as she continued to pull weeds and toss them into a pile.

"Aren't you lonely?" Rachel asked.

"I'm smart enough to know I won't be lonely as long as I don't forget who I am." Roz straightened up and pulled off the soft leather gloves she wore. "Strange as it may seem to you, Rachel, I think I'm a hell of a woman. I took good care of my girls and ran a clean house. I never told the secrets that my customers told me and I raised you to be as tough and as smart as I am." She paused to brush the dust from her skirt. "Aside from that, I raised myself because my mother died when I was a baby and my pa and brothers were too busy putting food on the table to pay much attention to me. I guess I was born lonely and got used to it like some folks get used to being blind or deaf."

Again Rachel swallowed. Deaf or blind. Loneliness did feel like that—a void where nothing existed but what she felt inside, a silence where sensation replaced the sound of simple conversation. She studied Roz's garden, searching for something to say and finding nothing appropriate to her mother's revelations. Roz had never spoken to her like that before, never revealed herself in a way that made her seem all too human and vulnerable.

"We've had a lot of weeds this year. . . ." Her voice faded as she realized how absurd it was to make small talk with her mother as if they were neighbors chatting over a fence.

"Is that why you're here, girl? To pull a weed from your pretty little town?"

"No. I came to pay you back . . . the money you gave me before I left." Rachel held out the same leather pouch Roz had given her the day they had buried Liddie. For seven years, she had counted out a share of her earnings to put into the bag. "According to Phoenix, you didn't bring much with you."

Roz ignored the money. "A few old dresses that no one would notice or try to steal."

"You can get whatever you need at the mercantile."

"You bet I can." She'd smiled then, the first Rachel had seen. "You know how everyone thought all my money went into my wardrobe?"

Rachel nodded.

"Well, it just goes to show that people can be right and stupid at the same time. I wore the same color because ten dresses can look like thirty if they're all the same color and you're handy with a needle. Hell, I'm so handy that I even knew how to sew money into the hems and linings of the ones that eventually wore out." Roz smiled then as she glanced at the bag bulging with money.

Another unexpected twist of a knife in Rachel's heart. She hadn't known that her mother could sew. Clothing had appeared on her bed from time to time and she'd assumed it came from the dressmaker. She'd believed the stories about Roz's wardrobe, that Roz was foolish and nearsighted in her extravagance. She should have known. She should have given it enough thought to realize that Roz's primary "business" was survival.

"My clothes . . . did you make them, too? Is that why you refused the hand-me-downs the church ladies tried to give me?"

Roz shrugged. "I hated wearing my brothers' hand-me-downs."

"You wanted me to have what you didn't," Rachel said, and waited for the answer. It seemed important to know the truth.

"Pride," Roz said flatly.

Pride. Roz's pride. Henry's pride. Her own pride that kept her from trying harder to hold him, to admit that she wanted to hold him. She was tired of it all.

Yet she gave in to it as she held out the bag again, refusing to ask more questions, telling herself it was too late and didn't matter anymore. "This money is yours, Roz. I always considered it a loan."

"Well, consider it your dowry," Roz snapped. "We're even, Rachel."

Even. How odd that her mother reflected Henry's attitude, though he had never said it in so many words. He simply made sure that whatever she did for him was promptly repaid in one way or another. The significance of the connection drifted through her mind, hovering just out of reach. She dropped the pouch into her apron pocket. "Yes . . . well . . . if you need anything . . ."

"You know, I'd forgotten how much I liked living here in the basin. Guess I had to at the time or I would have—" She shook her head. "It's important to retire in the right place. Retirement is the only thing in this life that lasts."

It was odd to hear her mother speak so. "You're giving up the—"

"I was respectable once, Rachel," she said, and the repetition of what Liddie had said as she lay dying stabbed Rachel with grief. She heard Roz continue, but her mother's voice seemed far away, removed somehow from the present. "A good little farmer's daughter. I liked making things grow."

Rachel remembered the pots of flowers Roz always had in her office and sitting room, the garden that had been a part of every "house" she'd owned. But truck gardens were practical and, more often than not, necessary in towns where the local storekeeper might be righteous enough to refuse trade with a brothel. And what woman didn't enjoy flowers? It wasn't as if Roz could expect the men in her life to present bouquets to her, not when she commanded the stiffest prices in the territory—appreciation enough for the temporary use of her body.

"This is your land and your town," Roz said as she bent to pluck another weed. "It's not big enough for both of us, but the basin is. I thought I'd move on next spring, find another place by the river—"

"It's big enough, Roz," Rachel said without having to think about it.

"Why? Because it was mine to begin with?"

"I don't know why."

"You'd better figure it out, girl. I won't stay here without good reason, and that man of yours—and how you feel about him—is one hell of a good reason for me to move on."

Rachel didn't respond. Her mother had ridiculed her dreams too often. And if she could present Roz with cause to remain in Promise, she would have to face her own reasons for wanting her to stay. She wasn't ready to make admissions, even to herself, that might invite more derision.

"You're not the first woman who's been torn between blood loyalty and the man she loves," Roz said.

"Doesn't seem like a tough choice. You obviously think he's worth it, and we both know that I'm not."

"Do you know what it's like to make a choice like that?" Rachel asked, unable to either admit or deny her emotions for Henry. She didn't know if what she felt for him was love, and if so, she didn't know why.

"You're learning, aren't you, Rachel?" Roz asked, avoiding Rachel's question.

"Yes, I'm learning."

"Too bad you haven't learned to be selfish. The choices are easier then."

"Are the consequences easier, too?"

"Depends on how many soft spots you have on your conscience. You either get tough or you get hurt." Turning, Roz walked toward the cabin, ending the conversation.

It had been the longest conversation they'd shared since that first day, yet Rachel felt as if it shouldn't be over and the answers she sought dangled like threads that would unravel her if she pulled them. She turned away to return home.

"Rachel."

She whirled around at the softness in Roz's voice, the tenderness, and decided that she had imagined it as she faced her mother. Roz's expression was tight, her eyes hard, and her mouth slanted with cynicism. It reminded Rachel of Henry, of how he looked when he revealed the soft spots in his conscience. She waited there, watching her mother, and wondered if Roz was about to pull a thread.

"I made a choice between keeping you and holding on to the man I thought I loved. There was a family that wanted you. If I'd known that you were the one who would suffer the consequences I wouldn't have been so selfish."

Shock stunned Rachel, then anger ripped through her. She fell apart with it, her emotions scattered in too many directions for her to pull them together. So many times, she'd needed to hear those words from Roz, any words that implied she wanted her daughter, that she cared. Now Rachel couldn't even understand them. "Who was this man, Roz? My father?"

"If you want to call him that. He was a Rebel soldier who'd deserted while his company was trying to invade Colorado. He wandered up here, found me, and took me to Denver City."

"I see. He wanted you to get rid of me and you kept me because you were *selfish*. And you regret it because *I suffered*. . . . and *not once* in eighteen years . . . *not once* in the seven years since I left, have you said or done anything to show it," Rachel said with a low ferocity that felt ripped out of her. The men who had visited her mother's house for an hour or an evening seemed more real to her than the idea of actually having a father. She should feel something for the man who fathered her, but she couldn't get a handle on anything tangible. It was too new after years of pretending it didn't matter, years of being afraid to know the truth. It didn't seem as important as what Roz had revealed about herself. It wasn't as important as hearing Roz's admission after a lifetime of wondering what was wrong with her that her mother didn't love her. It wasn't as consuming as the pain of knowing that maybe her mother had cared.

She took a step forward, but her legs felt disjointed, and she could barely see for the haze of anger blurring her eyes. "Why now, Roz?"

Abruptly Roz sank down on the step, a billow of old ivory cloth with no shape. "Why did I keep you? Because I wanted the same things you want—to not be alone in the world. To belong to someone. Or: Why did I tell you? Because maybe now, more than ever before, you need to know.''

''I needed to know every time you sent me to the attic . . . and every time we picked up stakes in the middle of the night. I needed to know when you gave me this money''—Rachel slapped the bulge in her pocket—''and you let me leave without so much as a good-bye. At some point after that, I learned to need something besides a mother.''

''You learned to rely on yourself, and to believe in yourself. You learned to be strong,'' Roz said with a note in her voice that sounded like pride. ''I told you once to make sure you were fighting for yourself and not someone else. Well, this is it, Rachel. I'll stay here as long as you let me because I *am* selfish. And as long as I'm here, you run a big risk of your Englishman finding out about you.''

''I'm aware of that.'' Instinct governed Rachel now. Her thoughts were too fragmented, her emotions too numb for her to control her responses. ''I told you that you can stay.''

''Out of duty?'' Roz snorted. ''I'll take what I can get, Rachel, but what about you? If I stay, you'll be fighting your husband for me, and you'll probably lose. If you tell me to leave, you'll be fighting him for yourself, and you just might win the prize . . . if you can call him that.''

Rachel retreated, one step, then another and another. She couldn't talk about this, couldn't argue with what seemed like logic when somewhere inside herself she knew that it wasn't logic at all. Not to her. ''You stay, Roz,'' she said, out of anger and a reasoning that she couldn't quite grasp. ''I want you to stay for me—'' Words failed her then and she turned away, walking with slow, measured steps when she would rather run. But she couldn't run—not from Roz or Henry or herself. She couldn't escape from the reckoning that was sure to come.

And she couldn't banish the thought that, like her mother, she had conceived a child in passion rather than love with a man who had made it clear he did not want to raise a child. A man who would leave as surely as her father had.

The trembling wouldn't stop as Rachel reached her house. The weakness in her limbs reminded her that she hadn't eaten. The calmness of her stomach suggested that it might be safe to do so now as it had not been earlier in the day. Neither had Henry eaten, and it was past time for lunch. It was easy to concentrate on physical needs, to perform the mindless task of preparing food, packing it in a basket, carrying it out to the vegetable garden where Henry was working. No doubt he was still grumbling about how she had turned him into a "bloody farmer." Thinking about Henry was easy now, a habit she had developed without realizing it. He was a part of her life. He was a part of her, though he would not like to know that. She'd been content to drift along, waiting for something to happen, not pressing him for more than a few chores and his attentions in bed, not pressing to understand what was happening inside herself.

It was time to make something happen. Roz had convinced her of that with her confessions, with her implications that she had wanted her daughter. Rachel didn't question whether it was true. Either her mother had lied by omission for all of Rachel's life, or she was lying now. At the moment it didn't matter. The wasted years mattered, when Rachel would have believed any hint of caring or affection. The deprivation and emptiness of those years mattered. She didn't think about whether it was too late for her and Roz. She had to do all she could

to make sure it would never be too late for herself and
Henry.

There were already too many loose threads in her life.

He was on his knees, his palms flat on his thighs and
his gaze on the ground in front of him. His sketch pad
lay beside him, the pages flipping in a lazy midafternoon
wind. Rachel approached him quietly and stood beside
him, allowing the drift of her skirt in the breeze to catch
his attention.

"What is this?" he asked, his voice a whisper.

She followed his gaze and saw the beginnings of a
pod sprouting from a young bush in the garden. They'd
been late in planting this year but the growth seemed to
be catching up to the season. "Snap beans."

"I planted this?"

"Yes."

"It's food."

"Yes."

"It's growing."

The awe in his voice was unmistakable, and she suddenly recalled the first time she had planted seeds and
watched day in, day out for signs of growth. But she'd
been a child, captivated by the wonders of life—even
that of a vegetable. She'd known that she had proven
herself in some way. She was useful and important.
She'd dragged Grace outside to look, and Grace had patted her head in approval.

Henry seemed like a child too, the way he stared and
stared at the growth, the way he reached out and stroked
it with his finger. But his movement was awkward and
the pod bent under his touch. He snatched his hand away
and glared at his fingers as if they were foreign to him.

Instinctively Rachel laid her hand on his head and
sifted her fingers through his hair.

His gaze jerked up to hers, followed her movements as she dropped to her knees beside him and adjusted the tiny pod to lay cradled in the fold of a leaf. "I was five when I planted my first garden. When the first growth appeared I told anyone who would listen that I had 'borned a cabbage.'"

His mouth twitched ever so slightly. "Cabbage for you and a string bean for me," he said gravely. "There's a certain logic in the geometry of it."

"Geometry?"

His mouth twitched again. "The study or science of shapes and solids, among other things."

"Oh." It took her a moment to comprehend the implication, and she chuckled at the image. "Then I think I should tend certain shapes and you . . . " Her sentence trailed off as he raised his head to stare at her. She realized her mistake. His comment had been improper and she had encouraged more of the same instead of blushing or changing the subject as a refined lady would have done. But it had been a natural response—the kind of banter that flew over the breakfast table in brothels.

"Farmyard humor from my oh-so-serious paragon of a wife? Perhaps I am corrupting you after all."

She felt corrupted—by the whimsical note in his voice, the smile that curved his mouth and crinkled the corners of his eyes. A genuine smile rather than the familiar derisive slant of lips and cold, blue glare. A beautiful smile, free of tension and dark, secret thoughts. *He* was beautiful, with the planes of his face highlighted by sunlight and creased by pleasure, his shirt over the firm muscles of his broad chest and shoulders smudged with dirt, his hands roughened by calluses that had been raw blisters a few weeks ago. She liked the way his fancy suspenders were frayed at the edges and his trousers were slightly baggy in the seat.

Perhaps she even loved him—for his instinctive acts of compassion to animals and children, his grumbling while he earned his calluses and aching muscles, for the way he questioned without seeming to show any interest at all, curious in spite of himself. And she loved the child in him that called out to the child within herself—both children who had never had the opportunity to be young.

She smiled back at him and trembled inside as his finger traced the curve of her mouth.

"Nourishment I presume." He nodded toward the basket, though his gaze remained fixed on her.

"Lunch," she said against his touch, her tongue tasting him as she spoke, and stared transfixed by his hooded gaze as he moved his hand from her mouth to his, licking the taste of her from the tip of his finger.

She shivered at the caw of a crow flying overhead and drew back to unfold the tablecloth that lay on top of their meal. "I'm late today," she said, and her voice sounded high and breathless.

"You were with the whore again."

The cloth slipped from her grasp and fluttered to the ground, perfectly spread on the grass bordering the garden. She peered up at him and saw neither tightness nor rebuke in his expression. "She is retiring here."

"Then it is fortunate that I am not."

"She bothers no one," Rachel said, avoiding his gaze as she laid out the meal, dividing and arranging the bread and meat just so, adding pieces of dried fruit and setting jars of water and cool, fresh milk beside each plate. She'd taken such care in choosing food that carried little scent to offend her appetite, yet it was the loathing in Henry's voice that robbed her of hunger.

Without further comment, he reclined on his side, supporting himself on one elbow and crooking one leg. "You are joining me?" he asked.

"Yes. My work is done early today." She gratefully embraced the change of subject.

"Your work is never done, Rachel." He bit into a sandwich of cold beef. "It is devilishly difficult to keep up with you."

"Why must you keep up?"

"To please myself."

The old derision and sarcasm were absent in his voice. He was different today, more unconstrained than she'd ever seen him, without mockery to shield him and anger to protect him. She prayed it would last through the afternoon.

"Maybe it will be easier for you to keep up with me once you move out of the soddy," she said, noting how he stilled suddenly, as if he were preparing to strike out.

"Why would I do that?"

"Because winter is coming. If it snows too much, you will be trapped in the house."

"Or trapped in the soddy?"

"No, I don't think you would feel trapped there as long as you had paints and canvases . . . and walls." She glanced at the barn with its huge mural on the side.

His gaze on her was narrowed and sharp. "You see too much, Rachel."

She shrugged. "Only the obvious."

"So I am being evicted."

"You are being relocated to a bedroom in the house with good light. I've already cleared it out and stripped and whitewashed the walls so you won't be distracted by wallpaper."

He stretched out on his back, then, and stared up at the sky. "You've thought of everything, I see."

"There were no other places, Henry. Every house and building is occupied, and the soddy is unsuitable—"

He held up his hand, touched his fingertips to her mouth—a simple gesture of conciliation rather than a caress. "Thank you, Rachel. Your tolerance is one gift I can neither refuse nor repay."

The stark simplicity of it choked off anything else she might have said. The strain in his voice was eloquent with vulnerability. She had moved him, touched him, and she wasn't sure how. He had changed in the past weeks and she wasn't sure why. She could only hope it was enough.

Without realizing it, she had eaten half a sandwich and drunk all of her milk. She felt Henry's regard as she pushed a crumb around on her plate and relinquished it to an ant crawling across the cloth. The small smile tipping up the corners of his mouth gave her the courage she needed to take another risk. "You don't have to come to my room anymore. I'm pregnant."

The smile faded. "I see. There is, I suppose, a bed in my garret?"

"No."

"It is not like you to commit such an oversight," he said tonelessly as he rolled to his side and stood up, looking down at her.

"There are two other bedrooms, if that's what you want." She breathed deeply, yet felt deprived of air. "I am hoping that you will choose to share mine."

"Rachel," he said with strained patience. "You just informed me that I did not have to come to your room again."

"You never *had* to, Henry. I never forced you to come, nor would I have."

He reached down and grasped her wrists, pulling her to her feet and shifted his hold to her shoulders, as if he would shake her. "You force me, madam, every time you are within my sight. You violate everything I believe in with your blasted honesty. You imprison me with your open arms."

It was thrilling, provocative, and frightening all at once to have him speak to her with such leashed emotion, to know that she inspired that in him, to know that she held him with more than legal documents and unspoken vows. The truth was as compelling in that moment as his hold on her. She wanted to violate all that he believed in, to force him to feel more than anger and contempt and suspicion. She wanted to embrace him in his darkness and pull him out of it. She wanted to hear him laugh. And she wanted to learn how to play with him. She wanted them to learn to play together.

She did love him.

Framing his face with her hands, she stared into the turbulence in his eyes. "I ask you, Henry, to share my bedroom with me. The choice is yours."

"Am I to understand that you are reluctantly giving me my freedom?"

"Yes."

He pulled her hands from his face and bent over her, his breath a drift of warmth on her cheek. "Are you fit?"

"Yes."

"Good." The world tilted and spun and before she could catch her breath she was draped over his shoulder and holding onto the waist of his trousers for balance. The ground blurred as he strode with her toward the house, forgetting the remains of their meal.

Her stomach lurched and spun. "Henry . . . stop . . . put me down."

He ignored her.

Darkness encroached at the edge of her vision. Out of desperation, she bunched the cloth of his pants in her fingers and tugged once, jerking up his pants until the crotch met the resistance of his body. "Hank! Stop . . . *please.*"

"Dammit, Rachel," he roared, and executed an odd sideways dance. "You're castrating me."

"Put me down," she countered.

He stopped and his grasp loosened as she tugged harder. But as soon as she released his pants to slip free, she felt the flat of his hand connect with her bottom. "Don't call me Hank." He continued to hold her as he lowered her to the ground, her body sliding against his, her skirt pulling up where it was caught between them.

"I'll call you worse than that if you cause me to lose the only meal I've eaten today," she replied breathlessly, and leaned back to smooth out her dress.

"You said you were fit."

"I am fit, but I am also carrying a child—in my stomach." She pointed at her belly. "What should we tell him when he is born lopsided? That his father insisted on carrying his mother as if she were a sack of flour?"

Entranced by his sudden bark of laughter, she closed her mouth and simply listened. She'd never heard him laugh before, never thought him capable of mischief or horseplay.

Again the world tilted as he lifted her—gently this time—and cradled her in his arms as he walked to the house. He opened the back door and carried her inside, through the kitchen, up the stairs into her bedroom. Her body slid downward, flowing like liquid against his as she made no attempt to separate herself from his embrace. "You seem pleased about the child," she said, testing his mood.

"I don't know what I feel about the child, Rachel."

"Then what are you doing? Why—"

He tipped up her chin, cupped it within one large hand. "I have done my duty for you, Luc, and the Ashford name. Now I am free to claim what you have promised me." His mouth hovered above hers. "Now I am here because it is what *I* want."

She couldn't move and didn't dare speak as he unbuttoned her dress and slipped it off her shoulders and
down her body, taking her petticoat and bloomers along
the way, his hands urgent, his breathing ragged. He
tossed her clothing across the room and tugged at his,
flinging each piece in a different direction the moment
it cleared his body. Not once did he touch her skin, yet
she felt desire melt and trickle between her legs and her
heart beat frantically in her chest.

He reached out to encircle her breast, his gaze studying her response as her nipples puckered and swelled
and her body shuddered with every breath. It seemed
like forever that they stood in the center of the room,
stripped down to flesh and sunlight, nothing between
them but freedom and need. Suddenly Rachel felt closer
to him than she ever had before, though a foot of air
separated them.

His hand trailed down the center of her body, lingering to trace the shape of her navel, then moving lower
to sift through springy curls and slide lower still. Her
knees buckled and wobbled as he found her, his fingers
slipping inside of her, stroking . . .

He withdrew with a slow, teasing caress and she saw
her moisture on his hand, felt it as he painted each nipple
then raised his hand to taste her on his fingertips. Arching her neck, she closed her eyes, presenting herself to
him with her arms at her sides, her palms open and facing him. Sensation rippled through her, wave after wave
of excitement as she felt his mouth on her breasts, one
then the other, with gentle bites and insistent tugs drawing the last bit of flavor from her flesh.

And still, he did not press his body to hers, but
touched her one small bit at a time—his mouth on hers,
his tongue teasing and playing with hers . . . his fingers
dipping into her and brushing her body with her own
mist . . . his lips skimming her neck and her ears and

down to her breasts again . . . the tip of him pressing at her navel, a rigid tether connecting them.

He swallowed her cry with his mouth, and his hands on her shoulders guided her backward, urging her to sit on the edge of the high bed as he stood between her outspread thighs, his head bent over her, drinking from her mouth as if he might never get enough.

She opened her eyes as air bathed her body, cooling the mist on her flesh. He loomed above her, still standing, still staring at her with drowsy, seductive eyes. His member was full and hard, reaching toward her, and his breath seemed to snap as she leaned forward to press a soft kiss in the center. She lay back, her hips still at the edge of the mattress, her legs open to receive him.

The afternoon faded as he advanced, entering her a little at a time, maddening her, tormenting her, beguiling her with the promise of fulfillment. She unfolded around him, conforming to his shape, absorbing him, then opened again to take more of him. It seemed an eternity as he stood above her, filling her and lifting her hips with his hands, guiding her movements to meet his smooth and gentle thrusts.

Slowly he drove her mad with need as he stroked rather than thrust, over and over again, pausing each time as if he savored every sensation and sought to prolong it. Slowly she met him, her legs embracing his waist, her hips rising and falling and rotating against him, her hands clutching the quilt, her gaze bound by his as she dissolved from the inside out and spasm after spasm carried her from one moment to the next.

With a groan, Henry gripped her hips, holding her still as he thrust and tensed and followed her into completion. And the moment where life met death and became renewal endured when she thought she could not survive one more wave of pleasure without drowning in her own senses.

Henry eased out of her, leaving her body as surely as he would leave the room . . . as he always left her to lie alone in her bed, surrounded by empty dreams and the scent of remembered passion.

She expected nothing more, anticipating only his absence, forcing herself not to cry out in protest as he released her hips and lowered her legs. It had been different this time—slow and easy and lingering, the sensations ebbing and flowing and all the more intense for the gentleness he had shown her, all the more profound because they had not hidden from one another behind closed eyes and darkness.

Again gripping the quilt, she stared up at him, waiting for him to pick up his clothing and walk away.

He stepped around the side of the bed and the mattress dipped with his weight as he sat up against the headboard, his back cushioned by pillows. Then his hands grasped her under her arms and he drew her upward, cradling her between his legs, her back supported by his chest, her head resting on his shoulder. He said nothing, but merely held her, his hands entwined with hers where they crossed over her midriff.

Closing her eyes, she held tears at bay, afraid to move or make a sound that might disturb the closeness he had established, concentrating instead on the feel of his perspiration-dampened flesh against hers, on the way his maleness lay relaxed beneath her bottom, on the sound of Henry's easy breathing as his cheek rubbed over her hair, seducing her with more than the promise of passion.

Exhaustion washed over her, and she succumbed willingly to the sanctuary of sleep, the respite from thoughts of what might be.

And when she awakened the next morning, she felt the warmth of his body surrounding her, the slow puff of his breath on her ear, the vibration of his whuffling snores against her back.

For the first time since she'd spoken vows of marriage, she felt like a wife.

20

Late August

I t was easier to think about what he didn't want.
Henry stood back from his current portrait of
Rachel, ignoring the second figure in the painting and
studied her newly rounded form—the hips that had widened a bit, the fuller breasts, the belly that protruded a
little more every day. The child she carried wasn't real
to him. It was a part of Rachel, belonging to her. And
though he painted the changes in her, he didn't really
see them.

He didn't want to see them, to acknowledge that what
she held within her body was a part of him. A part he
would leave behind. Perhaps that was why he'd delayed
moving into the house. When Rachel had told him of
the room she'd prepared for him, she'd touched him,
resurrected his need for understanding and acceptance of
what he was. And when she'd lain naked on her bed in
the afternoon light, staring at him so openly in her desire
for him, she'd shaken him, rearranging the patterns in

his mind until he felt valued rather than merely tolerated. Yesterday Rachel had shown respect for his art and honesty in her passion for him. Both were gifts that would be difficult to leave behind.

He wanted nothing from Rachel that couldn't be repaid, like the room she'd prepared for him. Perhaps she didn't know how much her gesture had meant to him. Perhaps she did. Either way, he couldn't risk owing her.

The light dimmed as a curtain of heavy clouds obscured the sun. It didn't matter. As soon as it dried, this canvas would join the dozen others covered with Rachel's likeness. A dozen likenesses that were not complete.

He didn't want to finish them, to see what they might reveal.

Phoenix had been far easier to paint. He'd rendered him in watercolor, a nebulous, almost transparent figure that seemed far more substantial than Rachel did in oil. But then Phoenix's impression on his life was straightforward, simple, and somehow, Henry knew that it would remain an impression, like a blurred thumbprint in clay. Someday Phoenix would simply be a memory. A friend who had moved on.

A friend. It was an alien concept, yet when applied to Phoenix, he felt no wariness or suspicion. Theirs was an easy companionship, more often than not spent in quiet moments of walking down the street or working side by side on one of Rachel's projects. Phoenix demanded nothing. And when the brawl had broken out in the saloon two months ago, it had been Phoenix who stood at his back, lending support—and fists—to the underdog in an uneven fight. Perhaps it was the recognition of a kindred spirit that eased Henry's acceptance of Phoenix. Perhaps it was because he knew that Phoenix would move on. There was freedom in knowing the unquestionable fate of an association. To know it could be no other way.

As it could be no other way with Rachel. He didn't want to believe it might be different with her, that he might not want to leave after five years. It had been unsettling enough that he hadn't been able to leave her yesterday, but had spent the night holding her in sleep, resting more peacefully than he had in years.

He dropped a light cloth over the easel yet continued to stare at it, seeing Rachel in his mind as she had been when they'd met, on the trail, in Finnigan's barn, surrounded by her friends. Friends to whom she gave trust and owed loyalty. Friends who were helping her build a future.

He didn't want friends like that.

Outside, the thunder and wind of a late-summer storm called to him. He enjoyed the Wyoming storms with their sound and fury and savage beauty. They reminded him of all that he felt yet could not express. They reminded him that peace and order were easily destroyed, that dreams were easily transformed into nightmares.

He did not want to forget that all that separated heaven from hell was the horizon.

Henry left the soddy and stood outside, watching the storm as rain drenched his clothes. The sky flashed with an eerie yellow glow and jagged bolts of lightning struck the ground, leaving an unending gloom in its wake. He glanced toward the house and saw illumination in the kitchen window framing Rachel as she prepared their evening meal. His gaze wandered to the parlor and found the orange and red flicker of a blaze in the fireplace, then returned to the kitchen.

Rachel stood at the window, watching him as she tucked a stray strand of hair behind her ear and tied her shawl more firmly about her shoulders. He tried to look away, to study the storm and memorize the exact shading of the clouds and angle of the trees as they bent in the wind. But all he could see was the warmth and welcome he saw through the windows.

"Rachel has invited me to dinner," Phoenix said from his side. He hadn't noticed Phoenix's approach, yet his presence didn't surprise Henry.

Henry nodded and turned back to the soddy, feeling cold suddenly. Funny, how he'd never minded the wind and rain before. Phoenix followed without invitation and stood in the center of the room, studying the paintings that leaned against the walls.

Henry scowled at his lack of objection to an invasion of what he considered his private "cave," his lack of discomfort at having Phoenix examine the renderings of his soul. In that moment he realized that he trusted Phoenix. In that, too, was freedom . . . to share without fearing violation of all that was important to him.

"These are older?" Phoenix asked as he pointed to the canvases along one wall.

"Yes."

"Your use of light is more pronounced in these." Phoenix moved to another set of paintings, seemingly at ease with demons and storms. "They are recent?"

"Yes." Henry stood immobile by the door, his gaze fixed on the paintings, seeing for the first time what Phoenix had seen immediately. There was more light, and more color, in the newer paintings. Why hadn't he noticed?

"You have a rare gift to render a mood as well as an image," Phoenix said as he began to walk around the room, picking up one canvas, comparing it to another. "Never have I seen this quality of luminosity."

"I wouldn't imagine that you've had the opportunity to see more than the requisite nude hanging above every bar in the territory."

"I have not always been in the territories," Phoenix said. "Europe offers many opportunities for artist and connoisseur alike."

"And which are you?" Henry asked, intrigued at this glimpse into the past of a man who never spoke of himself.

"Both, though my appreciation of art is far greater than my talent to produce it." A painting caught Phoenix's eye and he bent to see it more clearly. He shifted his position, moving from one canvas to another, discreetly passing over the nude of Rachel. "You don't know her yet."

"I know her," Henry said.

"Do you know that she is ill in the mornings?"

"She's expecting. Of course she's ill."

"Do you know that she is in love with you?"

Thunder crashed and lightning struck, but Henry neither saw nor heard the storm raging outside. He drew breath yet it burned his throat. "I have heard that women in her condition are often fanciful," he said with a forced air of indifference.

"Rachel is not fanciful. The last thing she wanted to do was love you."

"Of course she's fanciful," Henry said, lightly. The last thing he wanted to do was to take this conversation seriously. "Look around you. She takes in vagabonds. She's building a town and will populate it with her own children if need be. If that is not fancy I don't know what is."

"It's a need to belong. You of all people should understand that."

"I don't see why," Henry said. "For that matter I wonder why Rachel has such a need. She has a home and friends." Henry picked up a clean rag and dried his hair, hiding the tremble in his hands as it struck him that for the first time, he felt as if he, too, had a home and friends.

"You don't believe in love?" Phoenix asked.

"Of course I believe in love. I have seen men and women betray and cheat and kill for love. I have seen suicide committed in the name of love."

"Rachel won't betray you . . . though like all of us, she has secrets she is afraid to tell."

"I have no interest in her secrets," Henry replied. "Particularly the one you have just revealed."

"Her feelings are not a secret to anyone who sees her clearly." Phoenix nodded toward the portraits of Rachel. "Isn't that why you haven't finished these? Because you know what you will see?"

Henry's mouth flattened as he refused to respond. But the answer was there, in the paintings. He hadn't completed the portraits because he was afraid he *wouldn't* see Rachel's lack of guile, her spirit of giving. He was afraid that he might find that she was not what she seemed. His life with Rachel was a promise in itself— of peace and contentment, of discovery and satisfaction, of being more in Rachel's eyes than he had ever thought himself to be. Here, with her, he felt almost whole. But he knew how easily promises were broken, how quickly peace could be shattered. He knew that to accept love or to feel it was to accept despair.

He wanted no part of it—neither Rachel's love nor the hope he suddenly felt. Hope, like love, destroyed. Still, the feeling wouldn't go away. It sat in his thoughts like a garden that had bloomed under his care, a cow that gave milk at his touch, a need to live rather than exist.

He didn't want to deny that need anymore.

Phoenix turned to face him. "Cletus, Horace, and I leave tomorrow to hunt for winter meat. I won't be coming back."

The change of subject jarred him. The topic itself shook him loose from other thoughts. He'd expected Phoenix to leave. He hadn't expected to feel such an immediate sense of loss. He didn't know what to do with it, so he ignored it. "Does Rachel know?"

"Yes. I had hoped to help you move all this into the house tonight."

"What does your departure have to do with my moving into the house?"

"She needs you nearby."

"I am close."

"It would ease my mind to know you are together. Fear can feed on itself when you're alone."

"I'm sure Rachel appreciates your concern."

Phoenix breathed deeply, then reached for the door. "My concern isn't entirely for Rachel."

He couldn't follow as Phoenix left the soddy. Henry had to think, to fight against the weight and meaning of all that his friend had said. His steps dragged as he wandered around the room, studying the canvases as Phoenix had done, trying to see them through Phoenix's eyes. Love and hopelessness stared back at him from the ravaged features of his mother. Mockery and contempt twisted the face of his father—a demon's face corroded by depravity. In another, a whore rose above a boy like a gargoyle, ripping out what was left of his heart as he stared at the ceiling with tears of blood running from his eyes. And then there was Phoenix, sitting across from him at the poker table, grinning around a cheroot clamped between his teeth in the only painting that was not exaggerated. Odd that Phoenix had not taken particular note of his own likeness.

Henry knew he should go to the house, share the meal with Rachel and Phoenix, bid a proper farewell to the only friend he had ever had aside from Luc. But his appetite was gone, both for nourishment and prolonged farewells. The morning would be time enough to say good-bye. His shoulders heaved—once—and sudden

moisture trailed down his cheek. He glanced up at the
roof to check for leaks, yet there were none. He raised
his hand to his face, then touched his fingertips to his
tongue, tasting the salt of tears.

Bloody hell. He cursed over and over again as he
paced angrily about the soddy . . . because he hadn't
thought he had any grief left to shed. Because with every
loss another part of him became hollow, and he feared
that someday there would be nothing left inside himself
but emptiness.

He blinked rapidly and shoved the painting aside.
He'd denied his feelings before, refusing to acknowledge
that he'd been touched by one person or another. But
this was different. Phoenix was different. He had chosen
to be a friend with no ties or obligations of blood or
business, or convenience. He had set no conditions for
his loyalty as he'd stood at Henry's back. He had accepted Henry as he was without judgment, without trying to change him.

He would miss having such a friend. He would miss
Phoenix.

He turned away from the canvas and lifted the cloth
from the easel to reveal his newest painting of Rachel.
She stood beside Roz, the madonna and the whore, both
of them dressed identically in ivory, yet where one was
bald and looked as tattered and soiled as her gown, the
other stood with grace and dignity, her hair falling down
her back, her skin flawless and glowing with the touch
of the sun. In another painting, Rachel knelt in the garden, her hands mounding dirt around a stunted sprout,
nurturing it, coaxing it to grow.

He removed the canvas from the easel and replaced it
with a new one, larger than the others. An image took
form in his mind as he readied paints and brushes and
unearthed a clean palette. An image of Rachel, holding

a storm in her hands, taming the devil's tail, soothing away the fury.

Rachel, who was taming him with her honesty and her tranquility, humbling him with her patience and caring. Rachel, who took his nightmares away and gave him love instead.

He admitted it to himself—that she loved him. Her very honesty was proof. Submitting to her husband was one thing. Wanting him night after night, receiving him with desire, and giving and taking pleasure was quite another. Rachel did not lie beneath him with her eyes closed and her body slack. She openly studied him as if she saw something new in him each time he came to her. She moved with him, around him, as if she would absorb him into herself.

Perhaps she already had, for he was beginning to hope that love did not always bring despair. And if it did, he was beginning to wonder if it wasn't a small price to pay to be able to hold her through the night, to awaken naked beside her as if he had been reborn in the image she had of him.

It was time for him to move into the house.

Rachel did not see Henry for three days. By night, she watched the lamps pour light from the windows of the soddy as she waited for him to come to her. By day, she found the eggs gathered and the cows milked and saw Henry working in the garden before retreating to the soddy once more. She hadn't approached him to ask why he didn't come for meals . . . why he didn't come to her. She didn't want to learn that he no longer wanted a wife in the kitchen or a woman in the bedroom.

"Leave him be," Phoenix had counseled during dinner the night before he'd left.

But Phoenix was a man. He did not spend each morning with his head hanging over a bucket. Men sowed

their seeds and puffed out their chests while women let
out seams in their dresses and made endless trips to the
convenience. Men did as they pleased while women
were supposed to be virtuously patient and sweetly forgiving.

She slammed the kettle onto the stove and glared at
it because the water did not come to a boil fast enough.
Enough was enough. Henry had chosen to honor their
contract. "For better or worse, in hopelessness and in
hell," he had said. For five years he would be her husband. Well, it had only been five months and she had
yet to see "better." She'd been wasting precious energy
fearing "worse," and she felt wretched enough to believe that hell was around the next corner. If hopelessness was to be her fate, then better to hear him say it
now, while she felt righteous in her anger.

The front door slammed and she heard a vivid curse
come from the entry hall. Her ill temper fled before a
sudden burst of anticipation in her chest. She matched
Henry's curse at the flightiness of her moods as she listened to him clomp up the stairs. Bits of plaster dropped
from the ceiling as a crash above her head announced
his arrival in the bedroom she had made over for him.

With a step as light as she could manage, she tiptoed
to the doorway and peeked down the hall that stretched
the length of the house. The door was open and she saw
several crates piled on the porch, canvases sticking up
over the tops of some. Paintbrushes stuck up over the
top of another. A lone tube lay squashed on the floor,
red paint oozing from the end.

A footfall hit the top stair and she pulled back feeling
a little giddy—from heaving all morning, she told herself—and knowing her mouth was tipped in a foolish
grin for no sensible reason that she could think of.

Except that Henry was in the house for the first time
in three days, and he was apparently moving in.

Absently she grasped a corner of her apron to protect her hand and moved the now-whistling kettle to a shelf attached to the stove. He couldn't have had a proper breakfast, she thought, and selected two—no, four—eggs from the basket. The slice of ham she hadn't been able to eat would warm nicely, as would the biscuits she had made earlier in hope that her stomach would accept something before noon. It was a sop to her pride to give him warmed-over food. Why should she go to extra trouble for a man who went to no trouble at all to acknowledge her existence?

Perhaps he would enjoy some red-eye gravy. . . .

He deserved beans and hardtack.

Sighing, she sliced more ham and heated the frying pan.

The cursing continued as did the tromping in and out, up and down the stairs, the bumps and crashes. Not once did he announce himself in a more conventional way. Pride and self-pity joined forces to keep her from offering help or a ''good morning.''

But after an hour, she had no choice. The table was filled with fresh ham, eggs, gravy, and warmed-up biscuits. Her stomach grumbled at being empty, and she miraculously had an appetite for more than dry toast and chamomile tea. She had prepared breakfast for Henry, and he would eat it if she had to tie him down and feed it to him.

Gingerly she climbed the stairs, stepping and pausing to keep her stomach from lurching unnecessarily. Constant banging from inside the room drowned out her knocks on the door. Her hand hovered over the doorknob, then wrapped around the faceted crystal and turned. She pushed the door open and peered inside.

Henry was still cursing as he dropped one item while plucking another from a crate. Set precisely side by side, canvases leaned against the walls. She stared at them, shocked by the macabre renderings of people who looked like monsters, portraits of despondency and anger and suffering done in the colors of gloom and blood, and she felt as if Henry had captured their souls on canvas rather than their likeness. Wasted, tormented souls, like Benny in the alley, his mouth open in a soundless scream. There were people she didn't know and those she did; their eyes eloquent with weariness and misspent lives. Only Phoenix—with sorrow and gentleness and wisdom in his eyes—looked as he always did in a painting that was disturbingly normal compared to the others.

And then there was a young man she dimly recognized as Henry staring blankly at a ceiling while a monster grinned from the shadows and a hideous, clawed woman rode above him. She saw violation in that one, and somehow knew that the woman was a prostitute. Pain constricted her chest and sickness turned her stomach. She wanted to step back, run away, but the pictures held her in a trance of morbid fascination. She opened the door wider and took a step inside.

"Henry—"

He spun around to face her, but his gaze shot to a row of paintings beneath the window, and his body turned as if he were trying to reach them . . . to conceal them.

She glanced at the portraits and froze. They were all of herself—beautiful images as accurate as the one of Phoenix, only more perfect somehow. The colors were exquisite and the light in them seemed real, as if he had captured bits of the sun and moon and brushed them over the canvas. He had portrayed her as being beautiful and flawless . . .

But he had painted her without a soul.

21

—————————⇒◦ ◦⇐—————————

He'd painted her with no eyes.

She wrapped her arms around her waist as she stood there, too stunned to move as tears stung the back of her eyes. But she held them at bay, knowing that if she lost control, she might scream and never be able to stop.

"Why?" she whispered.

"Get out, Rachel." His mouth was tight, his eyes hard and forbidding.

"Is that how you see me?"

He didn't answer as he stood stock still, staring back at her.

"Is that how you see me?" she shouted, and his head jerked back as if she'd dealt him a blow. "Am I empty and shallow to you? A *shell*?"

Silence.

"Damn you, Henry, *answer me*." Control fell away from her then as pressure built in her eyes, her chest, and she shivered with a sudden chill. She backed away, reaching behind her for the door.

He moved, then, catching her by the arm as he slammed the door closed, imprisoning her in this hell of his own making. Saying nothing, he pushed her ahead of him, forcing her to look at his demons, one by one, and then the sightless, soulless angel in their midst.

"Isn't a shell what you bargained for in a husband, Rachel? Isn't what we have an empty marriage?"

He wouldn't allow her to turn to him, to see if his expression was as intense as his voice. Still, it calmed her to have a question she could answer, to fix her attention on something other than the macabre world Henry lived in. "That's what I bargained for," she agreed. "It's not enough."

"Now greed is something I can believe in. If I painted your eyes, Rachel, would I see avarice and deceit? Betrayal perhaps?"

She heard a whimper and realized it was hers, a tiny animal sound of pain. She could tell him the truth now, end the fear, begin the future with a clean slate—with or without Henry. She glanced at the painting of him as a young man and knew that she wouldn't take such a risk. "You would see love, Henry," she said quietly, with a steadiness in her voice she hadn't thought possible. It had been easy to make the admission in the face of other more devastating secrets yet to be told.

His arms wrapped more fully around her from behind, his hands crossing over her waist, his chin resting on the top of her head, preventing her from moving, from looking at him, keeping her close. "That is why I haven't completed the portraits of you." She felt his chest rise and fall, as if he were struggling for air, and then she heard him, a whisper that seemed raw with pain. "I don't want to see love in your eyes."

"You don't believe in love?"

"If I did not believe in it, I would not fear it." He guided her toward one of the other paintings—of a woman who had wasted to nothing. A woman with madness in her eyes. "Look carefully, Rachel, at a woman who loved her husband. She didn't know that it had the power to destroy her until she had sacrificed everything—her youth, her children, her sanity."

"No." It was all she could say in the face of what he had revealed. *Her children.* Her gaze slanted toward the picture of Henry as a young man—a picture of debasement and agony—and she knew then that he had good reason to hate whores.

"Oh, yes. My father enjoyed watching his mistress rape me, Rachel." With one hand, he forced her head to turn back to the image of the madwoman. "He brought her to my mother's house . . . to my bedchamber. And my mother heard me beg them to stop. She heard me retch and mewl like a baby. She heard me call out for her to stop them."

Betrayal. The word took on new meaning for Rachel. And in the midst of her horror, she heard Henry's voice, cold and devoid of life.

"But she loved my father. She catered to him in all things—the women he paid to serve him, the spectacles he forced her to watch, the way he indulged Luc and hated me."

"Where . . . where was Luc when—"

"Luc was sent on a social errand. God forbid that the heir to the title—and a sickly one at that—should be distressed in any way."

"He doesn't know." It relieved Rachel to know that Henry had not been abandoned by Luc.

"He knew as it was happening. He felt it though he was miles away and unable to return."

Something cold touched the base of Rachel's spine and moved upward, freezing her as Henry released her and pulled a canvas out from behind another, holding it up so she had to look at it. It was two faces of the same man, joined together at the back of the head, one portrayed with substance and texture, the other with a smooth blend of shadowy colors that blurred together.

"Luc and I share more than our mother's womb. We *feel* one another."

She stepped back at the anger she heard, and with only Henry's body visible beneath the portrait, it seemed that she looked upon one man with two heads. Again she stepped back.

"Do you comprehend, Rachel?" he said with a note of mockery. "Do you understand what it's like to feel pain and know it isn't yours? Or, worse, to know that even your thoughts aren't private . . . that is, when you're sure they *are* your thoughts and not someone else's?"

It was beyond comprehension, yet she believed him. It was a terrifying thing he told her, yet she was not afraid. When she'd first seen Henry and his brother together, she'd thought them two sides of the same man, yet that had been a false image. Henry was so much more than Luc's shadow. "You're not the same," she said aloud, unable to articulate her thoughts.

He laughed, then, a wrenching sound that shook her and made her cry out, once, before she clamped her hand over her mouth.

"Look at what you profess to love, Rachel," Henry said from behind the canvas. "Look closely at another form of madness . . . at the freak you have married."

In that moment she saw it all so clearly. In Henry's mother she did indeed see madness. In his father she saw evil. And in that misty image of her husband, she saw a man who was as afraid to look upon himself as he was to see love in her eyes. Afraid that if he did, he would perhaps see nothing but lies.

She snatched the painting from his hands and threw it aside, facing him for the first time since she'd tried to escape him. And then she clutched his arms as he had hers, turned him toward the hellish images he had created and stood behind him, unable to see over his shoulders. She didn't need to see. Not when she could feel the stiffness of his body as he obeyed her silent commands, the way he moved like a puppet beneath her hands. "*You* look, Henry," she said fiercely. "That is not love in your mother's eyes, but obsession, and I have seen it drive strong men to acts of madness. And your father—*look* at him. Pity him, for I doubt he ever once in his life knew what love is."

Henry trembled slightly then stiffened once more, but still, he didn't try to move away from her as she turned him toward the row of portraits of herself. "Look at *her,* Henry. She's beautiful and perfect. I am not. If you painted in the eyes, you would know that. You would see only a woman like any other who is lonely. You would see a woman who will never be complete until she knows that she is loved and accepted for what she is. You would see a woman who would do almost anything for you."

"Except sacrifice her soul," he said.

"Do you require it as proof of love?"

"No. It would prove nothing."

"Nothing but insanity," she said softly. "In spite of yourself, Henry, you know what love is. It's grieving for a helpless animal, and caring for a child no matter where or who he came from. It's forgiving your brother even though his good intentions led you in a direction you didn't want to take. And it's watering a bush with your tears because life means something to you." She stomped over to a corner and swept her hand toward the picture of Phoenix. "It's painting a friend as he really is because you respect him too much to distort his image.''

His head snapped up. "You see too much, Rachel."

"I only see *you*, Henry." She released him and turned toward the door. "As for that." She pointed at the discarded canvas. "It belongs on the compost heap. You and Luc are different from one another. And if you share feelings and sensations, then maybe it's because God knew you would need something to remind you that you are not alone." Her breath caught and she swiped at her eyes, aware for the first time that she was crying. "Oh, damn."

"There are those who think Luc and I are freaks of nature," he said, his gaze meeting hers with the same intensity she'd heard in his voice. A desperate intensity, as if he were waiting for something, yet afraid to hope it might exist.

"Then I'm a freak, too, because I've felt your pain and your anger and your fear. I've stumbled through your darkness. I didn't understand any of it until now. And now I feel it even more." Four steps took her to the door. Pausing, she bent her head, knowing she had to finish what she'd started by invading his world. She had to say it all.

She had to know what would come of it.

"I feel you when you're near, Henry. And maybe I see what you try so hard to conceal because I'm not afraid to know what you are . . . because I know that you are worth loving." She sighed and rubbed the bridge of her nose, then stepped into the hall. "Breakfast will be hot by the time you wash up."

Silence followed her down the stairs. Once in the kitchen, she heard his footsteps above her, moving back and forth, slowly, heavily. Working out of instinct and habit, she reheated what could be salvaged and threw the cold eggs into the slop bucket. And then she sank into a chair and stared at the dust motes dancing on beams of sunlight that slanted in through the window as tears continued to roll down her cheeks.

She felt drained and her limbs shook with weariness. What had she done? It had all seemed so clear a few minutes—or was it hours?—ago, yet now nothing made sense. Not what she'd found upstairs, nor what had been said. Only one thing was certain in her mind. Henry knew how she felt. She had one less secret to worry about.

An object flew out and down outside the window, landing, from the sound of it, in the flower bed. She recognized the shape of it and rose to look outside. Among her transplanted wildflowers lay a canvas on a twisted and splintered frame. A canvas with the two images of the same man. She glanced up at the ceiling and smiled. Henry had missed the compost heap by a good fifty yards. Wiping away the last of her tears, she sat down again. At least he had opened the window before he'd tossed out the painting. At least he had tossed it out.

For now, she decided that nothing else needed to make sense.

Henry tried to think rationally, to find some fragments of logic in the midst of his confusion as he'd paced the room after Rachel had gone. He tried to remember why he'd painted such portraits, why they were important to him. But there was only the echo of Rachel's words in his mind and the scent of lavender in the air. She'd been angry and hurt when she'd first seen the portraits of herself. And then she'd been angry and hurt when she'd seen the others and recognized them for what they were. She'd condemned his demons on his behalf. She'd cried for him.

She thought him worthy of being loved.

It had struck deeply, that pronouncement, exposing a lifetime of fear that perhaps his father had been right, that his mother had forsaken him with good reason, that if he and Luc were not tied together in mind and spirit, his brother, too, would leave him to rot in his own memories. At some point in his life, he had begun to believe in his own worthlessness and live down to the assessment. At some point he had convinced himself that he didn't care.

Until he had felt Rachel's fury and sorrow within himself. Until he'd felt guilt and shame that she should experience even a portion of what had plagued him all his life . . . all because she loved him. More important, because she loved him as he was.

Against all reason, he'd wanted to tell her that he loved her for all that she was—a truly honest woman filled with passion and compassion, a woman who was stronger than he in her ability to give without fear of losing too much of herself. But such words had been turned against him too often, daggers that pierced their bearer with lies and drew blood from his soul. Besides, he did not know the meaning of such words. Instead of playing Rachel false, he'd given her what she'd asked—an addition to the compost heap. With that gesture, he knew he had made an unspoken vow to her, and to himself.

The odors of ham and red-eye gravy and biscuits met him in the downstairs hall, drawing him to the kitchen. He paused in the doorway, silently watching Rachel, her gaze fixed on the window as she sat at the table with a whimsical smile curving up the corners of her mouth. Here was reason. In her was a promise he dared to hope would be kept.

She glanced up at him as he walked toward her, his gait slow and awkward with a sudden and irritating shyness. He winced at the still-damp streaks of tears on her face and reached out to wipe them away with his thumb. Her breath caught and she sighed as she turned her face into his palm, accepting his touch as she always did, without reservation. The sound of his voice and the ease with which he spoke surprised him.

"You humble me, Rachel."

Her mouth moved against his palm and he knew the pleasure of holding her smile within his hand.

"It wasn't my intention." She kissed his fingers, and he waited, knowing she would not leave it at that. "Though I'm sure you could use some humility."

He chuckled in pleasure as he withdrew from her side to take his place at the table. Pleasure that he should know her so well. Pleasure in her honesty that gave him freedom to trust her. "A man must leave his pride on the porch when you are near, Rachel."

"You took my suggestion about the painting," she said. "Why?"

He shrugged as he accepted the plate she had filled for him. "I find your vision of me more pleasing than my own."

"And that isn't pride?"

"No," he said, and stared down at his plate in the shyness that plagued him lately. "It is hope that you can convince me you are right." The words themselves tasted fresh and sweet on his tongue. How strange it was to speak candidly after so many years of hiding his feelings, even from himself.

Her expression fell into sadness, and she avoided his gaze. "Even when we have what we want, Henry, we live on hope."

"For what?"

"That we won't lose or inadvertently destroy what we hold most dear." She bent her head to her plate and took small bites of her breakfast, chewing slowly, each swallow followed by a deep, measured breath.

"*She's been ill,*" Phoenix had said, and Henry realized it was true in the way she approached her food as if she were stalking it, trying to trap it before it escaped her. He noticed then her hollow eyes and the delicacy of her form.

"The child plagues you," he said.

"No. My body plagues me."

"Will it pass?"

"I don't know. This is new to me."

"Have you consulted the other women?"

"The only woman here who has had a child is—" She shook her head and immediately clamped her hand over her mouth. "Excuse me." Pushing away from the table, she ran out the back door and bent over a bucket on the stoop.

Henry followed, standing helplessly beside her and flinching as she retched, her whole body heaving as if she were being turned inside out. "What can I do, Rachel?" he asked.

Her hand limply waved him away as she continued to toss up her socks.

Grimly he returned to the kitchen and dampened a cloth. It seemed unjust that a woman should suffer so for the results of a man's pleasure. Still, as he listened to Rachel pant and heave, he was grateful to be a man and therefore free from such affliction.

He found Rachel sitting on the stoop as if she had simply dropped where she stood. Tendrils of hair stuck to her temples and forehead in limp curls dampened by perspiration. Her face was eggshell pale and transparent, her eyes dull and weary. He thrust the cloth at her.

"How often does this happen?" he asked, ashamed that he should have to ask.

"Every day."

"Which woman in the settlement has had a child? I'll fetch her."

"Roz."

The whore. A vision of Benny bleeding in an alley, his body and clothes encrusted with filth, reminded him of how such women care for their children. "Then I shall take care of you. God knows what she did to her offspring."

"She raised her daughter as best she could," she said weakly, and gained her feet. "I can take care of myself, Henry."

"Then do so by taking to bed for the day."

"The dishes—"

"I'll do them," he said gruffly. "You've turned me into a farmer and merchant. Why not a scullery maid?"

Her mouth opened, shut, then opened again. "I was going to dust the furniture and clean the floor . . ."

"Ah, so I shall be promoted to parlor maid in the space of one day."

She made no comment, but merely averted her gaze from the remains of their meal as she passed by the table. Henry frowned at her lack of response and her lack of argument. He'd never seen anyone work as hard as Rachel, yet now she was all too willing to spend the day in bed—a certain sign that all was not well with her.

He cocked his head, listening to her slow progress as she climbed the stairs, the muted sound of her footfall in the bedroom, then silence. The sudden cessation of movement and sound alarmed him. Why hadn't he noticed her pale color and increasing frailty before? His knowledge of childbearing women was nonexistent, and Rachel had so much as admitted that hers was little better.

For the first time in years, he experienced fear for someone besides himself and Luc.

It would appear that Rachel was redeeming him after all.

. . .

How had he come to such a pass? Henry wondered as he fished around in the murky water for something to wash. He shuddered as a chunk of soggy biscuit floated past his arm followed by a slice of ham. Something was definitely wrong here. The plates were more coated with grease as he pulled them from the dishpan than when he'd put them in. Perhaps it was the soap. Rather than awaken Rachel to ask what he should use, he had, in desperation, retrieved a bar of lavender soap from the water closet. Still, he reasoned, if it cleaned bodies, it should work on tableware.

Perhaps he should have cleaned the food off the plates first. He pulled out a handful of slimy food, and plopped it into the slop bucket, belatedly trying to remember what Rachel had done after a meal.

More scum formed on top of the water and seemed to congeal around his wrists. He shuddered and snatched his hands from the pan. He couldn't recall a blasted thing besides the turn of her waist . . . or the sway of her derriere when she'd bent over to get something from . . . *under the sink!* Of course!

He crouched down and lifted the checked curtain covering the shelves beneath the sink. There was soap, and at the sight of it, he remembered that she rubbed it on a rag and then washed a dish when they were on the trail. He grimaced at the roughness of the lye concoction. Thinking himself to be ingenious, he shaved some off the bar and dumped the slivers into the water. Now that made more sense than soaping a cloth over and over again. It didn't work. The water was still foul and the dishes still came out coated with slime. He rooted around and discovered a package containing a powdery substance. It was labeled "Babbitt's Best Soap." He tossed a handful into the water and watched it float sluggishly on top of the grease.

Bloody hell. He had more important things to do than spend the day figuring out the proper scientific formula for washing breakfast dishes. And he absolutely refused to expose his ineptitude to Rachel.

An hour later, he led Rain into the kitchen and gestured toward the sink. Thank God the Indian woman seemed to understand English, though he had yet to hear her utter more than the occasional grunt or click of the tongue. In desperation, he had sought her out, explained that Rachel was ill and then damn near choked on his pride by admitting his failure to perform such a simple task. She'd had the temerity to grin at him when he'd all but begged her to keep his secret. Now her tongue clicked like the back legs of a cricket, over and over again as she emptied the sink and drew fresh, hot water from the reservoir on the side of the massive stove.

Hot water . . . of course. He'd forgotten that Rachel had always heated water for this purpose on the trail. He just hadn't paid attention whether she'd used water from the reservoir or from the pump once they'd arrived here.

Then she slipped a voluminous apron over his head, tied it at his waist, and pointed to the foaming water in the sink. Sighing, he followed her mimed directions. He had hoped she would take pity on him and do the deed herself.

This time around, what had taken him over an hour to botch was accomplished in less than half the time. He'd barely dried the last spoon when Rain handed him a rag and pot of beeswax and demonstrated the proper way to dust and polish the tables in the parlor. Evidently the wax must be applied with a circular motion, and if Rain's clucking was anything to go by, the circles must always go in the same direction. He didn't have the energy to ask why.

His ruin was complete when Rain spied a basket of soiled clothes and proceeded to instruct him—in sign language—in the science of stain removal and proper rinsing techniques. There was even an art to hanging the articles out on the clothesline.

A full dozen times, he had offered to pay Rain to do all the work and received a toothy grin and shake of her head in reply. His back hurt from bending over the sink, his shoulders ached from working beeswax and lemon oil into the furniture. His dignity was howling for mercy by the time he became hopelessly tangled in the legs of a pair of Rachel's pantalettes. No wonder men preferred to work in the fields and hunt for game and construct buildings.

Disengaging himself, he glowered at the woman. "Since I have provided you with so much amusement, madam, I trust you will honor your vow of silence."

Rain grunted, nodded, and turned away to return to the cabin she shared with Cletus. Henry thought he heard her chuckle but he couldn't be sure.

He rubbed the back of his neck, trudged into the house, and climbed the stairs, vowing to suggest that Luc double whatever he paid the scullery and housemaids on his estates. And then he decided that he would find a maid for Rachel so that he would never have to endure such torture again.

22

---◆◎◆---

S uch bliss! Rachel thought as she sat up in bed, her back against the headboard. Who cared if Henry had stuffed the pillows behind her so that she had to recline in a most awkward position, or that she had to roll back the two extra quilts he'd piled on her?

She'd never been pampered before.

The day had slipped away as she'd slept, only occasionally aware that Henry might be having trouble with the household chores. She'd given it no thought at all once she'd heard the back door slam and glanced out her bedroom window to see him run down the road toward town, then return with Rain in tow.

A metallic crash reverberated through the house, and she hoped he hadn't dropped the soup pot. Sighing, she turned up the wick on the lamp and opened her book. Whatever the problem, she was enjoying her rest too much to worry about it now.

Engrossed in her reading, she almost didn't hear
Henry climb the stairs or walk into the bedroom, and
had barely enough time to stuff the book beneath the
covers before he walked into her room. Forcing herself
to calm her frantic movements, she arranged the sheet
over it, hiding the book completely. How careless it had
been to read such a book with Henry in the house. How
humiliating it would be if he'd noticed the title or seen
her hide it so clumsily. She glanced up at him, finding
relief that he seemed oblivious to everything but balancing her meat platter—used as a tray to hold a plate of
food, a glass of milk, and a cup of tea. He stood beside
the bed, his eyes weary, a don't-say-a-word tightness to
his mouth. He smelled of scorched soup and lye soap.

She thought better of telling him how fetching he
looked in her apron, and tried to remember if he'd been
wearing it during his dash into town and back. If he had,
the men would surely needle about it him during one of
their poker games . . . especially if Henry was winning.

The tray tipped and wobbled as he bent down to
smooth the covers, and she held her breath until he set
it safely down beside her on the bed. He straightened
with slow, stiff movements and batted the skirt of the
apron out of his way.

"How do you feel?" he asked.

"Better. I've much enjoyed the rest, Henry. Thank
you." She sighed as she saw the beans and canned fruit
on her plate. He *had* spilled the soup . . . after he had
burned it.

She'd really been looking forward to that soup.

"I don't suppose you'll be fit by morning." His expression was hunted, his voice half hopeful, half resigned.

Images of complete destruction flashed through her
mind—of beef broth coating her clean floor, of food
stuck to her pristine stove, of dented pots and chipped

plates and heaven knew what else. Now she knew what it meant to be spoiled rotten, for she was feeling worse by the moment. "I'm well enough to make us a proper meal, Henry," she said, and swung her legs over the side of the bed.

"No!" He lifted her legs back onto the mattress and covered her back up with the quilts, avoiding her gaze as he fussed with covering her with the quilts and ineffectually patting out the wrinkles. "If the beans do not suit, I'll . . . think . . . I'll find something . . . else."

Obviously Henry didn't want her in the kitchen. If his hunted expression was anything to go by, the chaos downstairs must be worse than she thought. She could only hope it wasn't total destruction. Sighing, she obediently leaned forward to allow him to plump her pillows again. "The beans are fine. Why don't you join me?"

As he left the room, he mumbled something about preferring intoxication to sustenance.

Surprisingly, the beans tasted good, and she forgot her disappointment over the soup as one bite led to another until her plate was clean, the glass of milk drained. The sounds from the kitchen died down and she listened to Henry's footsteps, shuffling on the wood floors, then silenced as he crossed over the rugs scattered about.

After a few minutes, she realized that he must have gone into the parlor to indulge in a glass or three of whiskey. Absently she picked up her tea, sipped, and grimaced. He'd sugared it with a heavy hand and it was cold. She was debating whether to brave the chaos she imagined in the kitchen for a fresh cup of tea or to remain ignorant of the damage for as long as possible when her stomach churned. Leaning over the edge of the bed, she tasted the beans a second time as she gave up her meal to the chamber pot on the floor next to her, then, on wobbly legs, managed to get to the pitcher and bowl on a table by the window to clean her face and teeth. As she climbed back into bed, she heard Henry climb the stairs, approaching the bedroom rather than his workroom.

"You ate it all," he said with bemusement as he crossed the threshold and halted by the bed.

"I was hungry."

His gaze found the chamber pot, and his mouth slanted at one corner. "Ah, Rachel, your honesty unmans me. You could have prevaricated and hidden that to preserve what remains of my pride."

"It *was* delicious," she said.

He sighed and finished off the whiskey in the glass he held. "Too late. Humility has set in and become quite gangrenous." His brow knitted. "You did not drink your tea."

"Um . . . I took too long to eat and it grew cold."

"I'll fetch more."

She shook her head and patted the mattress. "Come to bed, Henry."

"Rain said you should have some before you retire for the night."

"Your presence will do more to soothe and warm me than tea," she argued softly.

"You are ill."

"No. I am lonely."

"You need—"

"I need your shoulder beneath my head . . . your heartbeat next to my ear. I need you, Henry." Unable to look at him in her brazen plea, she stared down at her hands, waiting for rejection, hoping for that final acceptance.

The rustle of clothing broke the silence, and the mattress dipped beneath his weight. She swallowed to clear the sudden obstruction from her throat. For the first time, she dared believe that perhaps the events of the day marked the beginning of a future for both of them.

Yet still she waited for him to draw closer to her, to touch and hold her. Nothing happened. Nothing stirred. She peered at Henry from the corner of her eye and clenched the quilt in her hands.

"What is this?" He pulled her book from beneath his shoulder and read the title. "*McGuffy's Reader*?" His frown deepened as he flipped through the pages.

She wanted to snatch it from his hands, to throw it in the fire. She wanted to crawl under the bed and hide from his inquiring gaze. All she could do was lean against the pillows and clutch at the covers as if they would save her from the certainty of Henry's scorn. How could she have forgotten the book?

"This is a schoolroom book. Are you so desperate for entertainment?"

Swallowing again, she held her eyes open and un-blinking to fight tears, lifted her chin in spite of its quiv-ering, tightened her mouth against sudden trembles. And she felt his stare boring into her, studying her. She had only two secrets, and foolishly, she had betrayed herself in one of them.

"I've seen a number of books in the house. Why do you read this?"

No convincing bluff came to mind. She wanted to lie, but didn't know how. It was easy to keep secrets through silence, yet she couldn't deny the truth once it was dis-covered.

"Rachel?"

"I read this so that someday I will be able to read all the others," she said firmly, defiantly, though she felt as if she were choking on the words.

"You're teaching yourself to read?"

She blinked once and turned her head away. "I learned my letters seven years ago, then my teacher died. Phoenix taught me how to print. I do the rest myself." She drew up her knees and wrapped her arms around

her legs, curling into a ball, protecting herself from the
dark and forbidding silence that followed.

"What of your parents?" he asked softly.

"My . . . mother taught me my sums and how to write
my name. She didn't have time for more."

"And your father?"

"He's gone. Please . . . I can't talk about it." She felt
him shift beside her but couldn't look, afraid to discover
derision or mockery on his face, afraid to find that he
was leaving her.

"I hated school, you know. My tutor swore that he
had to beat every letter and number into me. I became
a very good student in order to avoid his cane."

She peeked at him, then, and saw him lying on his
back, his hands laced beneath his head.

"I suppose I should be grateful to him," Henry continued in a conversational tone. "Since reading is one
of the few pleasures I have found in life . . . Rachel, will
you look at me?"

Against her will, she complied. He hadn't moved except to turn his head toward her. His gaze met hers, more
open and revealing than she had ever seen it.

"Will you allow me to share that pleasure with you,
Rachel . . . and to show you how to find it for yourself?"

"You want to teach me to read? Why?"

He raised a hand to stroke her braid, to trace each
winding strand with his forefinger, and the gentleness of
it chased away her fears.

"Because you have taught me how to dream again. It
pleases me to think I can give you something equally
special in return." With that, he rolled to his side and
reached for her, prying her hands away from their clasp
around her knees, drawing her down to lie against him,
her head on his shoulder, her cheek resting on his chest,
feeling the steady rhythm of his heartbeat. All she could

see was the primer laying open across his midriff, and to her, it seemed a symbol of yet another unspoken vow between them—a vow of trust and new beginnings.

Urgent shouts and galloping hoof beats split through the midnight peace, and from the window Rachel saw lights appear, one by one, in the windows down the street.

She slid out of bed, dragging the covers onto the floor as she grabbed her dress from the chair and pulled it over her head on her way to the door.

"What . . . ?" Henry called from behind her.

"Cletus is back."

"Can't we welcome him tomorrow?"

"He's alone and he wouldn't be coming in at a dead run in the dark unless something was wrong."

Henry said nothing more, but caught up with her in the entry hall, one hand pulling up his trousers, the other reaching for the doorknob, twisting it and jerking the door open, allowing her to run out onto the porch without breaking her stride.

Cletus slid off his horse and began walking him in a slow circle around the yard as he spoke between deep, heaving breaths. "Horse went down . . . don't know why . . . weren't no hole in the ground . . . legs just plumb folded up and the critter rolled when he fell."

"Where's Horace?" Rachel asked. "Is he hurt?"

The night chill cut into Rachel and her voice seemed to be an echo, blowing through her through her like a winter wind.

"Not Horace," Cletus mumbled. "He's hauling Phoenix in on a travois. I came to warn you."

Rachel shivered and wrapped her arms around her middle. Everything seemed to disappear—sight, sound, sensation—everything but fear and panic. *Phoenix on a travois.* That meant he'd been hurt. Badly hurt. "What happened?" she asked.

"I just told you. Damnedest thing I ever saw," Cletus said as he continued to cool down his mount. "His horse folded up like a fan and there weren't a hole or tangle in sight to trip him up. Phoenix tried to kick free but his spur caught in the stirrup and the horse rolled on him . . . stove in his ribs and don't know what else. He told us to leave him behind—"

"You shouldn't have moved him," Rachel said as she turned back to the house, acting on instinct rather than actual awareness, feeling nothing but an urgent sense of necessity to gather her basket of medicines and get to her friend. "Cletus, ride back and stop Horace. I'll follow."

"It's too late," Henry said from behind her. "Horace is coming in now."

She'd almost forgotten about Henry as he'd stood so still beside her, listening to Cletus. Henry who had found a friend in Phoenix. A friend, she guessed, who might very well be his first. The thought chased away panic, gave her energy and purpose. She would not have Henry lose more than he already had. She stood in the yard, one foot extended to carry her toward the street, her body angled toward the house, torn between needing to collect her supplies and wanting to get to Phoenix. She sobbed in frustration.

A hand clapped around her elbow and drew her into a solid embrace. Henry's arms held her tightly, and his hand cupped the back of her head, his fingers stroking her, calming her. "Tell me what you need. I'll bring it to you," he whispered, and she heard the slight tremble in his voice, the strain and hoarseness telling her how hard he was trying to control his own emotions.

Other men ran out of cabins and the bunkhouse, and Horace reined in his horse, then vaulted out of the saddle to help them unhitch the crude travois made of poles and blankets. As they carried Phoenix up the hill, she took a deep breath and left the shelter of Henry's arms. "Blankets, whiskey, and my basket."

The travois was set down at her feet and she fell to her knees, pulling back the blanket covering Phoenix. She couldn't cry out at his ashen complexion or the blood that trickled from his left ear, or the way his legs were twisted and shattered with bones sticking through the flesh. She couldn't speak for the silent prayers she offered up from her mind as she ran her hands over his body, hoping that Cletus had been wrong about Phoenix's injuries, hoping that she would find nothing worse than broken limbs. Hoping that he would open his eyes and speak to her.

Cletus wasn't wrong . . . and Phoenix didn't move. His heartbeat was light, sporadic, and his skin was cold as death.

"His skull is fractured," Henry said, his voice oddly calm, disturbing toneless. He laid the basket down and dropped to his knees. "What of his ribs?"

"It feels as if they're in pieces. I think . . . I think he's bleeding inside." She looked up at Henry, feeling useless in the face of such destruction. She didn't even know where to start.

Rain appeared with a large kettle of hot water, and Rachel met her black, fathomless stare.

"Get Roz," she said as she dampened a piece of cloth and began to wipe away the dried blood from Phoenix's ear and neck.

"No," Henry said.

"Get Roz," Rachel repeated, then spoke to Henry without looking at him as one of the men ran down the street. "She has more skill in healing . . . I don't even know what to do."

"Do nothing," a thready voice said from below her. "I'm already a dead man."

"Roz can help you, Phoenix," she said.

He stared up at her, his light eyes silvered by the moon, a mirror reflecting her own face back at her. "It's too late, Rachel."

"No. It can't be too late. Roz will help you. She has experience in mending—"

Phoenix raised his hand and pressed his fingers to her lips. "Hush, Rachel. I have waited for this, prayed for it." His face twisted in pain and seemed to become almost transparent. His thumb brushed at a tear on her cheek. "Don't cry. You made me remember what it was like to live. Henry reminded me of what it was like to have a friend." He held up his other hand to Henry, and Rachel saw their fingers fold around one another's palms in a uniquely male clasp. His hand fell away from her face.

"Damn you!" Rachel cried out. "How can you give up so easily? How can you want to die?"

Phoenix sighed and coughed and a trickle of blood ran from the corner of his mouth. "To find peace," he whispered.

Roz broke through the circle of onlookers and knelt across from Rachel, her hands expertly moving over Phoenix as Rachel's had done. Gently she eased her fingers around his head and under it, feeling her way, then sat back on her heels, her expression grim and bleak in the waning moonlight as she shook her head.

Time seemed to end as the breeze calmed. Rachel saw nothing but Phoenix through the tears that blurred her vision, felt nothing but her own helplessness and outrage. "No! You have to do something. You have to try."

"He's stove in, Rachel. His head—"

Roz was right. Rachel knew it, yet she couldn't give up, couldn't stop herself from taking the knife from

Phoenix's belt and sawing at his boot. Roz grasped her wrist and forced her hand away from Phoenix. "Let him be, girl. All you'll do is make it worse for him."

"I can't be like you, Mother. I can't let him die like you let Liddie die."

"Rachel," Phoenix said, an odd gurgle in his voice. He crooked his finger, a silent request for her to lean closer.

She bent over him, straining to hear his whisper.

"Do not betray yourself for me, Rachel. I have enough guilt to bear."

Dimly she knew what he meant, realized what she had said, but it didn't matter just then. Only the sadness and pain in Phoenix's face mattered. A drop of moisture fell on his cheek and then another, and she knew they were her tears. Again he raised his hand to brush her cheek.

"Do not grieve for me. I'm ready to escape the loneliness." He gazed past her to Henry. "Finish your paintings, my friend. Believe what you see . . . trust what you feel . . . then look at yourself . . . as you have never done before. Do . . . not walk . . . away . . . from . . . the . . . truth."

The moon disappeared and nothing stirred but the faint hiss of Phoenix's breath, fading as the world seemed to fade around her, leaving her in a void. She felt Henry beside her, saw his hand clasped around Phoenix's as if he would keep life from slipping away from his friend with his own strength of will. It could have been a moment, or it could have been forever as Phoenix lay staring at the sky, waiting as he always seemed to wait, for something only he could see or understand.

And then utter silence descended around them and Phoenix's eyes became dark and fathomless, blinded by death.

"I'm sorry, Rachel," Roz said.

Rachel didn't reply as she kept her gaze fixed on Phoenix, willing him to breathe, praying that his heart would beat, praying that they had all been wrong and he would live. She didn't notice the others walking away, one by one and in pairs. She wasn't aware that only Roz and Henry remained there, kneeling by the side of a friend as his spirit drifted toward the horizon.

A fresh breeze sang in the trees as dawn stole the darkness and left luminous shades of rose and lavender and gold in its place. The cock crowed faithfully and a cow bawled in the barn, breaking Henry's trance. In the light, dew glittered on blades of grass like tears that would not dry.

He stared at Phoenix, seeing the sadness that had shaped his features in life etched in his face for eternity. Rachel was still beside him, her head bowed, her fingers stroking the back of Phoenix's hand. And across from him was the whore, sitting on the ground as if she were rooted there, watching Rachel.

Somewhere in his mind, he remembered what had been said as Phoenix's blood soaked into the grass, but he could not make sense of it just yet. He knew that it was important, that he should feel something, yet he was numb, his thoughts centered on the friend he had lost, on the place in his life that would forever remain empty because of it.

Horace and Cletus approached from town and climbed the hill, and as if that were a signal, Rachel covered Phoenix with a blanket as fresh tears began to flow down her face. She wiped her nose with her sleeve, like a child, and just then she seemed like a child, defenseless, vulnerable, lost.

"We'll take him down and make a coffin," Horace said.

"Rain will fix him up for burying," Cletus added.

"No," Henry replied, his voice a croak.

"No," Rachel said at the same time.

"You two go find a good shade tree on a little rise and fix up a place for him," Roz said, shooing them away. "I'll fetch him some clean clothes from the bunkhouse."

Without another word, Henry slid his arms beneath Phoenix, lifted him and struggled to his feet, carrying him into the house and laying him out on the sofa. He heard Rachel walk into the kitchen, then the clang of pots. She returned with a kettle of hot water, a basin, and several pieces of toweling. Roz stepped in with a neatly folded pile of clothing.

Henry turned away and headed for the barn.

Mechanically, he collected a saw, hammer and nails, and carried them to the lumber stacked at one end of the barn.

Time passed without notice as he fitted newly cut pieces of wood to one another with as much precision as his limited skill allowed. Sweat beaded his brow and ran down his face, and he paused to yank off his shirt and tear a strip of fabric from the hem to tie around his forehead, caring nothing about the destruction of the finely tailored garment, caring only about getting through the day.

He glanced up at Rachel as she walked into the barn and rooted through the wood for two smooth lengths of wood, one longer than the other, then kneeled on a pile of hay and began to nail them together into a cross.

They didn't speak as they worked, nor did their glances meet. And as she began to painstakingly carve letters into the crosspiece of the marker, Henry felt the blessed numbness of shock give way to anger.

She hadn't told him she couldn't read—a small thing really. A breach of honesty easily ignored.

Mother, he had heard her call the whore. *Do not betray yourself,* Phoenix had whispered to her, a warning that had caused her to tremble. Henry had heard that, too, knowing then that it was true.

She raised her daughter as best she could, Rachel had said, one defense for the woman among many. It explained so much—Rachel's tolerance of the whore's presence, her affinity for the dregs of humanity, her need to advertise for a husband. A *respectable* husband. Of course she had settled for a man whose claim to respectability was in his name and bloodlines. Of course she had been a willing accomplice to his brother's blackmail in a cunning exploitation of his own desperation and apathy. And of course Rachel—who saw so much—had shown him what he needed to see, what he'd wanted to believe in.

His father's whore had violated his body, but Rachel had raped his soul with her betrayal.

23

━━━━━◆◦◆◦◆━━━━━

S he stood at the base of the lone spruce tree growing on a small rise in the ground, her fingers releasing granules of earth onto the bare wood of the
coffin, feeling as if she were burying her new beginning
along with Phoenix. Henry, too, tossed his handful of
dirt into the grave, his expression closed, his eyes as dark
as the moment. He hadn't spoken a word to her, nor had
he spared her more than a glance. Yet he had been beside
her all day since she had joined him in the barn. He'd
finished the coffin, then sat on the floor, his back to the
wall, his eyes closed as she had carved Phoenix's name
into a homemade cross.

They had gone back to the house, each holding an end
of the coffin, and Henry had stood by while she lined
the box with a feather tick and pillow. ''He told me once
that he wanted life and, at the end of it, a peaceful
death,'' she'd explained as she covered his body with a

homemade quilt. "I wish I could give him what he wanted."

Henry didn't answer, but fitted the lid over the coffin and nailed it shut, his mouth tight, his jaw clenched, wincing with every blow of the hammer, as if the nails were being hammered into him.

Roz had been there through it all, giving orders when they were needed, doing whatever had to be done without comment. Oddly, Rachel didn't resent her mother's intrusion. There had been comfort in Roz's silent support, a sense of safety.

The settlers of Promise drifted away, leaving Cletus and Horace to fill the grave. Henry helped, and she saw anger in his movements, the rigid control he exerted over his emotions. She knew the measure of her own pain, but could only imagine the depth of Henry's suffering at losing what he had so recently found in friendship and trust and perhaps the beginnings of love.

The sky blazed with sunset colors, nature's fire claiming Phoenix's spirit, and dirt flew about like ashes dancing in the wind.

It was over. Between one night and the next Rachel had buried another friend.

And hope had died.

She heard the sob and felt the next, building in her chest, rising in a lump to her throat, escaping in a harsh burst of grief as Cletus and Horace walked away with their shovels over their shoulders. Henry threw his own shovel away from him and stared down at the mound of newly turned earth. "Please look at me, Henry," she pleaded softly. "Please hold me." Another sob was wrenched from her, and she felt arms surround her, gather her close, and rock her back and forth. She smelled jasmine and held on tightly, finding release in deep, gasping sobs, and the clumsy tenderness of Roz's arms. She'd waited all her life to be held and rocked by her mother.

Through her tears she watched Henry walk away.

She cried because Phoenix was dead . . . because she was dying, too, as the Henry who had revealed himself to her over the last few months retreated back into a place as dark and cold as Phoenix's grave.

He met them at the door, barring entrance with his wide-legged stance and his arms braced on either side of the frame, his gaze cold and forbidding as he concentrated on Roz.

Roz snorted and, without further word, left Rachel alone with her husband.

Henry turned his back on Rachel as he walked into the house and began to climb the stairs.

From out of nowhere, anger struck Rachel. An anger that felt as old as she was. Yet she managed to hold it at bay, to speak calmly, in a voice that only trembled slightly. "If I could change what I have done, I would."

He paused, his foot raised to take another step, lowering it as he turned to face her. "What have you done, Rachel?" he asked. "I want to hear you say it. I want to be sure that you know."

The fury that continued to build prodded her, but still she denied it. "I did not tell you that my mother is—was—a whore."

"So, it is true," he mused as he sat on the top stair of the landing and propped his chin on his closed fist. "I couldn't credit it, you know—my oh-so-honest wife keeping such a thing from me. That honesty is what drew me to you. I had stumbled into marriage with a woman who didn't play at coyness, saying one thing while meaning another." His brows arched as he regarded her from the landing. "I suppose I should give

you credit for that. You were forthright enough. Your
lies remained unspoken. Tell me, Rachel, if I had inquired as to your parentage, what would you have said?''

"I would not have lied to you," she said.

"How clever you are to be so miserly with your
words. It gives the illusion of sincerity and inspires trust.
Even as that particular trait maddened me, it was also a
relief to know I wouldn't spend the next five years bored
senseless by the banal chatter women employ to hide
their secrets.'' He shook his head. "What a fool I was
to ignore the questions I wanted to ask. But then you
were so respectful of my privacy. If you did not pry into
my affairs, then I couldn't very well pry into yours. How
easily you led me to believe you were special when in
fact you are quite common.''

"I am not my mother, Henry."

"No, you are not," he agreed, and rose to continue
up the stairs. "You surpass her in your talent to barter
flesh. Much as I hate to admit it, she is more honest than
you are. At least she openly plies her trade.''

He disappeared around the corner of the landing, the
sound of his footsteps slow and even as the fall of dirt
over a coffin, the click of a door as firm as the final pat
of the shovel over a filled grave. And she stood alone
in the entryway, feeling only his coldness, seeing only
the emptiness that had been in his eyes.

Her empty stomach rolled and clenched within her,
and she covered her mouth with her hand as she ran to
the water closet to heave and wretch without results over
the commode. She had nothing left to lose.

Except her temper.

With mechanical precision, she cleaned her face,
brushed her teeth, and freed her hair from its braid, then
removed her shirtwaist, skirt, and bloomers. Wearing
only camisole and petticoat, stockings and garters, she

climbed the rear staircase and opened the door to the spare bedroom.

Henry sat on the edge of the bed, his hands clasped in the space between his outspread knees.

She paused in the threshold and leaned against the frame in a provocative pose designed to display the full rise of her breasts and the slight spread of her legs revealed in the light filtering through her petticoat. Deliberately she drew up the hem on one side and tucked it into the waistband to show the length of stockinged calf and a hint of curls between her bared thighs.

He stared at the doorway as if nothing was there. "I can't live with any more nightmares, Rachel," he said thickly.

"I know of your nightmares, Henry. I'll pay for them for the rest of my life." With a sway of her hips, she sauntered into the room and knelt in front of him, her fingers working free the buttons of his trousers . . . lingering over each one, her voice husky and provocative. "But now, for a little while . . ." She opened the last button and released him from confinement and stroked the length of him that grew rigid and full as her breath touched him with every word. ". . . For now, I will give you every man's dream of heaven."

She tasted him with her tongue, nipped at him with her lips and felt his tremble, heard his breath shudder.

He grasped her hair and yanked her head back. "Get out."

She smiled in spite of the pull on her hair, the strain in her neck, and she encircled him with her hands, stroking up and down, squeezing him gently, then stroking again. "No, not yet. Not until I show you what I learned at my mother's knee." Pain stabbed at her as she jerked her head from his hold and she bent over him once more. Her mouth covered him, toying with him, tasting and

drawing on him with gentle force, then releasing him.
"You want this, Henry." She held him between her
hands. "Look how much you want this." Sliding a hand
lower, she cradled his sac, raked it gently with the
tips of her fingers. "I used to think the male form was
ugly . . . grotesque . . . until I saw you." She ran her
tongue along the length of him. "I dreaded a man's
touch . . . until I felt you inside me." Her hand squeezed
and fondled him. "I hated my own body . . . until you
looked upon me . . . until you showed me how much you
wanted me. . . ."

She took him fully into her mouth once more, and his
hands cupped her head as it moved up and down and
around him, suckled him and claimed him completely as
her own passion melted in her belly and trickled between
her legs.

His hands brushed the straps of her camisole away,
pushed it down, lifted her breasts, his thumbs caressing
her nipples. And again she freed him and smiled up at
him, her lips parted and moist. "It's not a nightmare, is
it, Henry? Not with me. Not when you touch me. Not
when I do this. . . ." She raked him lightly with her
teeth.

"Tell me to stop, Henry . . . or tell me to go on."

He inhaled sharply and grimaced as he spoke. "Name
your price."

"Tell me what you want. Say it, Henry. I want to be
sure that you know."

"I want you." He groaned as if the words were
knives, shredding him.

She held him more tightly between her hands and then
replaced them with her mouth, taking him urgently now,
drawing on him faster and harder as he thrust his hips
upward, matching her rhythm . . . as he stiffened and his
hands tightened on her breasts while she drank deeply
of his passion.

The force of his release inflamed her, and she surrendered to the quickening in her belly, the hot racing of her blood, the moment when she could not breathe and she felt as if she were dissolving from the inside out at his feet.

It took all her strength to look up at him, to speak calmly. "They did it everywhere in the early days when Roz worked for others—in the receiving room, in the hallways, in the bedchambers with the doors open. I stopped drinking anything after lunch so I wouldn't have to use the necessary at night. So I wouldn't have to walk past them and see what they did to one another." She caught a breath and held it for a moment. "After a customer tried to peek up my skirts, Roz started locking me in whatever room was vacant that night—usually the pantry or a closet. Later we moved to Grace's house, and it had a nice, big attic. There was nothing else to do you see, except listen to the sounds and see the pictures of what they were doing in my mind. I learned to dream to drown out the ugliness."

She needed to tell him everything, praying that he might understand, and knowing he would not. She told him of fetching for the girls and listening to their carnal adventures, of becoming friends with some of them and learning from the ones with education. She told him about Liddie and her last day in Roz's house. "I dreamed of being like the ladies in town, with their nice houses and their last names that people spoke with respect. I wanted a husband—one man who came home to me every night and held my arm when we strolled down the street and opened doors for me. As I grew older, I realized that those women paid for the right to their names and their houses by cooking and cleaning and sewing, then sitting alone at night while their husbands visited my mother's house. It occurred to me that I could do the same. I could belong, too." Her voice

broke and she looked away from him. "Condemn me
for bartering flesh in exchange for respectability, Henry.
But do not judge me because a man promised my mother
the moon and left her alone with a baby to raise instead."

He shoved her away from him. "Damn you," he said,
and his voice was gritty, as if he had eaten dirt and was
trying to spit it out.

Deliberately, she placed her hands on his thighs,
kneading the still-taut muscles as she forced herself to
stand, forced herself not to cover her breasts, forced herself to look at him and skim her lips with her tongue.
"Why?" she asked. "Because I stopped being your wife
and became your whore? Isn't that what you want—
proof that whores do indeed beget whores?" She strolled
to the door, holding her back straight, her head high,
then glanced at him over her shoulder. "And remember,
Henry, that you enjoyed what I just did to you. Remember that it was not a nightmare."

It was his worst nightmare.

It plagued him through the night—images of himself
accepting her ministrations, enjoying them even as she
taunted him with his weakness for her. Memories of her
touch, the hot wetness of her mouth on him and her
coldness after he had lost control. Thoughts of all that
he should have done to stop her, to stop himself. He was
a man now, able to protect himself. No one had held
him down. No one had forced him. Even while his body
fell prey to her, he could have fought her with his mind,
fought her with indifference as she had once fought him
in a Cheyenne hotel room. If she had been a woman like
the one from his nightmares, or one like Roz, he could
have thrown her away from him.

Oh, God, why couldn't he see her as she really was?

A woman like Roz . . . He pressed his palms to his temples and shook his head, trying to see Rachel that way. But even with her scanty garb and provocative manner, she looked like Rachel, her face scrubbed clean and free of paint, her eyes wide and fixed and just a little bit frightened. She'd smelled like Rachel, too, a gentle, fresh scent of lavender and soap rather than the musk of men and a prostitute's heavy perfume. But she was practiced in the carnal arts and had employed them with calculation. She could barely read, yet she had seen more of men than any decent woman could claim.

After a customer tried to peek up my skirts, Roz started locking me in whatever room was vacant that night.

He closed his eyes and saw himself being violated by a whore. And then the image shifted and it was Rachel as a child, being mauled by a "customer." A child who had been born without innocence, yet had learned to dream in the darkness.

The image faded as exhaustion pulled him down into a black pit where demons slept. And when they awakened, they wore his face as they gathered about a child lying in the filth of an alley.

Abruptly he sat up and lit the oil lamp on the bedside table with shaking hands. He heard the sounds of retching in the next room until he wondered if there would be anything left of her come morning.

He wanted to go to her, to hold her head and wipe her brow. Each time he stopped himself. He owed her nothing but his time for five years. He wanted nothing from her but his freedom. He cursed himself for a liar as he lay on his stomach and buried his head in his arms, his shoulders heaving with grief for more than the loss of a friend.

. . .

Morning came with the familiar barnyard sounds and the slam of the kitchen door. His mind refused to function beyond the most fundamental thoughts. It was time to work. To milk the cows, curse at the hens, and share a moment of communion with the poor old rooster. Time to tend the garden and make things grow. Time to build onto Promise.

It was the way each day began for him, and for that always-queer moment when sleep mingled with awareness, yesterday was nothing but a blank in his memory. His eyes were gritty and his head pounded as he rose from the bed. He swallowed and winced at the rawness in his throat, and remembered Phoenix's pain, his death. He remembered Rachel uttering the word ''Mother'' and the shock of knowing it was addressed to Madam Roz. And he remembered the rest—Rachel pleading with him to hold her, to look at her, Rachel admitting her deceit without excuses, Rachel coming to him in the guise of a whore and leaving him to weep like a baby. How long had he stifled his anguish in the pillow?

Sunlight burned his eyes as he stood at the window, watching Rachel leave the henhouse and walk into the barn. Something twisted inside him to see her take up his chores as if he had already left her, seeing her go on without him.

With another curse, he strode from the room and made a quick stop in the water closet to wash up. It didn't help. His reflection showed black circles under bloodshot eyes. With two days' worth of growth on his face, he looked like the sots passed out in the Cheyenne saloons. He felt worse.

Rachel walked into the kitchen as he emerged from the water closet. She halted in the middle of the room, standing frozen for a moment before setting the basket of eggs on the table and placing the skillet on the stove. He studied her as she sliced bacon and laid the strips into the pan. From behind, she looked like an ordinary farm wife, her braid wrapped in a knot at the base of her neck, her shapeless dress faded and threadbare. But when she turned, he saw the delicacy of her features, the paleness of her skin, the shadows of defeat that had replaced the richness of summer in her eyes.

"When are you leaving?" she asked.

Leaving? It caught him by surprise. Oddly, he hadn't considered that, and wondered why not. "In five years," he replied.

Her head snapped up and she stared at him. "You're free to go, Henry. I will have my child and your name. I require nothing more."

"Ah, yes," he said as he sauntered to the table and sprawled indolently in a chair. "My name. As I recall, you will become a *respectable* widow if I should break our contract. Will you grieve, Rachel?"

"Yes, I will grieve," she answered with the damnable simplicity that both irritated and fascinated him.

"And then what? Will you take a lover . . . after a *respectable* mourning period?"

"I want no other lover, Henry." She removed the spitting bacon and expertly cracked an egg into the grease. Her face blanched as she pressed a hand to her stomach and averted her gaze from the white and yellow meat.

Bloody hell. "Have you eaten?" he asked.

"Tea and a biscuit."

"Which you have lost."

She nodded.

"Go to bed, Rachel," he said wearily.

She presented her back to him and clenched the edge of the sink. "Save your compassion for small animals and children, Henry. I can take care of myself."

Infuriated that she should take such exception to his concern, he retaliated. "Of course you can. You are all things to all people, working yourself into the ground, caring for injured madams and taking in wounded souls, building your own little empire to rule with a benevolent hand. One wonders what you are about, and why."

Whirling from the sink, she picked up a spatula and lifted the burned egg from the pan, sliding it onto a plate next to the strips of undercooked bacon and slamming the whole in front of him. "I am about the business of surviving because I have been given precious few other options. Eat your breakfast, Henry. If you are staying, there is work to be done."

Pushing the plate aside, he rose from the chair. "Self-pity, Rachel?"

"Why not?" she said as she stood her ground. "You certainly seem to find pleasure in it."

The chair slid across the floor as he shoved it out of his way and scooped her up in his arms to carry her into the parlor. "Then I suggest that you indulge yourself in a way that will be of benefit and pity the child who has no choice but to survive your ambitions." She flinched away from him and held herself rigid until he deposited her on the sofa and dropped a throw over her.

"Will you show such concern if the child is a girl, Henry? Or is your sympathy limited to the male children of whores?"

"My sympathy is wearing thin," he said, and strode out of the house. He had to get away from Rachel and her barbs that tore into him and poisoned his beliefs with doubt.

Do not walk away from the truth. Henry heard Phoenix's voice as clearly as if his friend walked beside him down the street. A useless piece of advice, he thought bitterly. The truth was all around him in pristine new buildings—not one of them with a false front—the untouched quality of the land around them. It looked both old and new with the natural foliage and trees allowed to grow free of human restraint in the settlement, the strict orderliness of the gardens, the bounce and purpose in the steps of the inhabitants though their aspects were ragged with time and wear. For a while he had begun to believe that it would live up to its name.

The truth was that it was a place like any other, where secrets were kept and promise was just another pretty word.

"Rachel's built a pretty town here."

The voice intruded into his thoughts, reminding him of why he stood in front of the small cabin. Roz stepped outside and sat in the rocking chair on the miniscule porch.

"It doesn't have that lived-in look yet, but I expect it will when we see children playing in the street. Too bad you won't be around. Still, Rachel should have known better. Men find out who she is and they always run the other way."

"Always? Don't they at least try to peek up her skirts?" Henry asked bitterly.

"Last one that tried it got his balls jammed up into his throat by her knee."

"Rachel is ill," he said, keeping his distance as an image of what Rachel had done to him the night before raced through his mind. A kick might have been more merciful than the way she had stripped him of pride and left it collecting dust on the floor.

"Don't fret over it. There's enough folks here to take care of her if need be."

"I see. I should have known that your touching display of maternal comfort yesterday was simply a whim of the moment. Still, it helped Rachel—" He extracted a coin from his pocket and flicked it in her direction. "No doubt you expect payment."

"I've been tarred and feathered and plucked. Anything you say to me is just so much pee in the wind."

Disgusted with her crudity and his momentary delusion that she might actually want to help Rachel, he turned away.

"Did you and Rachel stop at Finnigan's on your way up here?" she called.

Something in her voice stopped him. Something urgent, as if she were trying to hold him there. "We stopped at Finnigan's."

"Maeve's quite a woman—taking what life threw at her and making something of it. Her folks were gentry in the Carolinas. Her pa died in the war and her ma moved West during the Reconstruction. She married an old fart who liked little girls. He sold her to me when he was finished with her. I gave Maeve a choice—a fifty-dollar stake and freedom or work for me. She was one of my best girls."

He tasted bile at the picture Roz painted. It didn't seem possible that the plump, cheerful woman who looked as if she'd been born in a kitchen would be one of Roz's "best girls."

"Hard to believe, isn't it? There aren't more decent folk around than Maeve and Eamon. They work hard, and deal fairly. Come to think of it, Eamon is quite a man to stick with a worn-out hooker like her—God-fearing man that he is."

"What is your point?" he asked impatiently.

"No point exactly, unless it's that some women are born whores—like me. I like men and took pleasure in giving them what they couldn't get from their tight-laced wives. I got more pleasure in taking their money. Only way a woman alone can fight back is with money. Rachel knew it. She wasn't born a whore, so she bought herself a husband. She was smart enough to know that there aren't too many men like Eamon in the world. That man has a pure gift for seeing good in everything. Did you see the dandelion patch next to his barn? He won't pull 'em up . . . says they make the yard look happy.''

"I fail to see—"

"Yep, I know you do, so I'll tell you. Respectability is like those fancy fronts hiding dogtrot buildings. Anybody can have it if their pockets are full. Respect is something else. You got to have it for yourself, before anybody else will think you're worth theirs. Rachel respected herself enough to get away from the red-light district." She began to rock back and forth in the chair. "Then she fell in love with a highfalutin' piece of work and forgot that she was always more than what she came from. Seems to me like she lost on the deal."

His eyes narrowed, Henry stared at her, too dumbfounded to reply. He'd always thought of her kind as being too primordial in their instincts to recognize anything beyond their own depravity. Yet such a creature sat in her rocker on the porch of a simple cabin giving him a lecture on respect of all things. An avaricious creature who bent over in her chair to pick up the coin he'd tossed at her and roll it from one finger to the next and back again to finally rest in her palm. Now that he could understand.

"I repeat, madam: Rachel is ill. Name your price to care for her."

Roz gave him a shrewd look. "Give Rachel what she wants."

"She has what she wants," Henry said bitterly.

"You think you're what she wants? Well, think again, Hank. You're just the means to an end. There's only one thing she ever wanted, fool notion that it is."

"I grow weary of your backwoods philosophy, madam."

"All right." Roz nodded, and left the rocker to approach him.

He saw more than shrewdness then. He saw suffering and pride, a plea and a resignation that it would not be answered. He saw a human being. "Name your price," he repeated softly.

"Rachel loves me. She shouldn't, but she's got more heart than sense sometimes. Look at what she's done, building and growing and doing good for other people. Don't get me wrong. She's sincere. It's what she'd do regardless. But she thinks she needs something for me and for herself because she's a part of me. She believes what everyone has always said about her . . . because of me."

"Tell me," Henry said even more softly, caught, in spite of himself, by the wistful note in her voice, by the emotion in her expression. "What does she want?"

Roz's sigh caught on a breath and she whimpered, a raw, abrupt sound that ended almost as soon as it began. But on the heels of that sound was a single word that chilled him through to the bone. A word that had driven him for years until he'd learned that it was unattainable . . .

Redemption.

What a grand irony it was that he had feared corrupting Rachel, that she had promised not to try to redeem him. What a joke it was that he had thought himself redeemed in spite of her promise.

24

October

Henry was gone, vanished, it seemed, into his world of demons and nightmares. He appeared only to do the chores, take his meals, and politely inquire as to her health. And though his physical presence filled a room, his expression was closed to her and his gaze touched her only in passing.

He'd returned to the house that morning over two months ago to sit silent and brooding in a chair across from where she lay on the sofa. She hadn't tried to speak to him. She'd had neither the energy nor the will in the aftermath of her performance the night before. She'd acted out of anger rather than reason, and in the doing proved Henry's convictions to be well founded. She had played the whore for him, and she had been magnificent in the role . . . a natural.

Whores beget whores.

Henry's nightmare had become hers.

Roz had arrived within the hour, and Henry retreated upstairs to his room full of paints and canvases. It had been strange to have her mother fetch and carry for her, nurturing her as if she were a small child. And during quiet moments when Rachel had been able to keep her food down, Roz had helped her with her reading and writing. It had been stranger still, to feel as if she had finally been granted a childhood, and a mother, even for two months.

She and Roz had spoken little, yet it hadn't seemed necessary. Healing, Roz had gruffly commented one afternoon, took time and was best accomplished with a respite from the conversations and concerns of everyday life. Perhaps there had been a healing between herself and her mother. Their time together had been peaceful and free of old resentments. Their manner with one another was like that of new acquaintances who were learning about one another with reserve and caution. Neither of them talked of anything more personal than Rachel's health and Roz's garden.

Rachel knew that her health was improved and the sickness that had plagued her for the first five months of her pregnancy had finally left her, allowing her to pick up her life again. But, in spite of the renewed energy of her body and the reassurance that her child thrived and grew within her, weariness continued to shroud her mind and smother her spirit. She was aware of it, yet escaped responsibility by sleeping whenever time allowed. Her appetite for food had increased along with her constant exhaustion, and that, too, she regarded with little concern.

Since Roz had stopped coming every day, there was no one to notice what she did.

Being alone in the house with Henry for the last two months was to be completely alone for what seemed like eternity.

She sat in her bed, reluctant to leave after her afternoon nap, dreading the minutes when she would sit across the table from Henry, remembering and yearning for the closeness they had shared for such a short time.

He was in the garden now, preparing the earth for winter's siege. She'd forgotten to tell him that autumn in Wyoming was short and often capricious, appearing on a gypsy wind to pillage the land and carry away the vivid foliage, leaving drab brown grasses, bare trees, and dreary gray skies in its wake. Only the evergreens stood lush and full as hostages for the return of Spring.

They had lost the late vegetables to early storms, and everyone in Promise had worked from dawn until late in the night to save their communal grain crops. She barely noticed that today, the sky was clear and blue, that the air was balmy with the remains of summer. For her, winter had come the day Phoenix had died, and she had forced Henry to ask her to play the whore for him.

His voice reached her from the front porch as he conversed with Roz. Rachel tilted her head in curiosity. During Roz's rare visits to the house, Henry exchanged little conversation with her.

"Something has to be done," Roz said. "Or you'd might as well put her up in a Mason jar with the vegetables."

"She has done all the preserving, helped with the butchering and salting of meat, made new pillows and ticks for the beds." Henry's voice was cold, dispassionate. "She has earned her rest."

"Damn it, she's not resting. She's dying inside."

"How dramatic you are, madam. It looks to me as if she is like the hens, and simply sitting on her nest . . . roosting so to speak."

"Well, then, Hank, maybe you'd better see to your *hen*. There's more to being a rooster than fertilizing eggs . . . though on second thought I never met a man smart enough to know that.''

Rachel frowned and waited for Henry to explode. Even Roz dared much by calling him "Hank." But Henry let it pass without comment or sarcasm.

"What do you imagine Rachel needs from me, madam?"

"All she does is eat and sleep and *roost*. She'll be fat if it doesn't stop."

Was she getting fat? Rachel wondered as she glanced down at herself and ran her hands over her thighs, her stomach and breasts. No, not fat, though she noticed that her hips were fuller and her thighs were not as firm as they had been. She pulled her braid over her shoulder and twirled the end, then paused, her brows drawn together as she examined her hair. She kept it combed and neat, but she couldn't remember the last time she had given it the thorough brushing that had been a nightly ritual. It showed in the lack of luster and dryness of the strands that stood out stiffly from the leather thong holding the plaits in place.

"A certain increase in girth is to be expected, I believe," Henry said.

"And it's supposed to go away after the baby hatches. If Rachel isn't brought under control now, it won't happen, and you'll have to roll her down the hill to get her into town."

Control? Something shifted inside Rachel and climbed into her throat. Her breath came in short, shallow gasps. Suddenly she felt cold and clammy. She'd felt this before—as a child when men had approached her and asked her if she would like to play with them, and when she'd walked away after Liddie's death and found herself literally alone in the wilderness of a territory she had only seen from a window. She'd felt it when she'd first met Henry, and when Roz had moved to Promise.

It was blind unreasoning panic, clawing at her to be released.

"Your daughter, madam, is quite capable of taking care of herself along with half the territory if need be. She certainly doesn't need me to orchestrate her daily habits. As for control—"

Rachel raised her arms to cover her head as she'd done in the attic when brawling and gunshots broke out in her mother's house, muffling the sounds, stifling the scream of protest she could not make for fear that she would never stop screaming. *Control.* They were speaking of controlling her as if she were incapable and truly did belong on the shelf with the canned beans.

No! She held her breath and let it out, over and over again. She forced her hands to relax, her mind to escape its lethargy, to function. They would not control her. She had worked too hard and too long to keep from ending up like the girls who worked for her mother, surrendering themselves to a life that wasn't a life at all. Some of them had gone mad. She had seen it—women who became dolls to be arranged and toyed with, women who welcomed death . . . like Liddie. Suddenly she realized what her mother was trying to say, what her mother thought. She had to stop her from saying more to Henry, from reminding him . . . hurting him.

Somehow, Rachel managed to leave her bed and descend the stairs, to cross the entry and stand in the threshold of the door left open to admit the breeze.

"She's getting addled, Hank. I've seen it happen. Women just give up and their minds go someplace else."

They didn't see her as Henry and Roz faced one another at the top of the porch steps. She saw the grim set of Henry's mouth, the tightness of his jaw, and Rachel knew that she was too late, and Roz had inadvertently made him think of his own mother. Roz shouldn't have mentioned madness to him. Rachel had to stop her from saying more.

"And where would I go, Mother?"

Henry's head whipped around, his gaze focused on her for the first time in two months.

Roz raised her brows, a small smile tipping up the corners of her mouth. "Someplace better . . . where you can't feel. You know how it is, Rachel. You've seen it a time or two. Remember Jane—how she loved music, how she sang at the top of her lungs every time she screwed a customer, and then one day, she didn't stop singing?"

"Enough!" Henry shouted, and it sounded raw with barely suppressed anguish.

"Yes, enough, Roz," Rachel said, startled by the firm clarity of her voice. "I'm sure you have better things to do than fret over my health."

"My mistake, Rachel . . . guess I'd better be going."

As Roz strolled down the hill, Henry stared blindly at the mountains rising in layers behind the settlement, his hands clenched, his posture stiff.

"I'm not going mad, Henry," Rachel said softly.

He turned his gaze on her then, studying her closely with narrowed eyes.

"You thought so, too, didn't you?" she asked. "You just didn't want to admit it to Roz."

Silence.

"You needn't concern yourself," she said, feeling more calm and certainty than she had in a very long time. "We each have a place to retreat, you know. Roz has her garden. You have your paintings—"

"Then where have you been, Rachel?" It was a whisper, as if he didn't really want to ask.

Away from your scorn, she wanted to say, but kept silent as she walked out onto the porch and leaned forward over the rail to look out over the town at the base of the hill, the mountains that serrated the horizon on all sides, the water that flowed through her land, covered in some places near the banks by an early crust of ice. Bleak, gray clouds loomed in the near distance, a heavy curtain soon to be unfurled by the force of freezing winds. She smiled as it overtook the sun, dimming the afternoon light to pewter, then breathed deeply the scent of winter in air that grew increasingly cold and bitter. "I am where I have always been, Henry." She gestured toward the cabins and shops of Promise, the glow of firelight and lanterns spilling weakly from the windows. "But this time I am in an attic of my own choosing."

His face became as ashen as the sky as he took a step forward, toward her, his hand outstretched. So this, she thought dispassionately, was what fear looked like on Henry. She'd never seen it displayed so blatantly before, though she knew that it was always there, always a part of him, like his anger and tortured thoughts. Like the demons he carried with him, rendered on canvas in shades of blood and evil. She almost pitied him then, for the compassion that was so much a part of him, over-ruling his distaste for her.

"You needn't worry, Henry. If any man had the power to drive me mad, there were many others in my mother's house who could have accomplished it. No man shall ever have such power over me ... not even you."

He retreated the steps he had taken toward her. "Then your ... retreat is merely an indulgence of—"

"Despondency or perhaps self-pity due to unrequited love?" She interrupted, irritated that he considered her feelings to be slight. She shook her head. "No, Henry. I am *merely* indulging in new dreams."

She rubbed her arms and blindly stared at ahead as he disappeared around the side of the house and entered through the back door, avoiding her as he always did now, making her feel ugly and unclean.

New dreams and old nightmares. Henry was surrounded by them as he strode into his workroom, escaping Rachel and her verbal blows. He'd winced with each word she'd uttered on the porch, feeling the slash and bite of her certainty. It shouldn't have hurt—shouldn't have affected him at all to hear that she did not need him, that she would indeed go on without him, that she had already anticipated the necessity. He felt as if she had forced him from her life, as if every time she looked at him, she was seeing a memory rather than flesh and blood.

He felt like a memory, no more substantial than mist and fading smiles that would never return, like the portraits of Rachel that stood along one wall were depictions of memories, sightlessly and silently condemning him to a life of emptiness. Only Phoenix's portrait seemed alive as Phoenix was not, speaking to him, urging him to save himself.

Finish your paintings, my friend.

Henry had tried to complete his images of Rachel, but his talent failed him. He'd painted in the eyes on one portrait, then two, but they were dull and lifeless, as Rachel had been over the last two months . . . as he had felt until she'd spoken of new dreams that afternoon, and he had experienced fear as he'd never experienced it before. Fear that what Rachel saw from her portraits was what he would see in himself.

Nothing . . . nothing at all.

Believe what you see . . . trust what you feel . . .

He paced in front of his renderings of her, back and forth, studying each one, searching for answers. He'd captured her coaxing a plant to grow, as she had coaxed him to learn and to see with more than his memories; in

Finnigan's barn, magnificent and righteous in her anger
at him; standing next to Roz, their resemblance so obvious to him now, yet they were extremes of one another, like winter and summer were extremes of nature.

I am not my mother, Henry.

No, he admitted to himself, whatever Rachel was, she
was not her mother. How much easier it would be if she
were. In his mind, her greatest transgressions against him
were what she had done to him rather than what she
was.

Last was the painting of Rachel holding the storm in
her hands, as she had held him with her hands and
mouth, taming him, teaching him the difference between
violation and respect.

Tell me what you want.

I want you.

It was the truth. He still wanted her, healthy or ill, fat
or thin, in love and in anger. Without her he would live
in hopelessness and in hell. It was only left to discover
if living with Rachel would amount to the same thing.

. . . look at yourself . . . as you have never done before.

He'd been avoiding it—that look at himself, into himself. But Rachel's words drove him now, and he crossed
the hall to his bedroom to pluck a mirror off the wall.
Propping it up beside his easel, he picked up his palette
and brush and began a new portrait. A portrait of a
stranger who had come to life in Rachel's attic.

He spent the night alternately looking between his image in the mirror and the pristine surface of a blank
canvas.

He'd never seen such a thing. The sight of so much
snow amazed and fascinated him, and even the wind
seemed white, slanting the fall of snowflakes and picking
them up in elaborate plumes.

The winter storm had moved in overnight, quickly and stealthily, without the fanfare of thunder and the often spectacular exhibition of summer lightning. There was no violence, no force beyond the wind that howled and drove an appalling amount of snow against trees and buildings. Now Henry understood why everyone in Promise had worked so feverishly to store food and wood and oil, to repair shutters and roofs and perfect the seals on their doors as best they could. And as the snow drifted and piled up to amazing depths on the ground, he understood why Rachel had stocked so much fabric and yarn and hides. While they had spent much of the past three seasons working outside, he saw the danger of venturing far from hearth and home under such vicious conditions. He recognized how deadly winter could become if one did not have enough tasks to fill the months of isolation and confinement.

He frowned as the back door slammed, and glanced out the window, barely recognizing Rachel dressed in Levi's and boots, and a coat and hat made of a fur he'd never seen before. She bent against the wind, a coiled rope looped over her shoulder as she slowly unwound it, pulling it taut before taking another step toward the barn. He squinted, looking downward, and saw that one end of the rope was tied to an iron ring set into a post by the door.

She was going to milk the damned cows.

He stumbled over a tray set outside his door, and glared at the spilled coffee and trampled biscuit. Something lurched in his chest. *Kindness is a luxury and not to be wasted. . . . Mine will cost you nothing,* Rachel had once said. Did she have any idea of the high price her kindness had exacted from him?

Snagging an old coat from among many hanging on pegs by the door, he ran after her and slid off the top step to land in a drift that reached his shoulders. He grabbed the post and hauled himself to his feet, then held the rope for balance, and followed the trail Rachel had made in the thigh-high snow. His feet slid out from under him again as the rope pulled tighter, snapping from his grip. Rachel stood at the barn door, tying the other end to another post. He'd thought they were hitching posts for horses rather than people. Since Rachel was no longer attached to the rope, he used it for leverage and again followed her footsteps. Thank God the chicken house and barn were close to the house. He suspected it was due to careful planning.

He literally blew into the barn and found her milking the first cow. Without comment, he took care of the second. They leapfrogged one another, Rachel taking the third cow and him the fourth, then met one another's gaze over the stall dividers.

"Thank you," she said politely.

"My pleasure," he replied mocking their civility. "It is, after all, my assigned chore."

"Not anymore."

"I beg your pardon?"

"Horace is moving into the tack room."

"May I inquire as to the reason?"

"He says this winter will be unusually difficult, and volunteered to live here in case I couldn't get out."

I rather than *we*. "I see."

"No, but you will," she said. "If the weather gets worse and doesn't stop for a while, we won't be able to get here even with the rope to guide us. People have been known to freeze to death or be buried alive on their way to the outhouse."

"Surely you exaggerate."

"No."

No. "Bloody hell."

"If Horace is right, and he always is, we will be too cold to bleed."

Frigid air blasted them as Horace opened the door just enough to squeeze through. Given his bulk, it was a large opening. "Yep," he said, strolling up to them. "Hell's going to freeze over this year . . . we'd better get started."

"Doing what?" Henry asked feeling as if he had suddenly been mislaid in a foreign world.

"Fixin' me a cozy place. I ain't going to sleep with the critters, you know."

"It might be warmer with them," Rachel commented, and disappeared into the tack room.

Henry didn't like the sound of that.

The day passed with several trips to the house and back for foodstuffs, blankets, and containers of lamp oil. The large tack room was already equipped with not one, but two feather ticks on each of the two beds stacked one upon the other against a wall, as well as a supply of medicines and bandages—kept there, Rachel said, for emergencies. Henry didn't like the sound of that either. They made sure the old wood and coal stove was in working order and checked the hay that filled the loft to the rafters. At least, Horace quipped, water would be no problem. He'd have enough snow to melt to last until Judgment Day.

"I'm glad you insisted we store extra hay and feed, Horace," Rachel said. "I cleaned out all the milk cans, too, in case we're all snowbound. At least milk doesn't sour if it's frozen."

"I been thinkin', Rachel," Horace said, scratching his chin. "You bein' in the family way, you'll need your milk an' eggs. Now, I checked the henhouse an' stuffed blankets in the walls like I said I would, an' put a stove in there. Since it's attached to the barn, thought I'd knock a hole in the wall over there an' put in a door to pass the time. Might be I can rig up a rope from the loft to the house an' a pulley of sorts so's I can send milk an' eggs over to you if it gets bad enough. Otherwise I got my snowshoes."

Henry noticed them then—the oval paddlelike contraptions attached to Horace's boots.

"Mebbe you an' Hank here ought to start using 'em, too."

"Yes, I unpacked them this morning. I'll teach Henry how to use them," Rachel said. "Will you be all right here?"

"Don't see why not, Rachel. Here or alone in my cabin—ain't no difference, an' I got no feather mattresses there. I brought my sewin' an' knittin' and should do just fine."

"He sews and knits?" Henry asked when they were once again back at the house.

Rachel shrugged. "He says he learned how to knit when he was stuck in a dugout one winter with an old widow of a miner. As for sewing—most men who live alone know how to mend their own clothes."

"Oh." Henry stared at her cheeks, red from the wind and cold and her eyes drooping with weariness. She removed her coat and absently rubbed the small of her back.

"What in blazes kind of animal has fur like that?" he asked, his hand brushing the side of her breast as he fingered the dense brown pelt. She was rounder now, softer, and the feel of her stirred the awareness inside him—awareness that never faded, but sharpened with every thought of her, with every memory of holding her through the night and feeling as if she belonged there.

She stared down at his hand, then met his gaze when he lingered, the backs of his fingers moving up and down over the fullness of her breast. "Buffalo," she said, and stepped away to hang up the coat.

He glanced at his hand, still outstretched, touching nothing now but the winter air that had followed them into the house. In that moment, he felt lonelier than ever before. Abruptly lowering his hand, he, too, stepped back, and cleared the sudden thickness from his throat. "Ah," he said sagely. "I suppose you shot the buffalo, skinned it, tanned the hide and made the coat."

"Yes. The meat fed five of us for the winter."

"Why am I not surprised?" he asked the ceiling.

"I'll get dinner. We've barely eaten all day."

"I will cook for you, make a home for you, give you children—" he quoted musingly as he remembered the tray she'd left for him that morning. "What a good wife you are, Rachel. I wonder how many of your promises you are willing to keep." He didn't know why he pursued the subject, why he had such an urgent need to hear her answer. Logically, it seemed inappropriate under the circumstances. Inappropriate to the present state of their relationship and his ingrained disapproval of her. A disapproval that was becoming more and more difficult to justify and maintain. "I believe," he continued with studied nonchalance, "you also promised not to nag or deny me."

"Yes."

"Even now?"

She slammed down a crock of butter on the table between them. "Yes, even now. You have kept your part of our bargain by staying here. I will keep mine. Aside from that I was wondering how to approach you about sharing a bed. It would be best to close off the rooms we don't need to conserve firewood, and the nights will be less cold if we—"

"Yes, of course. I can see the practicality of sharing a bed," he snapped, fighting his disappointment over her lack of enthusiasm and the way she made it sound like another business proposition. Yet what had he expected? For her to fall at his feet and beg? Not Rachel. Not if he offered her a thousand towns on a platter. He flattened his palms on the table and leaned forward, meeting her gaze eye to eye. "Tell me, is there a price?"

He felt the sting in his cheek before he'd registered the lift of her hand, the swing of her arm across the table.

She gave a soft whimper, so soft and so brief that he thought he imagined it as she straightened, standing tall and calm in the face of his insult. "I could ask you the same thing, Henry. But on second thought, I prefer to use extra wood than to submit to your cruelty. Keep your room. We are both accustomed enough to living in the cold. In the spring I will take legal steps to terminate our relationship once and for all." Calmly she sliced bread and buttered it, then poured a large mug of coffee from the pot kept hot on the stove and carried the sparse meal up to her room and slammed the door.

Henry's appetite deserted him as he rubbed his cheek. Her slap had not hurt near as much as he had hurt himself with his callousness.

He climbed the rear staircase and paused at her door, expecting it to be locked against him. It opened easily.

Rachel sat curled in a chair by the fire wrapped in an old quilt, both hands cupped around the mug of coffee.

"I grow weary of your efforts to send me away, Mrs. Ashford. We have an agreement. It will not be broken."

"It is no longer an agreement, Henry, much less a marriage. It is a sentence neither of us deserve."

"Is it, Rachel?" he asked as he advanced toward her.

"Surely you would be happier elsewhere."

"I don't know," he admitted baldly. "Would you be happier if I were?"

"I'd like to think so, Henry. You make me feel tainted as I never felt in my mother's house."

"It was your choice to play the harlot, Rachel."

"Yes. And that is all I will ever be to you." She met his gaze. "Eventually that is all I will be to myself." Her voice snagged in her throat, a small, tearing sound that tore at the part of him that could not stop wanting her . . . loving her.

"Perhaps . . . I am wrong," he said as he raked his hand through his hair. "If I thought I could forget my doubts and forget you, I would leave. But I have to know, Rachel."

"*Perhaps* you're wrong? *You* have to know?" Her voice was low and bitter . . . condemning. "And I am to lie back with my legs spread while you ponder your dilemma, Henry? Am I to allow you to *use* me in your quest for truth?"

"You want me, Rachel." He winced at the sound and meaning of it—the raw desperation that denied him the proper words, the pride that kept his own mind from revealing itself to him, and the fear that wouldn't allow him to accept his own feelings.

"No, Henry. I love you, while you merely want me. The price is high enough for love. I will not pay for your urges, as well."

"You think I am not paying for your love, Rachel? Do you assume that wanting is such a simple thing—a matter of flesh rather than soul?" He stepped closer to her, leaning over and cupping her chin in his hand, to hold her face close to his. "You are more coward than I, Mrs. Ashford, for I am willing to pay any price to resolve what is between us . . . to find peace." Disgusted with himself and the confusion that rendered him a creature of emotion rather than reason, he released her and turned away, striding toward the door.

"Are you saying that you want to try?" she asked, halting his progress.

He struggled to find the answer, to understand and to give her as much honesty as he could find within himself. "You hold me, Rachel. I should hate you, but I don't. It should be easy to walk away and forget you, but I can't. Learning of your secret should have resolved what I feel for you, yet it hasn't." He inhaled deeply and looked away from her. "Yes, I think we both must try."

"All right, Henry," she said, "I will sell myself to you for the winter. I want this resolved as much as you do."

Sell . . . She would sell herself to him. It should have disgusted him, yet he could only view her capitulation as a reprieve. He should have felt satisfaction, yet all he felt was outrage that she should reduce herself to a thing to be bought and sold. Not Rachel. Never again. He didn't turn, not yet. Not until he heard the rest of it. "What of your terms, Rachel? A pound of flesh perhaps?" he goaded.

"No, Henry. Flesh is what you want, remember?" She tilted her head, a slight nod of acknowledgment. "Oh yes, and you want to try. You want truth and a clear conscience—"

"We both want peace, Rachel."

"Yes," she agreed, and seemed to wilt back into the chair. "I want to try, too. If it doesn't work, then we'll both be free." She smiled up at him, a feeble thing that barely curved her mouth and hadn't the strength to change the grimness in her eyes. "After all, I, too, have an aversion to whores."

Fury rose to strangle what was left of his reason. It was the worst thing she could have said. That it was true, he could not deny, and that, too, infuriated him. Hadn't he once accused Luc of prostituting him?

"Very well, Rachel. Since we are both of the same mind, I think we should begin *trying* now." He returned to her, driven by the demons she had awakened in him to lift her from her chair and stand her before him.

"Yes, Henry. Perhaps it won't take long for you to learn to hate me and for me to forget that I love you." She lifted her hand to unbutton her shirt.

They removed their own clothing, standing apart from one another, and he knew that his own expression was as cold and unyielding as hers. She studied him dispassionately as he touched and caressed her with calculation, knowing exactly what drew the greatest response from her. It was a mutual taking, harsh in its selfishness, explicit in carnality, unrefined in responses given with verbal urgings rather than soft moans and gentle sighs.

Suddenly she tore herself away from his embrace, her chest heaving, her eyes bleak. "I can't, Henry. Never again. Not like this." She backed away from him, and he followed, until she backed into a wall and could go no further. "This isn't trying, Henry. It's anger and punishment on both our parts. It means nothing. It is nothing."

"No, Rachel," he corrected, and stroked the side of her cheek with the back of his hand. "It began as nothing."

She turned her face away.

"I'm sorry, Rachel." His voice was rusty, the words seeming new to him. "I'm sorry," he repeated, tasting the concept and finding it palatable. "And you're right. You chase away my anger, Rachel, and I only punish myself." It hadn't been difficult at all to admit that he was wrong, and he found the courage to gather more words in his mind, to deliver them with honesty. "I know nothing of noble intentions, but you make me want to learn." He lowered his hand and stepped back, giving her room to leave him if that was her will.

She didn't move. "I only know what I have observed in my mother's house, Henry, and I wonder if you know any more than I about making love. I wonder if you know how to accept tenderness." Turning away, she folded back the covers on the bed and sat down, facing him. "Can we begin trying now to learn what might be possible?"

Banishing all thoughts of betrayal and suspicion for the moment, he went to her, wanting desperately to know more of the tenderness she spoke of.

She received him with arms that expressed the same desperation, holding him, her fingers stroking his hair over and over again in a gesture of comfort. But it had been too long since he'd received comfort and he felt awkward with such generosity, helpless with his sudden need for the soul-deep intimacy it offered. Lust was less demanding, less enduring in the mind and heart. Passion was all he could accept while his mind was full of doubt and his heart was still brittle from disuse.

Denying the anguish of such thoughts, he groaned and lowered her to lie on the bed and stretched out on his side next to her, supporting himself on one elbow as he began a slow exploration of her body, learning her as if it were the first time.

He caressed her with a light touch on her breasts and down to her waist, avoiding her belly and finding her thighs. He breathed deeply as she moved restlessly, trying to get closer to him, to touch him. "Shh," he murmured, hesitating as his hand hovered over her rounded stomach, reluctant to touch her there, yet needing to acknowledge that this, too, was a part of her. "Gently, Rachel," he whispered, and pressed his palm flat against her belly, stroking her flesh in slow circles. "I would not hurt you."

Staring up at him, she stilled, but to cover his hand with both of hers. "I know, Henry." she said with a sadness that shamed him with the knowledge that he had hurt her many times, that she expected him to hurt her again with silent anger and forced indifference.

He leaned over her, taking her mouth, shuddering as her tongue played with his and her hands provoked his body. He grew full and hard in her hands, aching for release. The pressure grew as she sat astride him, open-

ing over him, sheathing him as she rocked slowly, ag-
onizingly on him, teaching him that tenderness seduced
more completely than uncontrolled lust.

Like the blizzard that raged outside with whispers and
muted light rather than sound and fury, it was a gentle
storm of desire, a surrender to themselves rather than to
anger toward each other. And when they lay tangled on
the bed, Henry felt the satisfaction of passion well spent
and the loneliness of knowing that even now they hadn't
shared more than their bodies with one another.

Their anger might have dissolved, but fear and wariness remained.

25

Nothing had changed, yet everything was different.

Death came daily on a white wind, smothering the land and freezing its inhabitants, a clean, quick death that created casualties with a blast of wind or a blanket of snow. A deceitful death that filled its victims with a warm euphoria as it turned them into statues of ice that would shatter with a blow. And though they were warm and well fed inside the house, Henry felt brittle with the coldness between himself and Rachel.

A latticework of hemp criss-crossed the town, linking one dwelling with another and with the mercantile Rachel had stocked for just such an emergency. The outlying dwellings had been abandoned as citizens doubled up in the cabins surrounding the cluster of public buildings. Rachel's barn had become a Noah's Ark of sorts, sheltering as many animals as possible with two other men sharing in the work required to care for the stock

that could mean life or death for the community. The
balance of the animals had been moved into the bunkhouse where the townsfolk took turns seeing to their
welfare. Stubbornly Roz remained alone in her cabin.

Henry almost envied Roz for the peace and freedom
she seemed to find in her solitude.

He lay in bed watching Rachel brush her hair, her eyes
closed, her body visibly relaxing with every stroke. She
was almost finished now and would begin to braid the
thick strands and coil the whole into a heavy net at the
base of her neck. In her loose, white nightrail and the
mesh snood, she looked to him a fantasy from some
ancient tapestry, a lady clothed in ice and snow tending
her land and her people, taking pride in them as she no
longer took pride in herself. . . .

Because of him.

Dread was a live thing inside him as she fastened the
net and lowered the wick on the lamp in a ritual he had
begun to hate. Nightly she came to him, and nightly he
succumbed to the magic of her scent, her sighs, the love
she conveyed with every touch. But slowly, insidiously,
desire between them had become brittle with desperation. His response to her had begun to irritate rather than
excite him, separating mind from body as his sensibilities protested his surrender to pleasure rather than will.
And each night she rolled away from him as if he were
of no further use to her . . . as if she knew of his struggle
and didn't believe that she could possibly be of any more
use to him. Her remoteness left him nothing to hope for
but more moments of exhausting sex followed by a night
of sleepless torment.

*Perhaps it won't take long for you to learn to hate
me and for me to forget that I love you.* She'd said it as
if she believed nothing else was possible for them and
nothing was left but acceptance of the truth. It hadn't

occurred to him then that he would begin to hate himself. He'd never imagined that he would try so hard to keep her from forgetting that she loved him.

She left her place in front of the hearth and came to him, standing at the foot of the bed where firelight shone through the fabric of her gown, revealing lush breasts to caress and taste and long legs to wind around him. And then she slipped the buttons free from the tiny loops, one by one, until the gown fell open down the length of her body—a simple gesture that spoke of willingness and need rather than an attempt at seduction. Yet seduced he was, by the need to hold her any way he could until he found the courage to banish the nightmares that had been part of him for so long. He stared up at her, felt her withdrawal begin as it always did if he hesitated. She, too, he realized, was holding on to the only thing they had the courage to share.

The first thing he saw was her belly, a graceful curve outward to his artist's eye, a curve that aptly followed the perfect shape of an egg. He studied it, trying to envision the child within, and failed. The baby wasn't real to him. He didn't want it to be real. Not yet. Not when he feared that such a small part of himself would give Rachel more than he ever had. Yet in spite of his rejection of the child, in spite of the sensual skills that were so much a part of her, it was easier to envision Rachel as a mother than it was to believe she was a whore.

As he reached for her she slipped the nightdress from her shoulders, allowing it to fall to the floor. She ran her tongue over her lips as he stared at the provocative fullness of her breasts, cupping herself with her hands as she strolled around to the side of the bed and leaned over him, offering herself. It was different tonight. *She* was different in her aggressiveness, and the way she displayed herself with a more provocative air.

Abruptly he levered himself up to sit with his back to the headboard and met her gaze. "Why do you do this?" he asked.

"Time grows short and I grow larger," she said as she raised a knee to the bed, brushing his thigh. "And we must stop when I reached my seventh month." Her hand found him, tracing his rigid length through the sheet covering his hips. "I'm afraid to stop."

She came on top of him, fitting herself to him though he was still covered by the sheet. Her legs pressed into his sides and her hips rotated against him, the linen creating a rough friction that was both ecstasy and pain. She leaned over him, again offering her breasts to his mouth as she continued to incite him with the slow, maddening movement of her hips and the sweet torture of her nails raking his flat nipples. "Nothing will be left once we stop. This is all we have."

"There are other ways, Rachel." He tasted her with his tongue, gently raked her with his teeth, then took her into his mouth. She lifted as he grew more turgid and insistent beneath the sheet. Her neck arched backward as she eased downward again, taking the tip of him into her along with the cloth. He held her breast in his hands and his mouth drew on her, one nipple then the other, until all he could taste was Rachel.

"I can taste you as you have tasted me . . . drink from you as you drank from me. . . ."

She cried out as he urged her to lie down beside him, to open for him. There, too, he smelled lavender, a common enough scent, yet on Rachel it was as unique as she was. "I paint you every night, Rachel, while you're in my arms . . . with my hands, my mouth. . . ." He tasted her with his tongue, searching for her essence. She whimpered, but it wasn't enough. He stroked and drew on her deeper and harder until she moaned and twisted. He held her still, his hands around her legs with gentle firmness as she begged him to stop, as she writhed and arched and gasped in completion.

He leaned his head back against the smooth wood of the bed and closed his eyes, his breath harsh and burning in his throat, his teeth bared in a grimace of pain. He felt as if he would explode, yet could not. He felt drained though he was still hard and full. He felt the air as she slid the sheet away from him, felt her weight as she sat astride him, taking him into her fully this time without the restraint of cloth and caution, giving to him more than he had just taken from her.

"Come with me, Henry," she pleaded. "Escape with me. Be with me for a few moments more."

His mind cleared and his body sagged. He thrust upward but could no longer fill her, denying himself completion. He touched and caressed her as her hand cupped his sac, stroking him, urging his body to respond. He turned his head away and opened his eyes, both relieved and frustrated by the futility of it all. Still, she tried, employing tricks that were both shocking and evocative, silently pleading with him and with his body. Still, he did not, could not respond. Not to the woman who sought escape rather than fulfillment. Not when he knew that any woman who might follow her would merely be dancing upon him as if he were the grave for all the dreams Rachel had given him.

He grasped her wrists and jerked her hands from his body and waited for her to meet his gaze. "Don't ever beg again, Rachel."

Her face paled and her lips trembled. Defeat dulled the brightness of her eyes as she left him to curl up on her side facing away from him, and pulled the linens over her body, as if she had only now come to bed and nothing had happened.

It was just as well. He couldn't look at her right now. Not until he faced himself. He should leave her now, but he couldn't do that, either.

"I did this to you," she said.

"You did nothing, Rachel," he said.

"No," she said thickly, and he knew that tears were falling onto her pillow. "Nothing happened." Her shoulders shook beneath the sheet. "It's over."

He stared at the white plaster ceiling and listened to the spray of snow against the roof and windows as he pulled the sheet up. A spot of moisture on the linen touched him, and he remembered how Rachel had used the sheet as both barrier to his penetration and enticement to try. It was cold now—as cold as the passion that had bound them together for the past month.

Sighing, he forced himself to speak, to end the charade they had both played so desperately. "You misunderstand me, Rachel. I cannot hate you. I can only hate myself for thinking that this is enough. You try to make it enough and I try to forget that I love you. We can't try anymore. All we do is cultivate fear that each time will be the last."

She turned onto her back, her gaze fixed on the stones of the fireplace across from them. "We've succeeded well, haven't we, Henry?"

"No, we've failed. You cannot forget me, Rachel, no more than I could forget you."

"No more than you can forget what I am," she corrected.

"I know who you are, and that is sufficient."

"I see," she said.

"Do you? I wonder. I have made two discoveries since coming to your promised land, Rachel: that redemption must come from within, and that there is no escape from the truth . . . or from the past. I no longer have the desire to run away from either."

"Is it so easy to understand?"

"No," he said. "It's bloody hell. Perhaps we must survive that before we can learn how to live."

"You suffer from winter madness, Henry. You will think differently come spring."

"Then I pray that I shall never suffer from sanity again."

"You will go, Henry," she said softly, and extinguished the lantern on the table by her side, leaving only the glow of the fire in the grate to keep the darkness at bay. And through the night, Henry lay awake without moving, knowing that Rachel did the same. There was nowhere left to run—even in sleep.

Dawn gentled the wind and tamed the fall of snow to a whimsical dance in the air. The sky remained a luminous gray and the cold was forbidding as ever—nature's warning that her mercy was, like kindness, a luxury in the territories and not to be wasted. The inhabitants of Promise took note of the mercy and celebrated the temporary truce between man and nature.

Henry worked feverishly in his room, celebrating his birthday by honoring the dying request of a friend with the new images he had created on canvas. Images of revelation and promise and hope.

Without the howl of the wind, Henry could hear the notes of a harmonica drifting up from the settlement, playing an old English hymn. The clear notes of the out-of-tune piano in the mercantile joined in midway, and from another part of town, someone picked out the chords on a guitar. Downstairs, the clang and scrape of pots and kettles harmonized as Rachel cooked a meal.

Luc seemed close today and Henry wondered how he celebrated his thirty-third year of life. He closed his eyes and concentrated, yet he sensed little beyond a quiet thought and a soothing presence. Luc was well pleased.

Perhaps he knew that Henry was closer to finding peace than he'd ever been in his life. Perhaps it would give Luc peace, too.

Their shared birthday had always been a lonely time for them in their childhood as they'd watched the servants honor the occasion with small gifts and a special meal laced with good cheer. Their father drank his way through the family day, and their mother had always retired as soon as the meal ended.

The past no longer seemed real to Henry. Perhaps he had finally escaped his nightmares.

He studied the three paintings he'd completed over the past month and silently thanked Phoenix for giving him friendship and wisdom. He had the odd feeling that his friend studied the portraits over his shoulder, an invisible presence nodding in approval.

Knowing he could do no more, he left the workroom and descended the stairs, following the scent of coffee, which, oddly, was not coming from the kitchen. He found Rachel sitting in the parlor, a tray laden with a china serving pot, cups, saucers, and a plate of her special apple muffins. As he crossed the threshold, she poured coffee in a cup and buttered a muffin for him.

He sat beside her on the sofa and accepted his breakfast with a nod. Needing coffee more than food, he drained the cup and poured himself more. The silence was unnerving as she stared ahead, and he sensed an attitude of waiting in her manner. Suddenly he felt like an animal stalked by hunters while drinking at a stream. She sat straight and alert, reminding him of how she'd been on the trail during her turn at guarding their campsite.

"Happy birthday, Henry," she said and handed him a cloth-wrapped packet.

Bemused, he stared down at the parcel and smiled. A gift. That explained her manner. It wasn't wariness at all, but the shyness of apprehension that the offering would not be to his liking. Perhaps she had made him a pair of gloves or knitted him some woolen socks. He turned the packet over in his hands, savoring the anticipation of discovery and thinking of the gift he had for her in the pocket of the embroidered silk vest he had unearthed from his trunk for the occasion. A gift that was as much for himself as it was for her.

Soon all would be well. As soon as he formed the proper words and managed to get them out in the open. They lurked in his mind and his heart, yet only words of censure and mockery had ever come easily for him. It had been a problem, he reflected, causing harm when he'd meant otherwise—

"Open it, Henry," she said with a note of urgency, as if she could wait no longer.

Obeying, he removed the simple wrapping and the hair on the back of his neck prickled in warning. "What is this?"

She rose from the sofa and stood with her hands folded over her belly. "Your freedom . . . and mine. Look them over and tell me whether everything is there."

"Everything is here," he said carefully. "The marriage documents, our contracts—even your advertisement."

"Good." She took the papers from his hand and carried them to the fireplace, then fed them to the flames one by one. "We're done, Henry. All debts are paid in full. I will make sure that your brother knows I ended it against your will."

Numb with shock, he watched as the papers scorched and curled and burst into flame, then quickly crumbled into ashes that seemed to fly up the chimney. He'd cleaned that chimney, he thought inconsequentially. And he'd nearly fallen in while making sure that the draft was sufficient to draw smoke upward so it wouldn't pour back into the house. He'd done a damn fine job.

Swallowing, he blinked his eyes and looked away from Rachel. He couldn't seem to speak, or function at all for the pain of it. His life flashed through his mind— the only life that mattered to him. His life since meeting Rachel: hearing her call him an ass in the streets of Cheyenne; seeing her longingly touch a hat through a milliner's window; holding her while in the midst of a storm; playing with her in the garden; revealing his nightmares to her and receiving a dressing down for his trouble; hearing her defend her mother even though she had run from her to live or die in the wilderness.

There was nowhere left to run.

He was lost in the midst of Rachel's Promise.

"Are you all right?" she asked, and something ruptured inside him, purging him.

"I'm bloody fine," he said roughly. "I'm doing smashingly well . . . excellent in fact." He rose and paced the width of the parlor, then back again. "You gave me freedom—just what I've always wanted." Raking his hand through his hair, he patted his pocket, feeling the small package he'd put there. It wasn't enough for her. He understood that now. "There is something I've needed to do for a long time. You've given me freedom to do it." He paused in the doorway and turned back to her before climbing the stairs. "Thank you, Rachel, for releasing me from hell."

Rachel walked stiffly to the door, closing it gently and locking it as she listened to Henry crash about upstairs— packing, no doubt, to move into one of the dwellings in town while the weather permitted. From the speed of his footsteps going up and down the steps, the repeated opening and slamming of the front door as he went in and out, he couldn't leave her fast enough.

She'd done the right thing, the only thing possible to save them both from certain destruction. She'd given Henry the only thing he could accept from her. The only thing he'd value coming from the daughter of a whore. She had given him what no one else had given him.

It was over. She was safe in her attic once more.

She sat down on the edge of a chair, covered her mouth with her hands, and doubled over, her body rocking back and forth, over and over again.

"Rachel!"

The call came from the front of the house. Dully she lifted her head, yet remained in the chair, afraid to move, afraid to hear anything Henry might have to say. Then she smelled smoke, saw a yellow glow interrupt the bleak gray of the sky, heard the crackle and roar of flames. She ran to the window and raised it, feeling heat mixed with cold as a bonfire burned in the yard. A circle, almost perfect, formed around him where the snow melted, enclosing him in a ring of white reflecting orange and red and yellow, like an unfinished painting.

What had he done?

"Rachel Parrish! Come see what you have done." Henry held up a painting of a woman, her face grotesque in her madness, then tossed it into the fire. The wind began to race again and snow began to fall more heavily as he chose another painting from the pile at his feet and held it up. A painting of a young man—a boy really— lying beneath a whore, his eyes shut against the horror of violation, his mouth opened in a soundless scream, and at the edge of the canvas, a man stood, watching and laughing with lascivious glee. "These are my nightmares, Rachel." That, too, fed the blaze. One by one he showed her his paintings and one by one threw them into the flames.

And then he reached for the one she hated most, the one she feared most—a man with two faces, one solid

and real, the other little more than mist. It was the painting he'd tossed from the window of his room and left
to rot among her flowers. She remembered wanting to
move it to the compost heap, but Henry had stopped her,
telling her that every grave deserved a few flowers. It
had lain where he'd thrown it ever since, the paint crack-
ing under the heat of the sun, the frame warping from
the rain, the canvas becoming brittle in the cold.

As she had when she'd first seen the cursed painting,
she curled her fingers into her palm, wanting to run out
and snatch it from him, to rip it to shreds and to destroy
Henry's image of himself so that he could see himself
as he really was. Yet, she knew that she could not, that
it would mean nothing unless he destroyed it himself.

He held it as it began to burn, releasing it only when
the flames reached out for him, threatening to take him,
too. He laughed as he pulled away. "You see, Rachel?
You've ruined me for the demons. They can't stomach
a man who has the taste of redemption in his heart. I
belong to you. Only you can destroy me."

He raised another portrait—of her half naked and
kneeling in the middle of her bed, one finger touching
the tip of her breast, her other hand reaching out for him,
her lips parted in an unspoken plea . . . and nothing was
where her eyes should be.

"This, too, has become my nightmare, Rachel. Such
beauty, such pleading. I hated it when you begged. I
hated it more that you were willing to accept so little
from me. It's not enough. It has no meaning without
love, and understanding, and forgiveness." He threw it
into the fire. "We both deserve more, Rachel. We
bloody well deserve it all."

Then he reached for the last painting and held it above
his head. She took a step backward and sobbed at the
light and color and beauty of it. Again it was her, but
only her head surrounded by mist. She wore a fine hat

of luxurious felt and silken fabric, enhanced with lush feathers and a single, silk rose. The hat Henry had given her. And her eyes, *her eyes,* were wide and full of an innocence she had never felt, full of a love she'd barely recognized at the time. And in their depths was a reflection of Henry standing before her, his hand outstretched, his fingertips brushing hers.

"This is my dream, Rachel," he shouted loudly, as if he wanted the world to hear him. "A promise of life and hope and freedom. *You,* Rachel—your heart, your soul, in exchange for mine. We need no other bargain."

She stumbled backward and caught herself on the arm of a chair, toppling it.

"Rachel! Answer me!"

Sobbing, she took another step and another until the locked door barred her way, and she groped behind her, fumbling with the key, turning it, freeing herself.

"Do I burn my dream, Rachel?" he shouted. "Tell me, damn you! Do I burn my dream?"

She jerked the front door open, but his gaze was trained on the window of the parlor and he didn't see her. He stood so still, as the portrait slipped from his grasp, slowly, until it touched the ground and fire licked greedily at the corner. His head bent forward, and the wind began to howl as snow swirled around him in frenzied plumes like ghostly pagan dancers honoring a sacrifice before consuming it.

"Henry." She tried to shout, but her voice croaked in a half sob, half laugh, as she crossed the porch and held the rail to descend the steps. "Henry . . . no!" she cried out as she ran to him and plucked the painting away from the flames and set it against the hitching post.

He didn't move, as if he were frozen in place, and tears formed icicles on one cheek and ran freely down the other in the heat of the fire. She recognized him as the man she loved, the man who gave warmth and com-

passion to those too small and helpless to protect themselves, while standing in the cold and finding shelter in
the darkness of his own thoughts, unreachable, yet still
reaching out.

She cupped his face in her hands, forced him to look
at her. "Henry. Don't burn the painting. It's my dream,
too."

He shuddered and blinked. "Where did you go, Rachel? I saw you, then—" He grasped her elbows and
held her away from him, staring at her. "Where the
bloody hell did you go?"

"Nowhere, Henry. I just had to unlock the door to
my attic."

Dragging her into his arms, he enfolded her inside the
coat and rested his chin on her head. The coat wouldn't
close around her increased girth, but she was warm
enough in the midst of Henry's fire. "So we are both
free," he said, and the words were a rumble in his chest
beneath her ear.

"Yes, if you tell me why you gave me the hat."

He blinked. "It was a gift. The only gift I have given
you and you won't even touch it."

"Only a gift? Nothing else?"

"What else would it be?"

She bit her lip and glanced away. "Payment . . . for
that night in the hotel."

"Oh, God," he said, and grasped her shoulders, giving her a gentle shake. "You wanted it. I saw you touch
the window and knew you wanted it. I could see you
wearing it . . . like this—" He pointed to the painting
leaning against the post, and grimaced. "And your
damned sunbonnet kept poking me in the eye."

She laughed then, even as she felt tears freezing on
her cheeks. A gift. Such a simple, lovely concept. "I
didn't consider that. I'd . . . never received a gift before."

With one hand, he fumbled for something in his vest pocket, then held it concealed in his palm as he lifted her chin with his fist. "You love me, Rachel?"

"I do."

"Without fear? Without doubt or regret?"

"Love is a fearful thing, Henry, yet it does not allow fear or doubt or regret. It simply is, whether we want it or not."

"Do you want it? Do you want me?"

"Yes."

The wind captured his sigh and carried it away. "I have something that belongs to you." He opened his hand to reveal an exquisite band of rich gold, burnished by time and fashioned into a cutwork lace pattern so fine and intricate, she wondered at the skill of hands and brilliance of mind that could create such delicate beauty. And worked into the design were small rubies and diamonds.

"When I first saw it I thought of teardrops and blood," she whispered.

"We have shed enough of both, Rachel . . . will you accept this, wear it as it was meant to be worn?"

"I will. . . . Henry, I want to go inside," she said, distracted by the collection of heavily clothed people staring up at them from the doorways of their homes. And at the end of town, a woman stood alone, the ivory of her gown obscured by a layer of snow.

"Any particular reason?" Arching his neck, Henry opened his mouth to catch a snowflake on his tongue, then followed her gaze with his own. "Ah. You don't care to ease their boredom with our theatrics?"

Before she could reply, the baby kicked out and Henry frowned as he leaned back to look at her stomach. "What in blazes was that?"

"The . . . *our* child quickens," she said, watching him intently, gauging his reaction. He'd rarely acknowledged the existence of a baby, and then only in reference to her health. The child was her hope for the future, and it had been Henry's curse—the reason Luc had forced him to marry her in the first place.

"It must be a girl," he said in mock disgust. "Already she tries to kick any man who comes close."

"You know about that?"

"Roz told me. I have lived in fear of your anger ever since," he said in a confidential tone as he guided her into the house.

She stopped short in the entryway, her attention caught by a large canvas leaning against the banister.

"My promise to you, Rachel."

She leaned over to turn it around and stared. A man stared back at her—a whole man sitting in a vegetable garden, his hands buried in the earth. A man with substance and clarity, his eyes clear and brilliantly blue, his face both strong and elegant.

"I couldn't see myself, Rachel. Every time I tried, the picture was incomplete, faded and dull. I've never felt whole, you see. But when I added you to the scene—" He pointed to her image, soft and smiling beside him as she dropped a miniscule seed into a furrow. "—I became real, *complete*."

"I can see that," she whispered as she swiped at the tears melting on her face. She saw Henry as he should be. She saw him happy. Her finger traced the figures of man and woman, sharing the pleasure of nurturing life, sharing the joy of living. Then she traced the third, smaller person in the portrait, as real and happy as the others as she kneeled beside Henry and herself with a sketch pad on her lap.

"A girl, Henry?"

"Our daughter," he corrected. "As I envision her—with the best of each of us. She has your eyes, Rachel, open and honest and with a touch of summer in their depths. And she has my smile. I have rather a nice smile, you know." He puffed out his chest and lifted his chin, preening comically.

She gazed up at him, studying his mouth. "No, I don't know. It is your best-kept secret."

He sobered. "No more secrets, Rachel. They only corrupt the truth."

"As you have corrupted me," she said. "You have, you know. I didn't want to fall in love. I didn't want to enjoy a man's touch or crave his approval."

"I think, Mrs. Ashford, that our bargain is well met. You are corrupted and I am redeemed."

"I thought it was the other way around." She folded her hands over her belly.

"You were never in need of redemption, Rachel. As I remember, you told a certain prig of a doctor that Benny did not choose to be the son of a whore. Well, neither did you choose your mother, Rachel. I, however, have chosen to be an ass for far too long." Cupping her face, he kissed the corner of her mouth as his other hand rested over hers. "Accept it, Rachel. We are both quite disgustingly ordinary."

Ordinary. It was true, she realized. A man and a woman who had learned how to forgive themselves as well as each other. A husband and wife who had discovered that respect could only be bought with the truth and that love was a luxury not to be wasted. Sighing, she set the portrait on a table and studied it once more. "Henry, I'd like to go upstairs."

"Any particular reason?"

"Yes."

"Your eloquence overwhelms, Mrs. Ashford. Would you care to elaborate?" he said as he hooked his arm around her shoulders and brushed her cheek with his knuckles.

She nodded and kissed his fingers, drawing a smile from him, a genuine smile free of darker emotions. A smile that brought light to his eyes and offered an unspoken vow that was worth a thousand words.

Epilogue

I t had been one hell of a winter, with the inhabitants of Promise isolated in their homes as they watched snow pile up to the rooftops. The cattle they hadn't been able to bring in from pasture had frozen in their tracks, some standing, some lying down. Even the men had cried when they'd found the livestock in various postures of death. Somehow, the helplessness of the animals affected them more than the loss of both a source of money and food.

Rachel had lost her new bull, but, Roz reflected, she still had Hank.

The thaw had begun late and even now, the land was spotted with patches and drifts of crusty snow amid the spring growth. Despite the time of year, the air still had a bite to it.

The boredom of being alone for months on end had begun to get to her, and more than once Roz had wished that she'd moved in with Cletus and Rain. She hadn't found peace in solitude. She'd found herself—a stranger who had forgotten how to think beyond the next customer . . . the next dollar. She had nothing to do but sit alone with memories that didn't make the past look any softer and entertaining regrets that made it look a hell of a lot dirtier. Oddly enough, it had been Henry who had saved her from herself.

He'd shown up on her doorstep in early February, wearing Rachel's buffalo-hide coat that had been completely covered with snow in his trek down the hill, and his eyebrows were frozen into sharp little needles above his eyes. His lips were stiff and blue and as he spoke the words seemed to freeze solid in the air as they came out of his mouth.

"Hurry," he'd said. "The horse will freeze—"

"What am I hurrying for?" she'd asked as she peered out at the massive workhorse he'd used to pull an old sleigh down the hill.

"The baby comes early . . . Rachel needs you."

"Your words or hers, Hank?"

"She's calling for you. It's been hours and she's frightened."

"Uh-huh. You scared, too, Hank?"

"I'm bloody petrified," he'd roared. "Now will you come willingly or shall I carry you?"

By the time he'd finished blustering, she'd gathered a few items and wrapped them in a blanket. Impatiently Henry wrapped her in a blanket cloth coat, swathed her head with a wool throw she hadn't finished knitting, then, without ceremony, carried her outside and practically slung her into the sleigh.

"What scares you most, Hank?" she asked, deliberately tweaking his temper. She liked him best when he was out of control and acting human.

He'd just sat there for a minute, staring at the horse's rump, then he'd looked her full in the face for the first time since she'd come to town. "What scares me most, madam, is that Rachel is frightened."

Roz was sure she liked her daughter's husband then. He needed Rachel and he was smart enough to know it and decent enough to admit it.

Without another word, he'd taken up the reins and urged the horse to retrace its path back up the hill in the roofless tunnel that had been plowed through the snow by the sheer size and power of their mount. A trail of yarn marked their path to the house as the unfinished throw—still attached to a skein of yarn in her cabin— unraveled along the way. Hank had been in a bad way that day.

He'd been drunk by the time Lydia Grace Elizabeth Phoenix Ashford screamed her way into the world. Those crazy Englishmen surely did like to make sure their names were long enough to reach back a generation or two. Tradition or not, it was one hell of a handle for such a little baby to tote around.

Still, Roz had to admit she liked the Phoenix part because it had been Hank's idea and confirmed that, under all those glowers he shot her way, lurked a soft heart and sentimental nature. Rachel needed that. The baby deserved it. Roz supposed that having the names of Liddie and Grace and Henry's mother wouldn't hurt, either. All that really mattered was that Rachel's baby carried her father's last name . . . that she had a father who was going to stick around for a lifetime or two.

She heard the sound of a fiddle and a few good-natured shouts coming from the other end of town. The citizens of Promise were gathering on the hill, where Horace was turning a side of beef on a spit above a pit of burning coals. Everyone, including the men, carried a dish of food to contribute to the celebration. Roz had a feeling there would be a lot of beans and bacon on the

table. Sighing, she turned back toward the big house on
the hill.

Usually Roz hated parties. They reminded her too
much of the illusion she'd created night after night in
the brothel—of genteel entertainment with an elegant
spread of food and drinks, and high-toned music provided by a man she'd hired just to play the piano that
had cost her a fortune. She'd hated pretending that the
men who came were invited guests rather than customers
looking for a shot of pride to chase down their whiskey,
a taste of power to water down the boredom of living
with wives who hadn't the slightest notion of how to
keep their husbands interested.

But this party was different, with boards suspended
between sawhorses instead of tables, and early wildflowers decorating the landscape instead of flocked wallpaper, and a bright blue sky instead of a ceiling painted
with cherubs and naked women. The men had put up a
makeshift plank floor in front of the big house for dancing and some tuned up fiddles and harmonicas. Roz
swallowed and shook off recollections of similar cele-
brations with just her father and brothers and a stray
Indian or two.

Remembering hurt too much.

"May I escort you, madam?" A man appeared by her
side and crooked his arm. A handsome piece of goods
who wore his Levi's, cotton shirt, and black silk kerchief
as if they were the fanciest duds in the territory. What
with ranching and railroad speculation being so popular
among the European gentry, she'd seen her share of nobility in her time, but this man made them all look like
counterfeits.

She took his arm and sashayed by his side, impressed
in spite of herself. Who'd have thought that Madam Roz
would be escorted down the main street of town—any
town—on the arm of an earl?

Lucien Ashford, Earl of Fairleigh, had ridden into sight two days ago at the head of a procession of Herefords and cowpokes that all looked a little scrawny from the deprivations of the worst winter in history. He'd announced that he'd lost half his herd, and decided that ranching wasn't for him. Roz had never heard of cows being given as a christening gift, but what the hell. The critters were alive and little Liddie would be ensured of having steaks to gnaw on when she grew teeth.

"Rachel and Henry are getting on well," he said conversationally.

"From what Rachel told me you'd know that better than me."

"And what did she tell you, madam?"

Roz shrugged. "That you and Hank have some sort of telegraph system of your own. I'm not sure I believe it, but life's been pretty strange lately, so maybe it's true."

"It was," the earl said. "But it has become rather one-sided of late. It would appear that my brother is so full of his wife that he has little room for me in his thoughts."

"Does that bother you?"

"On the contrary, madam. I am pleased that my brother is no longer lonely and plagued by my concerns."

"What about you? Rachel and Hank didn't have that boy you wanted to inherit your title and looks like your brother won't be leaving the territory. Seems to me like you're the lonely one."

He smiled, and it was the nicest thing Roz had seen since Hank had smiled at her one day when she'd caught him washing dishes for Rachel. Damn but the two brothers looked alike.

"I have not given up hope for an heir."

"You think Rachel and Hank would give up a son to you?"

"No. I never did," he said with a sigh. "And I never had any intention of requiring such a sacrifice. Any male child of Henry's will inherit the title and estates regardless. What he does with them will be up to him. In any event, you know as well as I do, madam, that your daughter would give me what I wanted on her terms or not at all."

"I know, but wasn't sure you did," Roz said with a grin.

They climbed the hill and paused as the front door to the house opened. Everyone fell silent and gaped as Henry appeared on the porch, decked out in a fancy black suit and a black silk vest embroidered with gold threads. In concession to his new home, he wore a string tie and Stetson. He looked like a showboat gambler ready to fleece every sucker in sight.

"Sheeyut, Hank," Cletus said. "Ain't you slicker'n new mud?"

"Fancier'n them words he throws around," Horace agreed.

Rain nodded and grunted, whether in amusement or approval no one knew.

Rachel sure had found herself a fine-looking man, even if he did have enough airs to fart his way to China. It had been more entertaining than a medicine show to follow him around the house the last two months and irritate the hell out of him. The best part had been washing his silk underwear and commenting every chance she got on how it was pretty enough for him to wear outside his clothes. One day she'd barged into his painting room and strolled around, suggesting that he paint her. With exaggerated patience, he'd circled her, studying her face and figure, then calmly running his loaded brush from the bridge of her nose to her chin. She'd been so stunned, she'd stood still while he cupped her jaw and dabbed and stroked different colors down one side of her face.

"That's better," he'd said as he wiped the original stripe from her face, then held up a mirror for her inspection. "Will this do, madam?"

She'd studied the roses and feathers he'd rendered on the side of her face and nodded. She'd lightly touched her cheek, feeling the texture of the paint, pleased at the image she saw. It would do just fine. But she didn't tell Henry that. Instead, she propped her hand on a suggestively outthrust hip. "I had a customer once who would've got all hot and bothered over this. Too bad he's dead. He'd of paid me triple to prance around in front of him with nothing on but a coat of paint."

Without comment, he'd snorted and turned back to his canvas.

Again the crowd grew silent, expectant, as the front door opened. No one had seen the baby yet, though they'd heard her from time to time, squalling her lungs out. Only Rachel stepped outside, and a collective gasp rippled through the assembly. Even Hank was struck speechless.

She wore an ivory silk gown trimmed in a soft, peachy color at the bodice and hem. Though a little thicker, her waist dipped in below full breasts and above hips widened by childbirth. Her hair, the color of fall honey and rich, spring loam was upswept with a long, thick curl draped over her shoulder. Her eyes had a new shine to them, glimmering in the sunshine, soft brown and amber flecked with summer green. And on her head was the most beautiful hat Roz had ever seen—a creation of ivory and peach, of silk and feathers, its wide brim curved just so over her forehead and dipping provocatively over one side of her face.

No wonder the men were drooling all over themselves even as they gazed at her with reverence. They weren't used to having a real lady walk among them, kissing one cheek, patting another. Rachel should have stuck out like a sore thumb among the ragged group of misfits, but she didn't. Instead she looked as natural in their midst as fresh wildflowers looked natural in the midst of patches of dirty snow.

Feeling a little awed herself, Roz backed away to a secluded spot as the earl stepped forward to greet his brother and kiss Rachel's cheek. This beautiful, elegant creature came from her. This poised and confident woman whose hand rested so comfortably in the crook of her husband's arm was hers, the best of what Roz might have been, the embodiment of the dreams she'd believed in once upon a time. Roz had been the highest-priced hooker in the territory, but this woman who walked toward her in a drift of silk and serenity was the true reward. Not that Roz would admit it to anyone. She'd leave sentiment to Rachel and Hank.

Rain slipped into the house and returned carrying a large, padded basket. The earl and the other two women immediately rushed over to see the baby, and the men approached with shuffling, almost shy steps.

"Liddie is wearing the gown you made her, Mother," Rachel said as she and Hank drew up in front of her.

"I saw her earlier," Roz said. "Looks like you have a new dress, too."

"I found it in an old trunk. Was it yours?"

"Could be. I don't rightly remember." It was a lie, of course. But the memory pained her too much to voice without choking on her own regrets.

"It looks like a wedding gown," Henry commented, pinning her with a considering stare.

"It is . . . now that a bride is wearing it," Roz said, noting that Hank was getting that distracted look again, as if his mind were drifting and he was impatient to follow it. Rachel saw it, too, and smiled again.

"Your box is on the porch, Henry," she said, and before she finished the sentence, he was off chasing visions again.

Everyone gave him a wide berth as the party went on around him through the afternoon. The earl ate beans and guzzled moonshine with the best of them, then took to the dance floor to teach the others some fancy footwork he called a "country dance." It didn't take long for him to give up and learn the Virginia Reel instead.

After two hours, Rachel shifted uncomfortably in the pose Henry had insisted upon. Liddie stirred on Rachel's lap and puckered her mouth—a sure sign she was hungry and waking up from her nap. Roz's neck hurt, but she didn't want to move. She liked sitting beneath the tree with Rachel and the baby while Hank worked with watercolors and paper. These would likely be the most peaceful moments they'd ever share together.

He glanced up suddenly and studied the scene in front of him, then did the same with the tablet he'd set up on an easel. Just as suddenly, he stowed his brushes in a wooden box, snapped the lid shut, and picked up the tablet. He approached them slowly, his attention still on his work as he seemed to compare the image with the reality. But then he stopped in front of Rachel and held up the painting.

It was such a simple thing—a portrait of two women and a child, all dressed in ivory as they rested beneath a tree, unforgiving in its honesty. He'd done Liddie as she so often looked, with her eyes closed and her mouth pursed as she sucked in her sleep, her tiny hand instinctively opened against the pulse at Rachel's throat. Rachel sat with her back straight and her head high with the pride she'd paid for so dearly, her expression serene and focused on the man who asked nothing from her but dreams.

And beside Rachel and Liddie was Roz herself, with her white hair brushed away from her face and caught in a bun at the base of her neck. He hadn't smoothed over the crow's feet at the corners of her eyes or softened the line of her mouth. She didn't mind. She'd spent years covering up the scars of hard living. She'd earned the right to show her age, to enjoy the freedom it gave her.

"It's wonderful, Henry," Rachel said. "Thank you."

Roz turned her head away to hide her sigh. Rachel accepted what she saw in the painting—the intimacy of their poses, the resemblance they had to one another, the same weary knowledge that no mother should have to share with her daughter. Roz thought that maybe now, Rachel accepted her, too.

Hank shook his head as he examined the portrait one more time. "It's a gift, Rachel."

"I know ..." Rachel's voice trailed off as Henry held out the painting to Roz, and she stared at them with wide, unblinking eyes.

"For you, madam," Hank said.

Roz took the small watercolor portrait and held it by the corners, afraid to smudge the subtle colors, the quality of light that Henry captured. She was equally afraid to speak, to ruin the moment that she'd never thought to have. Yet she knew she had to say something. She had to let both Rachel and Hank know that she wanted more moments like this one.

All she could do was sniff and wipe her eyes with her sleeve. "Damn you, Hank. You always bring out the worst in me."

"The worst, madam?" He smiled and leaned over to capture a tear from her cheek. "I think not," he said as he rubbed the moisture between his fingers.

"Do you want Henry to frame it for you, Mother?" Rachel asked. "It will fit perfectly on the table your father made."

"You giving me permission to show it off, Rachel?" Roz asked, knowing it sounded churlish, yet needing to hear the answer, to know once and for all if there was hope of understanding between them.

"No," Rachel said softly. "I'm asking you to show it off."

Roz nodded. "You frame it up real nice, Hank . . . but keep it simple. I don't want folks to see anything but what's really there." She had to clear her throat then. "The music is real nice now that Horace and Cletus decided to play the same tune. Why don't you two go dance before Liddie wants her supper?"

Henry bowed gallantly at Roz, tucked Rachel's hand in the crook of his arm to lead her to the platform a few feet away, then swept her into his arms and whirled her around the plank floor. He flinched as a feather from her hat caught him in the eye. He rearranged Rachel in his arms and tried again, but the wide brim stabbed his chin. Roz saw his lips move, recognizing the curse he muttered as others took to the floor—Rain stomping in circles and chanting under her breath while men paired with men until each—including the earl—was granted a turn with the two remaining women.

Rachel and Henry swayed to a tune of their own at the edge of the platform until another feather brushed his nose. He sneezed and cursed and swept the hat from Rachel's head to hold it with both hands at the back of her waist.

"Damn it, am I to be forever plagued by your headgear?"

"Yes," she said as she leaned back to look at him, her expression solemn. "As long as we both shall live, Henry."

He closed his eyes for the space of a heartbeat and inhaled sharply, as if he were breathing in her vow, absorbing it, before meeting her gaze and making a vow of his own. "It is a price I shall gladly pay, Mrs. Ashford . . . that and more . . . always."

Rocking the basket to keep Liddie happy for a little while longer, Roz looked around her—at the mountains that sheltered them, the land that was rich in game and fertile soil and wild beauty, the growing settlement of shiny new buildings and worn-out people. And by the side of a muddy road was the sign that Hank had fixed earlier in the day.

PROMISE
population 30 36 32 39 41

Author's Note

The history of the American West is riddled with stories of strong women who went to extraordinary lengths to survive the hardships and deprivations of the times. They maintained hearth and home, farmed the land, raised the children, and in many cases outlived their men, only to find themselves without property or resources to continue the lives to which they had become accustomed.

It was not unusual for the male providers—and protectors—of a frontier family to leave home to hunt for food or travel great distances over hostile terrain in order to purchase supplies from the nearest trading post. Sometimes they never came back. Equally common were children orphaned when their parents died—as in Liddie's case—of either hardship or disease as they traversed the wilderness in search of the land of milk and honey on the western side of the Mississippi. Either way, wives and children were forced to fend for themselves however they could, as fourteen-year-old Roz was when her father and brothers disappeared while on a hunting expedition.

The social and economic conditions of the nineteenth century did not provide choices for these women, and the closest most of them came to having independence was to own their own shop—which required capital—find a husband, or in Roz's case, run a bordello. If Roz had not been ruined by a man who took advantage of her isolation in the Big Horn Basin, she might have been fortunate enough to escape the red-light district. I do not justify her choice but merely attempt to explain it.

When Esther Morris literally backed opposing candidates for the governorship of Wyoming Territory into a corner on the issue of voting rights for the fairer and "weaker" sex, women like Rachel found the courage to make choices previously reserved for men. William Bright was elected governor and was known to say that his wife would have made a better governor than himself. With that enlightened attitude, he pushed through legislation in 1869 that gave women equal rights for the first time in America. By the next year, women were serving on juries, held their own property, and Esther Morris, who had accomplished so much by giving a simple tea party, became the first woman justice of the peace in the world.

Though Fort Fetterman was a major supply post from 1867 to 1882, it was abandoned by the time Rachel met Luc and went through with the marriage. I chose to keep the fort in operation for a few years more rather than send Rachel off the beaten track. Also, because of the hardship the soldiers suffered on the frontier, Fort Fetterman provided Rachel with the means to make her fortune by selling hard-to-get items such as leather gloves and home-canned vegetables and livestock.

The Big Horn Basin is a special place in Wyoming, rich in game and ideal for farming and ranching. Because of its natural barrier of mountains on all sides, the basin was spared the conflict between Indians and white man, and enjoyed more temperate weather than the rest of the territory, while being largely unsettled until the late nineteenth century. Only a few ranches existed in the area, owned largely by English aristocrats looking for investments and excitement in the new world.

The winter of 1886–87 dealt a severe blow to the economic structure of Wyoming, its record cold and snowfall crippling the activities of the settlers and virtually decimating the great cattle herds of the region. With the wisdom and grit of a good heroine, Rachel employed foresight and fighting spirit to weather the almost constant storms that winter to ensure the survival of her people.

Though careful research was done in preparation for writing *Unspoken Vows,* I still must offer a disclaimer concerning certain alterations and exaggerations of historical facts in the interest of giving Rachel and Henry a break whenever possible. Heaven knows they had enough strikes against them.

My main goal, as always, is to present my readers with an entertaining story that depicts the courage of two people who strive to build a loving relationship and perhaps perform the greatest feat of heroism of all for man and woman—to accept love without fear and to give it without conditions. I hope I have succeeded.